THE LIGHTBRIDGE LEGACY SERIES

The Secret Half

Book One

Elayne
G. James

MISCHIEVOUS MUSE BOOKS

MISCHIEVOUS MUSE
Publishing Arts Alliance

The Secret Half: A Supernatural
Coming of Age Story - Book One
of The LightBridge Legacy Series
2nd Edition • November 2018
A Mischievous Muse Book
Los Angeles County, California, US

Cover Design by Gineve Lynnara

Library of Congress
Cataloging-in-Publication Data
James, Elayne G.
The Secret Half / Elayne G. James
Contemporary Fantasy / Adventure /
Coming-of-age / YA Fiction
Book One: The LightBridge Legacy Series

Trade Paperback ISBN: 9780982886588

Printed in the USA

PRAISE FOR THE SECRET HALF

"What do you get when you mix in some ancient magic, some preteen angst and destiny? The amazing first book of a trilogy that will have you turning pages late into the night! The characters are believable. The scenes are so rich with detail you can smell the desert and feel claustrophobic in New York. The plot has left me hoping the next book is already in stores! I will be following this author!"

- GoodReads Review

"This book is a rare find—a book that will influence, entertain, enlighten, intrigue and amuse. A book that can spark the imaginations of not only young minds, but readers of all ages, from all walks of life. This beautifully written coming-of-age story holds adventure, mystery, and wisdom in equal measure. I didn't just enjoy the book, I came away feeling that it has the power to inspire courage (the courage to be oneself) in the hearts and minds of its readers.

I believe many will identify with the inner and outer struggles of Ani Jasper, as she wrestles with who she is and who she's becoming, and I found the unusual supernatural dilemma she faces especially intriguing. The Lightbridge Legacy promises to be a wonderful, multi-faceted series, and I can't wait to read Book Two!"

-Ishara Kassirer Author of **Droplet's Journey: Life in the Flow**

*"What makes **The Lightbridge Legacy** [**The Secret Half**] so engaging is the well-developed characters and the warm yet complex relationships between them. Combine that with Ani's harrowing adventures in real life as well as in more magical/spiritual realms, and you have a story that, once begun, is nearly impossible to put down!"*

-Greg Conway, Musician and Composer

*"Elayne James' **The LightBridge Legacy** [**The Secret Half**] is one of those books that delivers that "feeling." An adventure that unfolds so inevitably that you cannot put the book down. A story that comes along so infrequently, in terms of its pure potential for having a positive influence on a generation, particularly because it's aimed at young readers.*

Ani, our almost shy, reluctant heroine is an extremely likable character—real, accessible; curious and intelligent, discovering her own personal power—or "powers," as the case may be - and grappling with the consequences of exercising those powers.

Reading this book just makes you feel good—like you can trust your instincts and make a difference in the world."

-E. J. Irons, Filmmaker

THE LIGHTBRIDGE LEGACY SERIES

BOOK ONE
THE SECRET HALF

BOOK TWO
THE HIDDEN GATES

BOOK THREE
THE LOST PATH

BOOK FOUR
THE DARK BELOW

For you.
You know who you are.
You're the one in the room who feels like
an alien from another planet—like who
you are is different from who everyone
else is, and there's nothing you can do
about it—like you have to hide your true
self because no one will ever understand.
You are not alone.
There are more of us than you know.
We are those who see things differently,
and can re-envision the world the way
it was meant to be. We are the misfits,
the out-of-the-box-thinkers, the freaks
and geeks, the artists and writers,
the philosophers of the future,
the way-finders and the
creators of things yet to be.
You may not believe this right now,
but just wait and see—we are what
this world needs, simply by you
being you, and by me being me.

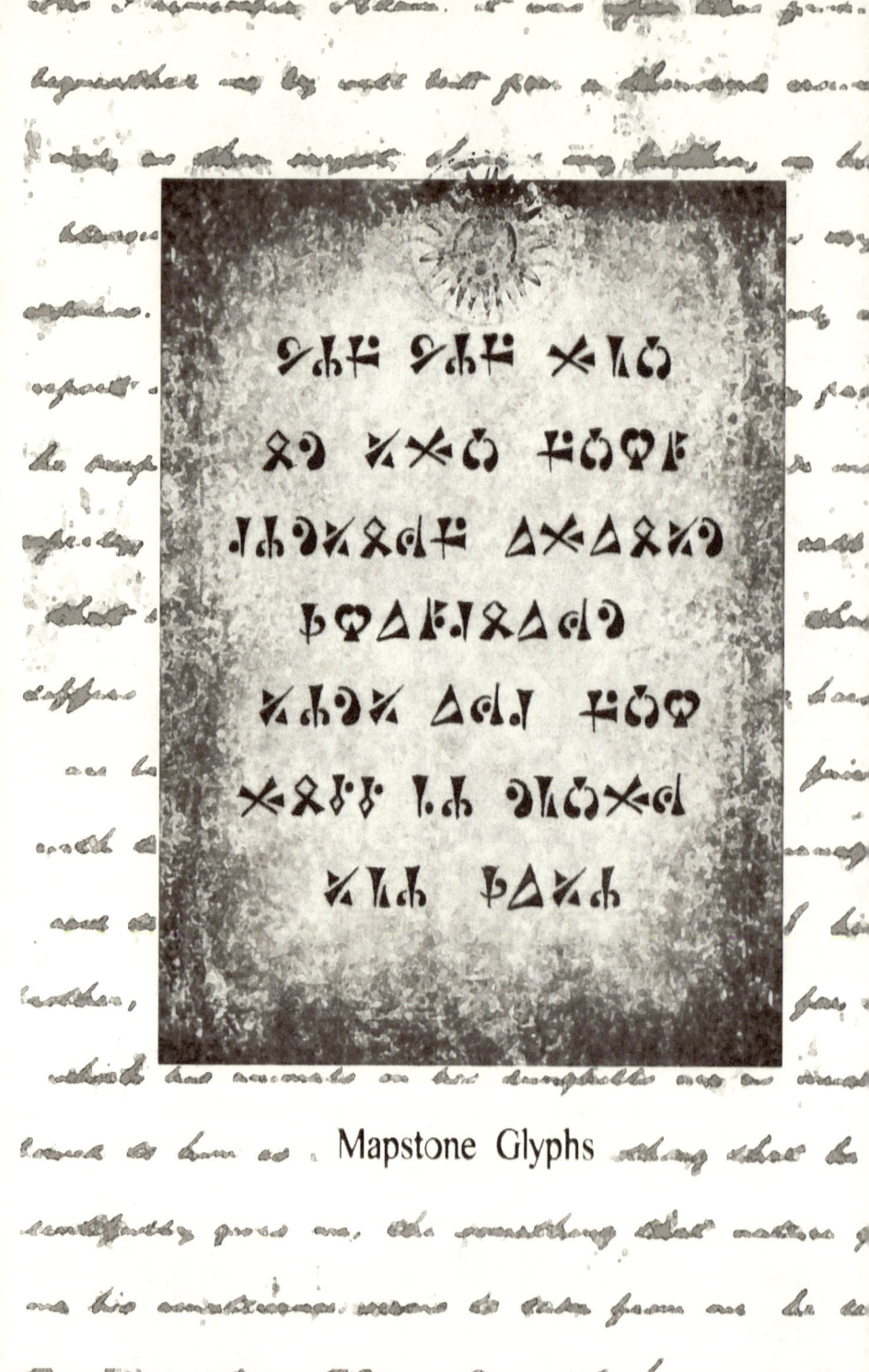

Mapstone Glyphs

The desert whispers
The city weeps
The mountain calls
The forest sleeps
The earth hums
Benieth your feet
Be still and listen
Until next we meet.

Xephero

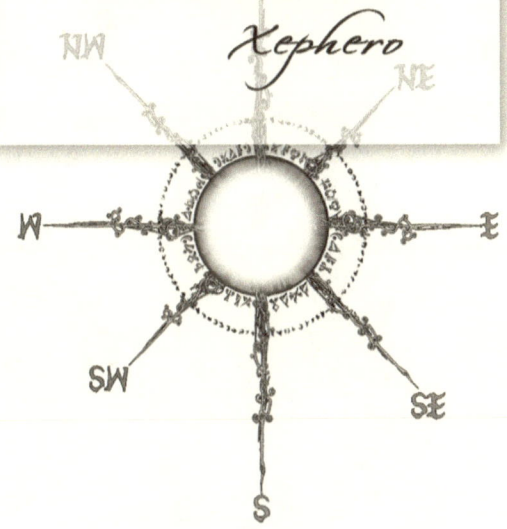

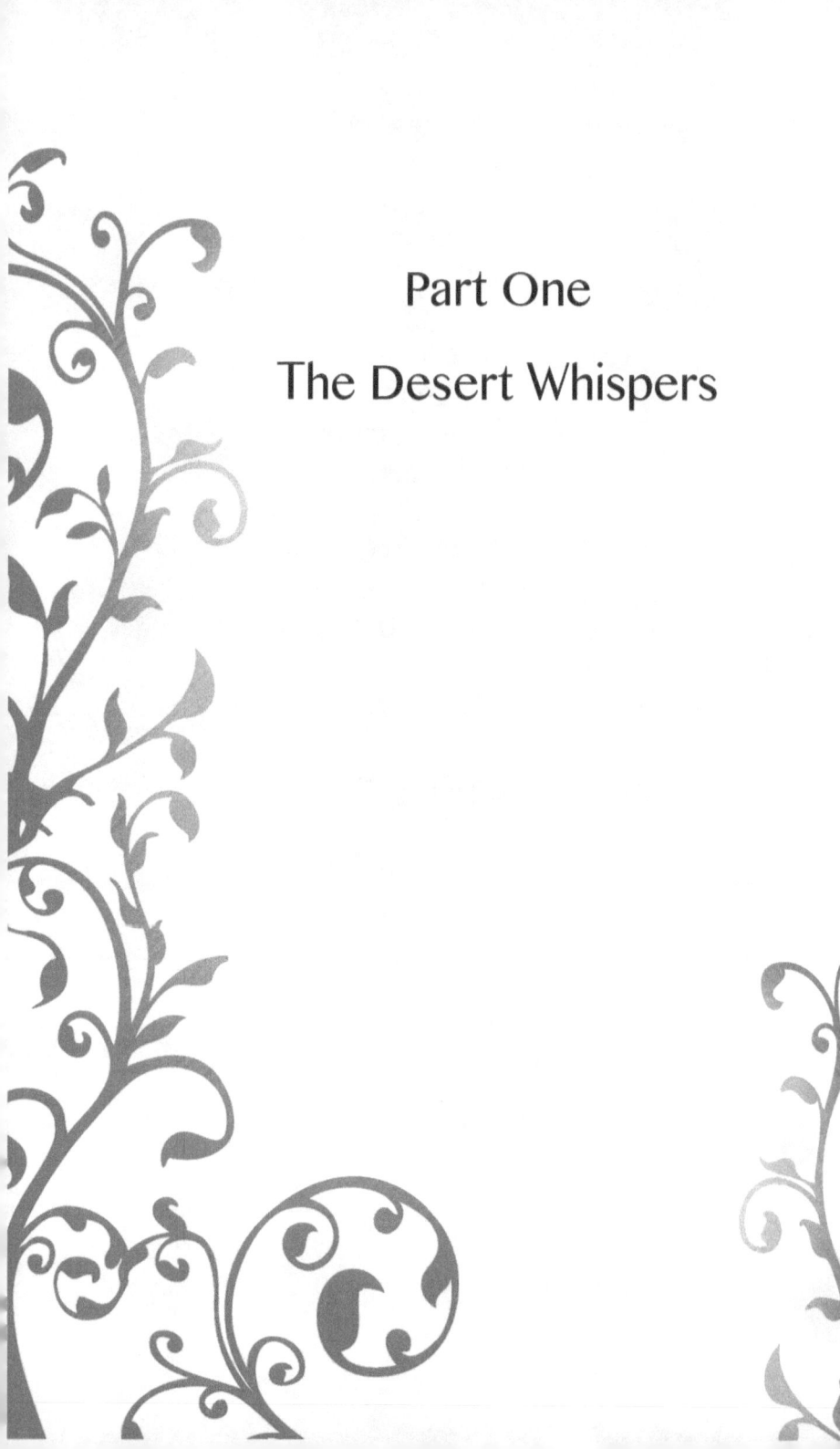

Part One

The Desert Whispers

The young apprentice glanced up from his transcribing as the old man materialized before him in a swirl of light.

"Our search," said the Master, "may finally be over."

The boy, who called himself Naviga, showed a hint of a smile. "You found him?"

"Her."

"Her?" Naviga could not hide his surprise. There had never been a female Light Master. Not in all the centuries the ancients had occupied Azimara.

"She senses the magic," said the Master, "but does not yet know she possesses it."

"Will you test her?"

"She will be tested." The Master moved to a carved sandstone box on a nearby shelf. He removed a smooth palm-sized stone and replaced the lid. "First she must recognize the Amnatah."

"And if she does not?"

The old man sunk into a nearby chair, suddenly weary. "Then our search must continue."

If the wind has a message for you, hear it.
If this storm has a warning for you, heed it.
If this voice speaks within, pay attention.
You will not learn if you do not first listen.

-Xephero ✣ Tome of the Zielfah Ri

CHAPTER ONE

ༀ

THE MAPSTONE & THE STRANGER

She didn't know why she left the path. Something deep down told her to abandon what was easy and familiar and venture into the nameless unknown. She held her breath, listening, waiting for the desert to tell her why she'd been brought here . . . to this precise place . . . at this exact moment.

And then she heard it—the beckoning. It called to her in wordless whispers the same way the canyon called, or the questing wind, or the path she walked every morning at dawn. But the power of this message was unlike any other. Vivid. Distinct. Absolute.

A speck of indigo caught her eye.

Bending down, she balanced on the balls of her feet to get a better look. As she brushed aside a bit of sand, flecks of silver flashed bright in the sun.

A gust of delight accompanied a quick inrush of breath. Familiar prickles tickled the back of her neck. It happened every time she was on the verge of making an important discovery. She loosened the clumped dirt around its edges and pried her newest treasure from the earth.

With the help of a little spit, she rubbed a spot clean with her thumb, revealing a surface as slick as glass. The stone, though obsidian black, possessed a murky water-like transparency. Brilliant veins of cobalt blue and aquamarine splintered through it like frozen lightning amidst tiny specks of silver, glistening stars in a midnight sky.

She ran a finger along its cool rounded edges. The shape seemed almost deliberate, as though carved to resemble the flame of a candle or a single teardrop. It fit perfectly in the palm of her hand, and tingled with aliveness—a distinct vibrational energy—the likes of which she had never before felt. This stone had secrets to tell. Ancient and awesome secrets.

There it was again, that fluttery feeling in the pit of her stomach. Her insides did a little dance whenever she unearthed a sample she knew her dad would approve of, but this time she felt something else too—something she could never tell her geologist father. Somehow, the stone called out to her. It *wanted* to be found.

Anani Jasper, or *Ani*, as her mother called her, had been finding stones for her parents' rock and gem shop for as long as she could remember. The shop, a windswept roadside tourist stop, occupied the front half of the Jasper family home in California's Mojave Desert. There, under her father's patient tutelage, Ani had learned to identify a wide variety of stones and minerals, memorizing each of their names and attributes. But this one had her stumped. She needed a second opinion.

Pocketing the stone in the red zippered sweat jacket she always wore on her excursions, she turned toward home. If anyone could identify this strange new specimen, it would be Dad.

As she followed the familiar path back to her house, she couldn't resist pulling it out of her pocket for a second look. She half expected it to do some kind of magic when she polished it with her sleeve. It may not be Aladdin's Lamp, but her father would give her plenty for it. She was sure of that. Even an average specimen earned her a dollar or two, and this one was far from average. Maybe she'd make enough to finally buy that book she'd been wanting; *The Magical Properties of Desert Stones, by E.B. Cummins*.

She first saw the book on the counter at Greyhawk's Gas and Garage. Her adopted Navajo grandfather, Kahetay Greyhawk, had shown her a copy of the book on one of their regular visits to repair the old Chevy pickup.

Kahetay explained that stones and other things of the earth

have their own kind of magic, and if you paid close enough attention, they would teach you. Ani longed to understand that magic and what it was trying to tell her.

"Hocus pocus hogwash!" her father had said when Ani asked for the book on her thirteenth birthday last May. It was his typical response to all things mystical, and just the sort of thing he would say if she told him this rock spoke to her. He'd call it "the curse of an over-active imagination," which was precisely how he categorized every unusual thing that had ever happened to her.

But Ani didn't let her dad's skepticism deter her. She found the idea of stones possessing some kind of magic, well, fascinating. Rocks were special. She knew it, and whether her father admitted it or not, he knew it too.

Clearing the top of a rise, Ani caught sight of her house in the distance, the only building for miles around. The winter sun crept higher in the early morning sky, coaxing the shapes and colors of the desert to come alive. Fire-reds and yellow-golds burst forth as cactus flowers opened to the light of the coming day.

As she made her way down the rocky slope, the stone grew warm in her palm, demanding her full attention. It seemed to pulsate against her fingers, a primordial heartbeat marking an ancient rhythm. She stopped and peered at it through squinted eyes, and in the stillness, heard the faint whispers again.

A dizzying swell of exhilaration rose within her. Ani held her breath to quell her excitement. She had to concentrate. Eyes closed, she focused her full attention on the stone, listening with her whole being as her grandfather had taught her, but still couldn't make out what the whispers were saying. And the more she tried, the more they eluded her.

Then as the last of the whispers faded away, she heard one distinct voice that rose above all the others and spoke as if it were her own thought. It said, "*Nohowee hah nokah*. I am here."

A shudder shot through her and in a sudden rush of energy she broke into a run. With the stone clenched tightly in her hand, she whizzed past rock, cactus and shrub, heading straight for her father's shop.

Breathing hard, she burst through the back door and ran straight up to the counter, only to be stopped short by an impassable barrier: her father's hand, held up like a stop sign, in an all-too-familiar don't-even-think-about-it gesture.

Jaw clenched, Ani stared at her father, hoping to convey the importance of what she had to show him, but it was no use. He wore his "serving the customer" face. His amiable manner and willingness to listen always put people at ease. Of course, that also meant they usually stayed and chatted longer than Ani wanted them to, but as her mother always said, it was good for business.

Ani peered up at the customer standing at the counter. He towered over her. His weather-sculpted face in combination with the wild snowy tangle that topped his head reminded Ani of a mountain in winter. He smelled of earth too—dirt, leaves, grass after a rainfall. Even the brown woven poncho that hung stiffly over his broad shoulders further corroborated his mountainness.

Sewn into the rough material of his poncho, a labyrinth of strange stylized animals and shadowy stone faces wove their way through an intricate web of maze-like borders and lines. It was unlike any of the Native American weaves she'd seen in her mother's anthropology books. She stood transfixed by the pattern for a moment and then looked up, not knowing how much time had passed.

Ani glanced at her father and then at the customer. It took an iron will not to interrupt them. She thought she would burst if she had to wait one minute longer.

Her will faltered. "Dad, I really need to show you something." She opened her hand to reveal the stone.

The customer looked down at Ani's rock. "Ah, that's a fascinating geological specimen you've got there." His accent was thick as ivy, but he spoke his words with deliberate clarity.

Ani smiled, pleased that her father would have to pay attention to her now. "I found it on my walk."

"Let's have a look," said her father, holding out his hand. "Hmmm. What have we here?" He inspected the stone with an old-fashioned magnifying glass. "Quite a find, Anani. Quite a find."

Her smile was triumphant. High praise indeed, coming from the expert himself.

"May I see it?" The stranger held out his hand. "With your permission, of course," he said, addressing Ani.

Ani nodded and her father placed the stone in the stranger's palm.

"What can I offer you for it?" asked the stranger. "Fifty?"

"Dollars?" asked Ani, astonished.

Her father peered at the customer, raising an eyebrow.

"The look of it pleases me," admitted the man, offering it back to Mr. Jasper.

4

Ani turned to her father. "Do you know what kind of stone it is?"

"Not off-hand," he said, peering at it through a lapidary's loupe, which offered a much stronger magnification. "Odd. I'll have to look it up."

She stared at her father, wide-eyed. This was the first time she'd brought home a specimen that prompted her father to consult what he called "The Geological Bible" which, he never failed to point out, was thoroughly devoid of any magical gibberish.

Stan Jasper opened the dusty four-inch thick reference book sitting on the back counter and flipped through the pages.

Feeling as though she might jump out of her skin, Ani waited for her father to find the name of her rock. And waited. And waited. She sensed the stranger's eyes upon her and began to fidget, trying to ignore his scrutiny, but something made her turn to look up at the man. His gaze met hers and for an instant time stood still. No sound. No movement. Just an odd floating sensation, like being suspended in water.

"It's not in there," said Mr. Jasper, jump-starting time again.

Ani turned her attention back to her father. "What? But it has to be. That book has every kind of rock there is."

"It's not in there," he repeated, as puzzled as his daughter. "Not like this anyway. A strange amalgamation of elements—onyx, smoky quartz, labradorite, traces of silver and lapis, even what looks like veins of aquamarine—all of which would not, to my knowledge, occur naturally in the same place, and certainly not in the same rock."

"I'll make it seventy," snapped the stranger.

Stan cleared his throat. "Well, I'm not certain of its value."

"Nor am I," said the stranger.

"It could very well be manmade," said her father, "given the odd combination of elements. It could be worth very little."

"That does not concern me," said the stranger.

Stan Jasper placed the rock on the counter and looked at his daughter. "Well, Ani? This man wants to buy your rock."

Ani was speechless. She stared at the rock, not wanting to give it up so soon. What if it was the only one like it in the whole world? What if it really was magic? Maybe the man could come back after she had a chance to polish it properly and look at it under optimum lighting conditions.

"Tell you what," said the stranger. "To help you decide, I'll make it an even hundred."

Ani's mouth fell open. "A hundred dollars? I've never even seen that much money."

The man smiled briefly, and then grew serious. "So it's a deal then?"

"No. I mean, I don't know. Can you come back next week—"

The man straightened, his voice now absent of previous cordiality. "I won't be by this way again."

A moment of silence passed as Ani picked up the rock and studied it, turning it over in her hands. The stranger continued to peer down at her with a questioning stare. She looked at him, wanting in that instant to run, not knowing why, but something held her there—some mysterious power the stranger seemed to have over her.

"Ani," pressed her father, "the man just offered you a hundred dollars for your rock. Don't you think you ought to give him an answer?"

"But Dad I—"

"This *is* a rock shop, honey. People come here to buy rocks."

"I know, but I just need some time to think about it."

"Well, that may be true," said her father, "but I'm sure this gentleman has better things to do with his time than wait for you to make up your mind."

He was right of course. She was being impolite by making him wait. And yet, the tall stranger didn't seem impatient at all. Actually, Ani got the feeling he would have stood there for an eternity if that were how long it took her to decide. She didn't want to give up the rock, but she didn't want to disappoint her father either.

"Yes or no, Ani."

"Alright, yes. I guess." Ani's heart sank the instant she heard herself agree to the stranger's offer. The customer produced a crisp one hundred dollar bill that seemed to materialize in his hand the instant Ani nodded her answer.

Frowning, she placed the stone in the stranger's palm. As he accepted it, the pulse of time altered once more and the shop blurred around her. The distant whispers she'd heard in the desert returned. The old man hummed a single note at the back of his throat and passed his hand over the surface of the stone in a slow deliberate arc.

Ani watched in astonishment as mysterious symbols emerged; characters of an ancient language surfacing from the depths of a crystal sea. She glanced up at the stranger, aghast. He met her gaze with a wry smile.

When she glanced again at the stone, the odd markings vanished and the whispers abruptly ceased. The stranger slowly wrapped his fingers around the rock, his hands so much larger than hers they concealed it completely.

"*So kraw ah Amna tah,*" said the tall man in a whisper only she could hear. "Remember the Mapstone."

The clang of the bell at the front door jolted Ani out of her trance. The stranger was leaving. The instant the door shut behind him, she knew she'd made a mistake. She didn't want the money. She wanted the stone.

She snatched the hundred-dollar bill out of her father's hand. "Hey mister, I changed my mind!" she called, waving the money in the air as she dashed out the door. But the desert stared back at her, a vast, silent void. There were no footprints in the sand. No car pulled out onto the dusty, desolate road. No sign that anyone had ever been there. The man had simply vanished and with him, her first true treasure.

*If we relinquish the need to understand,
and simply allow the mystery to be, we
can begin to accept the wisdom of the
unknowable. Paradoxically, it is usually
at this point that true understanding
becomes possible.*

-*Naviga* ✤ *Tome of the Zielfah Ri*

CHAPTER TWO

ૐ

THE PERSISTENCE OF SHADOWS

That evening when her mother called her downstairs for dinner, Ani didn't feel like eating. Usually, Ani was excited about the one meal a week her mother prepared. Though her father was an adequate cook, her mother's meals were special. Each of her recipes originated from a different exciting, exotic land. She'd prepare the food and dress the table in such an authentic way it almost felt like being on vacation. And while they ate, her mother would tell them all about the culture and the significance of the meal: why they used certain spices and ingredients, the mythical and medicinal qualities attributed to each dish, and the ancient lore behind the meal.

Ani loved hearing her mother's stories of exotic places and peoples. Some sounded so strange they seemed more like tales from other worlds. Ani's favorite stories though, were the ones her mother made up about some hidden tribe living in obscurity at the top of a mountain somewhere. To end these stories she'd always straighten in her chair and announce in her best newscaster voice, "Discovered by the famous anthropologist, Nan J. Jasper!"

Before her parents met, her mother had been in the graduate program at Columbia University in New York. Ani knew she'd given up being an anthropologist to raise a family, but Mom said she never regretted that decision, nor had she given up on her dream. She still kept up with the latest news and techniques through online courses.

Ani could smell the pungent scent of this week's special dinner cooking on the stove downstairs. She caught whiffs of sweet fried plantains and the thick lemony garlic aroma of Cuban chicken baking in the oven. She should have been hungry, but tonight, only one thing interested her.

Sitting at her desk, hovering over a large spiral-bound drawing tablet, Ani attempted to sketch the stone she'd found that morning, trying to recall every detail, every unique feature, but she just couldn't seem to get it right. The image was so clear in her mind, but when she tried to put it on paper, the thing just ended up looking like a messy black blob.

Why can't I get this? she thought, frustration mounting. She'd been sketching rocks and desert landscapes since the fourth grade, when her mother had given her art supplies for her 9th birthday—a set of charcoal pencils, a king-sized pad of charcoal paper, and an acrylic paint set complete with brushes and two blank canvases.

Ani didn't much care for the paints, but she loved the deep rich blacks and smooth greys of the charcoal pencils. The dark dust left behind as she sketched, usually ended up all over her hands and face, but it never really bothered her.

She ripped the top page off the spiral-bound tablet, threw it over her shoulder, and began again.

Each time she started over, she tried harder—pushed harder—breaking point after point until she was down to her last charcoal pencil, but the drawing never came into focus. Her memory of the—*what did the stranger call it?*—*the Mapstone*—was so vivid now it hurt. It cut into her thoughts like a razor blade cuts into flesh—smooth and quick and clean.

In her mind's eye, she again saw the symbols rise to the surface of the stone. Some primal part of her felt she should be able to read them, but their meaning remained just beyond reach. The harder she pushed the tip into the paper, the deeper the hate-storm boiled. Her body and mind, pushed beyond frustration now, bulleted straight into rage as her last charcoal point broke.

Thoughts went black. A thundering fury rioted inside her. In a fever pitch, she scribbled and scratched and struck the page, cutting deep black gashes into the paper until a face emerged, gruesome and vile.

She stared at it, blinking.

Impossibly, the image began to move on the page, at first seemingly confined to the parameters of the tablet, but like a wild animal caged, it began to fight its confinement. She watched in horror as it grew black arms and chard legs, screeching in agony until it broke free. The wretched creature rose up off the paper like a sickening, all-consuming shadow to envelop her. She gasped as it's black-mist fingers wrapped around her neck.

Ani clawed at her throat, heaved and convulsed, frantic for breath. The whoosh of blood through her veins, the final beats of her heart, the hiss of her last breath escaping, all throbbed against her ear drums for the final seconds of life.

She woke, gasping and coughing. Head pounding. Limbs numb and aching.

Taking great gulps of air, she calmed her racing heart. *Must have fallen asleep*, she thought, grasping at an explanation. She'd had bad dreams before, but this was no ordinary nightmare.

"Ani, honey, didn't you hear me calling? Dinner's almost ready. Time to wash up."

Ani glanced over her shoulder to find her mother standing in the doorway, dressed in her usual whitewashed blue jeans, white tucked blouse, and turquoise necklace. The site of her calmed Ani's frayed nerves.

"Um," Ani said trying to gather her wits, "I didn't here you. I was just, uh, concentrating, I guess." She looked down at her sketch, expecting a twisted mass of black gashes, but the drawing in front of her was . . . perfect. There, at the center of a pristinely white, smudgeless paper, was the Mapstone in full and beautiful detail, exactly as she remembered it. She touched the fresh charcoal on the page. It tingled on her fingertips.

"Have you fed Mobius today?" asked her mother. "He's been eyeing my side dishes again," said Nan with a grin, leaning against the doorjamb.

Her mom was one of those people who always seemed to be in a good mood. She took great pleasure in her studies, and she was constantly studying something: books, people, animals, plants, food. Her motto was, 'No matter where you are or what you're doing, there is always something around to learn from.'

"I'll feed Mobius in a sec," said Ani, looking at her blackened fingers. "I just need to, um, clean up."

"I'm happy to see you drawing again, Ani. It's been a while."

I may never draw again, Ani thought, trying to shake the nightmare from her mind.

"You two coming down soon?" asked her father, appearing behind his wife in the doorway. "It smells too good not to eat."

Looking at her mother and father, it was obvious to Ani where she got her coarse brown hair, dark eyes, olive skin, and plain features. Her father had the same dull qualities about his face. How many times had Ani wished she'd inherited her mother's fair skin and golden hair?

Aqua-blue eyes peered over Ani's shoulder at the sketch on her desk. "What'cha working on?" Her mother's jasmine-rose perfume spiced the air.

"It's the stone I found this morning," Ani answered.

"Let's see," said her father.

Ani held up the drawing.

"That's it," he said. "That's how it looked. Darndest thing I ever saw. Came straight out of the desert looking polished and perfect, as if it'd been sitting in a geologist's rock collection for years."

"It's beautiful, Ani. Good job with the detail and depth," said Mom, inspecting the sketch. "You found this on your trail?"

"Yeah, and then I lost it."

"You didn't lose it, Ani, you sold it. There's a big difference." Stan smiled proudly. "She got a cool hundred for it."

"Well well, a hundred dollars? What are you going to do with all that money?" Her mother began to weave Ani's long hair into a smooth braid down the center of her back. "Maybe it's time we opened a savings account for you."

"Maybe," said Ani. "I don't know. I haven't thought about it."

That was the honest truth. The money wasn't important. All that mattered was the rock, the stranger who bought it, and the questions he left behind. Why had he shown her the symbols? What did they mean? How could he have just vanished? And what was that nightmare about? Ani sighed, pinning the drawing up on her bulletin board. She may never know the answers.

"Well, I'm proud of you, Ani. You did great today," said her father on the way downstairs to the kitchen. "Soon you'll forget all about that rock, and you'll still have a hundred dollars in your pocket."

But Ani didn't forget. Later that night, after getting ready for bed, she knelt in front of her dresser, pulled the bottom drawer out, and carefully removed a small wooden treasure box from its hiding place. The box had been a gift from her grandmother before she died. 'Whatsoever you put in this box shall be safe for all time,' she'd said when she offered Ani the gift. She'd spoken the words like an enchantment, and Ani believed in their magic.

Her grandmother believed too. While she lived, she was the only family member Ani could talk to about such things. Grandma Kay winked imperceptibly whenever Ani received one of her father's lectures on why belief in magic was 'fanciful and rooted in ignorance.' She'd lean close and whisper, 'But we know differently, don't we dear.'

Thus far, Ani had but three protected items in her treasure box: a small heart-shaped sachet with the words 'Grandma's Love' embroidered on the front, a trilobite fossil souvenir from a trip she took with her dad a few years back, and a tiny pewter angel her mother had given her when she had pneumonia at the age of six.

As Ani placed the hundred-dollar bill in the box, she secretly wished it could be the stone instead. It belonged here in the company of her other treasures much more than a lifeless, magic-less, green piece of paper no matter how much it was worth. Now, all she had left of the stone was a memory. She glanced at her drawing tacked above the desk and knew what she had to do.

With charcoal pencil in hand, she took the drawing off the wall and added the strange glyphs that had appeared on the surface of the stone when the stranger passed his hand over it. Contrary to her experience inside her nightmare, she found it easy to recall and draw the ancient symbols, outlining them just below the sketch. Then, at the bottom of the page, she wrote one word—*Mapstone*.

Before closing her treasure box, she folded the drawing into quarters and placed it atop the other items kept safe by her grandmother's magic. With a sigh, she returned the box to its hiding place and climbed into bed.

When sleep finally came, she dreamed about the stone and the strange man who bought it. And the next night she dreamed of them again. And the next. And the next. Night after night. Always the same dream . . .

The stranger stood rigid on a hilltop. He held his hands open-palmed to the heavens as if in ceremony, but instead of sky, a canopy of rock hung overhead—the same type of rock as the Mapstone—jet black, glass-like, fractured by frozen blue-green lightning suspended amidst silver-fleck stars. In the absence of sun, the soft light came from everywhere, or nowhere, as if the air itself glowed.

As the stranger slowly lowered his arms, Ani saw that he clutched a curious metallic device in his right hand. Two luminescent spheres appeared at either end of a slender metal cylinder not more than six inches in length, casting a radiance that flooded the entire area with a light so brilliant it consumed all detail.

Momentary blindness sent a bolt of pain and panic through Ani. As the light subsided and her vision returned, she found herself unable to move. A second wave of panic eclipsed the first. What power this man held over her. The struggle against it, useless. When he summoned her, she could not refuse the call. Slowly, with the Mapstone in her hand, she ascended the slope, each step shakier than the last, until she reached the top.

She stood trembling before the stranger, weak and weary.

"What do you want?" she asked, the words barely spoken.

His gaze intensified as he held out the device, uttering words in a language she did not recognize, yet somehow understood.

"Take it," he said. "It is yours. Everything has changed for you now. And for me as well. Destiny awaits us both."

But when she reached out to take the object from him, the dream abruptly ended—in the most dreadful way—night after night.

"Ani? Are you feeling okay?" asked her mother before breakfast a week later.

Ani shrugged. Mom always knew when something was up. It was a bit annoying. "I'm okay," she said feebly.

"Got the blahs?"

"Yeah," said Ani, not wanting to talk about what was really bothering her.

"I know what you need," said mom, holding up a scrub brush and dishwashing soap.

"*Mom.*"

"It always helps to focus on something."

"Can't I just set the table?"

"Your father beat you to it. Come on." She gestured to the sink. "If you do the dishes while I finish cooking breakfast—"

"—There will be less to clean up after," finished Ani. "I know." She glowered, which only made her mom laugh.

Ani took the soap and scrub-brush to the sink, and ran hot

water into the washbasin, wishing they had a dishwasher like the rest of the civilized world.

"You'll feel better after you eat," said Mom. "We're having your favorite. Scrambled eggs with cheddar cheese and roasted potatoes, toast with cinnamon and honey."

"Well, if that isn't incentive, I don't know what is," said her father, joining the conversation. He picked up a dishtowel. "You rinse, I'll dry." He rolled up the towel and flicked it in Mom's direction to tease her.

Ani giggled. She liked it when Dad woke up in a good mood. He was pleasant enough most of the time, but every so often he showed a playful side that always lit up her mother's smile. They'd exchange private glances when they thought Ani wasn't looking. Secretly, she liked seeing the love they had for each other, and even though she'd never admit it to their faces, it was one of her favorite things about having decidedly dorky parents.

Within a few minutes, they were all sitting at the table, eating, laughing, talking of the coming day, and as her mother had promised, by the end of breakfast, Ani spirits had lifted and she was ready for school.

Though the nearest school was about sixty miles away, Ani didn't have quite that far to travel. In fact, her entire commute was less than 20 feet. She'd always liked homeschooling with Mom. Her favorite subjects were geography and history, but her mother could make any subject fun. She smiled as she remembered their first day of school together so many years ago.

"Welcome to the Nan. J. Jasper School for the Mineralogical Misunderstood," her mom had said with exaggerated significance. "Our first lesson will be The Psychology of Nose Picking. No wait, that can't be right. Oh yeah, it's the Quantum Affects of Phantom Farting. Hold on, that's next week. Let me just check my notes."

They laughed and laughed that first day and every day after that. She loved how Mom could make even the hard stuff seem easy. Ani may have wondered once or twice what it would be like to go to a real public school with kids her own age, but it was only a passing curiosity. She liked being the only student in class.

Ani decided not to tell her parents about the recurring dream that haunted her every time she closed her eyes. She didn't want them to make a big deal out of it. But when, a few days later, her father said he was going to Greyhawk's Gas and Garage for repairs, Ani jumped at the opportunity to go along. Her grandfather, Kahetay, would surely know what her dreams were trying to tell her. He had a way of knowing the meaning of things.

"We'll head out early tomorrow morning," her father had said after telling Ani she could go along. "But I want you dressed and ready to go by eight. The work on the truck will take some time and I want to be back home before dusk."

The next morning, after another fitful night's sleep— nightmares that came and went like mists in a dark forest—a strange high-pitched fizzing noise pulled Ani out of her dream-state and into a hazy awareness.

No, not fizzing, she thought sleepily, trying to focus her mind, *more like a clicking hiss.* It was such a strange sound that for a moment she considered the notion that she might still be dreaming, but when she opened her eyes all doubt vanished.

She found herself face to face with the source of the odd sound— a huge, scaly, green and gold, decidedly crafty six-foot long iguana.

Dreaming is one of the highest forms of communication known to man, wherein the soul speaks to itself in the secret code of the eternal.

-Solamas ❖ Tome of the Zielfah Ri

CHAPTER THREE

♈

THE WIND & THE DREAM-READING

Ani's eyes grew wide as the iguana's head bobbed inches from her nose. She let out a quick huff. "Mobius! You know you're not supposed to be on the bed! You scared me half to death. What am I going to do with you?"

Sooo sorrry, said the iguana in a low gravelly monotone.

Ani stared, aghast. The words just popped into her mind without a thought attached.

"Did you . . . did you just say something to me?" She rubbed the sleep from her eyes and focused her full attention on her reptilian friend.

Mobius had been a houseguest for a little over three years now, but he had never spoken to her before.

"Say that again," she demanded, feeling more than a bit foolish talking to an iguana.

Soooo sooorrry, repeated Mobius, this time even slower.

"That's what I thought you said." Ani squinted at the reptile.

Maybe, she thought, *this is one of those weird dreams that tricks you into thinking you're awake when you're really still—*

Asleeep? said Mobius, finishing her thought. *Noooo, you're awaaake.*

"Wait, you can hear *my* thoughts too?"

Of courssse.

Ani stared in disbelief. Maybe her imagination was playing tricks on her again.

Noooo, not that either, said the iguana.

"So," said Ani, sitting up in bed, "we're actually carrying on a real conversation right now?"

Ssseeems that waaay.

"But, you're an iguana!"

Mobius stared, unblinkingly. *Sssooo.*

"You mean you could talk this whole time but never said a word until just now?"

I taaalked. Yooou just didn't listen until nooow.

"Well, you can't just hop up on the bed and start talking. You might give someone a heart attack first thing in the morning and then Mom wouldn't let me keep you. And you know you're not allowed in my bedroom."

But it's waaaarm here, the iguana droned in earnest.

"You have your own bed with a heat lamp and everything."

His tail twitched. Even without words, she knew what that meant.

It's lonely downstaaairs. His thought had a touch of sadness to it.

Ani's heart softened. "Yeah, I guess it would be at night, with all the bedrooms upstairs."

"Ani, are you coming?" The impatient call came from downstairs.

"Just a sec, Dad," she called back, hopping out of bed to dash to the closet. "Shoot. I almost forgot. We're going to Kahetay's today!"

"Make it a quick sec!" yelled her father. "I don't want to be late."

"Coming!"

Ani glanced down at Mobius as she hastily tugged on a pair of blue jeans. "Can Mom and Dad hear you too?"

Naaah, only yoooou.

"Why only me?"

Dunno. Maybeee it's your birthdaaaaay.

"And why now after all this time?"

Dunno. Maybeee it's myyy birthdaaaaay.

Ani laughed. "This is just too weird." She went to the mirror and pulled her hair into a ponytail, securing it with a red hair tie.

"Anani!" This time it was Mom calling from the bottom of the stairs. "Your father's waiting in the truck. He's got the motor running. Better hurry."

"On my way!" she called back, throwing on a tank top and buttoning a long-sleeved shirt over it. A quick glance in the mirror confirmed her suspicions. "I look like the walking dead."

She scratched Mobius in his favorite spot under the chin.

"Sometimes I wish I could be an iguana like you. Then I could sleep all day and have lazy rainforest dreams instead of these awful nightmares."

But youuuu can't be an iguana like meeee, he said.

"Why not?" she asked, curious as to his reply.

Because you're a huuumaaan, answered Mobius, with infallible logic. *But as humans go,* he added, *you're okaaay.*

"Thanks," she said, secretly pleased to have the iguana' approval.

Mobius slowly turned, showing off its spiky dragon-scaled back, and then slid off the bed onto the floor. She heard a long drawn out *Seeee'ya 'round Ahhnee*, as the last few inches of his hefty two-foot tail disappeared through the doorway.

Ani smiled to herself. She had liked Mobius from the start, naming him after M.C. Escher's famous infinity illustration because the patterns the baby iguana left in the sand looked like figure eights. He seemed to approve of the name and from that point on, they were inseparable. Now that he could talk, or rather, she could understand him, it opened up whole new possibilities.

When Ani finally flew down the stairs, her mother was waiting with a lunch bag and travel mug for her father. "These muffins are to share with your dad, and there's orange juice for you too."

"Thanks Mom," said Ani, wondering what she would say about her daughter carrying on a conversation with a somewhat glib and disgruntled iguana.

Nan gave her a quick hug. "Have a good time. And remind Kahetay about dinner on Saturday. Six o'clock."

"I will." Ani dashed out the front door.

Her father sat in the old Chevy pick up, fingers tapping the steering wheel as the engine sputtered and coughed.

When she climbed into the passenger seat, he shot her a stern look. "I thought we agreed on eight o'clock."

"I was talking to Mobius," Ani replied matter-of-factly.

Her father put the truck in gear and pulled away from the house. "Got out of his cage again, did he?"

Ani nodded. "He said he wants to sleep upstairs."

"He's getting too big, Ani. Don't know how I ever let you talk me into keeping that thing."

"He would have died in the desert! Whoever let him go—"

"—probably wanted to get rid of him."

"Don't say that!"

"It's just a lizard, Ani."

"He's not just a lizard, he's my friend!"

"I really wish you could have some real friends. It can't be healthy never being around kids your own age."

Dad knew she didn't have the chance to make friends face to face, having no neighbors to play with, no playgrounds to play in. The only kids she ever talked to were the other homeschooled kids online and her two cousins in Vancouver whom she wrote to once a month, and saw only on the occasional Thanksgiving.

Ani figured her dad felt kind of responsible since it had been his idea to move to the desert in the first place. He brought up the subject every year around this time when the advance deposits for summer camp were due.

"I don't mind, Dad. Really. I like being alone," she told him, which was true. She didn't need to go to summer camp or play with other kids to have fun. Her imagination could take her anywhere she wanted to go—other places, other times, other worlds. She was never bored. And besides, she never really felt alone. Ever since she could remember, she'd had the feeling that someone else was there with her, always by her side. She used to have long conversations with him. Her parents called him an imaginary friend, but he always seemed real to Ani. When she was little, she even named him. She called him Eli, and together they had great imaginary adventures in far-off imaginary lands.

Her father frowned.

Here it comes.

"Have you thought about some kind of summer camp this year?"

Right on schedule. "Dad, you ask me that every year."

"And every year you tell me you don't want to go. But it's time to experience something new, Ani. "

"If you want me to experience something new, take me to the Grand Canyon."

"How do you know you won't like it? Or even love it? You'll never know unless you try. The friends you'd make there—"

"I don't need any new friends. I'm happy with things just the way they are."

"I understand that Kahetay is your best friend, and he's been a good friend to all of us, but it is important to have new adventures with other thirteen-year-old girls you can relate to."

"Do you think I'm like other thirteen-year-old girls, Dad? Do you think I have anything in common with them? I see how they are online. What they're interested in. I'm not like them and I don't need to be around them." Ani's voice raised in pitch as a subtle sense of dread crept up on her. "We don't have the money to send me to camp anyway."

"Well, there's the hundred you made off your rock, and we have some money saved up. Your mother and I talked it over—"

"No." Ani's stomach clenched. "Dad, I don't want to go."

"We think it's time. You need to be with kids your own age."

"No I don't."

"It's called Twin Moons Ranch. We checked out the website. It's in the Sierras. Beautiful place. Mountains. Rivers. Trees. Waterfalls. No desert heat. We think you'll really like it there."

"I really like it here. And besides, I'm too old for camp now."

"Twin Moons is a camp for kids your age, Ani. It will be a great experience. You'll see."

Panic vaporized her confidence. They were going to make her go. "Dad I . . . I want to stay here . . . in the desert, with you and mom and Kahetay, and Mobius."

"It will only be for a few weeks."

"Don't make me go."

"The decision has been made, Ani. Once you're there, you'll be glad you went."

"No, I won't."

"You will. You'll see. You're just going to have to trust us on this one."

"Dad, please."

"You're going, Anani, and that's final."

The cab of the truck fell silent but for the roar of the wind through the open windows. Ani couldn't bear the thought of leaving, even if only for a few weeks. Everything she loved was right here. She didn't need anything else. How could she make her father see? She had to figure out a way to change his mind.

At Greyhawk's Gas and Garage, Ani's father talked to the mechanic about the truck while Ani stood at the counter leafing through her grandfather's copy of *The Magical Properties of Desert Stones*. She tried to memorize the magical purpose of every stone, and wondered if Kahetay would someday teach her how to use them. Despite her desire to learn, Ani had never officially asked him to tutor her in the ways of magic, primarily because he had never officially claimed to know anything about it. But Ani had the feeling Kahetay knew many things he told no one about.

Quite a bit of mystery surrounded her grandfather; like the soundless way he walked, almost as if his feet never quite touched the ground, or the fact that he owned a garage, but not a car, and how he could tell what the weather would be like just by feeling the wind on his face, or how he could call a hawk down from the sky, simply by singing to it.

When her father approached, Ani quickly closed the book and pretended to be looking at a large map tacked up on the wall.

"Plotting your escape?" he asked with a chuckle.

"Yeah," she replied, playing along. "Which would be better? The highway or the canyon road?"

"Well, you'll have plenty of time to figure it out. The truck's going to take a few hours." He pointed to the lunch bag on the counter next to his daughter. "Are those your mother's muffins?"

She nodded, smiling at her father's childlike excitement. "I think I'll ask Kahetay if he wants to go for a walk. Save me one?"

"I'm not sure that's humanly possible. We're talking about Mom's baking here."

Ani laughed, turning toward the door. "I understand the risks."

Her father poured himself a cup of decaf from the coffeemaker on the counter and retrieved a honey-blackberry muffin, a look of sheer bliss further warming his usual pleasant expression. "Don't wander too far," he called over his shoulder. "And keep an eye on the time. I know how it goes when the two of you get to talkin'."

"Sure Dad," she said, having no true means of complying. He knew neither she nor Kahetay ever wore a watch. Desert time moved to the rhythms of the sun. It could not be rushed.

Ani peered around the corner and into the garage. No Kahetay. After searching the office and the break room, she headed for the supply room around back. She knew he went there sometimes to be alone. When she entered through the curtained doorway, the musky sweet smell of burning sage welcomed her, a scent that so often lingered in Kahetay's hair and clothing she had come to regard it as his own unique brand of cologne.

He stood at the center of the dimly lit stockroom. In his left hand, he held a small bowl of smoldering sage leaves, in his right, an eagle feather. With eyes closed, he turned to face each of the four directions waving the feather over the sage in a slow fanning motion. Smoke curled around his face and hands as he chanted softly to himself.

Ani knew not to disturb him. She recognized the strange and graceful movements of a Native American cleansing ritual. It was

21

something he did every day. He said it had to do with clearing away unwanted thoughts and negative energy, and that it paved the way for the body to heal itself. She found it beautiful to watch.

She studied his shadow-ridged face. There seemed an ancientness about him that belied his age. His long black hair, which fell nearly to his waist, had rivers of muted silver running through it. He claimed to have earned each strand with a life experience that left its mark on him, body and soul.

His chant complete, Kahetay opened his eyes to find Ani standing just inside the doorway.

"Anani." He spoke her name with a fondness reserved for old friends and gave her a warm hug. "I'm glad you came with your dad. It is good to see you."

Ani smiled up at her grandfather. He'd always been there for her, helping her, guiding her since even before she came into this world. She knew he wasn't her real grandfather. It was a title of honor bestowed upon him by her parents on the day she was born.

The way her mother told the story, they might have lost Ani had it not been for Kahetay. He had seen, in a vision, that there would be complications surrounding her birth. Three days before Nan had gone into labor, Kahetay came to the rock shop, insisting that she go to the hospital early.

It took some convincing, but finally they went, realizing that if there were any problems, even minor ones, the seventy-three miles between the rock shop and the nearest hospital would make it impossible to get urgent care. When Kahetay's dream became a reality, they were already at the hospital and received the help they needed to save Ani's life.

"You are carrying a burden, little one," said Kahetay, out of the silence. "A sadness weighs upon you."

"Dad is sending me away."

"To camp, yes. When he called about the truck yesterday, he mentioned it."

"But I'm not going to go."

"That is not the weight I sense. There is something else."

Ani nodded, remembering why she came. The nightmare.

He gestured toward the door. "The winter sun is bright and warm. The wind, gentle and cool. A perfect day for a walk, don't you think?"

Ani nodded again, her mouth tight.

Kahetay frowned. "What is it, little one?"

"I wanted to ask you about a dream I've been having. I was

hoping you could help me figure out what it means."

"Of course."

"And also something that happened this morning when I woke up."

His brows drew together. "What happened this morning?"

"Mobius . . . um . . . spoke to me. Not the way you and I speak, but inside my mind, like having thoughts that weren't my own."

"And what did Mobius say?"

"That he's been talking all along, I just wasn't listening."

Kahetay grinned. "That sounds like Mobius."

"He told me he wanted to sleep upstairs."

"Because it's lonely downstairs at night."

"Exactly. And he said as humans go, I'm okay."

"All in all, I'd say that's a pretty smart iguana you've got there."

"So I'm losing it, right?"

"No," he said, with a secret smile. "Actually one of the women in my tribe spoke with animals in much the same way. It was her gift. It could be yours as well."

"I don't think so."

"Why not? It's a wonderful gift. Animals are great teachers."

"I think it's just Mobius. Maybe because he lives with us. I don't know. But I've never heard any other animals talk."

"Or maybe it's like Mobius said; you just never listened before." After a pause, Kahetay added, "And your dream, was it about talking to animals?"

"No. I've talked to animals before in my dreams, but these dreams are different, not like any I've ever had."

"Ah, then," he said softly, leading her out of the stockroom and into the garage, "you can tell me all about it on our walk."

After a few words with the mechanic, they headed out the back door.

"And the dream always ends the same way," Ani told Kahetay as they approached a small patch of dunes. "I climb the hill to where the stranger is standing, and he gives me the metal thing, whatever it is—the one that's casting the weird light—and as I start to take it, the stranger closes his eyes. Then the wind comes up all storm-like, and everything disintegrates, molecule by molecule—turning into grains of sand. Then the sand turns black and everything is blown away by the storm—all of it—the man, the hill, the sky—and I'm left standing alone on this huge dark sand dune with this awful feeling like I'm responsible."

"Responsible for what?"

"Destroying everything."

"I see. And you're sure the man in your dream is the same man you saw in your father's shop?"

"Positive."

"What of the rock you sold him? The one with the strange markings? Was it also in your dream?"

"It was in my left hand the whole time. And the sky looked like it was made of the same stuff as the rock." Ani looked down at her feet as they walked. "Do you think the dream is telling me I did the wrong thing by selling the rock to the stranger?"

"I think perhaps it was meant for him all along. I don't believe he was there by chance."

"What do you mean?"

"You said he had a name for it. The Mapstone? And that when he received the rock, he made a motion with his hand that brought symbols to the surface?"

Ani nodded.

"Then it would appear he was already quite familiar with the stone and its unique properties. It would also seem he wanted you to know, or he would not have shown you."

"But why?"

"I do not know."

"And how could he have known I would find the rock? On that particular day? At that time? He was already there when I got back to the shop. Are you saying he was there to buy a rock I hadn't even found yet?"

"I'm saying it's possible he could have placed the rock in your path for you to find."

"But I strayed from the path that morning. There's no way he could have known where I would go. *I* didn't even know."

"Perhaps he has ways that are yet known to you."

"So he made sure I found the stone just so he could turn around and buy it back from me for a hundred dollars? Why would anyone do that?"

"I do not know."

"And why do I keep dreaming about him?"

"Tell me," said her grandfather, his voice a near whisper, "in these dreams, what is your sense of this stranger?"

"Well, at first I was afraid of him, but now—" Ani took a deep breath and let it out slowly, feeling suddenly tired. "I just want to know who he is. Why I keep having the dream. You know about this stuff, Kahetay. I've heard you talk about the meanings of dreams before. Can you tell me what this all means?"

He gestured for her to sit on a nearby rock at the base of a drift. "The images of your dream—" He stopped, considering, and then sat beside her before continuing. "Powerful symbolism—the climbing of the hill, the light at the top, the offering of magic—it says a lot about your readiness to take the next step in the evolution of self and soul, but," he bent to pick a tiny pebble from his leather sandal, "there may be more to it than that."

"What do you mean?"

"Perhaps this man and these images are not just symbols from your subconscious, but rather reflections, or visions of something authentic. Something real."

"Real?"

"I can not know for certain until I—" he broke off.

"Until you what?"

He hesitated, as if considering whether or not to finish his sentence. "Until I see it with my own eyes."

Ani pitched her grandfather a sideways glance. "How could *you* see *my* dream?"

Kahetay did not answer.

Ani waited. She knew not to fill the silences between them. Kahetay spoke only when the right words came.

Staring at the far horizon, he said, "Did I ever tell you the meaning of my name?"

"No."

"It is a word that represents the spirit of the wind. But this was not the name to which I was born. I received it when I turned twenty-one. I was still on the reservation, but I belonged to a group of individuals who did not entirely follow the Navajo ways. We were young and wanted to go beyond what our fathers had taught us. We called ourselves the *Nátah*, which is short for *Náá nátah déé*. It means 'from another place.' We acquired some—" he paused, searching again for the right words, "—unique skills. Each of us cultivated a different power."

"And yours has something to do with the wind?"

He nodded. "The Nátah believe it is only with the spirit of the wind that one can enter another's dream. As one of my *new skills*, I developed the ability to interpret dreams by direct experience."

"You mean you can get into other people's dreams and watch them?"

"When invited. Yes. It's the best way to comprehend the dream's message. I can have my own intuitive sense of your dream instead of relying on your description from memory. It is the use of words to describe a wordless world that ultimately fails us. With a dream-reading, no words need come between us."

"How does it work? Do I need to do anything?"

"The only essential ingredient to a successful dream-reading is trust. I will not be allowed to pass through the gateway of your secret world unless the surrender of complete trust is between us," he explained. "This is the way of the dream-reader. I must also surrender. I must also trust." He placed a fatherly hand on her shoulder. "So I must ask you now; do you trust me enough to share your inner experience with me?"

"Kahetay, you're my grandfather and my best friend. If it weren't for you, I might never have even been born. I trust you with all that I am." Love filled her heart and misted her eyes. "Remember when you told me about kindred spirits? Two people destined to know each other, sharing some common ground or life experience that will forever link them? That's what we are, you and I. Kindred spirits."

He gazed at her in reverence. "You are very wise, my friend."

"So what should I do?"

"You've only to fall asleep in my presence. I will do the rest."

"When can we start?"

At the crest of a sand dune, Ani stretched out, letting her limbs sink into the soft sand. The bluest of blue skies lazed above. Marshmallow clouds dangled from invisible strings.

The soothing tone of Kahetay's voice, the vivid colors of his words, painted an image of a beautiful garden in her mind. Her eyelids grew heavy and slowly closed. Cradled by the warm sand, cooled by a soft breeze and having slept only a few hours the night before, Ani drifted easily into sleep.

Again, she stood on the hill with the strange rock sky above, but this time she saw no sign of the stranger. She turned to search for him and stopped, amazed to find herself at the threshold of a magnificent stone city. Entering through a huge granite gateway, she followed a finely cut path of deep blue lazurite down into a maze of temples and terraced structures.

The narrowing path curved around a vast windowless edifice in the shape of a crescent moon, its points coming together to form an entryway. At each point a stone pillar stood broad and tall; chiseled sentinels inscribed with the same strange writing Ani had seen on the Mapstone. Try as she might, she could not read the message it held for her, but she knew someone who could.

Where was the stranger?

A chill ran through her, for the instant she thought of him, she could feel his presence. She spun around to find him standing behind her, not twenty feet from where she stood.

Again, he held out the metallic device and summoned her as he had always done, calling to her from within her own thoughts.

The small crystal spheres on either end of the device ignited, casting sidelong shadows in every direction. She stared, transfixed by the light as she started toward him.

Seconds passed in slow motion.

Drawing closer, closer, nearly close enough to touch, she extended her hand, palm face up, but as the old man held out the device, his gaze suddenly shifted to something beyond her. An expression of horror contorted his face. He stepped back and with one sweep of his arm, vanished in a burst of light.

Ani whirled around to see what had frightened the stranger away. There, standing at the entrance to the crescent moon temple was Kahetay, his posture so rigid it looked as though he'd been turned to stone.

When Ani woke it was late afternoon. Kahetay sat cross-legged on the sand beside her, head down, lips moving, soundlessly.

"Kahetay? Are you okay?"

He answered in a trembling voice. "Never before has my presence changed a dream. Never. This man in your dream, he knew I was there. He could see me." Kahetay turned to Ani, the look on his face even more somber than his usual serious expression. "Ani, I have seen this man before."

A shudder rippled through her. "What?"

"I have seen him in other people's dreams, but he has never seen me. Until now."

"Do you know who he is?"

"No, but he is always searching. Searching for someone or something. The Nátah call him the Soul Seeker."

If there was but one face of darkness, and
we had courage enough to look upon it,
we would find within it an image of our
own, for no man who carries the light of
life is without shadow.

-Xephero ✣ *Tome of the Zielfah Ri*

CHAPTER FOUR

ϒ

THE FACE OF DARKNESS

Ani shuddered. An inexplicable fear surged within. "The Soul Seeker?"

"He carries that luminous wand into people's dreams and holds the light up to their souls," said Kahetay. "When he doesn't find what he is looking for he moves on."

"What's he looking for?"

Kahetay didn't answer. Instead, he stood and offered his hand to help Ani to her feet.

They dusted themselves off and began walking back to the garage before he continued.

"The story among the Nátah is that he steals people's souls just before death, so that they will come to live with him in his great stone city in the afterlife. Many fear him because they believe if this were to happen, their souls would not be free to join with the Great Spirit. Some believe he is looking for the mark of death on a soul when he holds up the light. Others say it is a certain purity and sense of connection he seeks. There are even a few who actually believe he *is* the Great Spirit taking human form to conduct his quest."

Ani shuttered. A lump formed in the back of her throat as the realization hit her. She swallowed hard. "If the stories are true, then I might—" her voice cracked. She cleared her throat and summoned her courage. "Kahetay, am I . . . going to die?" The swirling, sinking uncertainty Ani felt when she thought of leaving behind all she had ever known pulled her down into a frightening kind of darkness. Without warning, Ani felt herself clinging to the edge of an abyss.

"Anani'nah, those stories were part of the Nátah's search for answers to questions they did not understand, stories that have taught my people to fear the Soul Seeker. I cannot deny the impact such tales have had upon me, but the truth may be very different." He stopped himself. A change came over his face, making him seem suddenly older. "I didn't mean to scare you."

"But what do *you* believe about the Soul Seeker?"

For a moment, the only sound was the rhythm of their feet on the dirt path. Ani knew not to press the question. If he had an answer, and she was meant to know, he would share it.

"I believe there are things in this world, and worlds beyond, that we have yet to comprehend. I believe this is one of those things."

"You're worried about something," said Ani. "What is it?"

"My thoughts are not yet clear. I will ask for further guidance. But by his reaction, it would seem the Soul Seeker regarded my presence in your dream as a threat, which leads me to wonder—

"Why would the appearance of someone who cares about me concern him unless he," she swallowed hard, "wants to take me?" said Ani, filling in the blank as Kahetay hesitated again.

"It was your dream, Granddaughter. What do your insides tell you?"

Ani stared at the ground, contemplating the question. She searched her heart as Kahetay had taught her. Years ago he'd shown her how to 'swallow the question,' and 'ask her body' for the answer. How does it feel inside you? Does it feel calm? Does it make you uneasy? Your body will tell you what is in your heart. She'd used the technique many times over the years. It always helped her make the right decision.

She closed her eyes, cleared her thoughts and then invoked an image of the stranger in her mind, but nothing came. No thought. No feeling. No answer. "It's not working," she huffed. "Why isn't it working?"

"You try too hard, little one. Release the effort and allow—

"I don't know how I feel about it," Ani spurt in frustration. "All

I know is that in my dreams, he only seems to want one thing—to give me the magic. Once he does, he vanishes. Every time."

"Then perhaps there is no danger," said Kahetay, glancing away so Ani could not read the concern in his eyes, but it was too late. She'd already seen it.

Ani waited a moment, hoping he would share his thoughts, but he remained stoic.

Finally he said, "If I were to interpret the images of your dream, I would say the hill you climb symbolizes a journey you will take and the challenges you will face. The man represents your guide on that journey. I believe the dream is a call. A summons."

"Then what's the light-thingy he's trying to give me?"

"The invitation."

"To what? What is that thing? You didn't get any sense about it?"

"Only that it is a talisman of some kind—an object that bestows magical powers on the soul who possesses it."

They reached the back porch of Greyhawk's Gas and Garage and sat on the concrete steps. Ani gazed into the distance toward the small stretch of dunes that met the blue sky with a silky smooth profile.

Her father pushed the screen door open behind them. "Perfect timing. Truck's done. Your man did a nice job, Kahetay. She runs great."

"He's the best in town."

"What town?" Stan laughed, glancing at the lonely truck stop with its single coffee shop, gas station, and small general store. He turned back to Kahetay. "Still comin' for dinner next weekend?"

"I'll be there," said Kahetay. "Saturday at six."

"Good. See you then." He looked at Ani. "Hungry? Let's pop next door for a quick bite to eat before we head back."

On the way home, Ani stared out the window, thinking about all Kahetay had said that afternoon. She knew he hadn't intended to scare her, but his words filled her with a numbing sense of dread as they tumbled over and over in her mind. She knew there was something he wasn't telling her; a piece of the story he wasn't willing to share. Maybe he thought he was protecting her, but she'd rather know, than not know. She knew that with too little information, her imagination could work against itself, making shadows into demons and dreams into nightmares.

She pulled her hair in front of her, absently combing out the tangles with her fingers as gusts from the open window created more. The wind vibrated in her ears, pounding out a mad rhythm inside her head. Ani rolled up the window and then glanced at her father. He hummed quietly to himself as he drove.

She sighed, wishing she could tell him about the dream-reading, wishing he could be the kind of father who would listen with an open mind, the kind of father who would take her seriously if she were to tell him about the stranger who haunted her dreams and perhaps threatened her very existence. But Ani knew he wouldn't believe her, and she would just end up feeling foolish.

Even her grandmother warned her about sharing such things with her father. "You mustn't speak of magic around your dad," she had said one morning in hushed tones, not long before she died. "He's a good man, but he has a kind of selective blindness. He can't see anything of the magical realm, and it has hardened his heart a bit." After stopping to catch her breath, she smiled feebly and then reached for Ani's hand. "You have a gift, my girl. Be glad of it. And protect it as you would a precious secret."

A few days later, her grandmother was gone, like a disappearing act performed by some cosmic magician. At the time, Ani didn't understand what had happened. She was only six. Nothing she loved had ever died before. Death was a new concept for her, but no one seemed capable of explaining what it was. Now, of course, she knew what death was, but she still didn't understand it.

Ani's eyes welled up against her will. She missed Grandma Kay, missed her gentleness, and the way she always seemed to understand. Would her grandmother be there, waiting for her on the other side when she, herself died? Ani's thoughts turned dark. What if the stories of the Nátah were true? What if the presence of the Soul Seeker in her dream really was a harbinger of death?

Desperate for a distraction, she forced her thoughts into a new direction, and tried to picture this ride home being just like any other. Ani always enjoyed the time she spent with her father in the old pick-up truck. It was pleasant, peaceful, and the desert landscape never failed to capture her imagination.

Shifting her focus from her reflection in the window to the desert beyond, Ani watched the sagebrush at the edge of the highway whoosh by in the failing light of dusk. Letting her vision blur, she allowed her mind to wander into a kind of daydream.

Floating outside her body, Ani looked down at herself and her father in the cab of the truck, speeding along the open highway. The scene looked as if she were viewing it through a pool of murky water. Almost instantly, Ani had a terrible sense that something was wrong, or would be soon, but what that something was, she did not know. Her eyes flashed to the window. They passed a mile marker sign—157—and a dirt road turnoff.

Nothing unusual. All was as it should be.

Then she saw it: a white wolf. It stood in the road up ahead. Not a coyote but an actual wolf, twice the size of any woodland wolf, its yellow eyes iridescent in the truck's high beams. They sped straight for it but the colossal creature just stood there, frozen, staring into the oncoming headlights.

Move, Ani thought, willing the wolf to safety. *Get out of the road!*

The wolf didn't flinch, and her father just kept on driving. Why wasn't he slowing down? They were nearly upon it now. How could he not see what was right in front of him?

Ani tried to speak, tried to warn him, but no sound escaped. With immense effort, she forced the words to the surface. "Look out!" she finally cried, but it was too late.

A horrible thud, the screeching of tires, blood spraying the windshield, and then—

Ani woke from her trance with a gasp.

Her father glanced over. "Is something wrong, honey?"

"Um, no, everything's fine," she lied. A numb tingling pricked her fingers and toes, and the pounding in her chest made it hard to breathe. Using a technique Kahetay had taught her to control panic in the face of danger, she began to slow her heart to a normal rate, one beat at a time. Taking three deep breaths, she concentrated on expanding the silence between beats by a millisecond each. When her body and heart had finally calmed, she replayed the ghastly images in her mind, trying to make sense of the scene.

This strange floating-outside-her-body experience had happened before, and each time, what she saw in her watery visions had come to pass. The first time it happened, Ani had seen herself caught in a sandstorm that nearly buried her alive. She didn't understand what she had witnessed or why. She didn't know it was a warning. Three hours later, on one of her afternoon rock hunts, the sandstorm hit her full-force, replaying the incident precisely as she had seen it.

Ani vowed that if she ever saw anything like that again, she would pay closer attention. Maybe she really could see the future.

When she thought about it though, the weird part was that these strange visions felt more like the remembrance of yesterdays, rather than the foretelling of tomorrows. It was as if she traveled into the future to recall some past event that hadn't happened yet. Kahetay called them *future memories*.

Ani thought about the white wolf. She could still see its glowing eyes staring straight at her as they—

She sat up straight in the cab, searched the view through the windshield, and in a flash, recognized the stretch of road they were on.

There, just ahead. Mile marker 157.

"Oh no. Not again. Dad! Turn on the headlights!"

"What?"

"You need to turn your high beams on and slow down! Now!"

He flipped on the headlights. "What's wrong, Ani?"

She couldn't very well tell her father she had seen the future and they were about to hit a wolf in the road. "Just slow down!"

He eased off the gas. "Are you going to tell me what this is all about?"

"There!" Ani pointed. "Look out!"

The animal appeared out of nowhere directly in front of them. Stan slammed the brakes to the floor, sending the truck into a skid. The screech of tires pierced the air. The smell of burning rubber filled the cab. He wrenched the steering wheel to the right, swerving just in time to avoid hitting the wolf head-on, but Ani heard a yelp.

"Stop! We hit him! Dad, stop the truck!"

In a cloud of dust, they came to a skidding halt on the dirt shoulder. Ani jumped out and dashed to the tailgate, searching the place in the road where she thought the wolf went down. It wasn't there. Her eyes swept the landscape. In the distance, she saw a spot of white moving slowly away. She squinted, trying to determine if it was limping, and then . . . it just . . . vanished.

She blinked. How could a wolf materialize in the middle of the road and then just disappear right before her eyes?

Daylight was all but gone. Perhaps a trick of the diminishing light? The darkening desert transformed into nebulous shades of grey and black. No movement. No sound. The eerie stillness raised the hair on the back of her neck.

She heard her father's swift tug on the parking brake. "Did you spot him?" he yelled from the cab.

"I think so," she called back. "He looked okay."

"How on earth did a white wolf get all the way out here?"

Ani didn't have an answer. The tingling in her hands began to subside, but her head still pounded. Suddenly her feet were made of lead. "Dad?"

"There's nothing we can do now, honey," called her father. "Get back in the truck."

Ani leaned on the tailgate to steady herself as a spell of vertigo hit full force. The desert grew colder and darker by the second. She couldn't seem to—

WHOOUMMM!

The sound, like a backward sonic boom, exploded inside her head. A wave of visual distortion rippled away from her in all directions, warping the landscape in ever-widening circles. Ani fell backward onto the truck and felt a sharp stab on the inside of her right ankle. She let out a shriek.

"Ani! Are you okay?" Her father bounded out of the truck.

"Something bit me!"

"Stay still, I'll get the flashlight!"

She didn't need the warning. Ani knew better than to move. Whatever bit her could still be there. The last thing she needed was to startle it again. One rattlesnake bite she might survive, but she had never heard of anyone her age surviving two.

She could feel the poison slowly burning its way up her leg. Silent tears rolled down her cheeks, and she began to shake uncontrollably.

The desert, which only hours before had felt peaceful and safe, now seemed a vast black void sucking her into oblivion.

"Daaaad!"

The air around her wavered, images bent and swirled, and out of the ground around her feet oozed a thick blood-black substance that carried with it the nauseating stench of burnt flesh.

Within the dark slithery surface emerged a face. Disembodied and contorted by the swirling ooze, the hideous visage of a demon creature materialized before her. Its agonizing screech shattered the silence of the desert.

"Daaaaad!" screamed Ani, but as she did, the liquid tar vanished—sucked back into the earth—and with it, the demon.

Her father appeared beside her, flashlight in hand, seconds after she'd called. To Ani, it seemed a lifetime. "What was that?"

He searched the area at her feet. "Whatever it was, it's gone now."

"No, the black stuff. The face. It came out of the ground. And that awful sound. You heard that, right?"

Her father's eyebrows drew together. "No, I didn't, honey. Let me see the bite." He shined the light on her foot. The beam illuminated a small, single welt. "Not a snake bite. That's good news at least. Let's get you home." He scooped her up, carried her back to the truck, and gently placed her in the passenger seat.

As he circled around to the driver's side, Ani's stomach turned inside out. She tried to bring her father's face into focus as he slipped behind the wheel. "Dad, I think I'm gonna be sick."

"Hold on, sweetie." He reached across her to roll down the passenger window. "Take deep breaths. The fresh air will help, but we need to get you home. Just hold on."

Ani stuck her head out the window while her father buckled her in. The crisp desert air cooled the beads of sweat on her forehead.

"Whh—?" She struggled to form the words. "What b-bit me?"

"Can't say for sure. Don't you worry, honey. It'll be okay." He tore out onto the highway, snatching a cell phone from the cup holder between the seats.

Ani watched her father through blurry eyes.

"Call Nan Jasper," her father commanded. He waited for the phone to connect. When the call failed to go through, he swore under his breath. "Contact Tom Mallow." He listened for the ring, nodded, then turn to his daughter and whispered, "Hang in there, sweetheart."

"Dad," Ani rasped, but the words barely escaped her lips. Mouth dry, skin fire, then ice, then fire again; she knew—knew she wasn't going to make it. *Too far. Too far.* The poison would work its way through her system long before they could reach a hospital. The Soul Seeker had won.

He held the phone to his ear. "Hey Tom, Stan Jasper," she heard her father say to the hello on the other end. "Can you give Doc Benson a call for me, send him out to the rock shop as soon as possible? Got a bit of a situation here." He paused. "No, it's my daughter." Another pause and then, "Not sure. Scorpion maybe."

He spoke in a calm, controlled tone, but Ani could hear the fear in his voice. She winced as a stab of pain shot up her leg.

"Yeah, there is. If you could call the house, give Mrs. J. the heads-up. I'm having trouble getting through. Tell her we'll be there in about 30 minutes." Pause. "Great. Thanks, Tom." Stan turned to his daughter. "Don't be scared, honey. Everything's going to be okay. I promise."

Ani heard her father's words, but they were far away now. Somewhere in the distance, the rattle of the old pick-up truck faded and Ani slipped into a milky white nothingness.

There is a place where all have been but none remember. It exists in the space between heartbeats. It lies beyond the known world and yet it is our truest home.

-Xephero ✦ Tome of the Zielfah Ri

CHAPTER FIVE

༓

THE WHITE WOLF REMEDY

Ani tossed and turned in fits of fever. Darkness came and went in waves of pain, as the scorpion's poison took hold of her mind. Images floated in and out, blurred faces hovered, then vanished. Words lingered unattached to sentences, drifting just beyond the reach of consciousness. She attempted to form words of her own but they slipped away, swirls in the mist. Trying to grasp even a single thought brought more pain than she could bear.

The slightest motion took tremendous effort, like swimming in a pool of thick, dark molasses. Finally overcome by exhaustion, she let go of the effort, let go of everything, and in that instant, the dissolution of consciousness was instantaneous and absolute.

Hovering between awareness and delirium, Ani discovered herself immersed in a vivid dream world, surrounded by vast fields of shimmering amber grass. Above, the sky glistened emerald green. A ruby red sun and an amethyst moon hung side by side over the crystal cut horizon. Beside her, a river of lapis blue fire appeared, carving a sinuous path through the landscape.

The shrill cry of a bird tore through the silence, drawing Ani's attention across the field. She noticed a single withered tree that she was sure hadn't been there before. Curious, she started toward it, and as she did, the tree began to transform.

With each step she took, it changed a little more.

Branches to arms.

Trunk to torso.

Roots to legs.

When the transformation was complete, a man stood before her, clothed in a robe of green and yellow leaves.

Ani squinted. She recognized his face. The stranger from the rock shop—the man who haunted her dreams—greeted her with a slight bend at the waist and a respectful tilt of the head. He spoke her full name in a single breath that she thought could have easily been the voice of the wind, "Anani'nah Jasper."

"It's you," she said, uncertain of her feelings at that moment— fear, fascination, curiosity, confusion, awe—all muddled her insides.

"Yes," answered the stranger.

"Where am I? What is this place?" She didn't wait for an answer. "Why are you doing this? Why did you bring me here?"

"Your assumption is false," said the stranger. "I have come for you, yes, but I did not bring you to this place."

"Are you the Soul Seeker?"

"That is what the Nátah call me. You may call me Xephero."

"So you've come for me? To take my soul?"

The bird that had drawn her attention earlier circled closer. Ani could see now that it was a hawk. The old man looked up and smiled before answering her question. "No. I only meant it is for you that I have come. Your soul is your own."

"So, I'm . . . not dying?"

"Not at the moment."

Relief washed over her. She exhaled, not realizing until that instant, that she'd been holding her breath. Ani peered at the man who, only seconds ago, had been a tree. With the threat of death dismissed, her curiosity took over.

"Who are you?" she asked. "Where do you come from?"

"I am what my people call an *Iye howah Koumfah*; a Light Master. I come from a place called *Azimara*. The place you have visited in your dreams."

"The stone city? It's real?"

"Yes. It is a place like no other."

"Where is this place?"

"You'll not find it on any map. But if it is your destiny, you *will* find it."

"I don't believe in destiny," said Ani, defiantly. "The future isn't fixed. I know because I've seen it. I've changed it."

"When you change the future, you do not defy destiny, you fulfill it."

Ani squinted. "What do you want with me? My grandfather

said that you—" She stopped herself, not wanting to voice any more false assumptions.

The stranger smiled inwardly and as he did, Ani felt a wash of warmth and approval from him that sent a tingle of well-being rippling through her soul. In its wake, it left behind a sensation of utter and complete joy. For a moment, Ani reveled in it, feeling an incontestable peace permeate her spirit.

No, she thought, forcing her mind to refocus. *Don't let your guard down. Resist. This could be how he lures people into a false sense of security.*

The stranger laughed as if she'd spoken the thought out loud.

"We have a word for that feeling of contentment you just experienced—*wi anham kar'ree*. The words mean *soul-bound*. It happens when you glimpse your true path."

"Or it could just be indigestion." Ani wondered if the old man knew the meaning o

The old man laughed again, and his laughter became a song that rang out through the fields before turning into the sound of the wind.

"I honor your caution, Ani Jasper. Such a trait will serve you well in the days ahead. I will tell you this. One part of Kahetay's story is true. I do use the *Zah iye howah* to see into people's souls."

"Zaw eye, huh?"

"Zah iye howah. It means bridge of light." He held up the palm-sized glowing scepter she remembered from her dreams.

"The individual who wields its power is called the *Iye howah Koumfah*," he said. "The Light Master."

The old man reached out somehow with his mind to douse the light emanating from the translucent spheres at either end.

Ani heard his thought, heard the command he used, but an instant later, she could not recall the word—if it was a word. It seemed more like an image or idea.

He offered her the metallic device.

Accepting it with both hands to assure she didn't drop it, she began to study its intricacies. On either side, engraved in silver, were the same glyph-like markings as those on the Mapstone, and on the massive pillars that marked the entrance to the crescent moon temple in the stone city. "What do these markings mean?"

"They are the written language of my people, which you will learn in due course. What you hold in your hands, Ani Jasper, is the most powerful magical object in this world or any other."

"Why? What does it do?"

"It employs light to create a bridge, a connection if you will, between any two things: people, places, objects, times, dimensions, even worlds. With it you can go anywhere in the known universe. It allows you to transcend the barriers of time and space . . . and mind. You could even mend molecules with it."

"So wait, you're saying this thing can take you anywhere you want to go, but instead you use it to get into people's dreams?" She found the idea disturbing. It was different with Kahetay. His dream-readings required permission, trust. Xephero entered uninvited. "What you're doing is wrong."

"What I do, child, I do because there is no other way." He held out his hand. The device vanished from her palm and reappeared in his own. "I have been searching a very long time for you."

"Me?" She took a step back. "Why?"

"You possess a unique soul signature, a very rare and powerful quality Azimarans call *Zielfah*.

"Zeal . . . fah? What's that?"

"It means double soul. There are very few Zielfah in this world. I have attempted to contact each of them, but you are the only one I could truly reach. The others are too young, or too old or simply refuse to believe. You are the only one who senses the magic within." He tucked the small crystal scepter into his robe—a robe that continued to change as they spoke. It had gone from leaves to twine to a brownish-green woven fabric.

"I am as you are," he continued, "a Zielfah. In this way we are connected. We share a common destiny."

"A moment ago you said 'if'. . . *if* it is my destiny."

"There is much for you to learn before your path is revealed. As you say, the future is not set. But I believe it is your destiny as it was mine. I only wish I had found you sooner. I have much to teach you, but there is little time left."

"What do you mean? Why?"

"Death. It is the only thing my magic cannot alter."

"I thought you said I wasn't dying."

"It is not you who nears the end of this journey."

"Are . . . are you dying?"

"This body no longer serves my purpose. Soon I will have no more use for it."

Ani felt an unexpected sadness for the man. She didn't know him, didn't even like him, and certainly didn't trust him, but she didn't want him to die.

"Death is not what you imagine it to be. It is not the end. Not for you, and not for me."

Ani took another step back, breath turning shallow, thoughts dark. "You want me to come with you," she uttered, "to the afterlife."

"No child. That is not who I am."

"Then why do you need me?"

"Only another double soul can wield the power of the Zah iye howah. Only another Zielfah can receive its legacy. I've searched countless souls to find you."

"But you said there are others, right? Maybe you can take one of them instead."

"You know the magic instinctively. They do not. You recognized the Mapstone when it was placed upon your path, and you didn't fear the dream when I came to you. I can say this of no other. And you are here, having this conversation with me in the *Interval*, a place that is not of your world, nor of mine. The others cannot even conceive of such a place."

"What did you call it?"

"The Interval. That is my name for it. My people have a more beautiful word for it. They call it *li aun twah ni*."

"Lee on twah nee," repeated Ani, trying out the words.

"It means, Web Between Worlds—the birthplace of light."

"But why do they call it a web?" said Ani, looking around at the tall amber grass. "Why not call it the field between worlds?"

"What you see around you is the manifestation of your own will. I saw something different when I first came. Now, for me, there are no images, only a magnificent web of light with strands that lead out in all directions. Each of them a new possibility, a new world."

"I still don't understand. What do I do with all of this?"

Xephero's image began to fade.

"Wait! Where are you going? I still have questions!"

"It is not I who leaves."

"I don't understand."

"Your apprehension is diluting your presence here. Concentrate on my voice. Let all other thoughts fall away."

Ani narrowed her gaze to Xephero's serene face, attempting to calm her jumbled emotions. She centered on the infinite depth of his sea-grey eyes, and let his focus strengthen her own.

"Listen to me," he said, speaking as a thought inside her mind, "there's something you must know." The Light Master's face darkened. "The Kalb has learned of your existence. He is more dangerous than you can possibly imagine. You mustn't use magic in your world. He can only find you when you use your powers."

"What powers?"

"Your future memories are part of Zielfah magic."

"But I don't do it on purpose."

"You can learn to control them. They are putting you in danger, Ani. You must stop."

"But they just come. I never know when it's going to happen."

"You must try to block them. The Kalb is more dangerous than anything your world has ever known. You encountered his essence first with the Mapstone sketch which you imbued with magic—"

"Wait. What?"

"—And then in the desert, just after the scorpion incident, where he tracked you through your future memory of the white wolf."

Ani shuddered. "That awful smelling black stuff that came out of the ground? That was him?"

Xephero nodded. "It is currently the only physical form he can manifest in your realm. But he will evolve as *your* powers evolve, *if* he has access to your magic."

"*My* magic?" said Ani. "This is insane."

"The scorpion too, was his device," Xephero continued. "He has the ability to command base life forms in your world. The lesser their intelligence, the easier it is for him to manipulate them."

"I don't understand any of this."

Xephero's voice began to grow faint along with his image. "I cannot protect you as long as you remain in your world. The only way to hide yourself from him is to cease the use of magic."

She could barely hear him now. "But I don't know how!"

A low crackling hiss started between her ears, growing steadily louder until she could barely hear her own voice. "I can't control it!" she shouted over the noise, but the old man's transparent form vanished.

Ani found herself on one of those strands of light Xephero spoke of, hurtling through time and space, worlds whizzing by in an impossible mesh of sights and sounds, faces and places, none of them familiar, none of them home. She had felt strangely calm in the Interval with Xephero but now, moving at the speed of light, she couldn't catch up to her own thoughts.

Surely she must be dying despite what Xephero had said. She desperately wanted to go back to that warm, golden field, that crystal cut sky.

A scream escaped her lungs. Guttural. Primal. An inconceivable cacophony of sounds whirled around her, inside her, growing louder and louder until—

THWAM! A great explosion of air and light turned in on itself, and then . . . utter silence.

The softness of her own bed beneath her quelled the dizzying sensation of falling backward. Her body tingled slightly, but no pain remained. Ani opened her eyes and tried to focus on her surroundings.

Back in her own room. Home. Walls. Windows. Pillows. Pictures. Home. Her father, asleep in a chair next to the window, snored lightly. The clear, clean light of morning filtering through the lace curtains painted patterns on his face.

Senses slowly returning, she breathed deep the sweet-scented air. The room smelled of memory; fresh cut roses and clean linens, chicken soup, and redwood. Mom must have opened the wooden chest at the foot of her bed, filled with baby clothes and crayon masterpieces, forever preserved—the type of things only mothers would keep. Ani wondered if her parents believed she was dying. She hated the idea of making them sad.

Then, feeling an odd warmth and weight on her hand, Ani looked down. Through the dissipating fog in her mind, she wasn't quite sure it was real, but there, at her side, was a large dog . . . no, a wolf. . . a *white* wolf—the same white wolf they had almost hit in the road that night in the desert. The presence of this wild animal in her bedroom should have startled her, but oddly, she felt no fear.

The large wolf leaned aside her bed, his head resting on her hand as if he had been there all along. In the afterhaze of unconsciousness, cognizant thought finally solidifying, she considered the possibility that she might be having another vision. Ani peered down at the white wolf. "Are you really here?" she whispered. " Or am I seeing things?"

The wolf lifted his head. "*Bit of both*," said a voice inside her thoughts.

"But *are* you real?" she asked, hoping for a more definitive answer.

"*If I were not, you wouldn't have found your way home.*"

"You brought me back?"

"*We're even now*," said the wolf. Seemingly satisfied with her recovery, the creature turned toward the door, pausing a moment before departing. "*Hathanya wa nua, Ani Jasper.*"

"Wait," Ani called. "I don't know what that means."

"Nan! She's waking up!" shouted her father, leaping to his feet.

"*It means, you're welcome*," answered the wolf. "*It means I honor you.*"

"Thank you," said Ani.

"*It means that too*," said the wolf, baring his teeth in what Ani chose to interpret as a smile.

"I understand," she said, knowing instinctively that he had been her anchor to this world and she was grateful.

The wolf said nothing more, vanishing in a shimmer of light.

"Understand what, honey?" said her mother, smoothing the covers around her.

"Mom. Dad." Ani looked up at her parents. She could tell they were searching for some sure sign that the delirium had broken with the fever. "How long have I been gone?"

"Gone, honey?" Her father's eyebrows drew together.

"You've been very sick, Ani," said her mother, tears welling in her eyes. "But you're alright now."

Her father stroked her hair. "Gave us quite a scare, little gem."

It must have been bad. Her father only called her *little gem* when he was worried about her. It was his nickname for her when she was a baby. "I'm sorry," said Ani. "I didn't mean to."

Her parents laughed. It was the kind of anxious laughter that came out sometimes instead of crying. Ani peered at her father. The corners of her mouth turned down. "Was it a scorpion?"

"Yes, but that was no ordinary desert scorpion. Doc Benson said your symptoms and the severity of your reaction were consistent with a much more venomous variety called *Tityus Obscurus*, which is only found in the Amazon rainforests. He had no explanation for how this could be possible, but he said you're a strong girl, fighting it the way you did."

"I'm just glad you're okay," said her mother.

"Are you hungry?" asked her father.

"Starved," said Ani, stomach growling in agreement.

Her father smiled through shining eyes. "That's what I've been waiting to hear. I have some soup on the stove. I'll heat it up." He turned to head down the stairs but paused a moment in the doorway, glancing over his shoulder. "I love you, Ani."

It broke Ani's heart to hear the fatigue and concern in her father's voice. "I love you too, Dad."

Her mother let out a quick breath and gathered Ani into her arms. "I almost lost you again."

"Again?" Ani tried to draw away, but her mother wouldn't let go. Ani could tell she was crying.

"I was so scared," she rasped.

"Mom. I'm okay. Everything's fine now. Right?" said Ani, not understanding why her mother was still upset.

Her mother withdrew, wiping her cheeks. "Right," she echoed.

But Ani could tell there was something else. Something she wasn't saying. "Mom? Are you okay?"

"I'm . . . I'm just glad you're alright. I love you so much. I don't know what I would do if—" She quickly composed herself. "Never mind. You're right. Everything's fine now."

Ani nodded, her eyelids drooping. "Mom, I'm kind of sleepy."

"Oh, of course, sweetie. Rest now, and when you wake up we'll have dinner ready for you."

Ani closed her eyes and let her thoughts drift away. With the persistence of vision, the outline of her mother's beautiful face, backlit by window light, faded slowly against her eyelids and the gift of sleep came soon after—dreamless, colorless bliss stretching into days and nights of rest and recovery.

When finally she regained her strength and had permission to go outside again, two weeks had passed. Ani made what she considered a 'sensible decision' to stay in and dedicate all her spare time to catching up on her schoolwork. She could spend all day online and no one would ask her to turn off the computer.

It was the perfect distraction.

When she finished one assignment, she started another.

Keeping her mind occupied seemed the only way to escape the feverish memories that lingered just beneath the surface of her awareness, threatening to consume her. Left to her own thoughts, all Ani could think about was the grotesque creature she watched claw its way out if her sketchbook the day she found the Mapstone, the same face she'd seen oozing out of the desert the night of the scorpion attack.

The Light Master had given her nightmare a name, the *Kalb*, and by doing so, had made it frighteningly real.

Now, when she fell asleep at night, it was the Kalb who haunted her dreams. When she woke, she found her sheets knotted in her hands, her pillow crumpled on the floor. She was fighting him . . . fighting the Kalb in her sleep. And the more she fought him, the more powerful he became.

Desperate for a reprieve, Ani tried to convince herself it was all a part of her delirium—not just the Kalb, but all of it—the Mapstone, the Web Between Worlds, Xephero, the stone city, the white wolf—all of it, even her conversations with Mobius. It seemed the only way to escape the nightmare was to deny any of it had ever happened.

And it almost worked.

Almost.

*There is a way of seeing that requires no
sight, a way of being that requires no breath,
a way of acceptance that releases us from the
constraints of our perceived limitations and
sets us on the path to authentic freedom.*

-Solamas ✦ Tome of the Zielfah Ri

CHAPTER SIX

ϓ

THE CLOUDLESS SKY

Ani pushed the darkness away again. The nightmares, thankfully, had abated, but every time she glanced at her charcoal pencils and drawing pad, she relived the horrible blackness that invaded her mind through the Mapstone sketch. Now charcoal pencils and drawing pad hovered over the trashcan as she finished cleaning her room. She wavered, but only for a moment, and then let them drop. The art supplies hit the metal bin with a clang.

"Anani!" a voice called from downstairs. "Kahetay's on the phone for you again!"

"I'm in the bathroom!" she lied.

She heard her father reciting his standard apology before he hung up. A moment later, he was standing in the doorway of her bedroom. "Do you want to talk about it?"

She donned a premeditated expression of innocence. "Talk about what?"

Her father leaned on the doorjamb and folded his arms across his chest. "Why you're avoiding your grandfather."

"I'm not avoiding him."

"It's been three weeks,—"

"—Three weeks, four days, six hours," snapped Ani.

"Do you know, when you were lying sick in bed, slipping in and out of consciousness, he came and sat with you? He didn't speak. He didn't sleep. He didn't eat. Just sat there in silence. I think he was praying."

"I didn't even know he was here."

"He never left your side."

"He wasn't here when I woke up."

"He left at daybreak, but before he went, he said that you would be okay."

"How did he know?"

"I didn't ask." The corners of her father's mouth turned down. "Listen, I've told him you're better, but he needs to hear it from you, Ani."

"I just don't feel like talking right now."

Ani knew her father wouldn't accept her excuse, but she couldn't tell him the real reason she didn't want to see Kahetay; she was afraid to find out it was all true. He would tell her that what she had been experiencing wasn't just some elaborate dream or fitful delusion. He would make her remember what she tried so desperately to forget. But as Kahetay once told her, 'refusing to accept who you are has unforeseen consequences.'

Despite her reluctance to venture outdoors, Ani rose early each morning to stare out her bedroom window at the vast and lonely desert. Once, it had been a terrain she knew extremely well. She had memorized every boulder, every bush and dry creek bed along the trail she herself had forged by walking nearly every day to the hill behind their house—a place she had discovered when she was just six years old and nicknamed Boulder Dash Hill, mimicking one of her father's favorite words, *balderdash*.

Her mother said even at an early age, Ani had the balance and poise of a cat, and as her legs grew longer, she found she could run like one. Faster and faster, she would sprint up that hill, taking great leaps from one boulder to the next, never breaking her stride. And when she reached the top, she always stood on the highest rock to receive her prize; a view that stretched out to forever. She never minded living a million miles from nowhere when she was at the top of Boulder Dash Hill.

Now, the desert she had loved so well seemed hostile and foreign. Once her friend, she felt the desert had betrayed her, and the bond between them was broken.

The scorpion changed everything. From that moment on, all she thought she knew had disintegrated, and she was now lost in the emptiness it left behind. Even the view from her window offered no solace.

Suddenly weary, Ani shuffled back to her bed and crawled under the covers. Sleep would let her forget. It had been her only refuge since the nightmares ceased. Maybe if she was lucky, she could sleep the whole day away, and when she woke again, it would be tomorrow.

Though her mother pestered her about it daily, another week went by before Ani finally ventured outside, "just to get some air," she told herself. She'd begun to feel claustrophobic in her little room above the rock shop. With a sudden and desperate need for open space, she mustered the courage to venture downstairs.

Ani slowly opened the sliding glass door at the rear of the house and stepped onto the back porch. No fence defined the yard, no rock borders, no boundaries of any kind, just a few feet of white concrete and the desert beyond.

Boulder Dash Hill could be seen from where she stood. It called to her faintly. She lingered on the concrete landing for a minute, as though it were an island surrounded by shark-infested waters.

This is silly, she told herself. *Am I really going to let one stupid scorpion ruin the whole desert for me?* She glanced back and saw her mother watching from the kitchen window, nodding her encouragement.

Okay. This is it.

She took a deep breath and stepped off the concrete slab onto the sandy dirt. A shudder of apprehension shot through her, but Mom was watching, and Ani didn't want to disappoint her. So she took another step and then another, and in this way, set out on the path to Boulder Dash Hill.

Following the well-worn, childhood-familiar trail, she searched instinctually for rocks and gems as she had done so many times before. But this time was different. She saw more. Heard more. Felt more. The whole desert seemed somehow more awake and alive. She knew then, another scorpion sting wasn't what she had feared. She stayed away from the desert for the same reason she'd stayed away from Kahetay. She knew it would make her remember, make her feel again.

The odd thing was, now she *wanted* to remember. Remember it all. Feel it all. The experience had changed her. It was a part of her now. Something she could no longer deny. Her reluctance to accept what she had been through made no sense to her now. Or maybe it made perfect sense. Her mind flew in circles like the grey hawk that seemed to stay just overhead as she walked. She glanced up as its shrill cry reverberated off the rocky slope in front of her. The magnificent bird circled once more and then landed atop the highest rock on Boulder Dash Hill.

Ani found herself running now, not away, as she once thought she might, but up . . . up the path to the top of the hill. Her feet knew the way, knew every step. She didn't have to think about it, or even see the trail. Instinct became her guide, and the rush of freedom it offered filled her with exuberance.

As she crested the hill she halted abruptly, out of breath and speechless. Where she expected to see the hawk, she found her grandfather instead, sitting cross-legged on one of the large, flat boulders, contemplating the sky.

Though she knew Kahetay had sensed her approach, he did not turn to look at her when he said, "You wouldn't know this, but today is the first day since you were sick that the sky has been totally blue. Most of the days have been grey, dark even. Now, you emerge from your hibernation and the clouds clear away. The sun shines."

"I'm sorry I didn't call you back," Ani said, shuffling her feet, tracing patterns in the sand.

"There is no need for an apology, little one. You had to journey inward before you could venture out. Sometimes we must find a dark place inside us to nurture the seed of self before pushing through to the surface again. It is the way of things in nature. It is wise to honor the wisdom of the earth."

"I wasn't honoring anything," admitted Ani. "I was afraid."

"And yet, here you are."

"I let my fear stop me. I forgot everything you taught me. All I did was run and hide."

"And what did you find when you were hiding?"

Ani thought for a moment. "More fear."

Kahetay, still gazing skyward said, "When it comes time for the seedling to emerge from the soil, it is not afraid to face the sky. But even if it were, could it choose not to grow?"

"You're saying I shouldn't have been afraid?"

"I'm saying life gives us opportunities to grow, whether we run and hide or hold our ground. And sometimes going within to face your darkness is the only way to step into the light."

"I missed you, Kahetay."

"And I, you, Granddaughter."

Ani closed her eyes to the sun, feeling its soothing warmth

upon her face. "I . . . thought I was dying."

"I know. I must confess something to you now," he said, soberly. "While you lay consumed by fever, I feared for your life as well. When I thought of our dream-reading, and the belief that the Soul-Seeker comes just before death, suddenly it all made terrible sense. He knew of the scorpion—maybe even sent the scorpion—and while you lay sick with fever, he intended to take your soul."

"But I—"

Kahetay brought his hand up to halt her words, then smoothed a long strand of hair behind one ear. "I fell prey to superstition. I, too, was in a dark place motivated by fear. I did something out of desperation I should never have done." He swallowed hard. "I intruded upon your inner world without permission. I did another dream-reading."

"While I was sick?"

"Yes. Your mother and father left me alone with you at my request. They trusted me. You trusted me. I betrayed all of you."

"Don't say that. It's not true."

"I have broken a sacred oath."

"You were only looking out for me. You thought a dream-reading might tell you why I wasn't waking up, right? You thought you might be able to help me, protect me."

Kahetay shifted his gaze from the cloudless sky to the ground where Ani's shadow stretched out between them. The silhouette of her long hair lifting and swirling in the gusty winds became a tangle of black snakes against the white sand. "I shouldn't have done it, regardless of my motivation."

"So then, you saw what I saw?" asked Ani, excited to hear another account of her strange experience in the Interval. "Did you hear what the stranger said? Do you think it's real, this Web Between Worlds?"

"What I saw, what I heard, was meant for you alone. This man is not what my people thought he was, and I am ashamed to admit I believed it, even for an instant. Ani, this stranger in your dreams, he is offering you a key. He has chosen you. He believes you are like him, a double-soul."

"What is this double-soul thing, and why does he think I'm one of them?"

"Sometimes children are conceived as twins, but only one is born. In rare cases, the result is two souls in one body, or what he calls Zielfah. My people have another word for it but the meaning, I believe, is the same. This may have been the reason he searched the dreams of the Nátah. Our knowledge of such a thing meant that it once existed among us."

Ani leaned back on a large rock, attempting to grasp this new information. How could she possibly be one of these Zielfahs?"

"The circumstances of your birth are not for me to tell," said Kahetay, knowing it would be her next question. "For such truths you must ask your mother and father."

Kahetay said nothing more. As they sat in silence listening to the wind, a small, banded gecko dashed out of a hole, scurried across Ani's foot, and stopped. Keeping very still, she watched the tiny creature. For a moment she saw the world through its eyes and understood the utter sense of connectedness it experienced with the earth, something that had eluded her in the weeks since her illness. By the slightest tilt of its head, Ani knew the gecko had sensed her presence, and though she tried to convey that there was no danger, it scurried off.

Kahetay had been watching. "You see differently now. Since the scorpion. You see with new clarity."

"It's . . . strange," she admitted.

"He teaches you already. He guides you even now."

"Kahetay," Ani said, her voice choked. "Who is he?"

"I don't know where he comes from, or where he goes when he leaves your dream, but he is asking you to follow him—follow what he believes is your destiny."

"If it's my destiny then won't it happen no matter what I do?"

"There are roads that lead to one's true path, and roads that lead to the *elsewheres* of life. It is still your decision to make."

"If he asked you, would *you* follow him?"

"I would," said Kahetay. "I believe what he is offering you is a precious gift. The gift of knowledge. Power. Wisdom. Magic. Just beware of one thing if you accept it. These gifts will not be free. You will be asked to give something in return."

"Like what?"

"That I can not answer, but he seeks you for a purpose, this much is clear. He needs you. And remember, you will need him as well."

"Why do I need him?"

"Where you will be going, if you choose this path, there are no signs to point the way. He is your roadmap. Do not presume to know. Ever."

"I still don't understand."

"It is not necessary for you to understand just now, but it is important that you remember, Granddaughter. Remember what I have told you."

"I will," Ani vowed.

He touched her arm. "I am not trying to scare you, little one. When you are truly ready to embrace your destiny, there will be no fear."

"I don't know about that."

"There is a sacred interconnectedness within all things, born of the first breath, in the heart of the universe. To swallow this knowing is to understand that all is one, and there is nothing outside yourself that can harm you."

"But how could that be true? There are lots of things that can hurt us, even kill us." She couldn't help but think of the Kalb who somehow sent a scorpion to kill her . . . one that came all the way from a rainforest in South America.

"When you exist at this expanded level of awareness," said Kahetay, "you learn of a deeper awareness. You begin to understand that there is no difference between you and the universe. All things, all people, all thoughts are but the Great Creator creating. This dance of creation has always been, is, and always will be. When you dance this dance, when this truth lives inside you, everything will change. My people call this expansion of consciousness *the dispelling of the Ninth Illusion*."

"The Illusion of Separateness," said Ani, recalling her grandfather's teachings.

Kahetay nodded.

"I remember," said Ani. "It's the final challenge of the Nátah initiation."

"Yes. And the most difficult. We each grow to adulthood with the understanding that everything is separate from everything else. It is simply a fact of the observable world. But it is a falsehood masquerading as truth, and that makes it a dangerous assumption."

Kahetay saw the doubt in her eyes. She could tell. He always paused to reconsider his words whenever he sensed her resistance, and that is exactly what he did now. Then after a silent exhalation, he continued—

"It takes a great leap of faith to let go of what we have been taught to believe, what we know to be true, in order to reach the deeper well of knowing and acceptance, and it is just such knowing and acceptance that is necessary to understand that separateness is an illusion."

Ani glanced down at her feet. The tickle of that tiny gecko still lingered there; a minute sense memory to confirm the interconnectedness of which Kahetay spoke.

That she understood. But she didn't really believe there was no difference between her and everything else in the world, and she certainly didn't believe there would be no danger in the world if she could somehow dispel the illusion of separateness. What about the Kalb? What about the Light Master's warning? Xephero seemed to think there was danger. Real danger. She could feel it in the old man's words. She could see it in his eyes. He was afraid for her. Afraid the Kalb would find her again.

Ani gave her grandfather a crooked smile. "I think I would fail the Nátah initiation test."

Kahetay smiled back. "No matter. You have your own path to walk. The path of the Zielfah. And it will have its own initiation."

A little stab of unease pressed at Ani's insides. There was something missing in Kahetay's words. A truth he seemed reluctant to share. How could he know so much about Xephero and his world, unless . . .

She stared at his profile. Maybe, just maybe, he knew these things because he was the same as her. "Kahetay? Did the Soul Seeker search your dreams too? Are you . . . a Zielfah?"

He studied the pattern in the rock beside him as if all the answers were written there. After a long silence, he returned his gaze to Ani. "No, Anani, I am not Zielfah."

She wanted to ask him how he knew the things he knew, but his eyes pleaded with her as if to say, *Allow me to keep just one of my secrets*?

"It's okay," Ani said with a sigh, "Xephero hasn't been back anyway. He hasn't visited a single dream since I saw him in the Web Between Worlds."

"Xephero?"

"That's what the stranger called himself."

"I see. Perhaps he is waiting for *you* to find him."

"Or maybe he has already found someone else."

"Is that your wish?"

"Yeah, it is," said Ani. "I'm glad the dreams and nightmares have stopped. Things are finally getting back to normal."

"Or perhaps the adventure has already begun," said Kahetay. "The Nátah have a saying; When the path stretches out before us, we must go where it leads."

"I'm not going anywhere. I'm staying right here," she said with dogged determination, but even as she spoke the words, she knew things would never again be the same.

If a man were allowed to gaze upon the map of his destiny, he may choose the unmarked road to avoid it, but then he is only a child, thinking blue is kinder than green.

-Xephero ✤ *Tome of the Zielfah Ri*

CHAPTER SEVEN

♈

THE FORK IN THE ROAD

Ani pushed the darkness away again. The nightmares, thankfully, had abated, but every time she glanced at her charcoal pencils and drawing pad, she relived the horrible darkness that invaded her mind through the Mapstone sketch. Now charcoal pencils and drawing pad hovered over the trashcan as she finished cleaning her room. She wavered, but only for a moment, and then let them drop. The art supplies hit the metal bin with a clang.

"Anani!" a voice called from downstairs. "Kahetay's on the phone for you again!"

"I'm in the bathroom!" she lied.

She heard her father reciting his standard apology before he hung up. A moment later, he was standing in the doorway of her bedroom. "Do you want to talk about it?"

She donned a premeditated expression of innocence. "Talk about what?"

Her father leaned on the doorjamb and folded his arms across his chest. "Why you're avoiding your grandfather."

"I'm not avoiding him."

"It's been three weeks,—"

"—Three weeks, four days, and six hours," snapped Ani.

"Do you know, when you were lying sick in bed, slipping in and out of consciousness, he came and sat with you? He didn't speak. He didn't sleep. He didn't eat. Just sat there in silence. I think he was praying."

"I didn't even know he was here."

"He never left your side."

"He wasn't here when I woke up."

"He left at daybreak, but before he went, he said that you would be okay."

"How did he know?"

"I didn't ask." The corners of her father's mouth turned down. "Listen, I've told him you're better, but he needs to hear it from you, Ani."

"I just don't feel like talking right now."

Ani knew her father wouldn't accept her excuse, but she couldn't tell him the real reason she didn't want to see Kahetay; she was afraid to find out it was all true. He would tell her that what she had been experiencing wasn't just some elaborate dream or fitful delusion. He would make her remember what she tried so desperately to forget.

Despite her reluctance to venture outdoors, Ani rose early each morning to stare out her bedroom window at the vast and lonely desert. Once, it had been a terrain she knew extremely well. She had memorized every boulder, every bush and dry creek bed along the trail she herself had forged by walking nearly every day to the hill behind their house—a place she had discovered when she was just six years old and nicknamed Boulder Dash Hill, mimicking one of her father's favorite words, *balderdash*.

Her mother said even at an early age, Ani had the balance and poise of a cat, and as her legs grew longer, she found she could run like one. Faster and faster, she would sprint up that hill, taking great leaps from one boulder to the next, never breaking her stride. And when she reached the top, she always stood on the highest rock to receive her prize; a view that stretched out to forever. She never minded living a million miles from nowhere when she was at the top of Boulder Dash Hill.

Now, the desert she had loved so well seemed hostile and foreign. Once her friend, she felt the desert had betrayed her, and the bond between them was broken.

The scorpion changed everything. From that moment on, all she thought she knew had disintegrated, and she was now lost in the emptiness it left behind. Even the view from her window offered no solace.

Suddenly weary, Ani shuffled back to her bed and crawled

under the covers. Sleep would let her forget. It had been her only refuge since the nightmares ceased. Maybe if she was lucky, she could sleep the whole day away, and when she woke again, it would be tomorrow.

Though her mother pestered her about it daily, another week went by before Ani finally ventured outside, "just to get some air," she told herself. She'd begun to feel claustrophobic in her little room above the rock shop. With a sudden and desperate need for open space, she mustered the courage to venture downstairs.

Ani slowly opened the sliding glass door at the rear of the house and stepped onto the back porch. No fence defined the yard, no rock borders, no boundaries of any kind, just a few feet of white concrete and the desert beyond.

Boulder Dash Hill could be seen from where she stood. It called to her faintly. She lingered on the concrete landing for a minute, as though it were an island surrounded by shark-infested waters.

This is silly, she told herself. *Am I really going to let one stupid scorpion ruin the whole desert for me?* She glanced back and saw her mother watching from the kitchen window, nodding her encouragement.

Okay. This is it.

She took a deep breath and stepped off the concrete slab onto the sandy dirt. A shudder of apprehension shot through her, but Mom was watching, and Ani didn't want to disappoint her. So she took another step and then another, and in this way, set out on the path to Boulder Dash Hill.

Following the well-worn, childhood-familiar trail, she searched instinctually for rocks and gems as she had done so many times before. But this time was different. She saw more. Heard more. Felt more. The whole desert seemed somehow more awake and alive. She knew then, another scorpion sting wasn't what she had feared. She stayed away from the desert for the same reason she'd stayed away from Kahetay. She knew it would make her remember, make her feel again.

The odd thing was, now she *wanted* to remember. Remember it all. Feel it all. The experience had changed her. It was a part of her now. Something she could no longer deny. Her reluctance to accept what she had been through made no sense to her now. Or maybe it made perfect sense. Her mind flew in circles like the grey hawk that seemed to stay just overhead as she walked. She glanced up as its shrill cry reverberated off the rocky slope in front of her. The magnificent bird circled once more and then landed atop the highest rock on Boulder Dash Hill.

Ani found herself running now, not away, as she once thought she might, but up . . . up the path to the top of the hill. Her feet knew the way, knew every step. She didn't have to think about it, or even see the trail. Instinct became her guide, and the rush of freedom it offered filled her with exuberance.

As she crested the hill she halted abruptly, out of breath and speechless. Where she expected to see the hawk, she found her grandfather instead, sitting cross-legged on one of the large, flat boulders, contemplating the sky.

Though she knew Kahetay had sensed her approach, he did not turn to look at her when he said, "You wouldn't know this, but today is the first day since you were sick that the sky has been totally blue. Most of the days have been grey, dark even. Now, you emerge from your hibernation and the clouds clear away. The sun shines."

"I'm sorry I didn't call you back," Ani said, shuffling her feet, tracing patterns in the sand.

"There is no need for an apology, little one. You had to journey inward before you could venture out. Sometimes we must find a dark place inside us to nurture the seed of self before pushing through to the surface again. It is the way of things in nature. It is wise to honor the wisdom of the earth."

"I wasn't honoring anything," admitted Ani. "I was afraid."

"And yet, here you are."

"I let my fear stop me. I forgot everything you taught me. All I did was run and hide."

"And what did you find when you were hiding?"

Ani thought for a moment. "More fear."

Kahetay, still gazing skyward said, "When it comes time for the seedling to emerge from the soil, it is not afraid to face the sky. But even if it were, could it choose not to grow?"

"You're saying I shouldn't have been afraid?"

"I'm saying life gives us opportunities to grow, whether we run and hide or hold our ground. And sometimes going within to face your darkness is the only way to step into the light."

"I missed you, Kahetay."

"And I, you, Granddaughter."

Ani closed her eyes to the sun, feeling its soothing warmth upon her face. "I . . . thought I was dying."

"I know. I must confess something to you now," he said,

soberly. "While you lay consumed by fever, I feared for your life as well. When I thought of our dream-reading, and the belief that the Soul-Seeker comes just before death, suddenly it all made terrible sense. He knew of the scorpion—maybe even sent the scorpion—and while you lay sick with fever, he intended to take your soul."

"But I—"

Kahetay brought his hand up to halt her words, then smoothed a long strand of hair behind one ear. "I fell prey to superstition. I, too, was in a dark place motivated by fear. I did something out of desperation I should never have done." He swallowed hard. "I intruded upon your inner world without permission. I did another dream-reading."

"While I was sick?"

"Yes. Your mother and father left me alone with you at my request. They trusted me. You trusted me. I betrayed all of you."

"Don't say that. It's not true."

"I have broken a sacred oath."

"You were only looking out for me. You thought a dream-reading might tell you why I wasn't waking up, right? You thought you might be able to help me, protect me."

Kahetay shifted his gaze from the cloudless sky to the ground where Ani's shadow stretched out between them. The silhouette of her long hair lifting and swirling in the gusty winds became a tangle of black snakes against the white sand. "I shouldn't have done it, regardless of my motivation."

"So then, you saw what I saw?" asked Ani, excited to hear another account of her strange experience in the Interval. "Did you hear what the stranger said? Do you think it's real, this Web Between Worlds?"

"What I saw, what I heard, was meant for you alone. This man is not what my people thought he was, and I am ashamed to admit I believed it, even for an instant. Ani, this stranger in your dreams, he is offering you a key. He has chosen you. He believes you are like him, a double-soul."

"What is this double-soul thing, and why does he think I'm one of them?"

"Sometimes children are conceived as twins, but only one is born. In rare cases, the result is two souls in one body, or what he calls Zielfah. My people have another word for it but the meaning, I believe, is the same. This may have been the reason he searched the dreams of the Nátah. Our knowledge of such a thing meant that it once existed among us."

Ani leaned back on a large rock, attempting to grasp this new information. How could she possibly be one of these Zielfahs?"

"The circumstances of your birth are not for me to tell," said Kahetay, knowing it would be her next question. "For such truths you must ask your mother and father."

Kahetay said nothing more. As they sat in silence listening to the wind, a small, banded gecko dashed out of a hole, scurried across Ani's foot, and stopped. Keeping very still, she watched the tiny creature. For a moment she saw the world through its eyes and understood the utter sense of connectedness it experienced with the earth, something that had eluded her in the weeks since her illness. By the slightest tilt of its head, Ani knew the gecko had sensed her presence, and though she tried to convey that there was no danger, it scurried off.

Kahetay had been watching. "You see differently now. Since the scorpion. You see with new clarity."

"It's . . . strange," she admitted.

"He teaches you already. He guides you even now."

"Kahetay," Ani said, her voice choked. "Who is he?"

"I don't know where he comes from, or where he goes when he leaves your dream, but he is asking you to follow him—follow what he believes is your destiny."

"If it's my destiny then won't it happen no matter what I do?"

"There are roads that lead to one's true path, and roads that lead to the *elsewheres* of life. It is still your decision to make."

"If he asked you, would *you* follow him?"

"I would," said Kahetay. "I believe what he is offering you is a precious gift. The gift of knowledge. Power. Wisdom. Magic. Just beware of one thing if you accept it. These gifts will not be free. You will be asked to give something in return."

"Like what?"

"That I can not answer, but he seeks you for a purpose, this much is clear. He needs you. And remember, you will need him as well."

"Why do I need him?"

"Where you will be going, if you choose this path, there are no signs to point the way. He is your roadmap. Do not presume to know. Ever."

"I still don't understand."

"It is not necessary for you to understand just now, but it is important that you remember, Granddaughter. Remember what I have told you."

"I will," Ani vowed.

He touched her arm. "I am not trying to scare you, little one.

When you are truly ready to embrace your destiny, there will be no fear."

"I don't know about that."

"There is a sacred interconnectedness within all things, born of the first breath, in the heart of the universe. To swallow this knowing is to understand that all is one, and there is nothing outside yourself that can harm you."

"But how could that be true? There are lots of things that can hurt us, even kill us." She couldn't help but think of the Kalb who somehow sent a scorpion to kill her . . . one that came all the way from a rainforest in South America.

"When you exist at this expanded level of awareness," said Kahetay, "you learn of a deeper awareness. You begin to understand that there is no difference between you and the universe. All things, all people, all thoughts are but the Great Creator creating. This dance of creation has always been, is, and always will be. When you dance this dance, when this truth lives inside you, everything will change. The Nátah call this expansion of consciousness *the dispelling of the Ninth Illusion.*"

"The Illusion of Separateness," said Ani, recalling her grandfather's teachings.

Kahetay nodded.

"I remember," said Ani. "It's the final challenge of the Nátah initiation."

"Yes. And the most difficult. We each grow to adulthood with the understanding that everything is separate from everything else. It is simply a fact of the observable world. But it is a falsehood masquerading as truth, and that makes it a dangerous assumption."

Kahetay saw the doubt in her eyes. She could tell. He always paused to reconsider his words whenever he sensed her resistance, and that is exactly what he did now. Then after a silent exhalation, he continued—

"It takes a great leap of faith to let go of what we have been taught to believe, what we know to be true, in order to reach the deeper well of knowing and acceptance, and it is just such knowing and acceptance that is necessary to understand that separateness is an illusion."

Ani glanced down at her feet. The tickle of that tiny gecko still lingered there; a minute sense memory to confirm the interconnectedness of which Kahetay spoke.

That she understood. But she didn't really believe there was no difference between her and everything else in the world, and she certainly didn't believe there would be no danger in the world if she could somehow dispel the illusion of separateness. What about the Kalb? What about the Light Master's warning? Xephero seemed to think there was danger. Real danger. She could feel it in the old man's words. She could see it in his eyes. He was afraid for her. Afraid the Kalb would find her again.

Ani gave her grandfather a crooked smile. "I think I would fail the Nátah initiation test."

Kahetay smiled back. "No matter. You have your own path to walk. The path of the Zielfah. And it will have its own initiation."

A little stab of unease pressed at Ani's insides. There was something missing in Kahetay's words. A truth he seemed reluctant to share. How could he know so much about Xephero and his world, unless . . .

She stared at his profile. Maybe, just maybe, he knew these things because he was the same as her. "Kahetay? Did the Soul Seeker search your dreams too? Are you . . . a Zielfah?"

He studied the pattern in the rock beside him as if all the answers were written there. After a long silence, he returned his gaze to Ani. "No, Anani, I am not Zielfah."

She wanted to ask him how he knew the things he knew, but his eyes pleaded with her as if to say, *Allow me to keep just one of my secrets*?

"It's okay," Ani said with a sigh, "Xephero hasn't been back anyway. He hasn't visited a single dream since I saw him in the Web Between Worlds."

"Xephero?"

"That's what the stranger called himself."

"I see. Perhaps he is waiting for *you* to find him."

"Or maybe he has already found someone else."

"Is that your wish?"

"Yeah, it is," said Ani. "I'm glad the dreams and nightmares have stopped. Things are finally getting back to normal."

"Or perhaps the adventure has already begun," said Kahetay. "The Nátah have a saying; When the path stretches out before us, we must go where it leads."

"I'm not going anywhere. I'm staying right here," she said with dogged determination, but even as she spoke the words, she knew things would never again be the same.

When the road takes you in a direction you never expected to go, it is time to open your eyes. Find the gift. Learn to see. To be a Light Master is to know that you always end up where you're meant to be.

-Xephero ❖ Tome of the Zielfah Ri

CHAPTER EIGHT

♈

THE TRUE PATH

Ani stood alone in the stillness of the rock shop, remembering. She picked up the Sherlock Holmes-style magnifying glass she'd peered through a thousand times. The shop looked distorted and strange through its convex glass. No longer familiar. No longer hers. She bent to examine one of the many bins. Dust had already started to collect on the tumbled stones. It had been her job to keep them clean, but there didn't seem to be much point now.

Running her fingers across the stones' smooth surfaces, she picked out a Rose Quartz and an Amethyst, pink and purple, her two favorites. She put them in her pocket along with a small, smooth black stone she had found and tumbled a few weeks back— a little part of the desert she could take with her.

Ani shuffled into the house and stood before Mobius' large wire mesh cage with its jungle milieu. She checked his favorite napping spot; the branch closest to the heat lamp, but he wasn't there.

For an anxious moment she thought he'd gotten out again and she pictured her father's infinite irritation at the delay it would cause.

Her eyes swept the length of the cage in a minor panic, but there he was hiding behind a rock down in the far corner, his tail poking out.

"If you're trying to make me feel bad," she said, "it's working."

The iguana didn't budge.

61

"I'm sorry you can't come with us, Mobi. Mom says you wouldn't like it in New York. She says it's cold and wet and our apartment is too small for your cage." Ani paused, hoping to hear his thoughts even though he wasn't speaking to her. "I wish I could stay here with you, really I do. I'm not going to like it there either."

His tail twitched the slightest bit.

"Mobius, say something. Please? I know you're upset, but please don't hate me. I'll come back. I promise."

"Ani" called her mother. "Kahetay's here."

Ani let out a sigh. "I have to go now. Won't you at least say goodbye?" Again she waited. Again, nothing. "Kahetay will take good care of you until I get back, okay? If you want to talk to him, I know he'll listen." She turned to go, then glanced back to her friend and whispered, "I'm sorry."

After taking one last look at the view out her bedroom window, a view that had been home to her heart for as long as she could remember, Ani descended the stairs and emerged from the house carrying a small brown paper bag marked *Mobius*.

While her father loaded the last of the boxes into the back of a large moving van, Ani found Kahetay helping Nan load the old Chevy.

"I need to talk to you about Mobius."

Kahetay placed the box he was carrying on the tailgate.

"He's . . . upset," said Ani.

"Understandable," said Kahetay.

"He's very sensitive, and gets moody sometimes, but if you pay attention to him, he gets better. He eats mostly fruits and vegetables, and he likes crickets for dessert." She jiggled the bag and it made a scratchy noise. "But don't give them to him if he's being cranky. And he hates his cage. He'll want to sleep in the bed with you 'cause it's warm, and sometimes 'cause he's lonely, but don't let him. It's bad manners and he knows it."

"Ani—"

She handed him the bag. "He'll try to get away with stuff because you're new, so keep—"

"Granddaughter," said Kahetay, smiling sadly, "we'll be fine. I'll take good care of him."

Ani fought the sadness creeping up into her throat. It was only for two years, she told herself. Seemed more like an eternity.

Kahetay reached out to touch her cheek.

"What am I going to do without the two of you?" said Ani, her eyes welling. "You're my only friends."

"You will have new friends."

"Not like you."

"On this, you speak true," said her grandfather. "You and I share a special bond, as strong as any blood-bond."

"I don't think I can do this, Kahetay."

He took her hand and sat her down on one of the tattered wooden benches situated to either side of the shop's front door, and then sat beside her. "Your mother and father have not told you the story of how you got your name."

"Um, no," she said, wiping a tear from her cheek.

Kahetay's eyes sparked into a soft smile. "I asked that they allow *me* the honor."

"Why?"

"It was I who named you."

"You did?" asked Ani. "Why didn't you ever tell me?"

"I waited for the moment when knowing would bring meaning. That moment is now."

Ani glanced over at her father, standing at the back of the old truck, securing a piece of teetering furniture with a strand of frayed rope. "I can't believe Mom and Dad let you name me."

"Because I saved your life, they believed the honor fell to me. And I was indeed honored to choose your name. The naming of a new soul is a sacred privilege and a great responsibility. After you were born, I went on a vision quest to ask the wind spirits what you would be called. Seven moons passed and there came a whisper."

"The wind whispered my name?" Ani thought of all the times the wind had whispered in her ears. A warm tingle rippled through her—the kind of tingle you get when something seems so right, so perfect, that there is no doubt of its validity.

Kahetay nodded. "*Aani'inii* in Navajo means *that which is true.*" My grandmother, Nahni, who's heart-light shown moon-bright even on the darkest of nights, appeared to me in the flames of the fire I had built to warm my bones. She said you and her were carved from the same stone. In her life, when she walked the earth, Nahni was a trailblazer, a person who cuts a path where no path was or ever has been. She was the bravest person I'd ever known . . . until you came."

"That can't be true," rasped Ani. "I'm not brave."

"You fought for life before you took your first breath, as did she. You have always made your own path. You were born a trailblazer like my grandmother. A way-finder. The path you must now walk may not be the one you'd have chosen for yourself, but it *will* be yours. You will make it your own. Your full name is Anani'nah. It means *true path.* This I know. You *are* brave, Anani'nah. You will always seek the truest path. And you will find your way."

"Not without you." She wrapped her arms around her grandfather vowing never to let go.

"Granddaughter," whispered Kahetay. "Nothing can separate us. If you call to me, I will hear. When the wind speaks of you, I will listen. And we will see each other in our dreams."

Kahetay pulled away and Ani let him go, realizing in that moment that no amount of wishing could stop what was happening. Her gaze fell to the ground along with her heart, shattering on impact.

"I made something for you," said Kahetay. "A journey gift." He held out a palm-sized wood carving of a hawk. "Something to remember me by."

"I could never forget you, Kahetay," Ani said, her voice breaking. She took the small sculpture and studied it. The whole thing stood no more than an inch and a half tall but the detail was exquisite. The hawk's wings spread in flight. Its talons grasped a flawless clear crystal with a perfect faceted point at either end.

He indicated the crystal. "Do you know what that is?"

"Quartz. Double-terminated," she said automatically.

"One end points to home," he said slowly, "the other to destiny. One need not be forsaken for the other."

"I understand," said Ani. It was true. She understood the meaning of his words, but her heart felt differently. "Thank you," she rasped. The current of emotion that rose up from the deepest places in her, threatened to sweep her away. "I'll keep it forever." She gave him a quick hug and turned away to hide her face.

Through her tears Ani watched her father flip the rock shop's open sign to closed on the front door. He locked the deadbolt, walked over to Kahetay, and handed him the keys.

"George McCray will be here by the end of the week to reopen," said Stan. He kicked the dirt in front of him. "Okay, well, I guess that's it then. Thanks for everything."

The two men shook hands and then turned as Nan emerged from the house with a small box of odds and ends.

"This is the last of it." She set the box on the hood of the old Chevy truck and spun around to face Kahetay. "Thank you for being such a good friend, especially to Ani. You have been both guide and grandfather to her. Protector and companion. You'll never know how much it has meant to us." She gave him a quick peck on the cheek and squeezed his shoulders with genuine affection. "We'll miss you," she said, retrieving the box. "Come visit us in New York, okay? You're welcome anytime. You will always be family."

As she hopped into the truck, she called, "All set?"

Ani climbed into the cab of the rental van—the bench seat stiff beneath her. It smelled of stale potato chips and beer.

Without looking back, Stan opened the driver's side door and slipped behind the wheel.

Ani frowned. "You okay, Dad?"

"Fine," he said, without so much as a glance in her direction. He started the engine but didn't put the van in gear.

She wanted to ask him what was wrong but she already knew the answer. Everything about this was wrong.

"Ani, why don't you go ride with your mother in the truck for now. I'm sure she'd enjoy the company."

"But I thought you said—"

"I know what I said." He looked straight ahead as if he were already driving away.

"But I want to stay with you."

"We have a long drive ahead of us. You'll be bored inside an hour. Go on. Ride with mom."

"Are you sure?"

Her father gave a quick nod. "You can ride with me tomorrow."

Ani climbed out of the cab, and then stood with her hand on the door, thinking he might change his mind.

He didn't.

Through the dirty windshield of the old truck, her mother waved her over.

Ani stood for a moment between the two vehicles. Between Mom and Dad. Between everything she'd ever known and everything she never wanted. And there was Kahetay, standing in front of the rock shop, unmoving . . . waiting for them to drive away before he turned and went back to the life he had thirteen years ago. The life he had before she was born.

It was too much.

Like being ripped apart from the inside out. That's how it felt.

Her grandfather crossed to where she stood. "Remember," he said softly. "You walk a true path, little one. Always."

Ani nodded, suddenly feeling like she was clinging to a high wire with no net below, hands aching, body shaking. Can't. Hold. On.

Nan rolled down her window. "Come on, sweetie, it's time."

With nothing more to say, Ani opened the passenger door of the pick-up, its rusty hinges protesting, and hopped in.

She took one last look at the rock shop, one last look at her grandfather, one last look at the only home she had ever known, then hung her head, squeezed her eyes shut, and . . . let go.

Part Two

The City Weeps

The apprentice frowned, turning to face the Master. "Something is wrong. What is it?"

"Do not concern yourself, Naviga. I am weak from the journey. That is all."

"But your journeys have never weakened you before."

"Many things occur that have not occurred before. A time of great change is upon us."

"Will you bring her here?"

"No. She must come on her own."

"You are not certain she is the one?"

"If she is not, then Azimara will fall. There is no other."

The young man stared wide-eyed at the old one. Never had he heard the Master speak with such finality. "What can I do?"

"Finish the translation. The Tome must be ready. She will need its wisdom if she is to survive the initiation."

Without protest, Navaga resumed his slow, precision scribing, concentrating on the conversion of each new word. "It will be ready."

If we shut our eyes to what is inside us, we forsake the wisdom of our own existence. To be a Light Master is to embrace the truth that we are all much more than we seem.

-Xephero ✧ Tome of the Zielfah Ri

CHAPTER NINE

♈

THE FACE IN THE MIRROR

By the time they rolled into New Jersey, a whole week had slogged by. Ani was sick of the road, sick of switching between her mother and father, sick of hearing how great or how bad it would be living in New York, but she hadn't uttered a word. Every time she thought about it, she heard her mother's voice in her head saying; 'In the entire breadth of human experience, there's never been a difficult situation that complaining could improve.' It was one of her mother's favorite quotes.

Every city they drove through, according to Nan, "paled in comparison to the city of New York." She raved about the school Ani would be attending, and the apartment they would be living in, the food, the culture, the Metropolitan Museum of Art, Central Park. She said there was no place like it on earth. She talked about it like it was her hometown, but actually Nan had grown up in Santa Fe, New Mexico.

"It won't be long now," she said pulling up to a stop light in Secaucus. "We're almost there. Just across the river."

Ani grimaced involuntarily.

Nan smiled. "You're going to love it here, honey. I promise. We'll finally have a normal life—live like other people. We'll even have real neighbors. You'll make new friends in no time."

Ani missed the desert already. She peered at the snow-covered concrete sidewalks with their square potted trees and missed her sun-drenched dirt path to Boulder Dash Hill. She gazed up at the thick cast of grey clouds above and missed her brilliant blue skies. She listened to the people shouting, cars honking, and missed the humbling quiet of the rocks and cactus. She even missed the tiny gecko that lived in the hole on top of the hill, and the grey hawk that always circled just above. She missed it all so much, and she hadn't even been in the city a whole day.

Ani caught her first glimpse of the New York City skyline just before crossing the Hudson River. The distant skyscrapers glistened in the light of the setting sun like a golden version of the Emerald City in the Wizard of Oz.

Nan let out an exaggerated sigh. "What a sight. Isn't she beautiful?"

Ani nodded to be polite. But all she could think about was that, from afar, the Emerald City also looked like a place where dreams came true, but once inside, Dorothy and her friends found they had been deceived. Ani wondered if New York would be that way for her mom.

When they finally crossed the river, they traveled not over it as she had expected, but actually under it. As they descended into the Lincoln Tunnel, yellow safety lights, like an electric yellow brick road, replaced the gleaming sunlight of the fading day. Ani felt uneasy at the thought of being underwater in a car. The idea that a hundred feet or more of river flowed above them was unsettling. *What if the tunnel springs a leak? What if the moving van breaks down and we can't reach the other side? We could be stuck down here forever. I don't even know how to swim.*

She glanced out the truck's back window to make sure Dad was still following. What if he took one look at the city and turned to head back to the desert?

Her father did a little four finger wave off the top of the steering wheel when he saw her, as he had done every time she turned around, but he never smiled. Ani was beginning to think he might never smile again.

Before she knew it, they had emerged on the other side of the river into another world. To Ani, it seemed like a land made for giants. Enormous structures rose up around them on all sides, disappearing into the twilight high above. Why would anyone build buildings so tall? Seemed selfish to block the sky for everyone else. Does no one care about the stars here? The desert sang to the morning sky with every sunrise, and to the night sky with the dance of a billion stars.

But as they continued to snake their way through the city at a crawl along with hundreds of other cars, Ani finally understood. New York didn't need the stars. It came with its own night sky.

As darkness fell, the city lights flickered on a thousand at a time, painting the darkening canvas with brilliant sparkling light. The stars had fallen from the sky and settled on every surface of the city. Ani gazed out her window in awe, feeling as if she were soaring in slow motion through an entirely new universe filled with planets and stars and galaxies and alien life forms.

They rattled down a neighborhood street in Morningside Heights in the old Chevy truck and double-parked in front of a dark, ancient, and distinctly spooky apartment building.

Please tell me this isn't where we're going to live.

Nan checked the address on her notepad and said, "This is it!"

Great. Ani shivered as much from the creepy vibe as from the chilled air permeating the truck's poorly sealed windows.

"So, what do you think?" asked Nan, bubbling with excitement.

Leaning forward to look through the grimy windshield, Ani's gaze traveled from the chipped marble stairs that met the sidewalk under a tired old streetlamp, to the top floor seven stories above.

Unable to think of anything nice to say, Ani said, "It's um, big."

"It's wonderful, isn't it? This place was considered positively luxurious in its day. Built in the early nineteen-hundreds."

That much is obvious.

Nan pointed to the triangular pattern etched in a row of rough stone tiles that separated one floor from the next. "That design is called Art Deco. Look at that detail. Lovely."

A scrolling wrought iron fire escape crept up one side of the building and down the other, clinging to stained limestone blocks. Elaborately etched double glass doors adorned the façade, their beauty infringed upon by several large cracks and what looked like a . . . bullet hole?

Ani's vivid imagination spontaneously manufactured an elaborately detailed scene that involved a cluster of mafia thugs in a shootout for territorial rights against a lone hero standing on the side of justice.

Noticing the lit name and date carved in the stonework above the entrance—Wakefield Hotel 1927—Ani said, "We're moving into a hotel?"

"No, silly. It started out as a hotel, but it was converted. In the forties, I think. They're apartments now, honey."

"I wonder how many ghosts have accumulated here over the last hundred years," said Ani, only half joking.

"You're not afraid of a few little ghosts, are you?"

"How should I know, I've never actually met one before."

Nan glanced in the rearview mirror. "I think that's your father. Here, put on a sweater. It's still quite chilly here in March."

Yeah, the snow on the ground is a dead giveaway. Ani pulled on one of her Mom's bulky fleece-lined cardigans.

Nan did the same, then wrapped a scarf around Ani's neck and topped her off with a knit cap.

"Okay, I'm warm. You can stop now."

Nan got out and locked the door. "I called ahead to make sure the power's on, so the lights and appliances should all be working. Internet too. Oh, and I asked the landlord. There's a boy in 11B who's about your age and a girl who lives down the hall from us. She's fourteen. Later on you can go meet them. We're in 36C. It's on the third floor."

Stan double-parked the moving van behind them, much to the agitation of the other drivers on the street. And a rusty white truck with two burly men riding in the back pulled up bumper to bumper with the van.

Ani watched as her father hopped out and exchanged a few words with the men. Then the three of them got straight to work unloading furniture and boxes in silence until both the van and the old Chevy pick-up were empty.

By the time they'd moved in, it was nearly midnight, and a light snow had begun to fall. They heated stale leftovers from a diner in New Jersey where they'd stopped for a late lunch, ate their dinner in silence, and then headed straight to bed.

When Ani asked her mother why she had been so quiet during the meal, Nan used the excuse that it had been a long day, but Ani could tell it was more than that. Mom and Dad hadn't said a word to each other since they left California. It was as if they'd all become strangers overnight.

"Listen sweetie," said Nan, "I know you don't want to be here, but just give it a chance, okay? Do you want to know what I do when I find myself in a less-than-desirable situation?"

Not really.

"I find one positive thing about the new situation. Just one. That's not hard, right? And once you find one thing that's good, it is usually easier to find the next good thing, and the next. Before you know it, you're happy with your new circumstance. Can you do that?"

"Find one thing that's good about moving to New York?" Ani thought about that for a moment. The only thing that came to mind was the Kalb. Since the burnt-flesh demon-creature had found her in the desert, where she was the only girl for hundreds of miles, maybe he'd have trouble locating her in New York City where she was one girl among thousands. But that was not something she could tell her mother, so she just shrugged and said, "Can I go to bed now?"

In her new room, Ani rummaged through the three large cardboard boxes labeled "Ani's Things" to find a very important lump of crumpled newspaper. She had insisted on packing it herself. It was the only thing she really cared about.

With the utmost care, she peeled away the layers to reveal her treasure box. One by one, she inspected the items inside to make sure nothing had been disturbed: grandma's embroidered heart, the tiny pewter angel, the trilobite fossil, the drawing of the Mapstone and the hundred-dollar bill—all intact. To these, she added Kahetay's wood carving of the hawk, the antique Sherlock Holmes-style magnifying glass from the rock shop, and the three polished stones from her pocket. It was all that she had left of her previous life.

She clutched the box to her chest, watching the snow fall outside her window with cruel indifference. She listened to the sirens screaming by on the street below, heedless of the brutal impact it had on her imagination. In her mind's eye, she saw each and every victim. Heart attack. Car accident. Domestic violence. Murder. And with each, another little part of her died a small insignificant death. The radiator under the sill rattled on, oblivious to her plight, wheezing like it was too old and too tired to go on living. How could she live here? How could she be happy in a place like this?

Do they expect me to just forget about Kahetay and Mobius? Forget home? Everything I've ever loved is back in the desert. How could they ask me to give that up?

Fighting tears, Ani went to the bathroom to brush her teeth wash her face. After scrubbing off the city grunge, she groped for a towel but found only a bare rack. One more reminder that she wasn't home.

Water dripped from her hair and chin as she stared at her reflection in the mirror.

She looked different. Empty. Anonymous.

But there was something else. She squinted at the image in the mirror, seeing, impossibly, another face—perfectly overlaid onto her own. It was strangely familiar, a face not unlike hers, but more boyish and resolute. He mimicked her solemn expression.

A tingle rippled through her as she realized who it was.

"Eli?" she whispered. "Is that you?"

Through her tears, she saw the face of her imaginary friend smile reassuringly. In the far reaches of her mind, she heard the words, "*Don't give up, Gemi, we'll get through this. It'll be okay.*"

"But how?" she said out loud. "How is it going to be okay?"

She wanted an answer. She *needed* an answer.

The boy in the mirror offered no explanation, just a sad smile.

A drop of water fell from a stray strand of hair to an eyelash.

She blinked.

He vanished.

"Don't go," she whispered. "Please come back. I need you."

She held very still, willing her friend to return. *Pleeeease,* she thought with all the focus and energy she could muster.

Her reflection was her own again. Yet the memory of his face, the comfort of his words, the reassuring tone of his voice, stayed with her.

Deep breath.

I can do this.

Another deep breath.

I'm not alone.

Long exhalation.

Everything is going to be okay.

As she walked back to her room, she felt her strength returning. The desert had taught her the first thing to do in any predicament was to stay positive, turn your disadvantages into advantages. Why should this situation be any different?

Could it be any harder than getting caught alone in a sandstorm when she was seven? Or backing slowly out of a rattlesnake den she'd happened upon when she was nine? Or the time she twisted her ankle and had to make a splint for herself in order to hike the rest of the way home? *This is a city. No scorpions. No sandstorms. No snakes. How hard could it be?*

Latching her treasure box, she placed it on the nightstand beside her bed. Tomorrow she would investigate the surrounding neighborhood.

From now on, the city was just another adventure. A different terrain to explore. New discoveries. New experiences.

She felt better already.

And with that, she turned out the light, crawled under the covers, and closed her eyes to sleep.

*Locating the shadows and that which
casts them is one way to embrace the
light.*

-Solamas ❖ *Tome of the Zielfah Ri*

CHAPTER TEN

ళ

THE SHADOW ON THE WALL
AND THE GIRL DOWN THE HALL

Ani watched as the first white-gold rays of morning sunlight streamed into her room. She stared at the strange pattern cast on the blank wall across from her bed. It had the shape of a dragon, but where the tail should have been there was a second head. The two ends of the dragon seemed to be fighting each other, one breathing fire at the other, not realizing they were one.

The shadow dragon crept down the wall and stretched across her bedspread with the rising of the sun. When it was no longer visible, she slid out from under the covers and sighed, missing Mobius.

Not wanting to search the boxes for her clothes, pulled on yesterday's jeans and yellow "Rocks Rule" t-shirt.

With her parents still asleep—Mom in the bedroom, and Dad on the couch where he had fallen asleep watching TV—she quietly slipped out the front, taking pains not to wake them.

Once out in the hall, Ani eased the front door closed and then stopped, her hand lingering on the knob. A nagging unease knotted her neck and shoulders. She had a sudden urge to go back to her room and read a good book.

No. She promised herself she would explore the city and that's what she intended to do. She could hear her dad saying, "never go back on a promise, especially one you make to yourself."

She snuck down the deserted hallway, tiptoeing until she reached the stairs, but stopped when she heard a man's voice coming from the last apartment on the right, yelling something about cigarettes. The door swung open and a young girl about Ani's age stumbled out into the hall. A pack of soggy cigarettes hit her in the head just before the door slammed shut.

"And don't come back until you can replace 'em," came a muffled, angry voice.

"Jerk!" yelled the girl. She kicked the closed door and then noticed Ani standing a few feet away. "What are you lookin' at?"

"I was just trying to find my way out."

"Escaping before the parentals wake?"

"Yeah, how'd you guess?"

The girl drew a sleeve across her forehead where the soggy cigarette pack had hit. "You're new."

Ani nodded. "Just moved in yesterday."

"Right. Little desert girl from California. Welcome to the big bad."

"The big bad what?"

"Oh man, you really have been living under a rock."

"Not exactly under it. My name is—"

"Keep it down. If Joe catches me standing around out here, I'm dead. Come on."

"Aren't the stairs that way?"

"Never use 'em if I can help it. Less chance of running into the groper."

"The what?"

"It's not a what, it's a who. And trust me, you don't wanna know. His name is Gus and he lives one floor down, in 11B, but he's always makin' up some excuse to come around. Everyone thinks he's a twelve-year-old boy, but really he's a reincarnated sleazebag from the 1970's." She pointed down the hall and said, "Escape hatch. This way."

Ani climbed out the fire escape window and into the frigid air, where the cool morning sun had all but melted last night's snow. She followed a tangle of bluntly cropped, tarnished blond hair down the noisy metal stairs. A few uncut strands whipped the girl's cheek as her eyes flashed behind her every few seconds. Ani had never seen such angry blue eyes. The girl's tomboyish qualities gave her the kind of "tough-kid" look Ani had only seen on TV.

When they reached the street, Ani ventured a question. "Who's Joe? Is he your dad?"

"Foster parent, and what business is it of yours?"

"None. I just . . . I mean . . . what was he mad at?"

"I tried to flush his cigarettes down the toilet. Now get lost, I have things to do."

The girl vanished around a corner, and Ani was left standing alone on the sidewalk. Letting out a breath of frustration, she glanced around. Everything looked foreign to her. Every sound was strange to her ears. But the desert had seemed huge and strange and frightening at first too, she reminded herself. After she got to know it, she grew to love it. Shouldn't she give New York the same chance? It was only fair.

So she set out to explore the city, marking her path as her father taught her, except now, instead of using little rock piles and sticks to indicate the way home, she used soda cans and candy wrappers and whatever else she found along the way.

By noon she was completely lost.

Standing on a corner in front of a little neighborhood market, Ani gazed up at a street sign hoping to recognize the name. Her eyes widened as they fell upon an oddly shaped billboard that topped a building at the far end of the street. It advertised a brand of Chinese tea. The upper edge was a cutout in the shape of a dragon—the same two-headed dragon that had inched across her bedroom wall that morning. It was the clue she had been looking for, but as she started toward it, the market doors flew open, and a girl barreled out, running smack into Ani.

A pair of familiar angry blue eyes now stared her in the face.

"What the . . . are you following me?"

Ani attempted to regain her equilibrium. "Huh? No."

"Then what are you doing here?"

"I'm . . . ahh . . . kind of . . . lost."

"Geez. You stupid or what?"

Before Ani could answer, a middle-aged Italian man burst through the door. "You little thief, give me back those cigarettes!"

"What cigarettes?" The girl passed the Marlboro pack behind her back to Ani and then showed the man her empty hands. "Go ahead. Search me."

The man shifted his focus to Ani, "Hand 'em over and I won't call the police."

Ani shot her new friend a panicked what-do-I-do-now look, and in one word, she answered. "Run!"

The two girls whirled around and sprinted down a backstreet, the storekeeper cursing behind them.

Three blocks later, they collapsed on a bus stop bench.

"Wow," the girl panted, "for a *Ponch*, you sure can run."

"A what?"

"You might come in handy after all."

"My name's Ani. What's yours?"

"CJ, but don't think that makes us friends, cuz it don't."

"Fine by me," said Ani. "I don't know how to be friends with anyone anyway."

"Really."

"I've never had a real friend. Not like you. Not my own age."

"Huh. We might actually have something in common."

A fat water drop hit Ani's nose. Then another. She looked up. The sun had gone. Dark clouds loomed overhead.

"Great," Ani muttered under her breath.

"Better get used to it, Ponch. This ain't the desert."

"Can you just tell me how to get back to our apartment?"

"Turn around, fog-brain."

Ani glanced over her shoulder. The Wakefield stood there snickering as if it'd been playing hide and seek with her all day. She rose, mumbled a self-conscious thanks, and crossed the street without looking back. She could hear CJ's robust laughter even after the lobby doors closed behind her. If all city kids were like CJ, she might as well go back to the desert and argue with Mobius about where to put his cage. There wasn't much chance of her making friends here.

In her room, she flopped backward onto the bed, exhausted. Her first day in the city had been eventful, but not very much fun.

"Ani!" said her mother through the gap in the door.

Ani hopped up to pull the door open. She intended to tell her mother everything that had happened that day as a perfect example of why they should pack up and move back to the desert, but the look on her mom's face stopped her.

"Mom? What's wrong?"

"Where have you been!"

"I just went exploring."

"This isn't the desert, Ani."

So I've been told.

"You can't leave without telling us where you're going."

"I didn't want to wake you."

"Wake me? I thought someone had snatched you right out of your bed!"

"Sorry."

Nan took in a deep breath, held it for a moment and then let it out slowly. "Listen, I realize all these changes will require an adjustment period. You're a very independent girl, and you had a lot of freedom in the desert, but things are different now. We need to know where you are at all times."

"I might as well be in prison," mumbled Ani.

"It's my fault for not explaining things to you earlier."

"What do you want me to do, wear one of those ankle bracelets that goes off whenever I get more than a hundred feet from the apartment?"

"You're not under house arrest, Ani. We just need to be informed. I've put a pad of paper by the front door. From now on, if you leave the house, you write a note. No exceptions. And I don't want you going outside the neighborhood. You can go as far as the school on one end and the park on the other. No further. Understood?"

Ani shrugged. She used to come and go as she pleased. She used to have a life of her own. She used to be free.

"Alright." Her mother's expression went from resolute to impish grin. "Now that we've got settled, I have a surprise for you."

"What," said Ani, making no attempt to hide her disinterest.

"Well," said her mother, looking around. "How do you like your new room?"

Ani shrugged again. "It's okay I guess."

"Well, the walls are a little bare, don't you think?" She reached around the door and produced a rolled-up poster.

"What's that?"

"I thought it would make you feel more at home." She held it out. "Open it."

Ani unrolled the poster and stared at one of the most beautiful landscape photographs she had ever seen—the desert at dawn showing off its golden radiance, the blue and purple mountains rising up in the distance—and through the branches of a single silhouetted yucca tree burst the light of the rising sun in a seven-pointed star.

"Do you like it?"

It only made her miss the desert more, but Ani nodded anyway.

Her mother smiled. "I knew you would." She opened her other hand, which held a box of pushpins, and together they hung the poster over Ani's bed. When they finished, her mother reached into her shirt pocket and pulled out a twenty-dollar bill.

"Here."

"What's this for?"

"Your father and I talked it over. You're going to need an allowance now that you'll be attending public school."

School. Ugh. Ani's stomach lurched. In two days she would start public school for the first time in her life, but instead of being excited as she had always imagined, the thought filled her with dread.

"Don't worry, honey. You'll be just fine."

"I know. It's everybody else I'm not so sure about."

"Did you meet the girl who lives across the hall? Maybe you'll see her in school on Monday."

That was precisely the sort of thing Ani was afraid of. CJ was more than just a bad influence. She stared at the twenty-dollar bill in her hands and knew instantly what she wanted to do with it.

"Oh, and you're going to need this," said her mother. "It's only for emergencies." She handed Ani a brand new cell phone.

"I don't—"

"Just keep it in your book bag." She slipped the phone into a side pocket of Ani's backpack. "We need a way to reach you. Your number is taped on the back. Mine and your father's numbers are already in your contacts. And don't forget to keep it charged."

A few minutes later, they were in the kitchen looking for anything that might resemble lunch.

"I'll run to the store," said Ani, jumping at the opportunity. "I know right where it is. I found it this morning. It's not far. Just a couple blocks down."

Nan glanced out the window. "Looks like it might rain."

"I'll be quick."

"Alright. I'll make a list. Oh, that reminds me, I went shopping!" She produced a white cotton bralette from a Macy's bag.

Ani cringed. "I'm not wearing that."

"You may not need it right this instant, Ani, but you will soon. You don't have to be embarrassed about being a late bloomer, sweetie. All girls get there eventually."

"Mom. Stop. You're just making it worse," grumbled Ani.

"And . . ." Nan pulled two raincoats, one large, and one small, from the same Macy's bag. "I got us matching raincoats!"

Could this day get any weirder? Ani looked at the black vinyl slickers, covered with tiny white polka-dots, lined with faux fur, and said, "No thanks. I'm good."

"You're going to need a decent coat, Ani. It rains a lot here."

"I'll be fine." *As long as I can escape this parallel universe.*

"Take it anyway." She held out the coat, flashing her stubborn you're-not-gonna-win-this-one smile.

Ani sighed and put it on, feeling overly conspicuous.

In the kitchen, her mother handed her a short shopping list with another twenty-dollar bill and asked Ani to bring back the change. "Come straight home, okay?"

"I will."

It didn't rain, but the day remained cold and dismal and grey. Halfway down the block Ani shed the raincoat, stashed it in her backpack and made her way to the corner market where she'd run into CJ earlier. After putting the milk and cheese and lunch meat on the counter, she asked the man at the cash register how much a pack of cigarettes costs.

"I can't sell you cigarettes, miss. And you shouldn't be smoking at your age anyway."

"I don't want to buy them," said Ani, annoyed, "I just want to pay for them."

The man peered at her, confused. Then recognition donned. "I see," he said. "And you think that will be the end of it?"

"It's not stealing if we pay for them, right?"

"I . . . suppose not."

"Then I would like to pay for one pack of cigarettes, please. With this." She handed him the twenty-dollar bill her mom had given her for allowance.

"You've already given me enough, miss."

"That's my mom's money. I want to pay for the cigarettes with my own."

The man narrowed his eyes on her again. "What is your name, young lady?"

"Ani Jasper, sir."

"I'm Mr. Cardello," he said, extending his hand, "but you can call me Sal."

She accepted the handshake.

"Very nice to meet you, Ani Jasper." The man nodded his approval. "You're okay in my book, kid."

Ani smiled. Her first real friend in the city.

Reality, as it's commonly perceived, is but one of many states of consciousness from which to choose. Its attributes are created by us, for us, to teach us the meaning and power of thought.

-Xephero ❖ Tome of the Zielfah Ri

CHAPTER ELEVEN

✝

DISRUPTION THEORY

It was the first day of school, but only for Ani. All the other students had found their classes and gotten their books months ago. She had just stepped into a whirlwind of kids headed every-which-way, all knowing exactly where they were going.

"You don't even know what grade you're in?" sassed a freckled face girl in glitter-specked sunglasses, after Ani stopped her in the hall. "What are you? An L.D.er?"

"I'm in 8th grade," said Ani. "I just don't know where to go. What's an L.D.er?"

"Learning Disabled classes are that way." The girl spoke very loud, as if Ani had suddenly become deaf.

"Thanks," said Ani, starting out in the direction that Freckles had indicated. Maybe she really had been placed in a learning disabled class. It would make sense. She didn't know anything she was supposed to know. A New York City public school clearly wasn't a place for kids who'd never been to school a day in their lives.

Finally, after the 2nd warning bell rang out and the halls emptied, a suited gentleman with greying hair and dimpled chin stopped Ani and asked her name.

"Ani Jasper, sir," she said, relieved that someone might be willing to help her.

"My name is Mr. Schuman. I'm the Vice Principal." He looked at a list of names on a clipboard and said, "I thought so. I can always spot the transfer students. You're in room 101."

"I know, but the numbers jump from 100 to 102."

He walked over to a door marked with a piece of paper taped to it that read "Janitor's Closet" and removed the makeshift sign. Behind it, the brass number plate read 101. "It's a little game they play on new kids." He opened the door for her. "Miss Witcott is your homeroom teacher. I think you will like her."

"Thank you, sir."

"You're very welcome, Miss Jasper."

Ani entered the room and took the only seat available, smack in the middle of the class. Slumping in her chair, she felt dozens of staring eyes upon her.

Just as she was desperately wishing she could disappear, the unfathomable happened; the teacher, presumably Miss Witcott, asked Ani to stand up.

"Students! I'd like your full attention please. Thank you. We have a new face in our class today. I'd like you to meet Annie," Miss Witcott said, mispronouncing Ani's name. "She has just moved here from the Mojave Desert. Does anyone know where that is?"

"California," a girl in the front row called out.

"That's right. The largest portion of the Mojave Desert is in the southeast region of California, with smaller parts in Nevada, Utah and Arizona. It occupies nearly fifty thousand square miles in the west and it's best known for its notorious Death Valley, which sits two hundred and eighty-two feet *below* sea level, the lowest elevation in all of North America."

"Who would want to live in a place called Death Valley?" said a girl in the third row.

"I would," said a guy with a tongue piercing and ink-blackened eyes, sitting in the far corner, looking like this might be his 3rd time repeating the 8th grade.

"Death Valley is just a small part of The Mojave," said Miss Witcott. "Needless the say, Annie has come a very long way to be here."

"Approximately two thousand, four hundred, and sixty-one miles," added the know-it-all in the front row.

"Thank you, Janey. Let's all welcome Annie to our class."

Ani rose from her seat at the teacher's urging. "Um, excuse me, Miss Witcott? My name is pronounced *Ahh*-nee, not Annie."

"Oh dear, I'm so sorry," she whispered. "Class, let's give *Ahhnee* a warm welcome."

Feeble applause spread through the room until a shout came from the back row. "What kind of name is *that*?"

A boy sitting to Ani's right reached up to tug on the long dark braid running down her back. "Maybe she's an *Injin*!"

Ani's jaw clenched. *That's the last time I braid my hair before school.*

"Ask her if she lived in a cliff dwelling," came another call from the back.

The class erupted. They whooped and hollered and mocked.

"My grandfather is a Navajo shaman," Ani yelled over the commotion. "He belongs to a proud people who deserve respect! You shouldn't make fun of things you don't know anything about!"

"Quiet down!" Miss Witcott bellowed, "I will not tolerate disrespectful behavior in my classroom!" but her words held no weight. The class rioted out of control.

Ani stiffened. A slow pressurized panic rose inside her. The young faces around her began a frightening metamorphosis. Teeth grew longer, sharper. Eyes widened and went blood red. Fingers sharpened into claws. These weren't children, they were goblins—evil, teeth gnashing, kid-eating goblins. Ani had once read how goblins could take the form of children to gain their trust, but she saw right through the disguise. She backed away as the goblins all laughed and poked and sniffed and fought over who got the first bite.

"I get the arm!"

"I'll take a leg."

"I got dibs on her head. I'll bet it's nice and crunchy!"

Ani bolted toward the door, heart hammering against her chest. She could have sworn she heard one of them yell, "Quick, the snack's getting away!" as she bounded out into the corridor.

She passed the principal's office and kept right on running—out the annex, across the playground, and down one of the many neighborhood streets that divided endless rows of brownstones. She didn't stop until she reached the Wakefield.

Ani burst into the lobby and halted abruptly, trying to catch her breath. So much for her first day of school.

On the third floor, she found CJ sitting in the hall with her back against her apartment door. She wondered if CJ bothered with school at all.

"Hey," said Ani, trying to sound casual. "What's up?" CJ didn't respond.

"Why are you sitting out in the hallway?"

"Leave me alone."

"No. I want to know what's wrong. You look . . . pale."

"It's none of your business," snapped CJ. "And what are you doing here anyway? Aren't you supposed to be in school like a good little *ponch*?"

"I got attacked."

"Yeah? Who attacked you?"

"More like *what*."

CJ shot her a questioning look, and Ani suddenly felt very foolish for letting her imagination get the best of her. They were just kids. And running away today only meant that it would be harder to face them tomorrow, and every day after that.

"It . . . was nothing," said Ani. "Sometimes I just, um, imagine things being worse than they really are."

"Well, in that school, things can get pretty bad for real."

"Pointy teeth and red glowy eyes bad?"

"Worse."

Ani decided not to ask what that meant. At this point, it'd be better not to know. She nodded and turned toward her apartment.

CJ stood. "Joe won't let me in. Can I use your bathroom?"

"Yeah, sure." Ani opened the door.

Her father sat at the computer in a makeshift office that took up the far corner of their sparse living room. He'd been squinting at the monitor since before she left for school that morning, and looked up as they entered, peering at them through that same squint.

"Hey Dad," she said in a casual tone, hoping he would be too distracted to notice the hour.

He glanced at his watch.

So much for *that* wish. Ani knew the next thing out of his mouth would be a question about why school had let out early, so she jumped in to fill the pause. "Dad, this is CJ. She got locked out of her apartment. She just needs to use our bathroom. Is that okay?"

"Oh. Sure. Nice to meet you, CJ. Glad to see Ani's made a new friend already."

CJ scoffed at the word *friend*, as she followed Ani down the hall. "You don't have to show me where it is. I can find it myself."

As CJ pushed past Ani to enter the bathroom, Ani noticed she held her left arm so tightly it forced a white handprint on the reddening skin. "Are you okay?"

"Never better."

Ani watched as she leaned over the sink, turned on the faucet and ran cold water over her arm. The water turned ruby red, streaking the white porcelain as blood flowed from a deep gash at her elbow.

Ani grimaced. "That looks bad."

"It's just a scratch, and besides it's—"

"I know, none of my business. But I'm the one who has to clean up the sink and that's not just a scratch. What happened?"

"Joe just gets a little carried away sometimes when he's mad. I can handle it."

"He cut you?"

"Hey, keep it down."

"Shouldn't we tell someone—"

"No. And don't go blabbing this all over the neighborhood either. It's my fifth foster home. If I mess this one up they'll throw me back in the *Fragh*."

"What's the Fragh?"

"Freak Central." Then to Ani's questioning silence she added, "Group home. It's like being in jail, only worse. No chance for parole." She turned off the water. "Got something I can use to—"

"Oh, yeah, hang on." Ani ran to the kitchen and returned with a full roll of paper towels. "I won't say anything. I promise."

CJ grabbed the roll out of Ani's hands. "If you do, you're dead. Got it?" said CJ glaring with an intensity that screamed *I'm not kidding*.

"Yeah," said Ani. "I got it. But you know, you don't have to do that."

"Do what?" CJ pressed a wad of paper towels to her arm.

"Threaten me. If I say I won't, I won't." Ani reached passed CJ to retrieve an oversized Band-Aid from the medicine cabinet, and applied it to CJ's cut. To Ani's surprise, she didn't protest.

"Whatever. I'm outta here." She pushed Ani out of the way and headed for the hall. "And don't follow me this time."

"I wasn't fol—"

CJ slammed the front door, rendering the rest of Ani's sentence pointless.

The next day, Ani left the Wakefield forty-five minutes early and walked to school in the grey half-light of dawn—the air so cold, her breath turned smoke-white as she exhaled. She didn't mind the cold. She was just glad it wasn't raining so that she didn't have to wear that ridiculous polka-dotted raincoat, which her mother had neatly folded and stashed in her backpack.

When she arrived at Miss Witcott's classroom, she opened the door and peeked in. The room was empty except for the teacher.

Miss Witcott smiled and waved her in. "I'm glad you're here, Ani. I was worried about you. How are you today?"

"I'm sorry I ran away yesterday," said Ani.

"The first day of school can be pretty scary, I know, and for you, even more so."

"Why?" Ani thought for a frightening moment Miss Witcott had called home and talked to Dad. She braced herself.

"Well, this is your first time in a public school, right? That's got to be a little overwhelming, I should think."

"Oh. You didn't call my dad?"

"I did, but only to make sure you got home safely. I didn't give him any details, he didn't ask, and you are back in school today, so there's nothing to worry about."

"Thank you, Miss Witcott."

"You just needed a little extra time to adjust to your new situation. But don't make a habit of running out, Ani, or there will be repercussions."

"That's fair," said Ani, deciding right then to consider Miss Witcott her second friend in the city, after Mr. Cardello.

"Tell you what," she said, brightening a bit, "as it turns out, I am also your Social Studies teacher, which happens to be your last class of the day. If you have trouble in any of your other classes, we can stay after for a few minutes and talk about it, alright?"

Ani nodded.

Miss Witcott went on to say that she spoke with the goblins about their 'unacceptable behavior' and assured Ani no one would bother her again. Then she offered Ani her pick of seats and Ani took the desk nearest the exit, just in case she had to make another quick escape.

Some who walk this world are born on the earth but not of the earth. Their bodies are here, but their souls are from elsewhere. These elsewhere people walk with ghosts and listen to the rhythms of the universe, but know not where they belong. None see . . . that I am one of them . . . that I am alone here.

-Naviga ✢ Tome of the Zielfah Ri

CHAPTER TWELVE

ऽ⟨

NOBODY KNOWS

After all the kids had filtered in, and attendance had been taken, Miss Witcott stood at the front of the room and said, "Class, take out your pencils and a blank sheet of paper. Settle down, settle down, this is not a pop quiz." She turned to write on the chalkboard. "I want you to write at the top, I AM____, and then fill in your name. Under that, I'd like you to introduce yourself. Write a paragraph or two about who you are, what you like to do, your hobbies, something that you would like to share with the class. We usually do this assignment at the beginning of the year to help us all get to know each other, but since it *is* the beginning of the year for Ani, we are going to do it now. It will help her get to know us better, and feel more comfortable here—maybe even make a new friend or two."

A new friend or two? thought Ani. *What are the chances of that happening now?*

Ani glanced around the room. They all glared at her.

A large girl in the back row, wearing a black jacket that matched her died black hair and makeup-blackened eyes, scribbled something on her paper and held it up so Ani could see.

It said: **I AM____gonna kick your ass.**

Keeping her head down, Ani tore a piece of lined paper from her notebook and began to write . . .

Okay, ya'know how sometimes when you're asleep you can't tell if you're dreaming or not because everything feels so completely real? Well, that's how it feels to be me... all the time. I never know if what I'm experiencing is real or not. But I think I'm slowly figuring out that it's ALL REAL, and that is the scariest thing I can think of. See, if it's all real, then I am in some deep dark shades of trouble with all kinds of bad mixed in.

I'm Anani'nah Jasper and I'm an elsewhere girl. I'm nearly fourteen, I'm an amateur geologist and a magical apprentice. I live in New York City, but I was born in the Mojave Desert. I don't feel I belong here. I don't think I belong anywhere.

I'm technically an only child because I lost my twin brother the day I was born, but if you want to know a secret, the truth is, I didn't really lose him because we are still together. Two souls. One body. Weird, I know. But kinda cool at the same time. It's called Zielfah which means "double soul" in Azimaran and because of it, I'm next in line for some fierce magical mojo I didn't ask for. Oh and get this... because I am the appointed 'heir apparent,' I have some equally fierce enemies that want me permanently deleted in the worst way. Mom and Dad don't know. Nobody knows. No one would believe me anyway.

So I live my life as if everything is normal, whatever that means. It's not easy when you're a freak like me. I get these, um, future memories—like strange visions where I go into the future and remember stuff that hasn't happened yet. That's weird, right? Oh, and back in the desert, I almost died from a scorpion sting, but that's how I met Xephero, this bizarro dude who calls himself the Light Master. He's the reason I'm in this mess of a life. It all started when he chose me to be the future keeper of his magic, but I don't want anything to do with it. Welcome to my world.

Ani paused to read what she had written. She didn't mean to tell the truth about herself. She meant to make up a bunch of stuff that made her sound like a normal girl, but once she began to write, well, it all just came out. She crumpled the paper into a ball and through it in the trashcan beside the door. Just as she took another sheet of paper from her desk to start again, the bell rang.

Guess I failed that assignment.

87

As it turned out, Miss Witcott was right about what she said that morning. No one bothered her in class that day. As a matter of fact, a whole week went by without anyone even glancing in her direction, without the teacher ever calling on her when she raised her hand, without anyone ever even saying hi . . . and not just in Miss Witcott's room, but in *all* her classes.

She had become invisible.

The only time anyone noticed her at all was when she returned to homeroom one rainy morning after leaving to get a drink of water. They all stared at her as if she were wearing a gorilla suit.

"Ani," said Miss Witcott as patiently as possible, "you must raise your hand and ask permission to leave this classroom. You can't just get up and walk out anytime you feel like it."

"Why not?" asked Ani, genuinely curious.

The class erupted in laughter.

"It's disruptive," said Miss Witcott, giving the rest of the class a disapproving look that quieted only a few.

The girl in the black jacket who'd held up the threatening note—whom Ani later learned was nicknamed Mad Millie— shouted from the back row, "Don't bother, Miss Witcott, she wouldn't know about things like manners, being raised in a cave and all."

Another rumble of laughter from the class.

Whatever possessed Ani to do what she did next was beyond her comprehension. In what could only be described as a monumental moronic lapse in judgment, she turned toward the back of the room and said in a clear, calm voice, "I'd rather live in a cave than the slimy mud pit you crawled out of."

As the roar of laughter jumped ten decibels, Mad Millie glared at Ani in silent rage. The sheer power of it forced Ani back into her seat. She never left the classroom again. Not even when she was desperate to use the restroom.

That afternoon, when the final bell rang and all the history quizzes had been collected, Miss Witcott asked Ani to stay after school so that they could "discuss something in private."

"Have a seat," said Miss Witcott, after the rest of the students had gone.

Ani sat quietly waiting for her reprimand. She began to construct an apology in her head, wondering why Millie wasn't also in trouble. It hardly seemed fair. After all, she started it.

"Ani, thank you for staying behind. I won't keep you long."

"I'm sorry about this morning in homeroom, Miss Witcott. I don't know why I said that. The words just came out. It won't happen again. I promise."

"Oh, yes, well, it was a very unfortunate incident," said Miss Witcott. "But you should know Ani, that in this school we don't tolerate bullies. We have been watching Millicent for a while now. Disciplinary measures have had no effect. And unfortunately, she targets the new kids a lot. Your response was, well, understandable, given the circumstances."

Ani relaxed a little.

"I'm not saying what you did was right, but I am proud of you for being brave enough to stand up for yourself."

Or stupid enough.

"It's more than most kids would do.
But that's not the reason I asked you to stay after. I wanted to talk to you about your marks on the quizzes."

"Oh. Did I mess up?"

"On the contrary. Your test scores are the highest in the class. That's what concerns me."

"But I thought getting good grades was the idea."

"No Ani, learning is the idea, and you don't seem challenged by the curriculum at all. I've spoken with your other teachers. They've reported similar results. You have been excelling in all your subjects."

"Is that wrong?"

"And then there's this." Miss Witcott opened her desk drawer and drew out a wadded up piece of paper.

Ani cringed. She knew exactly what it was. "You didn't read that, did you?"

"I did. It's very . . . creative," said Miss Witcott. "But Ani, the assignment was to write about yourself and share it with the class so they could get to know you. This is a work of fiction. Do you understand the difference?"

"I do. It wasn't what I intended to write," Ani mumbled, secretly relieved that her teacher assumed she'd made it all up. "It just, um, came out that way."

Miss Witcott nodded. "I read your file. It says you have a very vivid and active imagination."

"I'm sorry. It gets me in trouble sometimes."

"Don't apologize, Ani. An imagination is a wonderful thing. However, you must learn to discern when it is appropriate to use your imagination and when it is not." She held up the crumpled paper. "This is an example of the latter."

The corners of Ani's mouth turned down. "I understand."

Miss Witcott studied Ani's face for a moment. "I read in your file that your mother homeschooled you until now. Is that correct?"

"Yeah. That's probably why they put me in L.D. classes, but I think maybe I should be in regular classes."

"Ani, you *are* in the regular curriculum. Who told you that you were in Learning Disabled classes?"

"I just thought—" Ani stopped, embarrassed.

Miss Witcott smiled warmly. "I'd say your mother did a very fine job teaching you."

"She goes to school too," said Ani. "We study together. Back home we sometimes used her school books when mine were too boring."

"You studied college-level texts?"

"Not all the time. But Mom's books were my favorites."

"I see." Miss Witcott put Ani's crumpled essay back in her desk and shuffled a stack of papers in front of her. "Well, we'll just have to make an effort to find assignments that will interest you from now on, okay?"

Ani nodded, excited at the prospect.

"Thank you Ani, you can go now."

Ani rose from her chair. "So, I'm not in trouble?"

"No, you're not in trouble," said Miss Witcott with another one of her kindly smiles. "See you tomorrow."

Ani left Miss Witcott's classroom thinking maybe school wasn't so bad after all. She wasn't an L.D.er, and her marks were the best in the class. She couldn't wait to go home and tell Mom and Dad the news.

She stopped at her locker and then headed out. "Great," muttered Ani, hearing the now familiar pelt of raindrops on the roof. Pausing to put on her raincoat, she looked left, then right, to make sure she wouldn't be seen in it. The halls were deserted. She zipped up and headed for the main exit.

Just before she reached the double doors, a girl waiting in the shadows stepped in front of her, barring her way. Ani had never seen this girl before. The black she wore from shoulder to toe made her bleached-white hair stand out like neon. Bulky silver chains draped her waist, wrists and ankles. Ani tried to pass, but the girl grabbed the back of her raincoat.

"Where do you think you're going, *polka-dots*?"

Ani winced at the reference. If that became her nickname at school, she'd never forgive her mother. Regaining her composure, she glanced at the girl's chains. "Aren't those uncomfortable?" she said, attempting to keep her voice steady. "They look kinda heavy."

"I have a message for you," said the girl in a low voice.

Ani forced an exaggerated smile. "Secret admirer?"

The girl's face scrunched up as if she'd just swallowed something sour. "Nobody messes with Millie and gets away with it."

Ani's stomach clenched. "Millie who?" she asked, knowing full well who the girl meant.

"You've been warned."

"Casey, come on. We're going to Vin's."

The call came from a girl emerging from the restroom.

The Silver Chain Girl let go of Ani's coat, but not before pulling it up over her head. By the time Ani could see again, the girls were gone.

School just keeps getting better and better, she thought. How was it possible that since she'd arrived in New York, she had made more enemies than friends? In the desert, she had found only one true enemy. The Kalb.

Ani shuddered. Just thinking about the Kalb filled her with a sense of dread that chilled her, body and soul. At least with Mad Millie, she knew what she was dealing with. What frightened her most about the Kalb was not knowing what it could do to her, or where it would appear next.

Bullies at school were relatively simple in comparison. She could probably avoid them if she was careful. And although she couldn't tell anyone about the Kalb, she could certainly tell someone about Millie. Maybe if Mom and Dad knew how bad it was, they would reconsider the whole concept of public school.

By the time Ani got home, she had worked out exactly what she was going to say, but stopped short of the front door, halted by the muffled sound of angry voices. She listened for a moment, trying to make out what was being said.

She'd never heard her mother and father yell at one another before. Not like this. She couldn't understand the words, but their anger pierced her heart like shrapnel. Suddenly what she had to say didn't seem all that important.

CJ emerged from her apartment across the hall and stopped behind Ani to eavesdrop. "That's how it starts, you know," she said over Ani's shoulder.

"How what starts?"

"Divorce. First, they fight. Then they throw things. Then one of them throws the other out."

"You're wrong. They're just having an argument."

"All the signs are there, Ponch. Take my word for it. Before the divorce is final they'll have played tug-of-war with you, and you'll end up in two pieces."

"It doesn't happen that way to everyone."

"Go ahead. Walk in on 'em. The way I see it, you got two possible outcomes. Either they're so wrapped up in 'emselves that they don't even know you exist, or worse, they *do* notice you and use you for target practice."

"They'd never do that."

"Go ahead. Prove me wrong."

Ani opened the door and stepped inside the apartment. Her parents continued to shout at each other, completely unaware that she was there. She opened the door and stepped back out.

"Um, I'll talk to them later. They seem busy."

"Uh huh."

Ani slumped away, fully expecting CJ to laugh out loud.

She didn't.

As Ani walked the length of the hall, she realized she had nowhere to go. The rain had stopped, and a tiny patch of blue sky opened up, framed by the hall window.

It made her terribly homesick.

She crawled out onto the wet fire escape and stared at that patch of blue until the surrounding grey swallowed it up.

What was happening to her family?

She pulled a photograph from her back pocket—one she had carried with her every day since she left the desert. It was a picture of her grandfather. The only one ever taken of him, he said. It showed him standing on the edge of a cliff. Two others appeared in the picture, but they stood back a few feet from the edge. Kahetay was poised, looking like he was ready to jump.

Ani had asked him if she could keep the photograph because she loved the look on his face. It seemed like he understood, just then, all the secrets of the universe. He had the look of someone who was truly free. At one point, she asked him what he was thinking when they snapped the shot. He replied simply, "I was thinking about taking a leap of faith."

She stared at the photograph now, heart aching. Her friendship with Kahetay had made her world special, magical. Life was a discovery, a fantastic journey, and she knew no matter how strange and wonderful it all got, he would be there to guide her.

Now everything was different. There was no Kahetay, no Mobius, no Boulder Dash Hill, no rock shop. All the things that made her feel like she belonged were gone. She even caught herself wishing that awful scorpion could sting her again. Even that horrible fever was preferable to this loneliness. At least it had taken her to the Web Between Worlds, and she had come out of it feeling somehow more connected and alive. It had even brought her family closer together for a time.

Wait, back up, said a disembodied voice. *Did you just say the Web Between Worlds?*

Only when we have walked alone through the rocky canyon of self-perception, shall we see the mountain of judgment and doubt that enshrouds our true purpose.

-Naviga ✤ Tome of the Zielfah Ri

CHAPTER THIRTEEN

ᛣ

THE HOLLOW HOUSE

Glancing up with a start, Ani scanned her surroundings. Alone. She was alone. Well, except for a black and tan cat sitting on the window ledge just beyond the fire escape.

Yeah, it's me, said the fat cat. *I wasn't going to say anything. Just didn't seem worth the effort, what with the absolute drivel oozing from your brain. You know—typical human thoughts— poor me, why is this happening—blah, blah, blah. Boooorrrriing. But that last bit about the Web Between Worlds, now that's a real conversation starter.*

The cat spewed the string of words without so much as a pause. Its voice came to her as a steady stream of thoughts inside her head, the same way Mobius had spoken to her about his cage, the same way the white wolf had when he brought her back from the scorpion fever.

The cat's yellow opal eyes peered out of a black Egyptian mask. *So, are you getting any of this?* it asked, making its way from the window ledge to where Ani sat. *Hello? Girlie-girl? Knock knock. Anyone home?*

Ani realized she was staring agape, and quickly closed her mouth. She didn't think she would ever get used to animals talking to her. "Um, yeah," she said to the cat. "I can hear you."

"*Well now, that's a bonus. What makes you so special?*"

"I'm not special. If I was, I wouldn't be—"

"*—out here on the fire escape whining about your life? Oh, all humans do that. It's an evolution thing. Once they get it, they won't whine anymore.*"

"Get what?"

"*Nevermind,*" said the cat, dismissively. "*Hmm, you look like every other human.*" The cat sniffed the air, its whiskers twitching. "*You smell like every other human. So how come we can chat like it's Sunday at the bistro?*"

"I don't know," said Ani. "When I was in the Web Between Worlds this weird guy told me I was a Zielfah. Maybe it has something to do with that."

Zielfah? Never heard of it.

"Doesn't matter anyhow. Everything's different now."

Yeah, so I heard.

"What am I going to do? It's all gotten so messed up."

I suggest a nap. Nothing in this world a good nap can't cure.

"It's not that simple for human beings."

Well, maybe it should be, said the cat. *I've been around your species long enough to know that you complicate things needlessly. Your kind thrives on it. You should spend less time trying to figure things out and more time lazing in the sun. You'd feel much better.*

Ani shrugged. "I'll try."

Nah, you'll forget. That's what humans do. They forget everything they're told that can make a difference. The only things they remember are the bad stuff that scrambles their insides. The cat scratched behind one ear for a moment and then said, *Hey listen, since I've got your attention—and who knows how long that will last—I've always wondered about this bathing thing humans do. Why do you use a tub? You've got tongues, haven't you?*

"Yeah, but we use soap."

What's soap got to do with anything?

"Well, no one wants to lick soap. It tastes terrible. I should know. I put a bar of soap in my mouth once when I was really little."

What'd ya do that for?

"It was shaped like a strawberry. Smelled like one too. I wanted to see if it tasted like one."

Not too bright, are ya?

"Well, I was four. I'm smarter now."

One would hope. The tabby hopped up on the fire escape railing in a perfect balancing act.

"Are you leaving?"

You want me to stay?

"Sure."

Can't. Sorry. Time to hit snooze. There's a mandatory napping clause in my contract. See ya.

"Bye," said Ani, not entirely sure of the proper way to bid a cat farewell.

And just like that, her mind turned quiet, and she was alone again. Without the cat's strange conversation to distract her, Ani's thoughts returned to her parents. The weight of their anger crushed down upon her, constricting her heart. When she had listened through the door earlier, she'd been grateful that she couldn't understand what they were saying, but now she wanted to know, *had* to know, what the argument was about.

She rose, crawled back through the fire escape window, and returned to the apartment.

Finding the door ajar, she stopped for a moment, listening.

Nothing.

She edged the door open and slipped inside. Dusk had turned the apartment a lifeless shade of grey. No one had clicked on the lights.

"Mom? Dad?" she called. "Is anybody here?"

Silence swallowed her words. She went from room to room. Searched the hall table and then the kitchen counters. No note. Cell phones still on the charger. Car keys gone. What if CJ was right? What if her parents had been so angry they just left and forgot about her?

The apartment sagged. Even the furniture looked lonely. The fading light through curtainless windows made the room seem like it was slowly disappearing. *Might as well disappear*, she thought, *it will never be home*. To Ani, this apartment represented all that was wrong with their lives and she hated how it made her feel— like everything in her life was fake, standing in for the real thing she couldn't have.

In the kitchen, she tore the cellophane from a frozen dinner, placed it in the microwave, and stood staring into space as the food slowly turned circles inside. The memory of her mother's exotic cooking made the smell of the frozen dinner almost nauseating. She tried to imagine sitting around the table with her mother and father, eating dinner together like they used to, but she couldn't. Not here. Not in this cold, coffee-stained kitchen.

The microwave finally beeped and Ani removed the plastic tray. Fried Chicken, mashed potatoes, and peas. She hated peas.

Why do I always eat my peas? Because Mom told me when I was five to 'always eat your peas'?

For once, she would eat only what she wanted to eat. Why not? No one there to tell her not to.

Turned out to be a hollow victory though, tasteless as it all was. She didn't really want any of it.

The adjacent living room took on an eerie cast from the kitchen fluorescents. Corners filled with shadowy shapes that vanished in her peripheral vision. Her mind began to populate the shadows with ghosts—residents of the underworld come to prey on helpless girls with no parents to protect them. An eerie scratching sound coming from inside the walls sent her running through the apartment, heart pounding, switching on every lamp she could find to dispel the ghastly specters.

Once all the lights were on, her fear began to wane. She berated herself for being such a child. The scratching noise was probably just mice. Lots of old buildings had them.

She took a few deep breaths to calm her racing heart and sat at the computer to contact her two cousins in Vancouver. She told them how different New York was from her life in the Mojave, and how much she missed the desert. They replied, full of suggestions on how to make the city more enjoyable—shopping for clothes, getting a makeover at Macy's, skating in central park to meet boys—all of which only made Ani feel more out of place. She'd never done *girl stuff* like that before. It seemed silly to her and she knew that made her even more of a freak.

Ani turned off the computer and glanced at the clock. 10:30 p.m. and her parents still weren't home. Maybe this was how it was going to be. Maybe she'd be alone for the rest of her life.

In her room, she changed into her pajamas, remembering to take Kahetay's picture out of her jeans pocket before throwing them in the hamper. She propped the photo on her dresser and then crawled into bed. If her parents had left for good, she would go live with Kahetay in the Mojave where she belonged. If they didn't want her, then she didn't want them. Kahetay would take care of her, and he would never abandon her. She was certain of that. He would be there for her, protect her, always and forever.

Before shutting the light off, she opened her treasure box and removed the Mapstone sketch. If only it were the actual stone instead of a stupid piece of paper, she'd use its magic to change her life.

As she unfolded the paper and stared at the drawing, an odd feeling came over her.

Something was different.

Then she saw it.

The symbols she'd drawn under the stone were nearly gone. Only the faintest wisp of an outline remained. She ripped a page of notebook paper from her school binder and quickly copied the symbols just before they evaporated entirely.

A groan escaped her lips. She knew what was happening. Her drawing was slowly disappearing just like her life.

Another hour crept by before Ani finally closed her eyes, hoping for another dream of Xephero and the stone city, or of Kahetay and Boulder Dash Hill. Anything familiar. But what came instead . . . was another nightmare.

The ground shook. The sky grew dark and angry. Desert animals scurried about, searching for shelter.

Desperate to maintain her balance, Ani searched the horizon for anything to focus on that wasn't moving. The whole world crumbled around her. Out of the desolate land, Kahetay appeared, his hand outstretched. She knew if she could get to him, everything would be okay, but as she started toward him, a horrific ripping sound shattered her eardrums, sending a crackling pain through her body like a lightning-bolt seeking ground.

The moment she reached out to her grandfather, the earth tore open exposing a vast black chasm between them. "Kahetay!" she screamed. "Look out!"

He took a step back, lost his footing and tumbled into the rift. As the blackness swallowed him, Ani heard a chilling screech that froze her insides. It was there—the demon creature she had seen in the desert just before the scorpion stung her. The Kalb. *It* was the darkness that devoured her grandfather.

"Kaaaheeetaay!" The sound of her own voice thrust her out of the dream.

Suddenly wide-awake, Ani bolted out of bed. She dashed to the kitchen, grabbed the phone and dialed the number as fast as she could.

It rang.

"Come on, Kahetay," she said under her breath.

It rang again.

"Answer."

It continued to ring.

"Please. Please. Please be there."

She counted five more rings and then hung up. The clock over the stove read 3:00 a.m. What was the time difference again?

Maybe he's just asleep and can't hear the phone. She decided to wait a few hours and call again at daybreak.

At first, Ani hadn't noticed that the lights she'd left on when she went to bed had been turned off. She tiptoed to the entry hall. Yep. They were home. Dad's keys hung on the hook by the door, and Mom's purse sat on the hall table. They must have come home after she'd fallen asleep and decided not to wake her.

Didn't matter. All she cared about now was that Kahetay was safe.

For nearly four hours she tried to will herself back to sleep but it was useless. In her mind, she saw Kahetay fall, again and again, into the black abyss. What if he was really in danger and trying to reach out to her through her dreams?

He'd done it before.

She'd just turned eight. Kahetay had gone to Arizona to visit family but turned up missing a few days into the trip. He'd been exploring a small cave looking for petroglyphs from his ancestors when the entrance collapsed. Trapped and injured, he sent Ani his location in a dream. Her parents would never have found him had it not been for that message Ani received. Maybe this was the same. Maybe he needed her. Maybe he was dying and she was the only one who could save him.

Ani looked at the clock beside her bed. 6:45 a.m. It was Saturday, she reasoned. No school. She could use her hundred-dollar bill, plus the allowance she'd saved up, buy a bus ticket to California and call Kahetay again along the way. She grabbed the cell phone, suddenly glad her mother had given it to her.

After throwing on jeans, a t-shirt and shoes, she opened her treasure box, took the money and stashed it in her front pocket. She also snatched the Mapstone sketch off her nightstand, folded it and put it in her back pocket. Maybe Kahetay would know why the marks were disappearing. Grabbing her old red zippered sweat jacket off the hook, she headed for the front door.

The pad of paper on the entry table goaded her on the way out. She paused, picked up the pen to write a note and then stopped herself. If they could leave without a word, then so could she.

Ani headed down the hall without looking back and flew down the stairs two at a time. Reaching the first floor, she swung open the door to the lobby and stepped through.

For a moment she stood there, on the other side of the door. Confused. Breathing it in.

Kahetay.

He was here. The sweet earthy scent of his clothes lingered in the air. She followed the musky aroma down the first floor corridor to apartment 13A.

The nameplate on the door read *Sophia Delecort* in fancy letters. Underneath, the word *Manager* stood out like a declaration in bold type. Ani started to knock but the door crept open on its own. "Hello? Is anyone there?" she called. Sage smoke curled before her, inviting her in. She hesitated, then slipped inside, at once curious and cautious.

"Kahetay?" Even as she called out his name, she knew it was silly to think he would be there. How could he be? It was just someone burning sage incense. Still, her eyes searched the room.

The place tingled with enchantment.

High rounded ceilings depicting the night sky hovered above, complete with constellations and a mobile of the planets. Thick red velvet curtains blocked out the early morning light, but a brightly colored Tiffany lamp, with its stained-glass, lavender-winged dragonflies, lit the room with a warm welcoming glow.

Ani couldn't help herself. She tiptoed through the apartment, careful not to disturb the intriguing collection of oddities she now beheld. The walls, lined with shelves, supported all manner of curiosities—smooth river rocks and labyrinthine seashells, prismatic crystals and brilliantly polished gemstones. On one of the lower shelves, the gossamer husk of a snake draped next to the feathers of a great bird. Multi-hued candles, hand-made incense, and dried herbs tied with twine covered two small round tables.

Her skin tingled with a sense of awe and fascination.

These things. She knew . . . knew what it all meant.

This was the stuff of magic.

This collection belonged to someone very special.

Someone . . . magical.

What brave contrast to the bare walls of her own apartment. Every inch of space here hummed with meaning, every object sparkled with purpose. Even the air seemed energized.

Then came an echoed whisper . . . "Ahhnee." The voice, weak, toneless, haunting, sent a shiver through her. It was the murmur of a ghost.

The illusion of form is so complete, so powerful, so utterly convincing, that we fail to question it. Yet it is just such a question that is the starting place of all mystical understanding.

-*Xephero* ❖ *Tome of the Zielfah Ri*

CHAPTER FOURTEEN

ʊ

THE GREY HAWK & THE SOUL SECRET

Ani whirled around to find her grandfather standing in the open doorway. Relief washed over her.

"Kahetay! You're alright!" Ani ran and threw her arms around him. "Oh, I'm so glad you're here. I smelled the incense. I thought it was you. I was coming to find you. How did you know?"

"Ani," he said, breathless and shaking. He drew away from her and looked into her eyes. A bleak expression darkened his face.

"What is it?" Ani asked, finally seeing his utter exhaustion. "What's wrong?"

"I came to ask *you* that question," he rasped. "I had a dream about you, an alarming dream. The earth opened to swallow you."

Ani felt a chill at his words. "I had the same dream about you."

"I see." He thought for a moment. "If we have shared this dream, little one, then there is great significance in it. A message awaits our understanding. Tell me—"

"But I woke up only a few hours ago. If we had the same dream at the same time, how did you get here so fast?"

Kahetay peered down at her through narrowed eyes. "You must tell me everything."

It hadn't rained since yesterday, and the morning sun chose to make a rare appearance, breaking through pink streaked clouds, as

Ani and her grandfather strolled down the block. Ani had never seen a morning so beautiful in the city. It was as if Kahetay brought the clarity and colors of the desert with him wherever he went.

They found a small wedge-shaped patch of grass and sat with their backs against a lone maple tree. The crisp wind prodded and played with the sparse leaves above their heads as Kahetay listened to the details of Ani's dream. Finally he spoke.

"This dream we shared, it was not about me. My world remains the same. But the earth beneath you is shaking. Tell me."

Ani could hold it in no longer. The words came pouring out of her like tears. "I hate it here, Kahetay. I don't have any friends. Mom and Dad fight all the time. School is awful. Worse than awful. I want to go back with you."

"It is never a wise choice to travel backward," said Kahetay. "You can only see where you've been, not where you are going. Makes it very difficult to see where you need to be."

"I need to be with you, Kahetay."

"Not long before my turning, the moon offered to me a small fragment of her wisdom that I will share with you." Kahetay paused, closing his eyes. When he spoke again, his voice was soft and seasoned with memory. "I once walked the length of a vast dry grass field at midnight to reach what the Natah called The Gathering of Souls. The moon was round and full before me. It lit my path well. I walked sure-footed in the darkness of night."

Ani waited as Kahetay paused again. She knew there would be a teaching for her in this memory, but the message was not yet clear. She also knew from experience, that if she interrupted him with her eager questions, the lesson would be lost.

"When the Gathering was done and all words that needed speaking had been spoken, I journeyed home the same way I had come—back across the field I had traversed with confidence only an hour before—but this time I was not so sure-footed. This time the mother moon was not before me but behind me. Instead of lighting my way, she cast a black shadow on my path. *My* shadow. I stumbled on every stray rock and into every crack. I simply could not see the ground before me. I was defeated by my own shadow. It was a part of me I could not escape. It is a part of us all. And at times it will darken our path. The lesson I learned that night taught me to find a balance within the self. Our spirit walks an inner path, just as the bodies walk an outer path. The lesson is that even though we can not escape the shadow within us, we can choose to embrace its gifts and walk toward the light, or we can walk away from the light to stumble and fall."

"The moon has been behind me for a long time now, Kahetay. I need you to show me the way back."

"No. I am your past, little one. You must look to your future now."

Ani shook her head. "If this is what the future is going to be like, I'm not interested."

Kahetay reached for Ani's hand. "Extend your vision beyond the moment of discomfort. Your current circumstances will not remain so for long. Your dream portends great change."

"What kind of change?"

"I will no longer be able to come to you when you need me. The distance between us will be too vast to traverse. This is what the dream tells me. And that if you keep your balance, and walk toward the light, you will find your way."

"Does it mean my mom and dad are going to get a divorce? That's what CJ says."

"CJ?" Kahetay's left brow curled into a sideways question mark, a particular thing he did whenever his thoughts made a curious connection.

"Just a girl I met in our building."

"This girl, was she in your dream?"

"Not that I remember. Why?"

"She was in mine."

"CJ?"

"A girl your age with dark blond hair and a circular shaped scar on her right shoulder. She caught your hand as you slipped off the edge of a crevasse and pulled you to safety. You called her CJ."

"That can't be right. She would never help me. She doesn't even like me."

"Are you sure?"

"Positive. She lets me know it all the time. She's not a very nice person."

"Sometimes the gift of friendship comes in unexpected packages. Perhaps you should keep your heart open to the possibility."

"Not this time. If you met her, you'd agree."

Kahetay picked two leaves from the ground. One had traces of green, hinting of spring, the other showed patches of autumn red and winter brown. "Do you know what makes them different colors?"

"My teacher, Miss Witcott, says it's sugar."

Kahetay nodded. "They start out the same and slowly, with the changing of the seasons, they react to what is inside and reflect it on the outside. But they are still essentially the same. One gets more sugar, one gets less, but they belong to the same tree."

Ani understood what Kahetay was saying, but she wasn't about to make friends with someone who didn't want to be friends with her. She looked down at her feet. Gnarled roots protruded from the ground, pushing toward the path in a constant struggle for space. In places, the roots had lifted the concrete, breaking the thick slab in two.

"This tree doesn't belong here," she said. "It can't grow. It's a prisoner of this city."

"Ani, give it time. I know you feel you don't fit in—"

"It's more than that, Kahetay. It's tearing our family apart. I think if we stay here much longer, there'll be nothing left."

"You're stronger than you think. Find that strength and wisdom within. Draw upon it. It will teach you what you need to know."

"But what if my parents split up? What happens then?"

"Why fear what has not occurred?"

"Can you talk to them?"

"Your parents have their own path, Ani. You must allow them to walk it, just as they must allow you to walk yours."

"And you think mine has something to do with being a double-soul?"

"That is for you to decide."

"You knew I was a twin, didn't you?"

"Yes."

"Why didn't you tell me?"

A strong gust of wind swept in and shook the branches above them. Ani peered at her grandfather. He seemed to be deep in thought, eyes closed, face lifted to the wind.

"Kahetay?"

He slowly opened his eyes. "I've never told you this, but the vision I had of you before you were born, it spoke of path and a purpose . . . it foretold a destiny that only you could fulfill."

"What is my destiny? Can you tell me?"

"Only that it is important. And when your mother and father asked me to be your grandfather, I knew it was *my* destiny to guide you. You were only three days old, but already I saw something in you that spoke the truth of my vision." He reached out to touch her arm. "I made a promise to you that day, and I have kept it. But I have always known there would be another to take my place."

"No one could ever take your place, Kahetay."

"Not as your grandfather, no, but as your guide."

Just as quickly as the wind came, it departed, leaving behind an eerie calm. He looked at the leaves that had scattered at his feet.

"The wind tells me there are things to say." He gathered his long silver-black hair, and secured it with a strip of leather produced from his shirt pocket. "You asked me once about the Web Between Worlds—how I knew of it. I didn't answer you then. It was an experience I wished not to revisit. But I must answer you now, for it is pointless to argue with the wind. I know about the Web Between Worlds because . . . I have been there."

"What?" A rush of excitement coursed through her.

"Long before you were born."

"You went to the Web Between Worlds?"

He nodded almost imperceptibly. "I gained access through my own dreams."

"I don't understand," she said. Then, all at once, it dawned on her what he meant. "You . . . you did a dream-reading on yourself."

Kahetay nodded, his expression dark.

"How is that possible?"

"It requires being both witness and participant—being in two places at once."

"What did it feel like?"

"It felt like my spirit was being ripped apart."

Ani saw a deep and private pain cloud her grandfather's eyes. She wanted to go back in time and be there for him as he had always been there for her, but all she could do was listen.

"The Natah call it the hub of all existence, the center of the cosmos. They warned me of the danger, but I was young and just arrogant enough to think I could—" he stopped and took in his breath, the memory filling his eyes.

"Kahetay," she said softly. "What happened?"

"I was only there for a brief moment, seeing what I could not, should not see, going beyond what I was, to glimpse the infinite. And then I became . . . untethered, to earth, to life. I became lost for what seemed an eternity."

Ani knew, when she heard the word 'untethered,' that the same thing might have happened to her if not for the white wolf. He had brought her back. Even then, she knew the white wolf had been her tether to this world. She stared at Kahetay in amazement, questions crowding her mind.

"I didn't regain consciousness for a week," he continued, "and when finally I woke, I was mad for a time. I survived, but nearly lost everything for that glimpse." He raised his eyes to meet hers. "The experience has haunted me my entire life, but it has also given me strength. Just knowing the web of light is there changes everything."

"I know," said Ani in agreement.

"But for you it was different. You were meant to be there. You were invited. The stranger protected you. Guided you. He guides you still, though unseen. It is no longer my privilege. It is his. I need to let you go."

"What?" His last words came out of the blue, a sudden thunderstorm on a clear day.

Kahetay rose to his feet. "I must leave now. The wind is calling."

"No!"

"Someday you too will understand what is calling you. Someday you too will go."

Ani wanted to ask him, plead with him to stay, but she knew it wouldn't do any good. Kahetay never changed his mind. Once he stood to leave, that was it. He was like a hawk that way. Hawks don't hesitate. They take flight the instant the notion hits them. And they never look back.

"I love you, little one," he said. "I am proud of you and who you are becoming. Remember that."

His words had a sad, far away feeling to them. She stood to hug him good-bye, but in the two seconds it took to find her footing, he had vanished.

"Kahetay!" she called, eyes searching the path through the tiny park. She'd grown accustomed to Kahetay's strange ways, how he always managed to vanish when she wasn't looking, but this felt different. He had never said good-bye before. It felt . . . final. Like she'd never see him again. Like the hole in her heart just grew ten sizes.

Now she had no one.

She pulled the crumpled Mapstone sketch from her pocket and let out a heavy sigh. She didn't even get the chance to show it to him and ask him what it meant or why the symbols were disappearing.

Ani looked down at the folded sketch and squinted as a faint dark spot formed on a corner of the paper, showing through from the opposite side. Unfolding the page, Ani stared wide-eyed as the symbols began to return. Slowly, the glyphs burned their way across the bottom of the page, darkening the edges as they formed, but these weren't the ones she had drawn. It appeared to be the same language, yet the arrangement of symbols differed from the first set. These were new words!

Ani caught her breath.

"Another message!"

When you find yourself at a crossroads frozen with indecision, remember this; it is not the path asking you to make a choice, it is your soul asking you to listen to your heart.

-Naviga ✣ Tome of the Zielfah Ri

CHAPTER FIFTEEN

CALL OF THE GUARDIANS

Ani burst through the front door and found her mother in the kitchen making breakfast.

"Mom, I have to show you something!" she said, waving the folded drawing in the air. "You're not going to believe this!"

Her mother did not respond.

Ani could tell she was upset. "I know I didn't write a note, but it's okay. I was with Kahetay."

"I know."

"You do?"

"He came here first. I told him you were still asleep in your bed, but when I went to wake you . . . imagine how I felt to find you gone?"

"I don't have to imagine it," said Ani. "I know exactly how it feels. The same thing happened to me last night."

Nan pulled Ani's cell phone from an apron pocket. "Why didn't you take your phone with you like I told you to?"

"I just forgot. I was upset."

"Whenever you leave the house, you leave a note, and you take your phone. Those are the rules, Ani. The next time you break them, there will be consequences. Do you understand?"

"What about when *you* leave the house? What about when *you* break the rules? You didn't write a note last night! You didn't take *your* cell."

"Like you, I was upset. Your dad and I . . . She looked away for an instant, then turned her gaze back to Ani. "I had no idea you'd come home to an empty house. When I stormed out, your father was still here. I didn't think he would leave too. I didn't—"

Her mother stopped, turned off the stove and went to the kitchen table. "Come sit down."

Ani glanced around. Panic shot through her. "Where's Dad?"

"Come. Sit. We need to talk."

"About what?"

Nan pulled a chair out and waited. Ani slipped the folded drawing back in her pocket and sank down into the kitchen chair.

This was it.

She could feel it.

Her parents were getting a divorce.

CJ was right. It's all happening just as she said it would. Less than a month away from my fourteenth birthday and everything's falling apart.

"It will only be for a little while," her mom was saying. "It's the opportunity of a lifetime."

"What?" Ani asked, finally checking in to the conversation.

"It won't cost us a cent. The college is funding the whole trip."

"Trip?" Ani blinked. "Are we going somewhere?"

"It's just me this time, honey. Remember I told you about Professor Hayden? The man who arranged for me to return to Columbia and finish my degree? Well, he's sending a research team to South America, and he has personally requested me. It's really very exciting."

"You're leaving?"

"Only for a few weeks. Seven at the most."

"Seven weeks?"

"Max." She rose to stir a pot of oatmeal on the stove and then dished up two bowls. "A lost tribe has been discovered in the Amazon," she said. "According to local legend, they are direct descendants of what was once believed to be a mythical race called *Los Guardas*."

"The Guardians?"

"Good, Ani. You remember your Spanish."

"Not really," said Ani, sidestepping her mother's irritating praise. "So who are these Guardians?"

"Oh, stories about the Los Guardas have been passed down for generations. Now, for the first time, they're allowing contact with the outside world." She peeled a banana and sliced it over the two bowls. "They have agreed to allow a select group of individuals to live with them . . . just for a few weeks . . . to learn about their culture."

"Can't they send somebody else? Does it have to be you?"

"This is a rare opportunity, Ani. We'll be the first anthropologists to study their rituals and rites. The Peruvian people believe this tribe's lineage might actually predate the ancient Incas. A chance like this comes but once in a lifetime."

"And Dad's mad because he doesn't want you to go?"

Nan poured milk on the oatmeal, sprinkled cinnamon, and slid one of the bowls over to Ani. "He's upset, but I think he understands how important this is to me."

Ani studied her oatmeal. Only moments ago, her stomach was growling. Suddenly, she wasn't hungry.

"Oops," said Nan, hopping up. When she sat again, she had two spoons. "Sweetheart." She raised Ani's chin with an index finger. "You understand, don't you? Why I have to do this?"

"I get why you *want* to do it, but—"

"If I don't go, I'll regret it for the rest of my life."

"You're not coming back, are you. You and daddy are getting a divorce and you're not coming back."

"Ani, no. What would make you think such a thing?"

"I heard you fighting."

"Oh honey, adults fight sometimes. That doesn't mean—"

"You never used to fight."

"We're facing some new challenges, and that's never easy, but everything's going to be fine."

Ani didn't want to hear any more. All she wanted was to turn back the clock, erase the last few months, make everything good again. "I wish we'd never come here!" She pushed her bowl away and stood up. The milk sloshed onto the table. "I wish you'd never gone back to that stupid school! None of this would be happening!"

"Honey, listen to me."

"No!" Ani ran to her room, slammed the door and threw herself on the bed. Her whole world was spinning out of control and there was nothing she could do about it.

The knob turned and the door creaked open. "Can I come in?" Her mother stepped inside and closed the door.

"You don't know what it's been like for me," said Ani, refusing to look at her mother. "Coming here. Losing my only friends, and now losing you." She choked on the words.

Her mother sat on the edge of the bed. "Oh sweetheart, you're not losing me. I would never leave you. You know that. I love you more than anything in the world."

"Then don't do this," Ani pleaded. "Don't go. Not now."

"I don't think you understand how important this is. Opportunities like this just don't happen to people like me. Most anthropologists my age got their doctorates decades ago and have been working in the field for years. I need to do this, Anani. I wish I could be like other moms and attend PTA meetings and throw weekend pool parties, but I'm just not that person."

"I don't know any other moms," said Ani, "and I don't care if you're like them or not. I just want you to stay and be *my* mom."

"I'll never stop being your mom, sweetheart. Not even when you're fifty. And I'll never stop loving you. Never." She stretched out her arms. "Come here." She turned Ani toward her. "I love you so much."

Ani didn't hug her back. She thought if she could hold out a little longer, her mother might change her mind and stay. Silence filled the room like liquid lead.

Her mother drew away and sighed. A moment later, she burst out in her best circus voice, "Step right up! Get your answers here! Anything you want to know. Only five cents a question."

It was a silly game they played when Ani first started homeschooling. It always made her laugh, but not this time. She searched her mother's face. A seriousness lingered there despite her forced joviality.

"Okay," said Ani, leaning back on the headboard of her bed with her arms crossed on her chest, "where exactly are you going?"

"Cuzco for starters, in Peru."

"I know where Cuzco is, Mom. Geography's my best subject."

She gave a proud smile. "Yes, I do recall that."

"What are you going to do in Cuzco?"

"Listen to the stories the locals tell, learn all we can about the myth before meeting the Guardian tribe."

"Why are they called Guardians?"

"There's an ancient legend about a subterranean city located under Cuzco. No one's ever seen it, but the locals say this tribe guards the entrance."

"Who's going with you?"

"There will be three anthropologists, two archeologists, one linguist and a medical intern. Plus a guide and a cook that we'll pick up once we've arrived."

"Is it going to be dangerous?"

"Oh honey, I'll be fine."

"How do you know? You've never been there. You said no one's ever been where you're going."

"We won't go unprepared. We're taking tents and equipment, lamps, a stove, all kinds of things. Even a folding desk or two. Llamas will carry everything. Our camp will be very civilized."

"Civilized? Right. I doubt where you're going anything will be *civilized*. Are you taking a gun with you for protection?"

"Our guide will be armed in case we encounter any of the more aggressive indigenous wildlife. There's really nothing to worry about. We will be perfectly safe."

"Then can I go?"

"Oh sweetheart, you know the answer to that."

After a long pause, Ani filled her lungs with air and let it out all at once. "Okay," she said pushing back tears, "can I at least come with you to the airport?"

"I don't know if that's a good idea. You'd have to get up very early. And then go straight to school after."

"I don't care."

"You might care when you're falling asleep in class."

"I want to go."

"Alright, you can see me off. My flight leaves Monday morning, 5 a.m."

"This Monday? As in—the day after tomorrow? No. That's too soon."

"I know it's short notice, but it was all the prep time they could allot. The University wants to move quickly on this. They've taken care of everything. Travel supplies, plane tickets, transportation once we're there. We go in for our immunizations this afternoon. They even pushed our passports through. All I need is a good hat, a mosquito net, and I'm all set."

"But why can't you go next month? What's the difference?"

"These are a primitive people, Ani. They have granted us access but who knows how long that door will remain open. The research grant gives us a full seven weeks, but we might only be there seven days before they've had enough of us."

Ani's bottom lip turned down. "You'll miss my birthday."

"I know honey, but we'll just have to celebrate early, okay? How 'bout we start right now?"

Ani continued to pout.

"The time will go by just like that." Nan snapped her fingers and forced a smile. "You and dad will have fun together."

"Dad hates it here, and so do I."

"Well then, this will be a good chance for the two of you to venture out, find new things you like to do together. Then I'll be back, and school will be out. We'll have the whole summer together. We can go someplace special." She put her arm around Ani again, this time more like a pal than a mother. "Maybe we'll go camping upstate, just the two of us. Okay?"

"I guess."

Nan stood abruptly, plunged a hand deep into her front pocket and pulled out an ancient Roman coin. She sat down and offered the coin to her daughter. "As you know, I've carried this with me every day since my father gave it to me on the night he died. I want you to keep it safe for me, while I'm gone."

"No Mom, that's your lucky coin. You should take it with you."

"Keep it," she insisted, "as a reminder. That way you'll always know I'm coming home to you." She closed Ani's hands around the coin and then held them in her own. "You can put it in your magic treasure box. The one Grandma Kay gave you."

"You know about that?"

Her mother nodded. "She gave me a gift that very same day. She knew she was dying. She was giving away all her prized possessions."

"What did she give you?"

Nan hopped up, disappeared into the next room, and returned a moment later carrying a travel-size leather-bound journal, the kind with a thin leather strap that wound several times around its middle to keep its contents safe. She held it out.

"It's heavy," Ani said, feeling the weight of it in her hands. She stroked the soft leather cover and then opened it, expecting to find dark secrets hidden inside, the kind such an old and enchanting volume should contain. Ani's smile drooped. "It's blank."

Nan nodded, positively excited at the prospect. "It was my grandfather's. He saved it for what he called his 'great journey of exploration,' but he was always struggling with some illness and never mustered the strength for travel. He died having never ventured beyond the limits of his hometown."

The corners of Ani's mouth bent down. "That's sad."

"Oh, but the story now has a happy ending."

"How?"

"That day, when your Grandma Kay gave us these gifts, she told me Pappy's dream lives on in me. I'll never forget her words; 'It is just a seed in you at the moment,' she said, 'but someday you will go on a grand adventure, and you'll take this journal with you, and fill it with all the wonders you behold.' And she was right. I'm going to take Pappy's journal with me to Peru and chronicle the entire expedition. His 'great journey of exploration' has become mine."

"How did she know?" asked Ani. Then she remembered how Grandma Kay winked every time the subject of magic came up. "Mom, did Grandma know how to do magic?"

"Magic?" She gave a little laugh. "Well, if she did she kept it to herself. But I know she was a believer, and now, so am I."

Ani closed the book. A wave of desperation crested inside her. Nothing she could say would make her mother change her mind. She knew that now. Until this moment, she had held out for some miracle, thinking if she could find just the right words, she'd convince her mother to stay, but it wasn't going to happen. Like her grandfather said, 'You can try to fight destiny, but in the end, destiny always wins.'

"Okay, put away the scowl," said Nan. "Let's go shopping. It may be a whole month before I'll get the chance to do anything so cultured again."

Ani felt the last of her energy drain away. "I don't feel like shopping."

"Oh come on. This is New York City—shopping capital of the world."

Ani made a face that conveyed her disgust at the whole idea.

Nan retrieved Ani's coat from a hook on the door, held it out to her and said, "While we're out, we'll buy your birthday present, okay? Anything you want."

Ani opened her mouth to say 'I want to go with you to Peru' but her mother quickly added, "Within reason."

Nan draped the polka-dotted, fur-lined raincoat over Ani's shoulders. "Come on, honey. Let's have some fun. How often do you get to pick out your own birthday present?"

"Fine," Ani said, begrudgingly, "I want a raincoat without polka-dots."

Your path will have many obstacles, but even the largest of obstacles appear small when viewed from a higher vantage point. Always endeavor to rise above your own limited perceptions. The most powerful opposition will come from within.

-Solamas ✦ *Tome of the Zielfah Ri*

CHAPTER SIXTEEN

♈

AN UNEXPECTED ALLY

Monday morning came much too quickly. At dawn, they all piled into the cab of the old Chevy truck and then drove the entire route to the airport in silence.

While her father parked the truck, Ani followed her mother into the JFK International Terminal, secretly hoping someone would tell them Mom's flight had been cancelled or that she was too late and the plane had left without her.

No such luck. Everything seemed to be going according to plan—her mother's plan. There wasn't even a line to get through security.

Ani tried to be brave, but when the security gate attendant stopped her and told her she could not pass beyond without a ticket, Ani couldn't hold it in any longer.

"Mom, don't go. Please don't go."

"Oh honey, I know this is hard for you. It's hard for me too, but everything's going to be just fine."

"You keep saying that, but you don't know! You can't know! What if you're wrong?" A black fear swept through Ani—fear that she'd never see her mother again. An image kept running through her mind like an annoying re-run of some stupid late-night horror movie. She saw her mother sacrificed on a rock slab, blood dripping from her fingers, painted-skinned natives dancing around her broken body.

"Come here." She took Ani's hand, led her over to a padded bench and then sat beside her. "We've never really been apart, have we," she said, squeezing Ani's hand. "You want to know a secret? I'm scared too. As much as I want to do this, as much as I've dreamed of doing this, I've never traveled so far from home. Never even been out of the country. It's a scary thing to do what you've never done."

"It's not too late to change your mind," said Ani.

"But sometimes doing the thing you're afraid to do—challenging yourself to push past your fear—is the only way to grow, to be a better person, to live a more fulfilling life. If we always let fear stop us, then our lives and our hearts get smaller and smaller until eventually they become too small to contain anything meaningful."

"Mom, you think I don't understand, but I do," said Ani. "I get it. You want a bigger life. But you can do that here. It's why we came to New York, right? It *is* bigger now. You don't have to go away to do that."

"It's not just me who needs this. You and Dad need it too."

"You're wrong. We need you."

"We've been lucky, you and I, haven't we? We got to go to school together—in our own living room. How many mothers and daughters can say that? And I adored every minute of it. You were the bright light at the center of my world, but I knew I couldn't keep you there, keep you all to myself."

"Why not?"

"Oh Ani, you're growing up. You're turning into a beautiful young woman. You're going to have so many new experiences, learn things I can't teach you. You're going to make wonderful friends, find new things you like to do, meet a boy and fall in love for the first time. If I kept you from all that, you would eventually resent me for it."

"I don't care about all that."

"Someday, you will. Probably sooner than you think." She tucked a strand of hair behind Ani's right ear.

Ani stared at the silver and turquoise pendant hanging from the chain around her mother's neck—a Pueblo Indian design from her hometown in New Mexico. Her mother never took it off. Ani reached out to touch the stone at its center. "Mom, what if something happens to you over there? What if you never come back?"

"I'll be home before you know it."

A voice announced flight 243 bound for Lima, boarding in fifteen minutes.

"That's my plane. I have to go, sweetheart." She gave Ani a desperate hug. "You're my girl. I love you so much. Take care of your father, okay? He'll need your help around the house."

There were tears in her eyes when she rose.

"Mom!" Until that moment, Ani didn't really believe she would actually go through with it. "Mom, please!"

Nan dashed to the security entrance, placed her belongings on the conveyer belt and watched as they slid through the scanner. Before stepping through the portal, she turned and blew a kiss to her daughter. "I'll see you in seven weeks," she said, forcing a smile. "Or sooner!"

"No! Mom! Wait!"

"Be good!" Nan called out as she joined her colleagues waiting on the other side.

Desperation turned to anger. "I won't forgive you for this!" Ani screamed. "I won't!"

"I love you!" Nan called back. She covered her mouth for a moment, her hand trembling, and then turned away.

Ani instantly wished she could take back her words. Un-say them. But it was too late. She watched her mother headed toward the boarding gate with her research team.

Why wasn't Dad here to stop her? Ani knew parking the car was just an excuse. He didn't want to watch her go. But he should have been here. He should have tried to talk her out of it.

Nan waved good-bye one last time from the other side of the security portal and then disappeared down a corridor.

Feeling as if the wind had just been knocked out of her, Ani collapsed on the padded bench. Fighting the growing numbness inside, she stared at the floor, studying the interlocking pattern of red, blue and grey lines in the carpet until a pair of men's loafers stepped toe to toe with her red sneakers.

"Come on, Ani," said her father, holding out his hand. "Let's go. We need to get you to school."

Ani looked up, her eyes pleading. "I just want to stay a little while longer. Maybe the plane won't take off. Maybe she'll change her mind. Maybe—"

"Ani, nothing's going to change," he said, his voice stern, his face expressionless. "She's gone. It's time for us to go, too."

They made their way out of the terminal, not speaking, not looking anywhere but straight ahead, into the void.

The rest of the school day Ani spent in a fog thinking about her mother. How could she be on a plane flying to South America while Ani was stuck playing dodge-the-bullies at some stupid school in New York City? It seemed too cruel.

All day she had kept an eye out for the Silver Chain Girl and her little gang, ready to duck out of sight if she happened to see any of them in the hall or on the playground, but to her relief, she saw no sign of them. By the time the last bell rang, it had been a very long, exhausting day. Ani didn't think the day could get any worse . . . until of course, it did.

"Watch where you're going, idiot."

"Oops," said Ani. Then she saw who she'd just run into and blanched. Figures. The meanest girl in the school and Ani had just accidentally knocked her books to the floor.

"Pick 'em up, loser."

Ani smiled apologetically. "Sorry." She gazed up into the fat, round face of the girl from the back row in homeroom.

Twice Ani's size, with an even bigger attitude, Mad Millie stood with hands on hips and teeth bared. "You."

Ani gathered up the girl's books, but when she tried to hand them back, Millie knocked them out of her hands and sent them flying again.

"Pick 'em up!" said Millie, this time loud enough for everyone in the hall to hear.

As Ani got on her hands and knees, she saw Millie smiling to her friends and then felt a foot at her backside. A quick shove left Ani sprawled on the corridor floor. A wave of laughter and snickers rippled through the hallway.

"What's the matter, little girl? Gonna cry?" Millie mocked in a sing-songy voice. "You forgot one." She pointed to a stray textbook a few feet away.

As Ani reached for it, Millie kicked it out from under her hand and sent it sliding across the floor. "Fetch!"

The gathering crowd roared with laughter. When the laughter subsided, Ani slowly got to her feet. She knew she wasn't going to win with this girl. She might as well just get it over with—take the punch and go home to put ice on it.

Millie narrowed her dark eyes as Ani stood directly in front of her. "You got some kind of death wish or something?"

Her tone had changed, like the snarl of a wild animal that had spotted its next kill.

"Pick 'em up!" yelled Millie, her hair turning to eels, her teeth growing into fangs. "Pick 'em up or else!"

Ani was sure any second now yellow lightning bolts would shoot from Millie's eyes, but she refused to pick up the girl's books.

"Or else what?" said a familiar voice.

Ani spun around to find CJ standing in the corridor with her arms crossed and her boots firmly planted, looking like it might take the National Guard to move her.

Millie went pale. "This is between me and the snip, CJ. It's none of your business."

"It is now. You're in my way. So pick up your mess and get lost."

"And what if I don't? Huh? What are you going to do about it?"

CJ peeled off her leather jacket, exposing a circular scar on her right shoulder just as Kahetay had described. "You don't really want to find out, do you?"

Millie's eyes locked on CJ's in a razor-sharp glare, while her minions scrambled to pick up her schoolbooks.

"Do you?" snapped CJ with such authority Millie jumped back a step.

The large girl stood for a moment, obviously considering her options and then turned to her friends. She sniffed the air like a dog. "Hey. You guys smell something? Wow, something stinks. Let's get out of here before I puke."

As Millie casually strolled by CJ holding her nose, CJ stuck out her foot. Mad Millie crashed to the floor, all 200 pounds of her. The hallway hissed with astonished gasps.

Millie got to her feet and spun on CJ, fists clenched and ready for a fight, but Silver Chain Girl and the rest of Millie's gang crowded in around her and pulled her away.

Ani could hear Millie yelling obscenities, her voice amplified by the long corridor, as they ushered her out the double doors at the far end. Shouts of spectators calling for a fight died down as the doors swung shut behind them. The lingering group quickly dispersed. CJ and Ani were left standing alone in the hall.

"Thanks," said Ani, dusting herself off.

"I always pay my debts."

"You don't owe me anything, CJ."

"Not anymore I don't. You saved my butt with Mr. Cardello and the cigarettes. Now we're even. Don't expect it to happen again."

"I won't," said Ani, but CJ didn't hear her. She was already halfway down the hall, heading for the exit opposite the one Millie used. Ani ran to catch up.

"What do you want?" said CJ, pulling on her sweat jacket as they pushed through the doors and into the crisp spring air.

"Nothing," said Ani, squinting at the clarity of the bright day.

They walked in silence for a moment until CJ said, "You're not going to follow me all the way home like some lost dog, are you?"

"We live in the same building. I'd be going this way even if you weren't."

"Whatever."

"I don't see why I should have to take a different route home just because you happen to be going in the same direction."

"Just get out of my face."

Ani fell back a pace, but after a minute, skipped forward and fell in step beside CJ again, matching her hurried stride.

"Sheesh," said CJ, "is there some special needs part of your brain that requires you to be a complete *irkoid*?"

Ani pointed. "So how'd you get that scar on your shoulder?"

"I don't see why I should have to talk to you just 'cause we happen to be going the same direction," CJ said, mimicking Ani.

"I was only trying to make conversation."

"Well, don't."

"Just being friendly."

"Wha'do I gotta do, tattoo it on my forehead?" CJ halted, turned, and pushed her nose in Ani's face. "I. Don't. Want. To. Be. Friends."

"Fine. We won't be friends," said Ani, taking a step back. "So how'd you get that circular scar on your shoulder?"

"It's a burn. Use your imagination."

"At least you didn't say it's none of my business."

"You know," said CJ "you're really annoying sometimes. No, I take that back, you're really annoying all the time, and by the way, you were completely pathetic back there. You looked like you were just waiting for Millie to hit you."

"I was."

"And the last thing you should do is admit it."

"I've just never met anyone like Millie before," Ani said, stepping off the curb to cross the street.

Without a second thought, CJ grabbed the back of Ani's sweat jacket and pulled her out of the way of a car screeching around a blind corner. "Well, get used to it," said CJ, continuing the conversation as if she hadn't just saved Ani's life. "This place is full of Mad Millies, and if you don't know how to defend yourself, you won't last long."

Heart pounding, Ani stared at CJ, stunned into silence.

"I'm sayin' it like it is. Wimps don't stand a chance here. You'll have to get some street skills if you want to stay alive."

"So then," Ani perked up, "teach me how to fight?"

"No way. You're on your own, Ponch."

Ani huffed in frustration. "Why do you keep calling me that? What does it mean anyway?"

"Got it off the late-night 70's cop show reruns Joe watches. It means you always try to do the right thing and you say really stupid stuff."

"Maybe so, but you've had your whole life to get used to this. I've had a month. The worst thing that ever happened to me back home was a scorpion sting."

"No way. You were stung by a scorpion? Did it hurt?"

"Like mad. And then I got really sick and almost died."

"For real?"

Ani nodded, hoping CJ wouldn't press for details.

"Maybe you're not as big a wuss as I thought."

"Then why not teach me to fight?"

"Forget it." CJ snatched a stick off the sidewalk.

Ani drew back.

"Relax *dorf*. I'm not gonna hit'cha." CJ scraped the stick along a chain-link fence as they passed by a cluster of neighborhood basketball courts. Chink-chink. Chink-chink. Chink-chink. "Listen up," she said, finally. "I pick my fights. Where and when and why. Don't let nobody pick 'em for me. It's all about strategy. Getting the upper hand. If you want to learn something, learn that."

"But that won't help me if Millie's gang corners me again."

"Hey, I said you were on your own. I'm not gonna keep comin' to your rescue."

"I know," pouted Ani. So just give me a few pointers, something that will help me stand up to her, and I promise I'll leave you alone."

"A few pointers," CJ said suspiciously.

"Yeah. And then I swear I'll never bother you again."

"Never?"

"Never."

CJ immediately put her foot out and tripped Ani.

"Ow!" Ani grabbed onto the fence to keep from falling. "What'd you do that for?"

"Lesson number one," instructed CJ. "Never blink when there's someone within arm's reach. Always be lookin' out for it. You never know where it's gonna come from. Lesson concluded."

When a warrior fights his destiny, the battle is lost before it has begun. For a Light Master, resistance to truth in any form blocks the path to inner mastery.

-Xephero ✣ Tome of the Zielfah Ri

CHAPTER SEVENTEEN

STREETWISE

The next day after school Ani searched for CJ and found her exiting the school grounds, but this time she wasn't on her way home.

"Okay, I'm ready," said Ani.

"For what?"

"Lesson number two."

"Go home. Tell mommy you had a bad day. I'm sure she'll make it all better."

"My mom's gone. She's in Peru."

"And I'm supposed to care about that?"

"You said you'd show me a few things."

"And you said you'd leave me alone."

"Yeah, after you teach me how to fight."

"How did it go from 'showing you a few things' to teaching you how to fight?"

"Come on, CJ. Just give me something I can use the next time I have a problem with Millie."

"You're not gonna let this go."

"No."

"Okay, meet me in the park tomorrow after school. We'll see how serious you really are."

"How 'bout right now?"

"I'm busy."

"Where'ya goin'?"

"Do you ever stop asking questions?"

"No. Not as long as there's something more to know. My mom always says—"

"Spare me."

Ani followed CJ until she could see the 225th Street subway station ahead. "Umm, you're taking the subway?"

"Imagine that. A girl in New York taking the subway."

"Aren't they kind of dangerous?"

"You live in the big bad city now, Martha May. No more hayrides to the state fair."

"I'm not from the country," said Ani. "I've never been to a state fair, and I have no idea what a hayride is, but they don't have subways in the Mojave Desert, so how would I possibly know?"

"Well," said CJ, "I grew up ridin' the trains, and there's somethin' you gotta understand about the subway here before you can appreciate it."

"Okay."

"It doesn't just take people from place to place," said CJ, stopping at the entrance. "It connects us—all eight million of us—in a way nothing else can—like . . . blood running through our veins. And there's a whole world down there. Things no one sees. You just have to know where to look. But the best part—" She leaned in close. "—is the rats."

"Rats?"

"They have rats the size of opossums, whole communities of 'em livin' down there."

"Nah uh."

"You think I'm lyin'? I'll prove it. Come on."

"Um, no, I can't. My mom said not to go into any of the underground stations alone."

"You're not alone, moron. You're with me."

"I think she meant an adult."

"Didn't you say your mom's in Peru?"

"Yeah."

"Then how's she gonna know?"

Ani peered down the stairwell in front of them. "I really don't think I should."

"*Should* is not in my vocabulary. Listen, you said you wanted to know more. Well, here's your chance. Come on."

Ani followed CJ down a long flight of stairs and stood by as CJ scanned the crowd for what she called her 'next mark.'

Ani wasn't sure what that meant until she saw CJ steal a couple of MetroCards from some unsuspecting tourists. "CJ, that's—"

"Stealing? Well, give the girl a gold star."

"I was going to say wrong."

"The trick is to learn to spot the non-residentials. They just figure they lost it somewhere along the way and buy a new one. Never try to steal from a New Yorker. They've got 360 D.S.P."

"What's that?"

"Three-hundred-and-sixty degree sensory perception. We're practically born with it. It's like a city-sixth-sense."

As they pushed through the turnstiles and entered the 225th street station, Ani paused at the rim, amazed at the living art that moved and breathed before her. So many people packed together, all headed in different directions, yet not one individual ever ran into another. It was like a magnificently choreographed dance they had been rehearsing all their lives.

CJ didn't seem to notice. She was used to it. They all were. But Ani had never seen anything like it.

An exquisite counterpoint began to play out in Ani's mind between the vast, lonely, serenity of the desert, and the bustling, fearless diversity of the city. There was even music in the air, adding to the effect. A tattered group of men sang a cappella in four-part harmony, their beautiful voices reverberating through the tunnels like a haunting movie soundtrack.

Ani blinked, suddenly mindful of the fact that she was alone. She called out CJ's name, but in the din of the people and the roar of the approaching trains, her voice barely made a ripple.

She climbed the steps they had just descended, and scanned the crowd, trying to remember what CJ was wearing. Not red or blue or anything bright. She always wore drab colors, olive greens and muted browns. Then Ani remembered the jacket. That over-sized brown leather bomber jacket CJ never let out of her site. Maybe she could spot that—

"Hey!"

She not only heard the word, she felt it, as a wadded up hotdog wrapper hit the side of her face, leaving a mustard mark on her cheek.

"Over here, stupid," called CJ. "Come on, we're going to miss it."

"Miss what?"

"C Line. Let's go."

"CJ, I can't get on the train."

"Shut up and run!"

They slipped onto the southbound train and took two open seats near the door. The train immediately started to roll, leaving the station for the relative darkness of the subway tunnels.

Suddenly exhilarated at the idea of a mini-adventure, Ani watched the lights dotting the subway walls stream by until the next station came into view. She was impressed by the efficiency and speed of the station stops—the on and offloading of passengers—as she witnessed the ebb and flow of the New York City Transit System.

Gradually, Ani began to feel more at ease with it all and wondered why her mother had forbidden her to ride the trains. There didn't appear to be any real danger here. Everyone minded their own business, for the most part. Everyone except for one peculiar looking elderly gentleman down the aisle from them. His focus seemed to be entirely on CJ.

"CJ," whispered Ani. "That man is staring at you."

"So."

"Now he's gesturing. I think he's trying to get your attention."

CJ glanced up at the bearded gentleman. He wore a rumpled Creamsicle suit, a peach-colored tie and shoes to match. CJ cursed under her breath and then shouted, "What are you lookin' at, creepazoid?"

The man smiled. "You're very good."

"And you're very annoying," yelled CJ, "so why don't you go stare at someone your own age."

Unperturbed, the man rose and moved to the open seat directly behind them. "You're so good, even your little friend here doesn't see what you're doing."

"Oh? And what am I doing?"

"A good business by the looks of it."

Just as Ani opened her mouth to ask what he meant, the conductor announced the approach of 110th Street over the loudspeaker. The train slowed to a halt. A bell sounded, double doors parted, and a flood of people poured out into Cathedral Parkway Station.

After the car had emptied, the rumpled man hopped up to greet the boarding passengers with an overly friendly grin. He helped an elderly woman across the threshold and into her seat, complementing her new coif. He introduced himself to two businessmen and shook the hand of a third saying he recognized the man's face from last week's lecture, and then helped a young mother—baby on her hip and too many shopping bags on her arms—squeeze through the doors just as they were closing. He even pinched the baby's plump rosy cheek before plopping down in the seat next to CJ.

"So," he said, "how are your powers of observation?"

"That depends," said CJ.

"On?"

"On whether or not you're going to get outta my face and leave us the hell alone."

The man smiled. "I'm willing to bet you've already scoped the passengers and sized them up for potential profits."

Ani looked at CJ, waiting for an explanation, but she offered none. Instead, she turned to the grinning gentleman and sneered. "You need to mind your own business, old man."

"Tell you what," he said, pulling a crumpled fifty-dollar bill from his pocket. "There are eleven new people sitting in this section from the last two stops, including yourselves. All but the punk Asian girl in the black tights and the pretty redhead in the blue silk dress have got front pockets, do you concur?"

CJ ignored him.

"So we'll say fourteen front pockets all together, not counting the baby."

"You're not going away," said CJ. "Why is that?"

"I've hidden a fifty like this one in one of those front pockets. If you can find it before 59th Street, which is my stop, you can keep it."

CJ let out a *humph*. You're whacked, mister."

"Perhaps, but you'll be fifty dollars richer if you can find it in time."

"Seriously whacked."

"Hmmm. Crazy, maybe. Serious, definitely."

"You're willing to throw away fifty bucks just to watch me find it?"

"*If* you find it," he challenged.

"What's the catch?"

"No catch."

"There's always a catch."

"Not this time," said the man.

CJ glanced around. "So someone in this car has your money in their pocket."

"*Front* pocket," he reminded.

"What if they get off before your stop? There are six stops between now and 59th."

"Then they're fifty bucks richer, and you're not. I'd start with them if I were you." He nodded to the three suited businessmen.

"Why?"

"Because I ride this train every day, and I happened to know that the sweet, elderly woman, whose name is Mrs. McClurry, gets off with me at Columbus Circle and our young mother there lives in Washington Heights, so she'll be staying on after we get off. But I don't know much about the three businessmen."

CJ sneered. "You spoke to one of them as if you knew him."

"Ahh, I knew you were paying attention. The one on the left is an English Professor at Columbia University, but I have no idea of his destination. He's not a regular, which means he could be getting off at the next stop. Better get started."

CJ rose from her seat. "Okay old man, you're on."

"CJ, don't. It's not worth the risk," said Ani, but CJ ignored her.

"Watch this," whispered the bearded man as CJ made her way to where the businessmen sat. "Watch her go."

"Why are you encouraging her to steal?"

"It's not stealing when it's my money and I've simply asked her to retrieve it. You may need to open your mind to a broader interpretation of what it is to be daring and free."

"I have no idea what that means," said Ani.

"Perhaps not now, but you will." The old man pointed a knobby finger at CJ. "Keep an eye on your friend's left hand there. She's right-handed but she uses her left. Very adeptly, I might add."

Ani watched CJ work, astounded at her grace and skill. She'd never seen anyone pick someone's pocket before. It was a magic trick—pure slight of hand—and CJ was a master at it. She asked one businessman the time, then inquired as to the type of material his suit was made of, touching his lapel to sample the wool.

The old man gestured with his bearded chin. "Ah, there, you see? Already she knows it's not on the men."

It made Ani uncomfortable to watch. What if they got caught? They could get arrested. Maybe the bearded man was an undercover cop and this was how he caught subway thieves.

"Fascinating," he said, still studying CJ's moves.

Ani frowned. "I don't think I like you very much."

"Why do you say that?"

"I don't think you're a very nice person."

"Oh, but I am. Well, I am now." He chuckled to himself. "I mean I didn't use to be. Not at all. In fact, I used to be—" He stopped and glanced at CJ who had moved on to the elderly woman with the fancy hairdo. "I used to be *her*," he continued, "And someone once made me the same deal. It changed my life."

"Fifty dollars changed your life?"

"No, but the deal did."

"What deal?"

"You'll see."

Ani scrutinized the man more closely now. Although his suit could've been pulled out of a 1920's closet, it was by no means old and worn. In fact, it looked brand new, as if he had it tailored especially, even though his shirt collar was too tight. She could see the red chafing mark on his neck. His smile ignited the air. He observed CJ with the intent of a man on a quest.

"Watch her go," he whispered, pointing with his chin.

On her way back to her seat, CJ 'accidentally' knocked one of the packages out of the young mother's hand and apologized, picking it up and placing it back in her lap.

"Ah, she's a natural," the man said. "Like poetry."

Each time, CJ barely touched the person and yet, by the time they reached Columbus Station, she seemed convinced the fifty was not in any of their pockets. She sat down in a huff and shot the Creamsicle suit a look of disdain. The conductor announced their approach to 59th Street.

"You lied, old man."

"I did not," he said, suddenly sounding like an English barrister. "You simply failed."

"Then where is it?"

"I hid it in the one place I knew you would never think to look. Your own pocket."

CJ reached into her front pocket and pulled out the man's neatly folded fifty-dollar bill.

"You said it was in the pocket of someone who just got on the train."

"At the last *two* stations. That included the two of you."

"Your game sucks, old man."

"It pays to be a good listener, like your friend here."

CJ laughed. It wasn't a proper laugh, just a single, "Ha!"

"Even though you failed my challenge," said the man, "I will give you that fifty and this one as well," he waved a second fifty in the air, "if you agree to stop stealing for say . . . six months?"

"You're as crazy as you look," said CJ. "All I'd have to do is promise not to steal, take your money, and then do whatever I wanted. You'd never know the difference."

"But *you'd* know, and that's all that matters." He rose, smiling. "Well, this is where I get off." He held up the second fifty. "Do we have a deal?"

CJ snatched the second bill from the man's hand and slipped it into her pocket with the first.

"And now you have a choice. Just like that. You can choose to by drugs with that money—"

"I don't do drugs, old man."

"—*or* you can use it to change your life."

"Right. I'd need a lot more than that if I was ever gonna change my life. I don't think a hundred dollars is gonna make that big of a difference."

"Think again. That is the most powerful hundred dollars you will ever own. Before you got on this train, you lived your life thinking you didn't have a choice. Now you do. Choose well."

The man turned to Ani. "And as for you, whatever you are searching for, young lady, keep looking. You'll find it."

"Remember. Six months. No stealing," he said, pointing to CJ.

The doors opened.

"Have an enchanting life," he said, as he stepped out.

The doors closed.

Through the window, Ani could see the old guy waving good-bye. He was still smiling.

"Man there's a lot of crazies in this town," said CJ. "Gotta love New York." She sat and began inspecting the two fifty-dollar bills.

"What are you looking for?" asked Ani.

"A tell. They're probably fake."

"You think so?"

"Yeah, the geezer just likes screwin' with people's heads. No one gives away money just like that. Especially not here. You gotta be a certain kind of stupid to wave two fifties around and not care where they land."

"But he didn't. He used them to get you to stop stealing."

"And you'd have to be even more stupid to believe that."

"Maybe he's just rich and has nothing better to do with his money."

"Nah, he was a creep. I can spot 'em a mile away."

Ani wasn't so sure. Something about the old man's smile as they pulled away from the station made her feel differently about him. It wasn't the smile of a person who'd just played a trick on someone or had taken advantage of them in some way. It was, Ani thought with interest, the smile of a man who had just made a difference in the world.

And there was something else too. Something that seemed eerily familiar about the old man, even though she was sure she'd never met him before today. Maybe it was more that the old man seemed to know *her*. At the very least, he knew more than he let on, and for reasons Ani could not fathom, this man and their shared experience on the A train intrigued and disturbed her in equal proportions.

"Get up," said CJ, interrupting Ani's musings. "This is our stop. Fat-Rat-Central."

CJ was right about one thing. Here, the rats were huge, and ugly, *and* disgusting. The girls found a strategic spot to sit and watch the center platform between the subway tracks where scores of rats congregated around large collections of trash.

Ani wondered in passing if she would be able to hear what the rats were thinking. She listened for a minute or two within her mind but heard only her own thoughts. Though she was curious as to why, she realized she was glad of it. She didn't think rat thoughts would be very pleasant. All in all, it seemed like an achingly dismal existence.

CJ refused to go home until they had seen a rat fight. An hour later she got her wish. Two of the largest rats faced off in a battle for territory and food. Ani couldn't watch. She sat on a separate bench wishing she were far, far away. CJ seemed to enjoy her discomfort as much as she enjoyed the rodent rivals tearing at each other's throats. So this was considered entertainment here? She didn't think she would ever get used to living in the city.

Maybe this is some kind of test—thought Ani. *CJ's way of finding out if I'm tough enough to be taught street fighting.* Well, if it was, then she was failing, she knew that much. So Ani forced herself to watch and tried to look interested, but it was no use. CJ saw right through her act and finally, disgusted or disappointed, Ani wasn't sure which, she got up to go.

"I'll take reptiles over rodents any day," Ani said hoping CJ would ask why, so she could talk about her iguana, Mobius.

"Follow me," said CJ, heading away from the exit.

"I thought we were going home."

"I changed my mind."

"CJ—"

"Shut up and pay attention. I want to show you something. Something nobody ever sees."

In the evolution of a soul, there will be adventures disguised as challenges and challenges disguised as adventures. See all of them for what they are—opportunities to conquer fear.

-Xephero ✤ *Tome of the Zielfah Ri*

CHAPTER EIGHTEEN

ԁ

SUBTERRANEAN SECRETS

"What is it you want to show me?" asked Ani, hoping it wasn't more rats.

"It's a secret. You can't tell anyone. Got it?"

"I don't know about this, CJ. Is it—?"

"If you're about to ask me if it's dangerous, I'm gonna hit you."

"I was going to ask if it's close."

"Come on. Through here." CJ turned into a shallow alcove and stopped before a metal door covered in ancient graffiti.

Ani hesitated. "What's this?"

"It's a time portal."

"What?"

CJ patted the metal. "Door. Thing you walk through to get to somewhere else."

"I meant what's in there."

"It's just an empty maintenance room. Geez, you gotta relax. Don't you get tired of being afraid of everything all the time?"

"I just like to know what I'm getting myself into."

"Sometimes you gotta strike out without a map, Ponch."

CJ grabbed the handle and pulled. The door didn't budge.

Relieved, Ani shrugged. "It's probably locked."

"The lock's broken. Has been for years." CJ gave it a hefty tug. The door scraped the concrete floor as it opened. "Follow me." She drew a small flashlight from a hidden ledge and snapped it on.

Using its beam to point out an odd shaped door—as tall as it was wide—she said, "That's where we're going."

Ani squinted. "I've never seen a perfectly square door before."

Leaning into it with her shoulder, CJ slid the door open. Beyond lay a shadowy tunnel, also perfectly square.

"I'm willing to bet there's a lot of things you've never seen before," said CJ, "and what's at the end of this tunnel is definitely one of them. Come on."

Ani didn't move. "I don't think this is such a good idea," she said, wanting more than anything to go home. "Isn't this considered trespassing? We could get in serious trouble."

"Who's gonna know?" The tunnel echoed CJ's words and Ani's guttural response. "Quit worryin'. Anyone who knew about this place is long gone."

Ani tried to swallow. Her mouth had gone dry. "That just means if we get lost down here, they'll never find our rotting bodies."

"We're not gonna get lost. I know my way."

"You've done this before?"

"Dozens of times." She pointed the flashlight into the blackness and stepped through the door. "Where's your sense of adventure?"

There's that awful word again. Adventure. She was beginning to hate that word. People always used it to talk her into things she didn't want to do.

Ani took a deep breath and followed CJ into the dark, dank tunnel, knowing if she turned back now, CJ would consider her a complete coward and refuse to teach her how to fight. Maybe this was just another one of CJ's tests. Ani knew she'd failed the previous one. This might be her last chance to prove to CJ that she was a worthy pupil.

As they made their way, the tunnel began to curve to the left in a long slow arc. Ani struggled to keep her imagination in check. The darkness morphed into a blank canvas on which she painted endless gruesome scenes filled with hideous creatures. She tried not to think of the Kalb. Tried to push him out of her mind. But it was no use. This was the perfect place for a Kalb attack. Black on black. She'd never see it coming. He'd win without a fight. She hated the thought, but she couldn't stop herself from thinking it.

Fear crystallized. A slow, low droning started in her ears.

Gemi! Think about something else! Anything else!

Eli? She sent the thought out to the void.

I'm here.

Are we in danger? Can just thinking about the Kalb draw him here?

No, but fear is a powerful form of imagination. It can create something out of nothing. And that's a magic he can track!

How do I stop it?

Distraction, was all he said.

Ani tapped CJ on the shoulder. "Talk."

"About what?"

"I don't care. Anything."

"Ahhh, is little Ponchy afraid of the dark?"

You would be too, if you knew what I know. "Just talk. Tell me about this tunnel. Why is it here? What's it for?"

"I think it's an old access tunnel for maintenance," said CJ as she led the way. "Or maybe it was for carting in building supplies when they were constructing the first subways, but whatever it is, I'm pretty sure no one knows about it anymore."

"Why do you say that?"

"I met this guy, Bob. He works for the archives office where they keep all the old maps and blueprints of the city. He knew everything there was to know about the subway system and its history, but he didn't know about this tunnel. I'd stumbled on a secret—a forgotten part of the city. After that, I knew I had to follow it . . . to find out where it goes."

"And where does it go?"

"You'll see."

Even in the dark, Ani could tell CJ was smiling. She hoped it wasn't because of something scary or gross at the end, that CJ thought would be fun to show her just to get a reaction.

Whatever it was, Ani promised herself she wouldn't give CJ the satisfaction. She'd pretend it didn't bother her, no matter what it turned out to be. But what actually waited for her at the end of the tunnel, she could have never anticipated, nor what happened next.

The droning in her ears graduated to a roar, and with a sudden WOOSH, Ani . . . was . . . somewhere else.

Cold. Dark. Damp.

A slow drip-drip-drip of water echoed in the distance. Coarse black rock closed in on all sides. The mossy smell of erosion filled her nostrils, the taste of the air, metallic on her tongue.

Still in a tunnel, she thought, *but not in the subway. A cave. I'm in a cave.*

CJ walked just ahead. Ani squinted. *Different clothes. How could she suddenly be wearing different clothes? Wait, those are my clothes. Why would CJ be wearing my—*

"Hazool, keep up," called CJ. "We're not out of the freak zone yet. We need to stick together."

A teenage boy ran to join them, his face unfamiliar. "I had to take a piss," he said, zipping up muddy jeans.

"Marking your territory is not necessary," said CJ.

We're in a strange cave somewhere, with a strange boy who acts like he knows us, and . . . ooohhh, I am so totally in a future memory right now. Crap. Crap. Crap.

Ani's gaze swept her surroundings. *But what are we doing here? Are there actual caves in New York City? This doesn't make any sense. Why would a future memory show me something that can't possibly happen—*

A sharp CRACK split the air. The ground crumbled beneath her.

Ani plunged into a maelstrom of falling rock and violent confusion. Her mind went black.

"Ponch, keep up!" yelled CJ, snapping Ani out of her trance.

Ani shook off the terror and tumult of the vision. This was the first time a future memory hadn't shown *someone else* in danger. This time it was her. She was the one in danger. And like all her future memories, if she didn't stop it, someone was going to die. *She* was going to die. Ani gasped. "Oh no!"

"What?" said CJ.

"Ceej STOP!" Ani reached out and grabbed CJ's shoulder. The ring of illumination from her flashlight gleaned off an oily substance pooling in front of them. "Don't move!"

"It's just an oil slick, Ponch." CJ started to take a step.

"No! Stop! Go around it!"

"Why are you freakin' out? Are you really that scared of the dark?"

"You have no idea."

"Well get over it," she said, trudging forward. Her boots trampled the oily mess without incident.

"Nothing happened," said Ani, confused. "You're okay."

"Why wouldn't I be? Geez Ponch, you're acting even weirder than usual. D'you forget to take your idiot pill this morning?"

"Every time I have a future memory the Kalb finds me. Except this time." She looked at CJ.

"What are you babbling about now?"

"Nothing. Never mind. Forget it."

"Gladly."

A half-hour into their trek, they came to a place in the tunnel that widened out, with rusted metal support beams crisscrossing above their heads. At the end of this section was a large black door almost twice their height.

"Ready for this?" asked CJ with her hand on the oversized, century old, cast-iron latch.

Not even, thought Ani, but she smiled and said, "Sure."

CJ opened the door to an impossible sight. They stepped from the confining tunnel into a grand expanse.

Cool air whisked Ani's face. She gazed up in awe, blinking as her eyes adjusted to the new light. A high vaulted dome ceiling crowned the round room with majestic elegance. The walls, lined with gleaming blue and amber tiles, arched up to a multicolored, stained-glass skylight fit for a cathedral.

Ani caught her breath. Never in her life had she stood in the presence of something so magnificent. The place seemed sacred somehow, like she'd just stepped into a church, no . . . a cathedral, the kind she had only seen in pictures. But at the same time, there was a lingering wistful loneliness here.

Construction debris scattered about hinted at some minimal effort of restoration, but the century of dust that covered every surface and hung in the still air like ash, proved those efforts hadn't been recent.

Ani whispered in reverence, "What is this place?"

"It's an old abandoned subway station under city hall," said CJ. "Cool, huh? It's over a hundred years old."

"How could anyone abandon something so beautiful? I've never seen anything like it."

"Actually, New York City is full of this guy's work. Rafael somebody-or-other. Bob told me all about him. Once you know the look of his stuff, you can spot it all over the place—Grand Central Terminal, the church of Saint John the Divine, Carnegie Hall—the guy had mad skills." CJ looked up at the vaulted ceiling above. "He always did these colossal tiled archways, which made his stuff not only beautiful, but super strong, and fireproof too."

"You sure know a lot about this."

"My buddy Bob at the Archive office slapped all sorts of crazy random facts on me."

"Did he say why they abandoned it?"

CJ shrugged. "It had something to do with functionality or practicality. Bob said it didn't really get used all that much when it was a working station. And the loop had its own set of problems."

"The loop?"

"Come on. I'll show you."

Ani followed CJ down a flight of stairs and into another elaborately constructed chamber, which opened out to the subway platform and tunnel. Well-worn train tracks ran through another series of colorfully tiled archways, massive in scope, yet delicate in their perfectly balanced symmetry.

The scene was lit like a movie, thought Ani, with soft beams of dusty sunlight filtering through skylights high above, interspersed with shadowy pockets of colorless darkness. Inverted four-limbed brass chandeliers hung from the highest point between each arch, unlit and unadorned.

CJ pointed to a stretch of track that formed a large loop as it ran its course. "These tracks are still used by the 6 train. This is where they turn around. But they don't stop anymore." CJ paused a moment and then turned to look back at the mezzanine where they had just been. "I think this is my favorite place in all of New York. They abandoned it because it didn't suit their purpose, but they just don't get it."

Ani drew her gaze away from the stained glass window above their heads to peer at CJ. "Get what?"

"That it has its own purpose. It doesn't need them to give it purpose. It may be lost and forgotten, but the place is no less beautiful because of it. Maybe it's even more beautiful now, 'cause it's not filled with people coming and going who couldn't care less about it."

"I think it's kind of sad that no one sees it."

"I see it," said CJ.

"Maybe they should make it into a museum or something."

"They tried. It got stopped."

"That's too bad."

"No it's not. I'm glad they stopped it." CJ's tone grew cold.

"Why?"

"Just because no one cares about it, doesn't mean it's worthless. Turn it into a tourist trap and a whole different something will be lost. Its dignity. Its serenity. Its—"

"—secrecy," Ani finished. "You don't want anyone else to come here. You want to keep it all to yourself."

"Then why did I show it to you?"

"Beats me. Why did you?"

"I don't know, but now I wish I hadn't." CJ started back up the stairs.

"CJ, wait!"

"Just drop it. I don't know what I was thinking bringing you here. You can't understand. No one can."

Ani's heart sank as she realized what she'd just done. CJ had finally shared a part of herself, a part of her world. A secret. It was a gift of friendship, and Ani had just thrown it to the ground and stomped on it. "Wait. I'm sorry." She caught up to CJ at the top of the stairs. "You're right. This place is perfect just the way it is. I'm glad you showed it to me."

"Well, I'm not. I should have known better. You wanna ruin it just like everybody else."

"No, I don't."

"Yes, you do. You want to turn it into some stupid museum. Advertise it in neon. Let a thousand clueless tourists trample it every day until there's nothing left."

Ani lowered her voice to a near whisper even though there was no one else to hear. "I won't tell anyone your secret, CJ. I promise."

"You better not. You do and you're—"

"I know . . . dead."

"Got that right."

"Well, if I tell, you have my permission to kill me," said Ani, "as long as it's quick and relatively painless."

"No way," said CJ, turning the flashlight back on. She slipped through the big black door into the workmen's tunnel before adding, "I'm going to hang you by your toenails and watch as all the blood rushes to your head until it explodes."

"Great. Sounds like fun."

"It does, doesn't it?"

"Can I at least take an aspirin first?"

"Or, I know, I'll encase you in a huge block of ice with only your head sticking out, and just when you're about to die by freezing to death, I'll light your hair on fire."

"Can we talk about something else?"

"Or how 'bout . . ."

All the way back, CJ thought of more and more unusual and gruesome ways to accomplish Ani's demise, until there were no variations left. CJ's laughter echoed through the tunnel, and eventually Ani joined her.

When they finally arrived back at the Wakefield, it was dusk, and they were friends again. As they parted in the hall, CJ turned to Ani and said, "You still want that fight lesson?"

"Yeah," said Ani. "I do."

"Morningside Park. After school. Tomorrow. We'll see how tough you are."

"If you begin by picturing yourself succeeding you're half way to success. If you begin by picturing yourself failing, you have already failed. A failure of the imagination will be a hindrance to every step, for what you are able to envision you are able to achieve."

-Naviga ✤ Tome of the Zielfah Ri

CHAPTER NINETEEN

ᴕ

WORDWISE

After another silent breakfast of cold cereal with her father, another morning of wishing her mother was there to talk to—or even Mobius, who, in a single conversation, spoke more words than Dad had all week—after a cold night and an even colder morning, Ani was anxious to get to school. Things might not have gotten any better with Dad, but it was about to get a whole lot better at school. CJ would teach her to fight, and she'd finally be able to stand up to Mad Millie.

Ani knew Millie wasn't the type of person to let something like this go. What happened in the hall the other day was just the beginning. She'd be back, and next time, her little gang would make sure CJ wasn't around to help.

Millie's in for a big surprise, thought Ani, as she finished her soggy flakes. *Everything's gonna be different from here on out.*

That afternoon, following one more miserable day of duck and dodge, Ani left school and rushed straight to the park, excited about her first fight lesson and . . . scared to death. She didn't trust CJ not to hurt her just to make a point. But Ani had to know how to defend herself, and that was worth a little pain.

Or a lot.

But their meeting in the park didn't go as Ani had hoped. Not even close.

After waiting for over an hour, Ani was ready to give up and head home when CJ finally showed. She spent a little over five minutes demonstrating how to punch someone in the stomach so that the wind is knocked out of them and then said she had to go.

"Wait. That's it?"

"I got someplace I gotta be."

"How 'bout tomorrow?"

"Maybe," CJ called back.

"But I—" Ani stood with her mouth open, feeling like an idiot as CJ walked away. "What am I supposed to do now?" she muttered to herself.

Ani started home, angry at herself for believing. What did she expect? Did she think CJ was going to spend the whole afternoon with her? Did she think they would become best friends?

Her determined stride carried her halfway home before her anger began to wane. What was she doing? She had more important things to think about. Just that morning, she'd stashed the Mapstone sketch in her backpack, vowing to find someone who could help her decipher the new message, and that was precisely what she intended to do with the rest of her afternoon. Turning around, she headed in the opposite direction.

On Broadway and 114th, Ani found an old bookshop. The shingle out front read, *WordWise*. She cupped her hands on the glass and peered in.

Looks promising. The faded sign in the window advertised 'Rare Books, Ancient Studies, Extensive Selection of Historical Reference, Collectables & Original Volumes.' If she was going to find a way to decipher the Mapstone language, this seemed like the perfect place to start.

She pushed on the door and stepped inside the musty shop, setting off the sharp clang of a brass bell. The man at the counter looked up from his book with a disgruntled look, but made no comment.

Heading down one of the aisles, Ani felt the intense, almost magnetic pull of the books, as if they had some kind of magical power over her. The shop felt cool and cave-like. No natural light seeped in past the front counter, but it wasn't altogether dark. Torch-shaped wall sconces lit the stacks, flickering like real fire.

She strolled through the maze of shelves with a sense of wonder. This was exactly the kind of place that could hold keys to the past, answers to questions unasked . . . the kind of place that might, in one of its ancient volumes, hold the secret to the Mapstone, but which one? The sheer numbers overwhelmed her. If she was to find her way through this labyrinth, she was going to need a guide.

"Hello," she said as she approached the front counter. "My name is Ani Jasper."

The man closed his book without marking his place, squinted at her over wood-rimmed spectacles and said, "Welcome to WordWise. I'm Devon. Is there something I can help you with?"

"I hope so."

"What you see around you is the culmination of forty years of study and exploration in scholarly pursuits," he said. "If you are looking for comic books or the latest bestselling young adult novel, you've come to the wrong place. And if you've recently consumed any quantity of candy, or have anything sticky on your hands, I must insist you go in the back and wash them before touching anything in this shop."

Ani decided not to be put off by the man's derision. He was protecting his treasure. She could understand that. "I'd be a little protective too," she said in a respectful whisper, "if these were *my* books."

The man picked up his pipe and peered down at her from his place behind the mahogany counter. "Indeed."

Ani held out her hands. "Clean," she assured him. Then she glanced around the shop and said, "I like it here. It's . . . perfect."

The bookshop owner smiled with the unlit pipe clenched between his teeth. "I agree." He indicated the dark shelves with a nod. "This collection is a testament to a lifetime of learning. The best kind of life lived, in my humble opinion."

"So you've read all these books?"

"Every one of them. I didn't buy them to sell. I bought them to read. But when the collection grew too large for our modest home, my wife compelled me to open a bookshop, so here I am. I can tell you anything you want to know about any book here."

"Wow. I hope I know this much when I'm old." Ani cringed. She didn't mean to call the man old. But he didn't seem to mind.

"You will," he said, smiling again. "If you want to, you will."

"I was hoping you could help me with something," said Ani, pulling the Mapstone sketch from her backpack.

"I'll do my best."

She placed the sketch on the counter in front of the scholar. "I'm trying to find out what these symbols mean. Have you seen anything like this in any of your books?"

The man pushed his spectacles up onto the bridge of his nose. "Hmmm," he muttered. "I have an extensive ancient languages section in the back, but I don't believe I've ever seen anything quite like this. Not Arabic. Not quite Runic, though similar in structure. The contours are a bit more organic in nature—"

"Do you know what language it is?" Ani asked.

"No, I'm afraid I don't."

"So you can't tell me what it says?" She couldn't hide her disappointment.

"I'm sorry, no. But the repetition here," he pointed to one of the reoccurring symbols in the sequence, "and here, and here, seems to indicate the construct of an alphabetic writing system, rather than a logographic or symbolic system where each mark represents a whole word or concept. If that is indeed the case, if this is an alphabetic system, then with a large enough sample, a cipher or translation key could be devised."

"You mean like the Rosetta Stone?"

"Precisely." The man grabbed a loupe from a desk drawer to examine the symbols more closely. "So," he said, "is there more?"

"No. This is um . . . all I have." Ani said, thinking of the first Mapstone message she jotted down just before it disappeared. She didn't know why she lied. She just felt suddenly and inexplicably protective. Maybe the message was only for her. Maybe if someone else were to translate the Azimaran symbols, it would violate some sort of sacred law. What if it put him in danger? She couldn't chance it.

"I see," said the man. "And where did this come from?"

"I found it, or I guess you could say it found me."

"Fascinating." He ran his finger across the surface of the drawing. "Curious. The surface is raised slightly, but the words almost appear to have been burned into the paper." He returned his gaze to Ani. "If you would allow me to keep the sketch for a few days I have a friend at Columbia University who may be able to help."

"My mom goes there. She's an anthropologist."

"And what did she have to say about this?"

"She hasn't seen it yet. She's in Peru. She's there on a research expedition in the Amazon Jungle."

"Well, if you would permit me to take it to—"

"—Um, no, but thanks. I appreciate you taking the time to look at it."

"Are you sure? You won't be able to translate this on your own. You're going to need an expert."

"No thank you." Ani pulled the sketch out from under the man's fingers, folded it, and stashed it back in her backpack. "I apologize for the imposition."

"No imposition. Come by anytime."

"I have to go," she said and headed for the exit. Just before she pushed the door open, she glanced back and saw the man pluck a fountain pen from its marble base and doodled the Mapstone markings on the back of a blank receipt. He stared at the symbols, lost in thought.

"Don't be surprised if those marks you just made disappear on you," said Ani.

He looked up. "What?"

Ani shrugged. "Never mind."

"Hey," he said, "if you're determined to tackle this thing on your own, you should probably try the library."

Ani stopped. The library! Of course! It was the perfect place to solve a word puzzle. Why didn't she think of that? "Is there one near here?"

"Sure there is," said the man, as if it was a ridiculous question. "About a block down the street. Go out to the sidewalk and make a right. It will be on your left. You can't miss it." He did a quick absentminded wave as he studied the note he'd made and then watched in astonishment as the symbols began to disappear. The man took a step back, knocking over a cup of pencils and pens.

Ani smiled as she left the bookshop and headed for the library, more determined than ever to decipher the Mapstone. Maybe the symbols belonged to some long forgotten alphabet, perhaps Mayan or Aztec—two of her favorite history subjects in her homeschool curriculum.

Now her schoolwork would have to wait. Deciphering the Mapstone was more important. She didn't care if it took all night. She had to solve this mystery.

Besides, it wasn't as if anyone waited for her back at the apartment. These days, Dad didn't even notice when she came home late. As long as she didn't interrupt him while he was watching the news or reading the paper, he didn't seem to care.

She found the library easily enough. Never had she seen so many books in all her life. She could spend months in here and never get bored. But at the moment, she needed to keep her mind on the task at hand. Taking her cue from the bookshop owner, she decided to start with Ancient Languages.

Her search produced no results.

She moved on to History, Anthropology, Archaeology, all with the same outcome. She looked up Hieroglyphs, Petroglyphs, Tachygraphy, which she'd never even heard of before, and even spent some time looking through books on Secret Societies, fantasizing for a foolish moment that it could be a coded language invented by members of the Illuminati for their clandestine communications.

While in the reference section, she decided to look up the word *Kalb* in *The Dictionary of Magical Creatures* and *The Encyclopedia of Mythology*. Not one mention of anything named Kalb or any monster that could penetrate the mind and altered its molecular structure to become a stinking, black, slithering goo. She shivered at the thought of Xephero's warning; the Kalb would come after her the next time she had a future memory. But she had no way of controlling how or when her visions would appear. And how could she defend herself against something if she didn't even know what it was?

Frustrated, she returned to the Mapstone sketch. She showed the sketch to the librarians at the reference desk who were supposed to know the answer to nearly any question. No one had a clue what the symbols meant. One of them even suggested Ani had made them up.

Translating this thing wasn't going to be easy, if it was even possible at all. But Ani was getting used to impossible things, like ancient writing showing up and disappearing on its own, or animals talking, or fight lessons from a girl who didn't really care if she lived or died.

She headed back to the reference section to continue her search. She grabbed an anthology of fabled underground city stories, a book called *The True Origins of the Atlantis Myth*, and a series about history's obscure references to lost places that may or may not have existed.

With an armful of books, she made her way to a free table, spilled them across its surface, and began paging through the thick volumes.

An hour later she was no closer to a solution then she had been when she came in.

Propping her head on her fist, Ani sighed. Eyes drowsing, her mind began to wander, and her thoughts drifted into a dream.

She stood again amid the opalescent structures of the stone city. A white stone fountain rose up before her, the majestic centerpiece of a town square. Ani listened in the stillness to the tinkling song of water drops as they fell from tier to tier and danced on the surface of the pool at its base. She closed her eyes to take in its subtle music, but felt more than just the serenity of the fountain; someone else was there.

Her eyes flashed open, searching for the presence she had sensed. At first glimpse, the stone city appeared deserted, but then she saw him; a teenage boy standing tall on a rooftop high above the square, watching her with fierce intent.

"Who are you?" Ani called out. "Why are you watching me?"

The teen did not move, but inside her mind she heard the words:

I am Naviga. I am he who prepares the Tome of the Zielfah Ri for your arrival. I am the translator of languages so that you will understand. I am the Light Master's apprentice until you come to replace me. I am the teacher of small things as the Master is the teacher of great things. Together we will teach you all you must know.

Questions raced through Ani's mind, but as she began to ask them, a soft tap on her shoulder pulled her out of her doze.

She stood and whirled about, surprising a young library assistant.

The color drained from the girl's face. One hand went to her heart, and the other to her rolling metal book cart, which she used to steady herself as she stumbled backward.

"Oh, I didn't mean to startle you," said Ani. "Are you okay?"

The young woman stuttered out an apology. "I—I'm sorry to disturb you miss," she said in a small voice, her demure demeanor offset by her wide-eyed expression. "I, um, overheard you speaking at the reference desk earlier. I caught a glimpse of your sketch, but I had to wait for my break before I could speak to you."

Ani held out the Mapstone sketch. "This?"

"Yes."

"I'm looking for any reference to this writing," said Ani. "I'm trying to translate it. Do you know what language it is?"

"No," she said, her complexion ashen.

"Do you want to sit down?" Ani pulled out a chair.

"No. I only have a few minutes left. I . . . I need to show you something. Can you come with me now?"

"If we continue to see what has been seen, think what has been thought, do what has been done, we fall into a kind of soul-slumber, becoming aimless sleepwalkers moving through half-lived lives. To become fully awakened, we must reach beyond the world of everyday thoughts and things, to make each step a vibrant new discovery."

-Solamas ✦ Tome of the Zielfah Ri

CHAPTER NINETEEN

♈

LOST LIKE ME

The library assistant motioned for Ani to gather her things and follow. As they made their way through the stacks to the far side of the library, she explained in whispers . . .

"There's a book here called, *Places I Have Seen that No One Believes* by a man named Nikolai Katella. It's in a separate section of titles by local writers, so you wouldn't necessarily think to look there, but well, there's um, a photograph I think you'll want to see."

"I don't have a library card," said Ani. "Is that okay?"

"You don't need a library card to look at it, but you'll need one if you want to check it out."

"How do I get one?"

"You'll have to come back tomorrow. Ask the front desk."

They arrived at a small shelf of books on random subjects by authors few had ever heard of. The assistant pulled a tattered skinny paperback from its nook and handed it to Ani.

On the washed out cover was a hazy photograph of a man in his mid-30's sporting a weathered fedora, matching leather vest, and scuffed explorer boots laced to the knees. An antiquated pair of binoculars hung around his neck. He stood next to a large stone etched in ancient symbols.

"I know the photograph is not very good and the detail is blurred," said the assistant, "but don't the markings on that rock look a little like the symbols in your sketch?"

Ani squinted. "Yeah, they do! Where was this photo taken? Does it say?"

"On the inside flap it says the cover photo is referenced in chapter four, but—"

Ani opened the book to chapter four, excitement fizzing in her middle. "It's—"

"Gone. That's what I'm trying to tell you. Someone ripped out the pages. Who would do something like that to a library book?"

"Is there another copy?" Ani asked, a growing desperation taking hold.

The assistant glanced around as if she were a fugitive running from the law. "No. This is the only one, and I checked. The book is out of print. The author only pressed a hundred of them. I checked all the libraries. This is the only copy in the system."

Ani turned the book over to look at the back cover and found another portrait of the author. In this photo, he posed in front of etched glass double doors. "I need to talk to this author. You said he's local?"

"He was. He died a long time ago. That picture is from the 1930's."

"Wait," said Ani, squinting at the design in the glass behind the author. "I know this place."

"Yeah, it's here in Morningside Heights."

"No, I mean, I live there."

"You live at the Wakefield?" Her eyes widened. "Is it haunted like they say? I've heard stories. You know the author, Katella, was shot just after this photograph was taken, right there on the front steps, but he didn't die that day. They saved his life and he went back to Peru a year and never to be heard from again. They say he worked for the mob but the book doesn't talk about that."

Just then, a woman wearing an expression as stern and stuffy as her starched grey business suit appeared at the end of the row and cleared her throat.

"I have to go," uttered the assistant under her breath, and with that, she disappeared in the stacks, followed by her starched supervisor.

Hoping she didn't get the girl in too much trouble, Ani found an open seat and began to read the book. The author, Nikolai Katella, was an American explorer who attended Yale where he became inspired by the work of Hiram Bingham, the man credited with the discovery of Machu Picchu in 1911. Most of the book seemed to be written in Katella's own hand, perhaps reproduced from his expedition journals, although, interspersed throughout, were short, typed 'clarification notes.'

It was all very interesting, but there didn't seem to be any further mention of the rock on the cover or its secret writings.

Ani had no clue how long she'd been reading until someone tapped her on the shoulder and asked her to gather up her things because the library was closing.

Ani nodded, but when she returned the faded and forgotten book to its lonely spot on the shelf, she noticed the gap in the middle where the missing chapter used to be.

Faint whispers—like the whispers of the desert wind back home—called to her again, but this time they seem to be coming from the book. She couldn't leave. Not yet. There was something in this book that she needed to see.

She glanced left, then right. Everyone had gone. The library was empty. She took the book and turned to the torn section one last time. Upon closer inspection, she noticed a small frayed portion of one of the missing pages had remained attached at the book's spine, and on that ripped remnant, half a word was showing. The first 4 letters of that word were A-z-i-m.

"Azimara," whispered Ani. "That could be Azimara." And the curved line below it looked like it may have belonged to a hand-drawn map.

It might not be much, Ani thought, *but at least it's something.*

She looked at the front cover again and narrowed in on the author's face. "What happened to you?" she whispered. "Did you find Azimara?" She turned to the final page of the book and read the last paragraph.

> **Nicolai Katella disappeared while on a return expedition to the Amazon jungle and was never found. After an extensive search, he was presumed dead. This book, based on his notes and photographs from the first expedition, was compiled, edited, and published by friend and colleague, Todd Maiser.**

A new fear pressed on her. *What if they killed him because of what he learned over there? What if anyone who get's too close to the Guardians' secret is in danger? What if they already have Mom?* It suddenly occurred to Ani that flashing the Mapstone sketch all over the city to track down its meaning might not have been the smartest thing to do.

Another tap on her shoulder, this one more decisive, jolted her attention away from the book.

Ani stiffened as she peered up at a uniformed man with a New York Public Library nametag on his chest. "The library is closed, miss. You need to leave now."

"Oh. Okay." Ani grabbed her backpack from the table nearby, and started toward the door.

"Don't forget your coat, miss. You're going to need it out there."

Ani turned. The security guard held out her new polka-dot-less raincoat—the one her mother had bought her the day before leaving for Peru. Nan had called it "drab and lifeless"—a combination of muted teal and brown with two rows of vertical zippers as its only embellishment. Ani thought the look of it fit her perfectly.

"Thanks," she said, taking the coat. "I would have been sad to lose it. It was a birthday present from my mom."

Turned out the security guard was right. She did need her coat, for as she pushed her way through the library's heavy front doors, the blustery spring air chilled her bones. Ani wrapped her coat tightly around her and started home.

Something she hadn't considered; there was a definite downside to staying late at the library. She had to walk home alone, in the dark, in New York City. She was pretty sure she knew the way, but everything looked different at night.

She reached into her backpack for the cell phone her mother had given her but stopped short. *No, you can do this*, she told herself. *Don't be a wimp. If you call Dad every time you feel a little lost, you'll never prove to him that you're okay out on your own. Then CJ will have been right about you all along.*

Ani started home, trying to imagine what CJ would do—how it felt to be fearless. She tried to think like CJ . . . *be* CJ. And maybe some of CJ's courage had rubbed off on her after all, because her trek home wasn't nearly as scary as she expected it to be.

Like her subway experience, Ani observed the ebb and flow of the city streets, the stop and go of traffic, the shoppers in and out of stores, and after a few blocks, it really didn't seem all that frightening anymore. In fact, compared to scorpions, the Kalb, and Mad Millie, the streets of New York seemed almost tame.

As she walked on, new confidence and strength flooded in, conquering her insecurity the way mastering a new skill conquers diffidence. By the time she'd journeyed halfway home, she'd become invincible.

Ani decided *this* was the way she wanted to feel all the time. She hated being afraid. No more, she vowed. *I'm done running away. I will learn how to protect myself from the Kalb, and as far as Mad Millie is concerned, well, if CJ doesn't want to teach me how to fight, then I will ask Dad to enroll me in a self-defense class.* One way or another, she was going to feel safe again.

Before she reached her neighborhood, however, she faced a different type of challenge altogether. If she had listened to the news that morning, it might have cautioned her about the coming storm, it might have told her to stay inside. But Ani hadn't heard the warnings.

Shortly after she left the library, it had begun to sprinkle, but she was used to that. What she hadn't counted on was the speed at which it developed into a genuine downpour.

The cell phone suddenly seemed like a very good idea. She stopped, fished it out of her backpack, and clicked it on. Nothing. She hit the button again. Still nothing. She shook it and held the button down until her finger hurt. Dead. How long had it been since she'd charged the battery? "Damn." She threw it back in her bag, gathered her wits, and quicken her pace.

Violent winds and stinging rain now fought her every step. Even with her raincoat zipped all the way up and her hood pulled down as far as it would go, she was utterly drenched inside and out within the span of a few minutes.

Determined not to let it conquer her, she pressed on, but one wrong turn, and suddenly nothing looked familiar.

She tried retracing her footsteps. Didn't help. She would have asked someone for assistance, had there been a soul around, but the streets were deserted. Even the taxi drivers seemed to have abandoned their routes on the flooded neighborhood roads.

Stopping at an intersection, she turned and turned again.

"Not lost," she told herself, "just misplaced." It's what mom always said when searching for something she couldn't find. 'It's not lost, it's just misplaced.' Ani swallowed her fear and began to repeat, "Not lost. Not lost. Not lost."

How long had she been wandering without direction? How far from home had she strayed searching for something, anything familiar.

Cold. Wet. Exhausted. Every part of her ached. The rain beat down so hard now it finally brought her to her knees. She squinted but it was pointless; the buildings on the street were a blur. *How can I find my way home if I can't see anything?*

Tears welled up as she wished for her mother. The thought came unbidden and tore at her insides.

Tears only made it harder to see. She whisked them away, but more came. And once started, they couldn't be stopped.

The force of it blindsided her. The deluge of emotion. Like drowning. Like dying. Lungs ached for oxygen. Gasps sent stabs through her ribcage. It wasn't about being lost. It wasn't about being cold or wet or scared. The storm raged inside her now. No refuge. No hope. No one to save her.

Rain pounded. Time passed. Maybe minutes. Maybe hours. Her sobs, at last, began to subside.

With her face buried in her hands, it took a moment to realize it—to come back to her outer senses, but it was there again—that feeling of a presence, of being watched. She opened her eyes and peered through the blur of her tears. Holding her breath, she listened for movement, but her ears were useless. The roar of the downpour drowned out all sound.

She squinted at a form taking shape only a few yards away.

"Who's there?" she called out. "Is someone there?"

No answer came, but the form inched closer—close enough to see that it was an animal of some kind—large enough to be as tall as she, on her knees.

The rhythm of her heart sped, but she didn't flinch. Nowhere to run. Not fast enough to evade a four-legged, and certainly not in her present condition. *Better at this point to appear as non-threatening as possible*, she thought.

Muscles throbbed as she stiffened, attempting to remain perfectly still. The puddle at her knees deepened by the second. How much longer before the torrent swept them both away?

The shape slowly took on more detail. Squinting as it crept closer, she could see now that it was . . . a wolf . . . a white wolf, and then she knew—somehow she just knew. Relief washed over her as fear dissolved. It was the white wolf they had almost hit in the road, the white wolf that had brought her back from the scorpion fever.

"It's you," she said.

The wolf stopped in front of her, just beyond reach.

She extended her hand as a gesture of trust. The wolf stepped forward to let her hand rest on his head.

"But, how did you get here?"

The wolf remained silent.

"Have you come to help me? Can you guide me home?"

The wolf turned to leave.

"Don't go! Please don't go."

He glanced back at her.

"Oh, you want me to follow you." Ani rose, but immediately collapsed, unprepared for the weakness in her legs, the extra weight of sopping clothes, and the power of the driving rain on her back.

Finding her footing on the second try, she sloshed over to the wolf and stopped by his side. She placed her hand on his back and whispered, "Thank you."

They crossed the flooded intersection together, step by step, fighting the storm's rage with all the strength they possessed.

When finally they reached the other side, Ani stumbled up the curb and into an abandoned storefront. They took shelter in its covered entrance.

The wolf bowed his head and vanished.

"No! Wait!" she screamed, "I thought you were going to help me! I still have no idea how to get home!"

She collapsed next to a pile of rubbish, defeated and shivering uncontrollably.

Then the rubbish heap moved.

Ani shrieked and sprang to her feet, holding her hands out in front of her as if the gesture offered some iota of protection.

A soggy head of hair popped out of the trash. "Mine! Get out! I was here first! Here first." The man's face, smudged with dirt and grime, contorted in anger.

"Oh, I'm sorry. I didn't mean to intrude." Ani took a step back as the man bared his teeth in a guttural growl.

"Get out! This is my place! My place. Mine," the man yelled, his voice, rough and strained, his right eye twitching with an involuntary tick.

"No need to get upset. You can have it. Really. It's all yours. I just wanted to get out of the rain for a sec." Ani backed up another step. A few more and she'd be out in the storm again.

"You don't fool me!" said the vagrant. "You're here to take my house away from me. I know your kind. If I don't give it up, you'll burn it down! Down to the ground. With me and my family inside. You'll take everything. Everything!"

"Is that what happened to you? Did you lose your family?"

"I won't let you do it! Not this time! I'll kill you if I have to!"

"No. No. I'm just a girl. Lost and trying to get home."

"Lost. Lost like me? Everything lost."

"I don't suppose you know where the Wakefield is?"

The man snarled.

"Right. I'll just go now." As she began to feel the spatter of rain at her back, she heard the man muttering something under his breath.

"Wakefield Nick. Wakefield Nick. Wakefield Nick."

"Do you know someone who lives at the Wakefield?"

"Oh, oh, oh, you mean Nick? Everybody knows Nick."

Ani took a step toward the man. "He lives at the Wakefield Apartments?"

"Used to. Not anymore. Not alive anymore. Dead now. Yeah, dead now. But he's still there. Still there. He leaves food out for us sometimes."

"How can he leave food out for you if he's—?"

"Dead? Finds a way. Always finds a way. Good man, Nick. Wakefield Nick."

"Can you tell me how to get there? To Nick's place, I mean?"

"Not if you're one of them."

"One of who?"

"Nick has enemies. Nick has friends. Which are you?"

"Oh, friend, definitely," said Ani. "Neighbors actually."

"Neighbors lost. Lost and trying to get back."

"Yes. Exactly. Can you tell me how to get there?"

"Can. Will. Will and can. Easy. Go a different path. Unseen. Unknown. You can't see because you look for what you know. But that is done now. Don't search for the known way. Search for the new. See what I see. Go where I go. Step how I step. You'll get through."

Ani listened to a list of convoluted directions, thanked him and promptly set out, hoping the man, crazy as he sounded, actually knew where the Wakefield stood. As she left she could hear him repeating, "Wakefield Nick. Wakefield Nick."

Still nothing looked familiar, but Ani followed the directions faithfully, releasing, as instructed, all preconceived notions on how to find her way home.

Under this, over that. Left at the stack of wooden crates, right when you smell rotten fish. Barkin' Jaxx will want a pet, but

151

won't bite. Nope. Keep on when you see the red neon sign. Ask Porch Sittin' Sadie for a word. She points the way if you give her a word back. Make it a good one. Around, up, down, in, and never mind a key; the rusty gate will open. Tell 'em you know Nick, they'll let you through.

Ani took it all in with a modicum of dark fascination, realizing that by "stepping how he stepped," she glimpsed a world very different from her own. A world never seen, never shown, never known except by those who belong to it. It was a side of the city that didn't shine, yet had its own light, its own sense of community, and a surprising measure of kindness.

Finally, to her utter amazement, Ani caught sight of a landmark she recognized—Mr. Cardello's corner market.

Elation came first. Then relief. Then a desperate longing to be warm, safe and dry. "Thanks Nick!" She broke into a run and didn't stop until she reached home.

Ani stood for a moment at her front door, dripping on the mat, waiting for her heart to stop pounding. She whisked the water from her face and turned the knob.

Leaving wet footprints on the carpet, she tiptoed into the apartment, hoping not to wake—

"Dad!" For once, her father wasn't asleep in front of the television, or busy at the computer. Unfortunately.

He sat stiff on the couch, cell phone in his lap, his expression grim, his hair and clothes as wet as hers.

Ani cleared her throat. "Is um, everything okay?"

"No, Ani, everything's not okay." He looked at the phone in his lap.

"I . . . I tried to call. My phone was dead. I'm . . . sorry."

For a long time he just sat there staring at the phone.

Ani fidgeted where she stood.

Finally he spoke. "Just because I'm no longer here when you get home, doesn't mean you can do whatever you want after school, and come home whenever you feel like it. I had no idea where you were. You could have been hurt, or kidnapped, or—"

"You were out looking for me?"

Her father growled under his breath. "Where have you been?"

"The library," answered Ani. "Studying."

"Studying," he repeated as if he expected a different answer.

He didn't seem to notice she was soaking wet and shivering, or if he did, he didn't care. After another long silence he said, still frowning, "Are you hungry?"

She thought for a moment. All she wanted to do was get out of these wet clothes and crawl under the covers to get warm. "Um, no, not really."

"Then go to your room."

She hesitated, wishing she could say something, anything, to make it all better, then mumbled another apology and shuffled off to her bedroom.

Ani plugged her cell's wall charger into the only outlet in the room, just below the only window in the room, then connected her phone and placed it on the sill, vowing never to let the battery go dead again.

In the bathroom, she peeled off her sopping clothes, toweled dry, and put on her softest pajamas, feeling grateful for the roof over her head. Before returning to her bedroom, she glanced at her reflection, but didn't recognize the girl in the mirror. She'd been replaced with someone hollow. Someone who used to be sure-footed. Someone who used to know the path. Now she was someone else. Someone who gets lost in the rain. Someone who's afraid of shadows. Someone who isn't sure of anything anymore.

Ani turned down the covers, mimicking her mother's bedtime ritual, wishing she were here to kiss her daughter goodnight.

As she shut off the bedside lamp, a flash of lightning drew her attention to the window.

She placed her hand on the cold glass. "Where are you, Mom," she whispered, gazing out at the bitter storm.

Another flash of lightning illuminated her phone on the sill. She picked it up and stared at the glowing screen. "Call Mom."

The phone began to ring. There was a strange clicking sound and then a moment of silence. "Mom?"

"You have reached Nan J. Jasper," said the voice message. "I'm currently in the Amazon and can not be reached, but if you would leave a message I'll ring you when I return."

"Mom," said Ani into the phone, "where are you? Why weren't you on the plane? We need you. I need you. I can't do this without you. I tried. Really I did, but . . . I don't know how. I miss you so much. Just come home, Mom," she rasped between sobs. "Come home."

Yes, there is strength inherent in opposition,
but there is greater strength in union. There
is always a key, hidden as it may be . . . to
unlock the ally within the heart of an enemy.

-Solamas ✣ Tome of the Zielfah Ri

CHAPTER TWENTY-ONE

ᡡ

A FIGHTING CHANCE

When Ani returned to Morningside Park the next day for her second after-school fight lesson, she wondered if CJ would bother showing up at all. While she waited in the drizzle, she worked on her if-you-don't-want-to-do-this-it's-fine speech, but this time, when CJ finally came, they spent nearly an hour together. Grateful for the distraction from her own thoughts, Ani threw herself into the lesson and even began to enjoy the challenge.

The next afternoon, when CJ showed up, she spent a little longer with Ani, and the next, even longer, until by the end of the week, their sessions had stretched to nearly two hours.

It was exactly what Ani needed.

With each passing day she grew stronger, and with that strength came a sense of determination she'd never before experienced. Even her muscles aching after a workout felt like an accomplishment. The pain was something she earned, something she was proud of. She could feel herself getting tougher and she liked it.

There was, however, one thing that made her very curious. Each time CJ left the park she headed in a different direction. She never went straight home.

Ani wondered where she was off to every night, imagining her friend involved in all sorts of mischief, but thought it best not to ask.

Though many things about CJ remained a mystery, Ani had begun to understand her self-defense tutor a little better. CJ was tough, but not like Millie who made a show of her meanness to get attention. CJ was the kind of tough that came from getting kicked around so much that you finally start to fight back. For Ani, it was something that only happened in movies, until now.

As the days dragged on, Ani's budding friendship with CJ helped take her mind off her mother trudging through the Amazon Jungle, surrounded by snakes big enough to devour a grown man—or woman. She spent less and less time at home with her father, who no longer seemed interested in much of anything when he returned from work. He had taken a minimum wage job working for Mr. Cardello as an inventory clerk at the corner market, which he called, 'a necessary distraction,' but Ani could tell it was depleting his spirit.

When Ani asked her father how it was going, he said, "One job is as good as the next if you can't do the work you're meant to do." He did admit to liking Mr. Cardello though, who offered him the position after a conversation they'd had one morning while waiting for Ani to pick out school supplies.

As Ani browsed, she couldn't help eavesdropping on the two men. They talked about being reluctant transplants, both having moved away from a place they thought would be their home 'until their dying day.' For Mr. Cardello it was Italy, for Dad, the Mojave Desert, two very different places, but the result was the same.

Ani learned something about her father that day, as she listened to the men talk candidly about their regrets. She realized the problem wasn't that he was angry about being in New York. It was that he felt displaced . . . lost. He felt how she felt. Ani thought maybe just knowing that would make things easier, but it didn't. It only made it more heartbreaking.

In the weeks that followed, Ani watched the light dim in her father's eyes a little more each day. She hated the awkward tension between them. And after the night of the storm, things only got worse. They spoke to each other in short, curt sentences, never saying anything kind or even remotely friendly to one another.

Something had broken between them, and she didn't know how to fix it.

Her daily fight lessons continued, and Ani tried to learn everything she could from CJ, but after the first week or so, she never seemed to get any better. She came home with a fresh bruise every night and took to wearing long-sleeved t-shirts to hide them, but she refused to give up. And although CJ seemed mildly impressed with Ani's dedication, Ani figured she was probably the worst street fighter CJ had ever seen.

On the following Saturday, after nearly spraining her arm during a particularly rough sparring match the afternoon before, Ani showed up at CJ's door for another lesson and learned that her suspicions were correct.

"Whoa, wait a minute," said CJ, stepping out into the hall. "That's it. We're done."

"My arm's fine, CJ. Come on."

"It's not just the arm. Face it, Ponch. You suck at this. It's not who you are."

"But I still need to protect myself, don't I?"

"You got a brain. You can use that to get yourself out of trouble."

"But—"

"Forget it. We're done. You said you wouldn't bug me about it."

"Yeah, okay."

"You know," said CJ, "I underestimated you. You're tougher then I thought."

"Thanks."

"But you still suck."

"I know. Um, you want to come out anyway? Just to hang."

"Sure. Whatever. Anything's better than this."

Ani heard a man yelling at the TV through the closed door of CJ's apartment.

"His team is losing," said CJ, "and the beer's almost gone. Not a good combination."

They sat on the curb out in front of the Wakefield, CJ biting off her fingernails and spitting them on the ground.

"Okay," started Ani, "I know the deal was, 'You teach me how to fight, and I leave you alone' but, well, I just want you to know if you ever need my help with anything, all you need to do is ask, 'k?"

CJ shot her a severe look.

"I know. I know. You don't need anybody. I just wanted to offer anyway."

"Got that right. I don't need nobody's help. But as long as you're offering, there is one thing you could do."

"Anything. Name it."

"My math and science homework."

"You want me to tutor you?"

"I don't need no stupid tutor."

"You want me to do your homework for you?"

"You said anything. It'd be cake for a pencil-head like you."

"But you won't learn anything if I do it."

"And I'll get good grades. Perfect."

"I'll help. But I won't do your homework for you," said Ani. "Take it or leave it."

"Fine. But that means you still owe me."

"I don't think that's how it works."

"Don't you ever get tired of being the perfect little Ponch all the time? I bet you're one of those kids who has got their whole life planned out. You probably even know what shoes you're gonna wear to your college graduation. Which is it? Harvard or Yale?"

"I wouldn't mind going to college someday," said Ani, feebly. "I think it could be fun."

"Only brain-mops like *you* would think staying in school half your life could be *fun*."

"I don't have it all worked out, CJ. When I was little I thought I would work in my dad's rock shop and take over for him when he retired, but that was before we came here. Before I found out—" Ani stopped herself. "The truth is, I don't know what I want to be when I grow up. Or even *if* I'll grow up. I don't even know what I want to be right now. I've never had a plan or a dream or even a wish. I can't see myself doing anything, actually, and I have a scary-vivid imagination so not being able to imagine a future for myself is really weird."

"Weird is definitely the word *I'd* choose to describe you."

"At this point I only know what I *don't* want to be."

"And that is . . . ?"

"Dead," said Ani. What she really wanted to say was, *I don't want to be devoured by a demon called the Kalb and live in eternal darkness for the rest of my short and painful life*, but since that was not an option, the only word that came out was *dead*.

For once, CJ didn't have a snarky comeback. After a moment, she said, "I can't imagine a future for myself either. Come on. I need to steal a Coke. Gotta keep old Mr. Cardello on his toes."

Ani hesitated. "You promised that man on the train you wouldn't steal."

"Promises to crazy people don't count."

"What happened to the two fifties he gave you?"

"Like I said. Fake."

"CJ, my dad works for Mr. Cardello now. I'm not—"

"Relax. I was just kidding. I hit the jackpot this morning. Found a fiver in the couch. I always search the cushions after Joe falls asleep drunk on the sofa."

They walked to the store, bought sodas and candy bars, and ate them on the way back.

"CJ?" said Ani, as they walked. "How long have you been living at the Wakefield?"

"Going on three years. Longest I've ever lived anywhere. Why?"

"I was just wondering—"

"If you're gonna lecture me about Joe, don't. It might not be the picture-perfect home *you're* used to, but it works for us. He needs the monthly check, and I need to be left alone. I'm not going to go play house with some fake mom and dad who paint my room pink and serve dinner from all five food groups. And I'm sure as hell not gonna to pretend to be somebody's daughter. Not my style, Ponch."

"I know."

"Actually, things weren't so bad in the beginning, but after Darla left—that was his wife's name, Darla, she's the one who wanted a kid in the house—after she split, Joe started hittin' the liquor cabinet at the top of the hour, every hour. I figure Child Services would have split us up if they knew. So I make sure they don't find out."

"How do you do that?"

"Every time they come for an inspection, I clean up the apartment, make sure Joe's sober for an hour and tell them Darla is out shopping or something. I put girly stuff around the living room, like flowers, so they can see she's been there. And I smile a lot like I'm actually happy."

"Why would you go to all that trouble to stay with a man who is hurting you?"

"Listen. Just because it doesn't fit your sugarcoated Ozzie and Harriet version of what a family should look like, doesn't mean—" She broke off.

Ani shot her confused look. "Who are Ozzie and Harriet?"

"Look, it's my home. So keep your big fat mouth shut about it."

"CJ, I wasn't going to say anything about your situation."

Actually, Ani *had* thought about saying something. She'd even considered calling social services to report Joe, but she knew CJ would never forgive her.

"Okay, then what?"

"I was going to ask if you knew the woman who lives downstairs in 13A? The sign on the door says she's the manager."

"That spooky old bag? You'll stay away from her if you know what's good for ya."

"Why?"

"Ever heard the story of Hansel and Gretel? Well, she's the one that builds the gingerbread house to lure kids in just before she eats 'em."

"Oh come on, be serious."

"I am. She's some kind of witch or something."

"You think she can really do magic?" Ani felt a surge of excitement.

"Haven't you ever wondered why we're the only two kids in the building? Well, there used to be more—a lot more—'til she moved in. One by one they've all disappeared."

"Disappeared? Or moved away?"

"Even Gus the Groper is gone. I'm tellin' ya, stay clear of that place unless you want to end up pickled in one of those jars of hers."

"Have you ever um, seen any ghosts here?" Ani asked as they crossed the street to the Wakefield.

"Who have you been talking to?"

"Nobody."

"I've heard the stories," said CJ. "But I don't believe in ghosts. You're not buyin' into all this crap are you?"

"Just curious."

They approached the Wakefield, but just before climbing the front steps, CJ turned.

Ani stopped. "Where are you going?"

"Got a favor to do a friend. See ya."

"Who're these friends you keep talking about?" called Ani across the widening expanse between them. "I've never seen any of them."

"And you never will," CJ called back. She flashed Ani a rare smile and disappeared around the corner.

Ani glanced up at the bay window that belonged to the manager's apartment. A familiar looking fat cat sprawled on the sill, basking in the white sunlight. If CJ was right—if Sophia Delecort really did know magic—then maybe she could help with the problem at school *and* with the Kalb. A new sense of hope and determination took hold. If self-defense lessons couldn't protect her, maybe magic could.

There is a basic order to magic. One must unlearn what is false before one can learn what is true.

-Xephero ✤ *Tome of the Zielfah Ri*

CHAPTER TWENTY-TWO

ᵧ

A QUESTION OF MAGIC

Standing in the corridor, trying to muster the courage to knock on the door of apartment 13A, Ani stared at the little brass nameplate that spelled out *Sophia Delecort*. She was losing her nerve. A manager of an apartment building as big as this would surely be busy. She wouldn't have time for curious girls like Ani, coming around to ask if she was a—

What are you doing here! The deep voice boomed out of nowhere, angry and invasive inside her mind. Ani jumped back, ready to apologize for the intrusion until she saw there was no one around.

Something furry brushed against her legs. The black and tan cat she'd met on the fire escape now sat on the manager's doorstep, looking as if he owned the place.

Well, well, 'tis herself, said the cat, *Did I startle you?* He sounded pleased. *That was my big 'voice of authority.' I've been working on it a while now. What'da'ya think? Pretty good, huh?*

"Very effective," said Ani, annoyed at the cat's insensitivity.

Gotta tell'ya, it scares away the dogs in the neighborhood. Love to watch 'em scatter. Endless entertainment.

"How did you get out here? I just saw you in the window."

Oh, I have my ways. What are you doing loitering in the hall?

"I wasn't loitering."

Looked that way to me.

"So, is this where you live?"

"You two know each other?" said another voice, this one soft and friendly, with a distinctly British inflection. It belonged to a woman in a long flowing skirt, pleated gauze blouse and broad-brimmed hat who approached from the stairs. "I was in the garden," she said, lifting the basket of greens on her arm.

"I didn't know there was a garden here," said Ani.

"Oh yes, I wouldn't care to live anywhere without a garden. It's the English in me, I suppose."

This is my human, Sophie, said the cat matter-of-factly.

Ani smiled at the woman. "Are you Mrs. Delecort?"

"Yes, but please, call me Sophie."

Told'ja, said the cat.

"My name is Ani Jasper. I live upstairs. Third floor."

"Yes, I know. You're Nan and Stanley Jasper's daughter. Moved in middle of March."

"Yes ma'am. Am I disturbing you?"

"No. Not in the slightest." The woman shook her head and her long, grey hair bounced at the ends in a playful dance. Around her neck, on a braided serpentine chain, hung a large teardrop shaped ruby encircled by an antiqued silver bezel. The faceted gemstone glinted with its own inner light, catching Ani's attention every time the old woman moved.

"Would you like to come in, dear?"

Ani hesitated. "If it's okay."

"Certainly."

Sophie opened the door and Ani stepped inside. The place looked just as enchanting as the first time she'd seen it. But there were things she saw now that she hadn't noticed before: a tapestry on the wall of a radiant woman holding a beam of moonlight, an old-fashioned phonograph with a thick, black vinyl record on its turntable, brightly colored playing cards depicting what looked like mythological scenes, laid out on a velvet-draped table in a hopscotch pattern. Ani's eyes lingered a moment on the cards.

Sophie said, "They're called Tarot." She pronounced the word 'tah-roe,' with emphasis on the second syllable. Sophie smiled. "They weren't out the last time you were here."

Ani stiffened. "But, I've never been h—"

"The truth, dear, if you please," said Sophie severing her lie.

She really is a witch, thought Ani, peering at the old woman. *No telling what else she knows.* Ani cleared her throat. "I'm sorry. I was only here for a second. I was looking for someone. How—"

"How did I know you'd been here?"

Ani frowned at the cat.

Don't look at me, he said. *I don't tattle.*

Sophie gestured to the couch, and Ani sat.

"The house recognizes you," she said simply, as if that settled the matter. "Would you like some tea and biscuits?" Before Ani could answer she added, "Tell you what. There might be some oatmeal cookies in the kitchen if we're fortunate. They're your favorite, are they not?"

"Yes, but how did you know that?"

"Oh, lucky guess, I suppose," she said with a wink, but the grin she flashed as she spoke the words admitted to a different story. "Back in a flash," she added, "and then you can tell me the reason for your visit."

When Sophie left the room, the tabby jumped into the high-backed red velvet chair across from Ani. *Sooo whadda'ya think?*

"She seems very nice," said Ani.

Yeah, she's okay. For a human.

"I know an iguana who once said the same thing about me."

Never met a reptile I didn't dislike, said the cat, cryptically.

"His name was Mobius," said Ani. "He was my best friend back home."

How very unfortunate for you, said the cat. *He was right though. You seem pretty cool for a human . . . seeing as how we can converse and all.*

"Can Sophie hear you too?"

Nah. She talks to me all the time, but she's not like you if that's what ya' mean.

"It's just that she seems to know things, so I thought maybe—"

She has other ways of knowing, said the cat. *We do alright, but I do wish you'd tell her I don't like brussels sprouts.*

"Brussels sprouts?" Ani crinkled her nose.

Yeah, she thinks I should be a vegetarian like her.

"Yuck."

Tell me about it, said the fat cat. *I didn't get this beautiful belly eating shrubbery!*

"I know where you can get some big fat rats," said Ani thinking about the subway.

Plenty of those right here in this building.

Ani shuddered at the thought, remembering the scratching sounds she'd heard in the walls the night she had come home to an empty apartment.

Sophie entered carrying an ornate silver tray. On it was a plate of cookies, milk and sugar, a pot of tea, and two fine china cups. She placed everything on an antique serving cart.

"Solomon. Off the chair," said Sophie, without so much as a glance in the cat's direction.

Ani laughed. "So that's your name. Solomon. It fits you."

"I'm sorry," said Sophie. "I don't have soda pop or anything of the sort. I don't get many young visitors here."

Or, Ani thought, *they don't stay long.*

The old woman regarded her for a moment. "The other kids told you to be afraid of me, yes?"

Ani nodded, embarrassed that she'd been caught thinking such a silly thought.

"But you're not, are you." She phrased this as a statement rather than a question.

"No," answered Ani. *Curious maybe, but not afraid.*

"And why is that, do you suppose?"

Ani shrugged. "Solomon says you're okay."

Sophie smiled. "Well, then I guess it's good to have friends who can vouch for you. Biscuit?" She held out a plate of cookies.

"Um, sure." She took a quick bite and placed the remaining portion on the small plate Sophie had given her. "Thank you," she said, remembering her manners at the last second.

"Don't worry, my dear. There's no poison in them. Well, not much anyway." Sophie smiled and returned to the cart to pour two cups of tea. "This is called Darjeeling. I happened upon it during my travels in India and Africa. It has since become my favorite."

"I want to travel someday," said Ani. "Explore the world." *Like Mom.*

"I'll wager you miss your mum. How long has she been away now?"

"Five weeks." said Ani. "She's coming home in two weeks!"

"That is excellent news." Sophie plopped sugar cubes into their cups, added a little milk, and stirred each with a tiny gold spoon.

"Solomon. Chair," she repeated. "You know it's off limits."

That's precisely why I sit in it, said the cat.

Ani giggled.

With a swish of his tail, the fat cat jumped onto the couch.

Sophie handed Ani her tea, and then sank down into the soft velvet chair with her own cup, relaxing with a sigh. "We play this game every day, and neither of us tire of it. We have a good life here, don't we Solomon?"

Instead of answering, Solomon jumped into Ani's lap and settled in with a loud purr.

Now it was Sophie's turn to laugh. "Oh, I see how it is. You two have quite a rapport, don't you? King Solomon doesn't take to just anyone. Consider yourself bestowed upon."

"We met out on the fire escape," said Ani. "We had a nice chat."

"I see. No introductions necessary."

"I like your apartment," said Ani, glancing around the rich-toned room. "You have beautiful things." *Magical things.*

"Thank you," said the old woman. "This used to be what they called the common room—a kind of meeting place for all the guests to sit and have afternoon tea—back when it was a hotel in the 1920's. It was the only room with a fireplace, so I kept it for myself when I bought the building a few years back."

"You own the Wakefield?"

"Indeed. I chose it for its reputation. Its history brought the price down considerably."

"What history?"

"Why, ghosts, of course. They come with the territory when you're buying a structure as old as this. But these ghosts were particularly energetic."

"There are ghosts here?" asked Ani, pretending this was the first she'd heard of it.

"Oh, not anymore. I had a good chat with each of them. Well, mostly I just listened."

"Ghosts talk?" Ani asked, taking a sip of tea.

"Only when they have something that needs to be said," said Sophie. "They were quite pleased to find someone who would listen to their stories. After that, they were more than happy to be on their way. Most people, dead or alive, just want to be heard."

"You're serious."

"Perfectly. You saw the bullet hole in the front door, yes? Nick. He was the most reluctant to go."

"Wakefield Nick," Ani muttered.

"Yes, that's what they called him, back in the day." Sophie eyed Ani with a questioning look. "A real *gangstery* fellow, he was. I had to promise not to fix the glass in the front door before he'd agree to leave."

"Why doesn't he want you to fix the glass?"

"Well, you see, as long as that bullet hole is there, the kids in the neighborhood will continue to tell his story. He simply wants to be remembered."

It's true, Solomon said with a yawn, *every word*.

"He also insisted I put food out front for some of the homeless folk in the neighborhood. There's a tiny door under the stairs—"

"I wondered what that was for," said Ani.

"It's a throwback from the 'good old days.' Postmen used it to deliver packages to the hotel. Nick left sandwiches inside for the needy on the block."

"That was thoughtful of him," said Ani.

"Oh, he may have been entrenched with the Mob, but he was a good man at heart. It wasn't his choice, you see. The Mafia. You might say he was born into it."

"Was Nick also an explorer?"

"That was his passion, yes, but not his vocation, much to his disappointment. I am told it was also how he met his end—

"In the Amazon," added Ani.

"Yes, but he absolutely refuses to talk about it."

Ani's hopes deflated.

"You seem to know quite a lot about our Nick."

"There's a book in the library about an American explorer who went to Peru, Nicolai Katella. That's his real name, isn't it?"

"It is indeed. A book? How extraordinary. I had no idea."

"I think he may have gone the same place my mom went."

"Ah," said Sophie. "And you thought I might ask him about it."

Ani nodded and took another sip of tea.

"Well, we aren't conversing much these days anyway. Oh, he still comes around now and again to check up on me. He's the protective sort, you see. He doesn't admit to it though. Says he's just making sure I haven't fixed the glass, and that I'm keeping up with the sandwiches, of course, but I know better. It's always the protective ones who have the most difficulty letting go. They want to stay and make sure all is right with their little corner of the world."

"What does he look like?" asked Ani, recalling the hazy photos on the cover of the book.

"I can't rightly say. I don't actually *see* ghosts."

"Then how do you know they're real?"

"I suppose it would all depend on your definition of *real*."

"I mean how do you know you haven't imagined them?"

"Never question your experiences with other realms, my dear. They are as valid as this one."

"But," persisted Ani, "I sometimes have trouble telling the difference between my imagination and what's really happening."

"The imagination is our greatest mechanism for grasping the unimaginable."

Ani blinked. This woman talked in riddles.

"Hmm, perhaps we should stick to more congenial topics of conversation for now. So, what brings you here on this fine Saturday afternoon, Ani Jasper?"

"Oh, I . . . was just um . . . curious."

"The truth dear, if you please."

It was a bit unnerving the way this woman always knew when Ani was about to say something less than truthful, but the compassion in her voice and the kindness in her eyes spoke more of acceptance than judgment, and that put Ani's mind at ease. "I came to ask you a question."

"Sounds rather serious."

"It is."

"Right then." Sophie straightened in her chair. "I'll answer to the best of my ability."

"Are you a—" Ani suddenly lost her nerve. If she asked her question and the answer was no, then Sophie might be offended and that was the last thing Ani wanted.

"It's alright, love. At the beginning of all great discovery there is first a question."

Ani studied Sophie's face. Tiny gold sparks in her eyes glistened every time she smiled, and she smiled a lot. Ani decided she liked Sophie and hoped that they would become friends. And the best way to start a friendship was with honesty. "Okay." Ani swallowed. "Are you um, a witch? The good kind, I mean?"

Sophie thought for a moment. "Well, I don't use the title, but I am familiar with the magical arts, if that is what you're asking." She looked at Ani with the inner glow of some private humor. "Was that all you wanted to know?"

"No, I want to learn. I know about desert magic, but I want to know more about your kind of magic. You know, spells and stuff. I need to know what it is, how it works."

"I see." Sophie took a slow sip of tea. "Well, those are some pretty big questions."

"But I need an answer. It's very important."

"What is magic? That's something each person must answer for themselves."

"Why? Can't you tell me?"

"I can tell you what it means to me, why I chose this path, but I cannot tell you what magic is. It's as individual as a fingerprint and just as complex."

Solomon stretched lavishly, turned a few circles and curled into a perfect oval, waiting for Ani to stroke his back. Another loud purr indicated his approval of her technique. "Can you use magic to defend yourself?"

"Against what?"

"Against something or someone who's trying to hurt you." Sophie's gaze was piercing. "Are you in trouble, dear?"

"No, I'm not in trouble. I was just um, wondering about it."

Sophie frowned. "The truth, remember? There's no need for deception. You'll not be judged."

Ani just couldn't bring herself to talk about the Kalb. Not yet. This was too important. She'd have to start with Mad Millie and work up to the scarier stuff after they had gotten to know and trust each other.

The old woman reached for Ani's hand. "What is it, dear? What has frightened you so?"

"I want to win a fight," Ani blurted out, jerking her hand away. "At school. I want to be stronger than I am. Can magic help me do that?"

The old woman took in a deep breath, exhaled slowly and said, "Knowing magic *can* make you stronger, inside. It will not insure that you win a fight, but it can teach you how to avoid drawing a fight into your realm of experience."

Ani grimaced. "Too late."

Sophie gave her a look of grave concern.

"I didn't go looking for trouble, honest, it just found me. Is there anything you can teach me that will help?"

Sophie rose from her chair and glided over to a brimming bookshelf. She took up a paper pinwheel and held it out. "Tell me what you see?"

Ani's mouth tightened. She wasn't getting what she came for, and she didn't want to play games. The old woman waited for her answer. Ani looked at the pinwheel and said, "Red and blue dots."

Sophie gave the wheel a spin. "And now?"

"Purple circles."

"Nothing is as separate as it seems, Ani. People, events—past, present, future—everything is connected. Magic is a way of seeing. It's about seeing the bigger picture, where the dots connect." She handed Ani the pinwheel and began clearing the cups and saucers from the coffee table.

"Okay then," said Ani, not wanting the afternoon to be over, "how do I learn to see like that?"

"Open your eyes. Look around you."

"At what?"

"Everything," said Sophie, leading Ani to the door. "A rose, a face, a tree, the palm of your hand."

"But those are just ordinary things." Ani glanced down at her hand. "I see them every day."

"When you can look upon the ordinary and see the extraordinary," said Sophie, "then you will have started on the path to true magic." She touched Ani's palm, and there, before her eyes, a painted rose appeared, its stem winding around her thumb before fading away. It tingled like tiny bubbles popping on her skin.

"Start where you are," whispered Sophie. "Start simple." Learn to see your world in a new way, and you will begin to understand."

That night Ani fell asleep thinking about the conversation she'd had with Sophie, excited that she might be able to learn real magic. She wondered what it would be like to cast a spell and have it actually work. If she could get Sophie to teach her a protection spell to keep Mad Millie away, then she wouldn't need to worry about defending herself. It seemed like the perfect solution to her problem. No one gets hurt.

Ani felt a growing exhilaration at the prospect. She even pictured herself casting a spell in front of Millie, manifesting an impenetrable barrier. She saw Millie throw a punch that stopped six inches away, crushing her knuckles on the invisible wall between them. She pictured Millie's eyes growing wide with the realization that there was nothing she could do. Ani smiled as she watched it all in her mind's eye. The sensation of power surged within her. She could feel herself becoming invincible. Maybe if Sophie's magic was strong enough it could even protect her against the Kalb.

As Ani mused about the possibilities, she became aware of a spot on the wall across from her bed. Something about it wasn't right. A four-inch hairline crack in the plaster began to split and grow, expanding until it was over a foot long. She stared for a moment in fascination. Did New York have earthquakes like California? And if so, why wasn't anything shaking?

In a shaft of light from the near-full moon out her window, she watched the plaster at the center of the crack chip away as if something pushed at it from inside the wall. The area around the crack began to discolor, and out of the opening oozed a thick, blood-swirled, black sludge.

"No. No, not again."

A hideous screech cut her thought. The unmistakable stench of burnt flesh accosted her senses, burned her throat and lungs, as the blackness grew and began to spread across her room. Ani looked down to see the scorpion scar on her ankle rip open and excrete the same foul-smelling ooze. A fiery agony crept slowly up her leg and sent shards of intense pain through her body.

Panic immobilized her.

This can't be happening. Then she remembered the warning Xephero had given her in the Web Between Worlds—not to use magic—that it would call the creature.

But I wasn't using magic, she pleaded. *I was only fantasizing about it.*

Ani's heartbeat tripled.

The dark substance consumed everything it touched. It bled out of every crevice now, covering the floor, the ceiling, the window, the walls, until it engulfed the entire room in a blistering blackness.

The searing pain crippled her mind. *No way out. No way out.*

Gemi, it's the Kalb! He's found us! said a frantic voice inside her mind. *The light! Turn on the light!*

Ani grabbed hold of those words like a lifeline. With extreme effort, she focused her thoughts through the pain.

Something about a light. Something she was supposed to do. She didn't understand. "Light?" she rasped. "What light? All. I. See. Is. Darkness." She forced the words out between gasps of agony. Speaking aloud tore at her throat as if the words themselves were knives.

No, said the voice inside, *The lamp! Switch on the lamp beside the bed!*

This time she understood. Fighting with all her strength to free an arm from the sticky goo, she groped for the lamp on the bedside table, nearly knocking it to the floor. She found the switch and just managed to click it on before the bloody black tar engulfed her completely.

A harsh yellow light flooded the room and with it, the blackness dissolved in a sulfurous mist. Ani choked and wheezed as the pain inside her relented.

Panic subsiding, eyes adjusting to the blunt brightness of the lamplight, she scanned the room. The walls were back to stark white. The floor, hardwood slats again. The glass in the window, clear. Not even a hint of the rank smell lingered in the air.

Another waking-nightmare. But this one was different. The pain. The pain was real. The ache in her ankle and legs, the burn of her skin, her sore throat . . . all lingering proof that she hadn't imagined or dreamed it. They were getting worse.

Confused, Ani rose and tested her wobbly legs. She tottered to the bathroom, using the wall for support. In the bathroom, she drank a full glass of water, filled it again and drank another. It felt like she could have kept drinking for days and would still be thirsty.

Not wanting to go back to her bedroom, she shuffled to the living room and found her father asleep on the couch again. Not until this very moment, did she understand—understand why her father always slept on the couch. The master bedroom reminded him of mom. It held all her things in suspended animation, awaiting her return.

Too much there.

Too many memories for him to bear.

Ani sunk into the chair beside the couch. Just being near him calmed her fears.

She sat there for a time, watching her father sleep, wondering if he ever had nightmares like hers. *Maybe it only happened to kids,* she thought. *Maybe when you grow up, you stop seeing frightening things in your sleep that seem so real you can't forget them even after you wake up.*

But, nightmare or not, the Kalb was real and so was the danger.

For the first time since all this "hocus-pocus" began, she didn't wish she could tell her father what was happening to her. Facing the darkness alone wasn't something she wanted to do, but watching him sleep so peacefully there, she realized it was better that he didn't know. It seemed unfair to put him through the worry of knowing, when he could do nothing to protect her from the Kalb. How could he keep her safe when he didn't even believe that such an evil existed?

There was something else to consider too. Something she hadn't thought of before. What if telling her father about the Kalb put him in danger? Could the Kalb harm those around her? Ani knew fathers were supposed to protect their daughters, but maybe it was the other way around now. Maybe it was up to *her* to protect *him.*

When finally she returned to her room, she paused to examine the crack in the wall where it had all started. Not a trace of black. She checked the scar on her ankle. Completely healed. She shuddered at the sense memory. The Kalb had found a way to get to her without using her future memories, and not just in her mind, but in the real world. That thought frightened her even more than the darkness that had nearly devoured her.

It is what we fear most that will propel us to our greatest discovery if we have the courage to dance in the fire and then leave the ashes behind.

-Solamas ✣ *Tome of the Zielfah Ri*

CHAPTER TWENTY-THREE

ϓ

ELI'S RIVER

Ani dreaded the thought of another nightmare, but she forced herself back to bed. It took another hour of staring at the crack in the wall before she managed to close her eyes, but when sleep finally came, she dreamed of her imaginary childhood friend, Eli. She had all but forgotten about the time they spent together playing in the sand out behind the rock shop, building elaborate miniature cities out of rocks and sticks, complete with houses, parks, and even tiny flowing rivers.

It was on the bank of one of those hand-made rivers that Ani now found herself. Eli stood on a rock in the middle, white water rushing around him. He looked different, older than she remembered, taller, like the Eli she saw briefly in the mirror her first night in the new apartment. Not at all the round-faced, chubby boy she used to play with. Only his eyes remained the same—the sparkling mischievous eyes of a fourteen-year-old boy about to play a trick on his kid sister.

Ani wasn't sure she liked the new Eli. The handsome young man who stood before her was unfamiliar and intimidating. If he was really her imaginary friend, why didn't she imagine him the same?

Then all at once she understood. *She* had grown older too. He was her age. Ani smiled. Her imaginary friend had been growing up with her all along. Changing as she changed. The thought seemed comforting somehow.

"Hey there!" called Eli. "I knew you'd come! Recognize it?" His arms stretched wide. "It's our river!" The water rushed around him, violent in its struggle to circumvent the many obstacles in its path.

"Eli!" Ani shouted. "Stay there! Don't try to cross! I'll get a rope!"

Eli was laughing now, or maybe singing, she wasn't sure which. "Gem, watch!" He leapt into the air, and with his feet barely touching the river rocks, skipped effortlessly over to where she stood. "Impressed?" He grinned so wide she could see every one of his perfectly white teeth.

"You could have slipped! You could have fallen in!" Ani was feeling something she had never felt before. The thought of losing him terrified her.

Eli read her thoughts. "You can never lose me, Sis. You know that."

"The currents in the river are dangerous, Eli. You could have—" Ani stopped. It'd taken a few seconds for his words to sink in. He called her sis. He'd never done that before. She froze for an instant, peering at him through new eyes. He did look like her. Why hadn't she noticed it before? He had the same dark hair, the same hazel eyes. "You're . . . you're my brother!"

"Well, it's about freaking time."

"My *twin* brother!"

"Oh, so that's why we look so much alike. Always wondered." Ani pretended to pout. "You're making fun of me."

"Well, if you can't make fun of your sister . . . "

"Are you . . . real?"

"As real as you are."

"But you're—"

"Dead? Yeah, I know, but that doesn't make me any less real."

She stared at him in disbelief. "Why didn't you tell me? All the times we played together. You never said a word about being my brother."

"I knew you'd figure it out sooner or later. Took'ya long enough though. Didn't you ever wonder why I always called you Gem?"

"No. I thought it was because of Dad. He always used to call me Little Gem."

"It's short for Gemini, silly. You know, the twins constellation?"

Ani's voice raised in pitch and volume. "They said you were my imaginary friend. They said you weren't real. They said I would grow out of it."

"And like a dummy you believed 'em. That's why I couldn't come around anymore. 'Cause you started believing I didn't exist. After that, I could only visit you in dreams."

"But even the dreams stopped."

"No, they didn't. You just stopped remembering them."

"You could have said something," she pouted.

"I can't make you remember me, Sis. That's not how it works."

"Well, you could have tried."

"I did. I tried to prove to you that I wasn't just a part of your imagination."

"How?"

He took her hand into his—it was as solid as any hand—and they began to walk along the river. "Sometimes," he said, "when you're upset, or afraid, or experiencing strong emotion, I can get you to hear me, even see me."

"That was you in the mirror, the day we arrived in New York?"

"Yep."

"And that was you I heard when the Kalb attacked me in my room? When he came through the crack in the wall?"

"Oh man. That black stuff. Nasty business."

"How did you know turning on the light would work?"

"I didn't. It was just a hunch. Since he found you by the use of your imagination—when you were picturing fighting Millie with Sophie's magic—I figured he might be using your imagination to get to you. I remembered when we were little, whenever you were afraid of monsters in the dark, Mom would come in, turn on a light, and they'd all go away. Our imaginations can fill the darkness with all sorts of stuff that can't hold up to the light of day."

"So I just imagined the whole thing?"

"Oh no. The experience was definitely real. But the Kalb was controlling you, making you see things that weren't there, so I thought maybe if you saw what really was there, he would lose his hold on you, and it worked."

"But the pain—I didn't imagine that. It was unbearable."

"I know. I felt it too."

"You feel pain?"

"I feel everything you feel. It's just that I can detach myself from it a little easier than you can. This Kalb thing is strong, Gemi. We have to figure out how to keep him from finding us."

"I don't even understand what the Kalb is."

"Neither do I. All I know is he wants to end the legacy and possess the LightBridge for himself," said Eli. "And because we've been chosen as the next heirs in the lineage, he'll do whatever he can to destroy us. And he's getting stronger."

"We?"

"What?"

"You said *we* have been chosen."

"We, as in you and me. It takes two, remember? Double soul?"

"You're . . . you're my second soul!"

"Of course I am," he said, kicking a pinecone into the river. "What did you think I was? A ghost?"

"Well, up until a minute ago, you were just my imaginary friend."

"If I were imaginary, Xephero would have passed us right by. You wouldn't be Zielfah and we wouldn't have been the successors to the LightBridge legacy."

"I don't want to be anyone's successor," said Ani. "Can't we just resign or something?"

Eli stopped, turned and looked directly into her eyes. An effervescent tingle radiated through her entire body. It felt like looking into infinity. Every molecule of her being recognized the soul connection they shared. Powerful. Timeless. Transformative.

Ani finally understood what it truly meant to be Zielfah.

"It'll be okay, Gem. I promise. Xephero will teach us."

"He scares me, Eli."

"Xephero? It's the hair, right? Crazy wizard hair."

"I'm talking about the Kalb."

"Geez, Sis. You really need to get a sense of humor, you know that? I'm dead and I still have one."

"It's not funny, Eli."

His expression turned serious. "I know. The Kalb scares me too, Gemi. Where I am, there's nothing evil. No darkness. No pain or suffering. You get used to that. You get used to things always being true and good. But the Kalb, that's as evil as it gets."

Ani shuttered.

"You wouldn't know this, but from up here everything looks different," said Eli. "We can see the light in things, in people, plants, animals, even in rocks and mountains. There's light in everything that's alive. But not the Kalb. I don't know how it's possible, but there is no light in that thing at all. It is pure darkness."

The thought sickened her. "How do we fight pure darkness?"

"Well for starters, you can't use magic. You can't even picture using magic."

"But I was going to ask Sophie to teach me a protection spell, one powerful enough to—"

"No, Gem, you can't. Xephero warned us about that. It's like a signal he can hone in on."

"I thought when Xephero said that, he meant only my future memories."

"No, *any* use of magic will call the Kalb. Even just the idea of it. Tonight proved that."

"But I think Sophie can help—"

"No magic, Sis. Promise me."

Ani huffed in frustration. "Okay, okay, I promise."

Eli let out a sigh of relief, and they continued up river.

"What about when I talk to animals? Is that magic?"

"No, it's like Kahetay said. It's your gift. Something you were just born with."

Relieved, Ani relaxed a bit, but the Kalb's attack, and the sense memory of pain and fear that came with it, stayed with her.

"So," she said, pressing on, "aside from the 'no magic rule' how do we protect ourselves?"

"The Kalb is powerful I know," said Eli, "but I think we can learn to block him, mentally I mean. We don't need magic for that. With practice, we can stop him from getting into your mind like he did tonight, but that still leaves his physical manifestation, which I haven't a clue how to stop."

"What is that black stuff anyway?"

"As far as I can tell, it's him, just in an altered form. It's the only way he can reach into our world . . . for now. When he's in that state he is limited in what he can do, but make no mistake, he can still kill us."

"What about Dad? Is he in danger? Just by being around me?"

"I don't know, but I don't think so. The Kalb only seems to want us. Unless—"

"Unless what?"

"Well, let's just say, I hope no one gets in the Kalb's way the next time he comes after us."

Next time. Ugh. "I'm just glad you were there tonight to save me, Eli. I never want to go through that again." Ani hugged her brother, wishing this dream of theirs would never end.

"I will always be with you, Sis."

"Promise?"

"Always." Eli stopped beneath a large oak tree. "This is my favorite spot on the river. I come here a lot." He pointed to a perfectly flat rock on the bank, with room enough for the both of them to sit upon. A warm, sweet breeze prodded and played with the leaves above their heads, creating intricate patterns of light that danced at their feet.

Ani smiled at her brother. "It's perfect."

They sat on the bank of the river, peeled off their shoes and plunged their feet into the cool, clear water.

After a long silence, Eli threw a rock into the river. "Our grandfather used to skip stones on the lake near his house in Ohio. Did you know that? He was really good at it too. Best in the county. They used to have contests. He always won."

"How do you know that?"

"He told me so. He's here, you know. His name is Eli too."

"You were named after Grandpa Elijah?"

"Well, it'd be a pretty strange coincidence if I wasn't, considering we have the same name. He's quite the character. You'd really like him, Gem."

"Can you bring him to our river sometime?"

"If he'll come. He likes lakes better than rivers."

They talked for hours about all the places they would go and all the things they would do together when they were finally grown.

It felt good to be there. It felt right. Ani knew she would never be alone as long as she could have this place with Eli. She promised Eli, promised herself, that this time when she woke she would remember him . . . remember all of it.

*If we communicate what is inside us, we will
be empowered by it. If we do not, we will be
depleted by it. We must tend the garden
within if we wish to grow.*

-Naviga ✤ Tome of the Zielfah Ri

CHAPTER TWENTY-FOUR

ᛦ

THE TRUTH OF SILENCE

The clank of spoons on cereal bowls perforated the breakfast table silence. Ani felt numb. Memories of Eli flooded her mind; all the talks they'd had since the day he appeared by her side on her first walk alone to Boulder Dash Hill, all the times they'd met in the sky and flown together in dreams, and all the cities they built of water and sand, every memory came rushing back to her.

Then came the details of their talk by the river last night; the promise she had made to remember. Her imaginary friend, the boy she had called Eli, was her brother. Her twin. Clearly, that was the message of the dream. But was it true? There was only one way to know for sure. She looked at her father across the breakfast table. "What were you going to name him?"

Stan glanced up from his cereal. "What?"

"What were you going to name him?" Ani repeated.

"Who?"

Ani glanced at the scar on her arm. "My twin brother."

He returned to his cereal. "I don't remember."

"Was it Eli?"

His expression hardened. "Who told you that?"

"You were going to name him after Grandpa Elijah."

"What does it matter now? They're both dead."

The pain and resentment in his voice poured out of him like bitter poison. She knew what it all meant. She couldn't deny it any longer. "You wanted it to be me, didn't you?"

"What are you talking about, Ani?"

"You wish I had died instead of Eli!" Ani gasped. She hadn't intended to ask the question. Not like that. But it had been gnawing at her insides ever since Mom had explained the circumstances of her birth . . . since the day she learned her father chose to risk his daughter's life in order to save his son. If Mom hadn't overruled that decision, they might both be dead.

"Why don't you just admit it!" she screamed.

"Eat your cereal," he said in a low snarl.

"No," said Ani staring back with equal intensity. "I have to know. You wanted Eli—"

"Of course I wanted Eli to live! He was my son for God's sake!"

Ani's insides went cold. "You blame *me*."

"That's ridiculous. How could I blame you?"

"I was the one who lived. You hate me for that!"

"Dammit, Ani! That's enough!" His fist hit the table with such force his spoon went flying across the kitchen floor.

She blanched as his rage hit her full force. He took in a quick breath as if to yell again, but instead rose from his chair, picked up the spoon, threw it in the sink and, without saying another word, retreated to the living room.

Ani sat very still for a moment, thoughts screaming in her head. *He doesn't care. He doesn't want me. He never did.*

The leaky faucet over the kitchen sink dripped in relentless rhythm, tapping out the seconds as the chasm between them grew. Back home, in the desert, they'd had the rock shop to bring them together, but they'd never really had each other, had they?

And now, they had nothing.

In the weeks to come, Ani and her father slipped into a solemn silence, broken only by brief conversations about dinner, chores, or school. All Ani could do was hope that her mother's return would dissolve the impenetrable wall that had risen between them, but that hope seemed further and further away with each passing day.

The only word they received from Peru was a single plain white postcard, delivered over a month after Nan and the research team had left New York, saying things were fine. But things at home were far from fine.

On the days she wasn't with CJ, Ani spent her afternoons downstairs with Sophie. It was the only place she felt truly welcome, and it meant she didn't have to go home to face her father until after dark, since Sophie told him she'd see to it that 'Ani stayed out of trouble' after school. Ani appreciated Sophie's intercession. Apparently, it was as much a relief to her father as it was to her, because he never again questioned her coming home late.

Sadly, Ani's 14th birthday came and went without celebration. The poorly wrapped sweater she received from her father seemed more like an apology than a present, but at least he remembered. Nobody else even knew it was her birthday. She hoped beyond hope that a birthday card postmarked from Peru would arrive in the mail. It was her only birthday wish, but it didn't come true.

One particularly gloomy Sunday afternoon a week or so later, Sophie invited Ani to tea. She made cucumber sandwiches, which she called an "English tradition," and they spent the afternoon sharing their past. Ani talked about her home in the Mojave, her friends there, Mobius and her grandfather, Kahetay, and how much she missed them. Sophie spoke fondly of her late husband, Everett, who was "as rare as the northern lights," she said, "a dedicated scientist who believed in the existence of the soul."

Sophie told Ani of her adventures as a nurse in her early years and the lives she saved in Africa. And Solomon, sitting on the old woman's lap, interjected a comment here and there, which only Ani heard, but mostly he just purred as Sophie absent-mindedly stroked his back.

The afternoon seeped by, and all the details flowed together like watercolors on a paper canvas.

Toward the end of the day, as the sun began to set, Ani opened her backpack and removed the folded piece of paper she had been carrying with her a full month now. She had already told Sophie about Xephero and her dreams of the stone city, about the LightBridge and the Mapstone, about the scorpion and the Kalb, but she hadn't yet shared the sketch.

"What have you got there?" asked Sophie, one eyebrow raised.

"Something I've been wanting to show you."

As Ani presented the drawing to her friend, she wasn't sure what she expected, but knew she'd be disappointed if Sophie offered the same vacant reaction she'd received from everyone else.

"I don't know why I waited so long to show you," said Ani, suddenly feeling the delay as a kind of betrayal. "I've been trying to translate it, but—" Ani stopped when she saw her friend's expression.

Sophie stared at the sketch, her face registering a strange mixture of recognition and confusion.

"Sophie? What is it?"

She pointed at the bottom of the page. "These symbols. I've seen them somewhere before."

Excitement surged. "Do you know what they mean?"

Sophie shook her head. "I'm sorry, love, I don't. Where did you get this sketch?"

"I drew it. Well, the rock part anyway. The symbols just appeared there. I did the first set from memory, but not these."

"What do you mean you did the first set from memory?"

"They were on the Mapstone, or I guess, kind of inside it really. It's hard to explain. Xephero, the old man who bought the stone, showed me."

"The man in your dreams?"

"Yeah."

Sophie returned her gaze to the sketch, one hand hovering above it. "And you say these symbols appeared here on their own?"

"This set, yeah, after the first set disappeared. I know how it sounds, but I'm not making it up. I swear."

"I believe you."

"You do?"

She traced the symbols with an index finger as if reading Braille. "Ani, may I keep your sketch for a few days?"

Ani frowned.

"I'll take good care of it. You have my word."

Ani nodded, hesitantly. "What are you going to do with it?"

"I would just like to sit with it a while. I know I have seen these symbols before. I just don't remember where."

"Will you let me know when you figure it out?"

"Of course I will. Thank you for sharing this with me." Sophie smiled and changed the subject. "So how are things with your father? Any change?"

"No," said Ani. "We can't talk to each other. We don't even know how without mom around."

"Your mother will be home soon, yes?"

Ani nodded, her countenance brightening momentarily. "She's coming home. Next week. But I don't think I can stand one more day of this, let alone a whole week. I hate what's happening to us. Whenever I try to talk to him I only make things worse. It's like he's turned into someone I don't even know. Ever since we left the desert, he's been . . . " Ani stopped, not really knowing how to finish the sentence. She didn't understand any of it.

Sophie retrieved Ani's red sweat jacket from the ornate wooden coat rack in the corner and draped it over Ani's shoulders.

"Your father comes from a place where there's always sun," she said. "Here, the buildings scrape the sky and we walk mostly in their shadows. If one is not careful, those shadows can seep into the soul." She glanced at the majestic grandfather clock that stood near the front door like a royal sentinel. "Come. There's something I would like to share with you." Sophie took Ani's hand and led her out the front door, down the hall and into the old elevator with its cast iron latticework and swollen wood-slatted floor.

Ani grimaced. "This thing feels like it could break any second."

Sophie grinned. "It's been around longer than both of us."

"That's what worries me."

"Learn to trust what has withstood the test of time, Ani Jasper." She swung the steel latticework gate to its catch and pushed the "Up" button.

Ani watched the tarnished brass indicator above the door as it slowly inched its way past one, two, three, four . . .

"Your father is facing his own challenges," said Sophie. "Perhaps he needs time to work out how he feels about all these changes."

"I get that," said Ani, "but he doesn't care how I feel. I'm going through it too."

The brass indicator stopped just past seven, pointing to what looked like a fancy letter R. When the elevator halted Sophie said, "Some passages appear dark upon first glance." She slid open the elevator gate to reveal a dim hallway with a narrow door at its end. Golden light seeped through its cracks. "But the destination—" she said, leading Ani to the end of the hall, "—can be glorious."

Sophie pushed open the door and they emerged into a blaze of color.

Ani caught her breath. She stood before the most spectacular garden she'd ever seen, blooming in celebration of spring, enchanted by the glistening amber light of the setting sun.

"It can be that way with the distance between two people as well," Sophie continued. "It can look dark and hopeless until someone opens a door."

"I can't open the door, Sophie. He won't let me."

"The door you need to open, my dear, is in your own heart."

Ani fell silent, wishing she fully understood what Sophie was saying, but it all just seemed like pretty words to her. Real life didn't work that way.

Sophie picked a bright yellow daffodil from a terracotta tub of wildflowers and offered it to her young friend. "This," she gestured to the vibrant life growing all around her, "is how I keep the shadows at bay."

"It's the most wonderful thing I've ever seen," said Ani. "I wish—" Again she stopped herself.

Sophie took her hand and led her through the garden to the alabaster wall at its edge. "I think if you could see inside your father's heart, you'd find he's just as scared as you are."

"Scared? Of what?"

"Of losing your mother. Of losing *you*. Maybe even of losing himself."

"All I want is for him to be happy."

"Then tell him how you feel."

"I've tried. He won't listen, Sophie. It doesn't matter what I say."

The old woman pointed to the distant horizon and said, "The sun is setting, is it not?"

Ani nodded.

"And tomorrow it will rise again. The morning will come and there will be a new day with all its infinite possibilities. Don't ever forget that, my dear." She took in a deep breath and let it out slowly. "Breathe in the day, Ani. You can create magic with breath and intention."

Ani took in a breath, feeling a little silly, but then, without understanding why, she began to feel better.

"What will you choose?" asked Sophie. "To see only that the sun sets? Or to believe it will rise again tomorrow? It's all in the choosing."

Ani watched the sun sink slowly behind the jagged silhouette of the city skyline. "You're saying there's still hope?"

"There is."

"But what do I do?"

"Just tell him you love him. That's always a good start."

Ani nodded.

"Go on now. He'll be wondering where you are."

"No he won't. He doesn't care if I'm there or not."

"Well, Solomon will certainly be wondering where I am. It's getting close to dinnertime. Go talk to your father. I'm just going to take a moment to say good-bye to this beautiful day."

Ani turned to go and then stopped and glanced back at the old woman bathed in the fiery glow of a perfect sunset.

"Sophie?"

"Yes love?"

"He told me to tell you he doesn't like brussels sprouts."

"Who?"

"Solomon."

*Change. It's not only inevitable, it is preferable
to the alternative—stagnation. Learn this and
cease to resist.*

-Xephero ✤ Tome of the Zielfah Ri

CHAPTER TWENTY-FIVE

༓

SOPHIE'S SONG

The day of her mother's return, Ani woke at dawn feeling better than she had in months. After breakfast, her father asked her to take the garbage out and she didn't even mind. Then he actually offered to help her with it.

"No, I got it, but thanks." Ani smiled. Things were already getting better.

In the hall, she ran into CJ.

"What are you smiling at? Did you win the lottery or something?"

"Even better," said Ani. "My mom's coming home from Peru today. We're meeting her at the airport."

"Ehh. Two parents instead of one. That just means twice the trouble. I'd rather win the lottery."

"Not me. Mom's coming back. Everything's going to be better."

"Yeah, good luck with that."

"Thanks," said Ani without hesitation. Nothing was going to ruin her good mood today.

On the way to the airport, Ani could feel the excitement bubbling up inside. Mom would have amazing stories to tell about the Amazon and the Guardians. The three of them would talk around the dinner table like they used to. And everything would finally get back to normal. They'd be a family again.

Even dad's sullen mood had begun to lighten. She knew once Mom was home, he would be back to his old self again.

They got to the airport early and waited almost an hour for her mother's plane to arrive and disembark, but when the passengers finally filtered into the baggage claim area, Nan wasn't among them.

When her father inquired, a flight agent from the airline said Nan J. Jasper never boarded the plane in Lima, and they gave up her seat to standby. The woman said this as if it meant nothing, as if it wasn't devastating news.

"What about the rest of the team?" asked her father. "Did the others get on the plane? There were seven of them."

"What are their names?" said the flight agent. "I can check the manifest."

"I don't know their names. She never told me their names. They would have had seats together though. Booked by the University. Dr. Nathaniel Hayden. Columbia University. Can you just tell me—"

"I would need their names, sir."

"Yes, of course. I understand."

Then seeing her father's dejection, the flight agent's tone changed. She looked at the monitor and whispered, "I can tell you this. The standby tickets we gave away in Lima were a group of seven seats, all together, which usually means they were booked at the same time."

"And my wife's seat was one of the seven? Nan J. Jasper?"

She checked the monitor again. "Yes. 8B. Right in the middle."

"So none of them got on the flight," he mumbled.

"What about the next flight?" said Ani. "If she missed this flight wouldn't she be on the next flight?"

"If they arrived late in Lima they could have been bumped to the next available seats, which would be . . . " she checked the screen, "8268 bound for LaGuardia. That flight are already enroute, and . . ." she hit a few keys, "there is no passenger with the name Jasper on board."

"Can you tell me when the next inbound flight from Lima will be arriving?"

"Not until Monday, I'm afraid."

"Thank you. We won't take up any more of your time," said her father, sounding like the life had just drained from his spirit.

"Dad, I need your cell phone. I left mine at home."

"Ani, she won't answer."

"You don't know that! We have to try!"

"Ani—"

"I *need* to call her. Dad, please."

"Alright." He grabbed his phone off its belt clip "Call Nan," he said into the phone, and then handed it to Ani.

She waited while it rang. It went straight to voicemail. Ani listened to the sound of her mother's sweet words and then after the beep, said, "Mom? Where are you? We're at the airport. You weren't on the plane. Please call us back when you get this and tell us that you're alright. I love you. I miss you."

"Ani." Stan took the phone from his daughter. "You don't think I haven't tried calling her? I call her every day, hoping beyond hope that somehow the call will go through and she'll answer." He shut off the phone, and put it back on its clip. "We're going home now."

"Something's happened to her. I know it," cried Ani, on their way back from the airport.

"You don't know any such thing," said her father. "Don't let that imagination of yours run wild."

"You don't even care. Not about me, or Mom."

"Ani, you know that's not true."

"Then do something!"

"Your mother's just been delayed, that's all." He unlocked the front door to their apartment, entered and hung the truck keys on the hook above the hall table. "There could be a thousand reasons why she didn't catch that planc."

"Yeah, including something being wrong."

"Nothing's wrong," he said, opening the refrigerator. "Don't you have finals to study for?"

"She's in trouble, Dad. I know it. We have to do something."

"You heard the airline. She'll probably be on Monday's flight."

"And if she's not?"

"Then I'll call the University. Maybe they extended they're stay. Nan did say they had the option of extending the expedition. Maybe things are going so well that they decided to work a few more weeks."

"Then they would have sent word to the University. To Professor Hayden. Call them."

"It's Saturday, Ani. Dr. Hayden won't be in his office until Monday morning. We can talk to him then."

"What if that's too late? What if she's lost and dying somewhere in the Amazon jungle? Would you even care?"

"Now stop it! I know you want your mother back. I want her back too. But there's nothing we can do right now, so drop it."

Ani opened her mouth, but her father held up his hand.

"I mean it, Ani. Drop it!"

"Fine." She marched out the front door, crossed the hall to CJ's apartment and rapped her knuckles hard on the door. No one answered. She knocked again.

A man's gruff voice snarled through the closed door. "What do you want?"

"Can CJ come out?"

"She's busy." Heavy footsteps k-thunked away.

Ani stood alone in the hall, staring at the mahogany wainscoting that ran the length of the corridor. Tiny detailed faces carved into its molding seemed to come alive, each with its own personality, its own sad story of how it got stuck in the wall. Ani sighed. She didn't want to know. She didn't care about anyone else's story anymore.

She just wanted out of her own.

Crossing back to her apartment, she pushed open the front door and peeked inside. Her father sat at the computer desk in the living room, focused on the rock shop's financial statements. She crept by unnoticed, slipped into her parent's bedroom and quietly shut the door.

At the closet, Ani tugged one of her mother's cashmere sweaters from its hanger, brought it up to her nose and inhaled deeply. The scent of jasmine-rose filled her senses, drawing her mother's essence closer than any photograph could.

"Mom, where are you?" The words came out in a choked whisper.

She stood in front of the antique vanity her mother had insisted they bring to the city, and dusted the surface with a finger, inviting a memory. They used to sit in front of this mirror nearly every morning, Ani stroking her mother's gold silken hair with a silver hairbrush that was both too big and too heavy for her tiny hands. It was one of their favorite things to do.

Why did everything have to change? They were together. They were happy. They were a family.

And now . . .

Ani sat and gazed into the mirror, searching for any trace of her mother's face, but all she saw was her own boring reflection. She hated her dark eyes and olive skin, her annoying rosy cheeks, and her coarse brown hair that always looked messy. It was obvious to Ani where she got her plain features. Her father had the same dull qualities about his face. How many times had Ani wished she'd inherited her mother's fair skin and golden hair? Couldn't she at least have gotten her mother's crystal blue eyes?

The vanity's top center drawer slid open with a slight tug. Alongside a matching comb, Ani found her mother's silver hairbrush, worn and tarnished with age. It seemed smaller in her hand now, but the feel of it brought back so many moments frozen in time. A tear fell onto the soft white bristles. Slowly, Ani reached up, pulled free the hair-tie at the back of her neck, and began to brush her own hair in long, slow strokes. The tears rolled down her cheeks.

Without warning, the bedroom door flew open with such force it crashed into the wall behind it, crumbling the plaster.

"What are you doing?" yelled Stan. "I didn't give you permission to be in here!"

Her father's voice was so harsh Ani jumped out of her seat, toppling the little stool.

"Dad, I—"

"What are you doing in here?" he repeated.

"Nothing." She wanted to tell him how much she missed Mom. She wanted to ask him if he felt the same way. Lost. Empty.

"If you're not going to study," he said sternly, "then I want you to catch up on your chores. You can start with the laundry." He pointed to the mound of dirty clothes in the hamper.

Ani grabbed the basket and headed for the door.

When she heard her father call her name she stopped, hoping he might make amends. Then maybe they could finally talk. But he didn't say a word, just tossed a bottle of laundry soap and a jar of coins on top of the heap.

"Dad—"

"Get going. It's Saturday. If you wait too long, the washers will all be full."

Ani ran out of the apartment and all the way down to the basement. She threw the clothes on the concrete floor. *Why won't he listen? Why can't he see how hard this is for me? He doesn't even care.*

"Hello there."

Ani whirled around to find Sophie standing in the doorway of the laundry room clutching her own hamper.

"Are you alright, child? Your face is as red as one of my summer tomatoes."

"Sophie, I don't think I can do this."

"Do what, love?"

"All of it. Living here in the city with my dad. School. My mom half way across the world."

Sophie glided over to Ani. "I understand. A girl needs her mother."

Ani could hold it in no longer. "She wasn't on the plane. None of them were. What if something's really happened to her?"

"Oh, you mustn't think like that, dear one."

"I can't help it," cried Ani, tears filling her eyes again. "I want my mom back."

"Of course you do."

"What am I gonna do, Sophie? What if she never comes back?"

"You and your mother are very close, aren't you?"

"We were until all this anthropology business started up. We did everything together."

"Sometimes when we love someone very much, we are surprised, and maybe even a little hurt, when we find out they have dreams that do not include us."

"She's my mom. How could she just leave me all alone?"

"She didn't, love. She left you with your father."

"He doesn't want me. He never wanted me. He wanted Eli!"

Sophie blinked. "Eli?"

"My twin brother. He had to die so I could live." Ani sobbed uncontrollably. "They should have saved him, not me!"

"Oh child, shhhh." Sophie took Ani into her arms and, gently rocking her, began to sing. Her sweet voice echoed faintly off the empty concrete walls of the basement . . .

> *"A song to dry your tears.*
> *A song to soothe your fears.*
> *This melody surrounds you.*
> *Lifts you and enfolds you.*
> *To heal a heart that's broken.*
> *In truth these words are spoken . . .*
>
> *You are loved. You are loved. You are loved.*
>
> *Take my hand, I'll guide your way.*
> *No truer friend, you'll find this day.*
> *We'll walk from darkness into light.*
> *The shadows but a memory of night.*
>
> *Beyond any doubt, beyond any dream.*
> *Beyond all that is or has seemed . . .*
>
> *You are loved. You are loved. You are loved."*

Over and over she sang this simple tune until all Ani's tears were dried.

"Now, shall we clean some clothes?" Sophie asked after a long soothing silence. "I always find it helps to clear my head when I take the time to do the laundry. Can't rush it, you see. It is what it is and you have to just let it be. Wash. Rinse. Dry. It has to go through all the cycles."

Sophie started separating the colors from the whites. "It was better in the old days, when you had to do the work yourself. No machines to do for you, robbing you of the teachings."

Ani rubbed her eyes. "I love you, Sophie."

"I love you too, dear one."

So they stuffed the t-shirts and jeans, socks and underwear into the washers, pushed the coins in to start, and waited for the buzzer to go off.

And while they waited, Sophie taught Ani her Love song.

When life doesn't go according to planned, we must look for wisdom, strength and purpose along the unchosen way.

-Naviga ✢ Tome of the Zielfah Ri

CHAPTER TWENTY-SIX

ᴕ

THE UNCHOSEN WAY

Monday arrived, as did the next flight from Lima, but Nan Jasper wasn't on it, nor was her research team.

They drove straight from the airport to the university to meet with Professor Hayden, but when Ani pulled her passenger side door open, her father insisted she stay in the truck.

"No. I want to go with you."

"Stay here." He shot her a stern look. "No arguments. I'll be quick."

He returned 10 minutes later, slipped behind the wheel, and sat staring out the window at the parking lot.

"Dad? What did Professor Hayden say?"

"No news."

"That's it? No news?"

"He said the option of an extension was part of the expedition agreement. There's nothing they can do until the extension time has lapsed."

"How long is that?"

"Three weeks."

"Three more weeks?"

"I showed him this." He handed Ani her mother's postcard.

"What did he say?"

"That they were in touch with the research team the first week they were there, but haven't heard from them since. He said the lack of communication was expected, due to the remote location." Stan started the engine. "All we can do is wait."

After that, the days all melted into each other. Every day they called the airline and the university, and every day they were told the same thing. No news.

When the last day of school came, Ani searched for CJ but never found her. After the final bell rang, Ani breathed a sigh of relief. No more homework, no more tests, *and* no more Mad Millie. She had managed to stay clear of Millie and her gang for weeks now. Another half hour and she'd be home free.

Because she stayed after to help Miss Witcott take down her bulletin boards, most of the students had already left by the time Ani went to clear out her locker in the silent corridor.

Her thoughts automatically turned to her mother. They hadn't received any word as to why the research team remained in Peru. The University continued to assert that there was nothing to be alarmed about, but Ani knew differently.

Now that school was out, Ani planned to ask her father if they could go to the university together and get them to mount a search-and-rescue effort. Ani wasn't going to stop until they listened to her.

She finished cramming the contents of her locker into her backpack and slammed the yellow metal door.

"Well, look who's happy to be leavin'. Thought you'd get away bruise free, eh?" Mad Millie loomed over her.

Ani looked left and then right.

"No one around to do your fightin' for ya this time."

Out of the corner of her eye, Ani saw the Silver Chain Girl and five others stroll out of the girl's bathroom.

Millie smiled. "Just in case you were thinkin' about bolting."

"I wasn't," said Ani trying to recall everything CJ taught her. Duck. Punch. Trip. Kick. Her hands clenched into fists.

Millie leaned in and said in a low, controlled tone, "I'm gonna kick your ass."

Ani tried to stand a little taller. "Go ahead and try."

Millie threw a look to her friends. "Oooh, the snip thinks she can fight now." The gang laughed.

"You know," said the Silver Chain Girl, "you're 'bout to have a whole lotta hurt."

"Where do you guys get your material?" said Ani. "Watch a lot of old gangster movies, by any chance?"

Millie casually strolled over to the drinking fountain and took a long sip of water.

Impatience took hold, twisting Ani's will. She wasn't going to get out of it this time, but she wasn't about to stand around and wait for it either. "Let's just get this over with, Millie."

The Silver Chain Girl laughed. "Hear that Mill? The snip's askin' for it. Let's not disappoint her."

All at once Millie swung around and spit a mouthful of water into Ani's face.

Caught off guard, Ani's hands went up too late. As she tried to wipe her eyes, she felt Millie's booted foot plunge into her stomach. She doubled over in pain, trying to gasp, but her lungs refused to take in air. Millie didn't wait for her to recover. Another kick sent Ani crashing to the concrete floor. A sharp stab shot through her left shoulder, but she stopped herself from crying out.

Ani looked up through blurry eyes as the corridor began to spin.

The lockers went transparent . . . then the girls. Then the entire school rippled away as if someone had thrown a stone into a reflection pool.

No, Ani thought. *Not here. Not now.*

With all her will, she tried to block the oncoming future memory, but failed. The scene around her disintegrated, replaced with a hazy vision of a point in time yet to occur.

Ani quickly took in her new surroundings. The Wakefield? Why had the vision taken her home? She stood in the hallway outside her apartment. A sinister calm pervaded. Then something told her to turn around, like the touch of an icy finger on her shoulder.

The door to CJ's apartment stood wide open. As Ani walked the 20 feet or so of hallway between them, the walls contorted, the floor warped, and her legs grew weaker with every step. She found CJ sprawled on the carpet in the entryway, bloodied and unconscious.

"CJ!"

Ani knelt beside her friend to feel for a pulse. She felt three faint beats of CJ's heart and then . . . nothing.

"Oh God, no! CJ. Don't die. Please don't die."

No amount of pleading would change the fact. CJ was dead. Blood pooled around her head. She'd been hit from behind, but by the look of it, that was only the final blow. The cuts and bruises on her arms, legs, and face proved she had put up a good fight . . . and lost.

Ani gasped and the vision evaporated.

As her eyes refocused and the yellow metal of the lockers again solidified, she knew only one thing. CJ was in trouble and she had to help her. If she didn't get to her soon, her friend, her only friend, would be dead.

At once, she saw Millie's foot thrust forward again, but before it bruised her ribs, Ani grabbed it. With one quick snap, Ani twisted it with all her strength. A shriek of pain reverberated through the corridor as Millie went down hard, nearly landing on top of her. In a flash, Ani rolled out of the way and Millie hit the concrete beside her.

Within seconds, Ani was back on her feet. The girls who'd been watching closed in. Eyes flashing to the ground, Ani scooped up her backpack and swung it around her to widen the circle. The girls stepped back, but didn't break formation.

"What is that?" said the Silver Chain Girl in complete revulsion. She pointed to the place on the floor Ani had just been.

A crimson-black mass formed before their eyes.

Ani caught the foul stench of burnt flesh. With a sinking feeling she realized the Kalb had tracked her future memory of CJ.

"Is that blood?" one of the younger girls asked.

"Keep away!" screamed Ani. "Don't touch it!"

The girls began to back away as they watched the dark pool spread at an unnatural rate.

The Silver Chain Girl recoiled. "That's not blood!"

"It's just a trick," yelled Millie, still on the floor holding her ankle.

"No!" yelled Ani. "Millie! Don't let it touch you!"

"Get her!" Millie screamed and two of her minions caught Ani's arms, holding her in place.

Ani labored against them, trying desperately to reason with them, but the girls' attention was elsewhere. Ani followed their gaze as they stared in horror at the black ooze. The Kalb had chosen Millie as its target.

"Millie!" yelled Ani. "Get up! Get out of its path!"

The warning came too late.

In an instant, the Kalb had utterly encircled her. Millie screamed as the putrid tar slithered up her arms and legs. She fought against it, trying to get free but the dark sticky substance grew thick and rubbery, holding her to the floor. The circling girls shrieked in terror.

"Help me!" yelled Millie. "Get it off me!"

The girls, some screaming, some crying, didn't move.

Like black quicksand slowly taking her down, Millie began to sink into the floor.

Ani struggled to break free, but they still had her arms. "Let me go! I have to help her!"

The Silver Chain Girl yelled over the screaming, "Let her go!" but the horrified girls didn't hear her.

"It's taking her!" Ani shouted. "Can't you see, it thinks she's me!"

"What is that stuff?" yelled the Silver Chain Girl. "What's happening to her?"

Ani's insides rioted. "She's going to die if you don't let me help her!"

The Silver Chain Girl yanked her friends away. "Back off! Let her help Mill!"

By the time the girls let go, the Kalb had Millie's entire body in its grasp. Tears streaming down her face, arms flailing above her head, her terrified screams had become unintelligible.

"Millie! Give me your hand!" Ani thrust out an arm. "Millie!" she repeated, "take my hand!" Ani couldn't stretch any further. She knew if she got too close, the Kalb would have them both. "Millie! Please! I'm trying to help you!"

Finally, Millie heard Ani's plea. Gasping her last breath before the black ooze took her under, she made a frantic grab for Ani's hand and took hold with such desperate force she knocked Ani off balance.

Ani went down fast. Face first.

Gulped in air to hold her breath. Last-ditch attempt to clutch the final moments of life.

One thought. Only one thought raced through her. *If I die, Millie dies! CJ dies! I can't let this hap—*

Mid-plunge, Ani just . . . stopped.

One second, freefall, the next, frozen.

For a moment, her brain could not make sense of it—suspended in mid-air, caught between the last minute and the next, hovering over the Kalb's dark oily surface.

Confusion lasted but an instant. Clothes taut around her middle like a sling—her brain began to put it together. One of the girls must have caught the back of her t-shirt. Someone just saved her life.

"Don't let go!" yelled The Silver Chain Girl. "Don't let Mill go!"

Ani reached with both hands and tightened her grip on Millie.

Pulled from behind, her shirt stretched as far as it would go, Ani yanked as hard as she could but Millie didn't budge.

"She's not moving!" yelled Ani, flashing a wild look at the rest of Millie's gang. "We need help!"

"Help us pull, dammit!" screamed the Silver Chain Girl.

Ani felt hands go around her ankles.

All six girls heaved. Once. Twice. Millie moved only a few inches.

Another heavy tug and her face cleared the surface. Mill gasped for air. Inch by inch, they managed to drag Millie free of the Kalb's grasp until her entire body lay limp on the corridor floor, dripping in black sludge, and smelling of rotted corpses.

The girls held their noses as Ani and the Silver Chain Girl hovered over Millie.

"Mill! Are you okay? Can you hear me?"

"I can hear you, Jo," she said, still trying to catch her breath. "Stop yelling. I'm not deaf."

"Can you sit up?" asked Ani.

"I think so." She wiped tar from her eyes, and they helped her to a sitting position.

The instant the Kalb realized it failed to capture its prey, it quickly retreated back into the floor, and a moment later the foul-smelling substance was gone. Not even a trace of it remained on Millie's clothes.

"What the hell was that?" gasped Millie with a knife-edged gaze aimed at Ani.

"I . . ." Ani hesitated. "I don't know."

"You're lying."

"No really. I don't know." It was the honest truth. She had no clue what the Kalb actually was, or where it came from. All she knew was that Millie nearly just died in her place.

Millie got to her feet with the Silver Chain Girl's help. "You better start talkin' or else—"

"I can't tell you what I don't know!"

"Oh, you know, and you're gonna tell me what the hell just happened or you're gonna wish you'd never come to this school."

"Already do." Ani's eyes flashed another 360. The girls no longer had her surrounded. They gathered around Millie, leaving Ani the perfect chance for escape. All she cared about now was getting to CJ. She grabbed her backpack and sprang from the group, heading straight for the double doors.

"Get her!" yelled Millie.

A few of the girls tore after her, but they were no match for Ani's long stride and natural speed. By the time she'd crossed the schoolyard and slipped through the hole on the chain link fence, they'd given up pursuit.

Ani headed straight for the Wakefield, praying it wasn't too late, her vision of CJ's death playing over and over in her mind.

*We are conditioned to believe that our lives are
shaped by what happens to us, but in truth, life
is shaped by what happens inside us. The power
of our thoughts and beliefs can change any
experience into a transformational awakening
or a prison of our own making.*

-Naviga ❖ Tome of the Zielfah Ri

CHAPTER TWENTY-SEVEN

ㅜ

THE GIANT'S ASSAULT

A gut-wrenching scream came from inside CJ's apartment. At
least that meant she was still alive. Ani ran the length of the
corridor in seconds and stopped at her door. "CJ!"

Another scream, louder this time, and more shrill, shook Ani
to the core. Dropping her backpack in the hall, Ani burst into the
apartment.

"CJ!" she cried, darting from room to room. "CJ! Where are
you?"

Another scream, even more blood curdling than the last.

Ani smashed through the kitchen door and found CJ pinned to
the floor by a giant of a man. Thrashing and shrieking like a
trapped wild animal, CJ fought the intruder, her arms turning
purple under his fierce grip. The giant shot Ani a vicious glance,
his angry eyes piercing a mass of matted black hair.

Without thinking, Ani lunged at the two of them, screaming
and hitting, but the giant swatted her away like some annoying
little insect, sending her sailing across the kitchen floor. With a
thud, her back hit the refrigerator door, rattling the glass inside.

In an instant she was on her feet again. She vaulted onto the
man's back, hanging on by his hair.

"Let go of her!" Ani screamed. "Leave her alone!"

The giant bolted upright and roared, trying to scratch the pest off his back. In that moment of distraction, CJ got free.

The giant grabbed Ani's arm, nearly dislocating her shoulder, and slammed her to the floor. Through squinted eyes, Ani saw CJ snatch a cast-iron skillet from the sink and—THWACK!—clobbered him over the head with it, which only served to make him angrier. He turned on CJ, his bloodless lips stretched tight over rotting teeth. She dropped the pan and ran, but the giant didn't chase her. Instead, he whirled on Ani.

Sprawled on the linoleum, every inch of her body aching, Ani willed her limbs to move. She scrambled backward, shuffling along the floor until she felt the kitchen cabinets at her back. A hideous grin marred the giant's face as he closed in. If she had to die, at least she'd die saving a friend.

"Hey pizza-face," CJ called from the doorway. She leaned in, chucked an ashtray at the giant's head and took off running again. This time the giant took the bait. He roared her name, the sound of it reverberating in the empty kitchen, and chased her through the apartment.

Ani stumbled to her feet—too fast—fell against the counter and braced herself to let the dizziness pass.

Equilibrium returning, she searched the kitchen in a frenzy for anything she could use to defend herself, opening every cupboard and drawer. All empty. Nobody lives here. Then she flashed on an idea. She'd seen it on the way in. It just might work.

She dashed toward the living room window, leapt into the air, and grabbed two fistfuls of crushed green velour. Down came the entire floor-length curtain, rod and all, and Ani with it, piling into a dusty heap on the stained beige carpet.

Bursting free, Ani gathered the drapery into her arms, sprinted through the apartment and found CJ cornered in the master bedroom. Ani snuck up behind the colossal man and threw the mountain of thick material over his head.

In a flash, CJ snatched the curtain cord and jumped onto the man's back. Caught off balance, he crashed to the floor like timber in a forest.

In a maneuver fit for a rodeo prize, CJ roped the giant as he struggled to get free, wrapping the twisted cord round and round, first his head, then his legs. As she tied his feet with the last of it, the giant bucked her off his back and she rolled to safety. The man's muffled threats penetrated the folds as he fought against CJ's expert restraints.

"Where did you learn to do that?" asked Ani, impressed.

"It won't hold him for long. We need to get out of here. Now!"

The two girls bolted toward the door.

"Wait," yelled CJ, "my jacket!"

"Leave it!"

"No way. It's the only thing that's mine." CJ bolted back to her bedroom, grabbed her leather bomber jacket and ran. Following Ani out the front door, she slammed it shut behind them.

They dashed to the end of the hall, heading for the fire escape, but CJ stopped short of the window. Ani knew something was wrong. CJ never hesitated.

"You okay?"

"So," said CJ, in a dazed tone, "you finally got to meet Joe."

"*That* was your foster father?"

CJ tried to answer but only gibberish came out. Her eyes started to roll back in her head.

"Hold on," said Ani, putting an arm around CJ just in time to keep her from collapsing. "I'm gonna get you some help." She pushed the button to call the old elevator.

"No hospitals, Ponch. They'll take me back. I can't . . . I can't go back." CJ slurred the words but Ani understood. "Promise me. No hospitals. No cops."

"Okay," said Ani. "I promise."

Ani banged on the door of apartment 13A, trying to keep CJ upright. Sophie answered wrapped in a midnight blue velvet shawl that made the blood red ruby around her neck stand out like a beacon in the night.

"Please Sophie, we need your help. CJ's hurt."

"Oh dear, come in! Quickly!" They laid CJ on the sofa. "What happened?" Sophie put a gentle hand on CJ's forehead just as she lost consciousness.

"Can you help her?" asked Ani, breathless.

Sophie brushed the hair from CJ's face and gasped at the bruises. "We need to get her to the hospital, Ani. And a police report will need to be filed. What hap—"

"No! They'll take her away. They'll put her in some awful group home or worse. CJ would rather die than go back there."

"Better a group home than this."

"No, Sophie. I promised. No police and no hospitals."

"Ani, she needs to be checked by a doctor."

"I promised. I can't break my promise to her. That's what everyone has done. Her whole life people have lied to her. I can't."

"I understand, but—"

"There must be something you can do. You said you used to be a nurse."

"Oh my dear, that was long ago."

"Please. Just try."

The corners of Sophie's mouth tightened.

"Please," pleaded Ani. "I know you can help her."

Sophie peered at CJ.

Ani could feel her reluctance. "If you call anyone, we'll just leave before they get here."

Sophie sighed in resignation. "Alright. I'll see what I can do." She sat on the edge of the sofa. "For the moment. Then we shall see."

Ani wiped her eyes. "Thank you."

"Well," she said, examining CJ's arms and legs, "there doesn't seem to be any broken bones. But there could be internal injuries." She rose, shaking her head. "I have something to take the swelling down but without a proper examination we won't be able to determine—"

"Can't you use your magic to heal her?"

"Ani, you must understand—"

"You told me you once used a healing spell on Solomon. You said it worked. Can't the same spell work for CJ?"

Sophie took in a deep breath and let it out slowly, studying the fierce intent on Ani's face. "I'll do what I can. But I'm going to call a good friend of mine. She's a doctor." Sophie raised a hand to halt Ani's protest before it was spoken. "She has a private practice. I can tell her no documents. No forms. CJ's injuries won't go on record. For now. But we will need to talk about this later." She glanced at the clock, and then disappeared into the kitchen.

Ani collapsed in a high-backed chair and listened to Sophie place the call. The words exchanged seemed to adequately convey CJ's wishes.

When Sophie finally returned, she carried a makeshift first-aid kit and a tall glass of clear liquid.

"This is for you," she said, holding the glass out to Ani. "I want you to drink the whole thing."

"What is it?"

"Water. Nothing more. But water is what you need right now, dear one. You've been through an ordeal. It will help ground you. Drink."

Ani obeyed. The instant the cooling liquid hit the back of her throat she began to feel better. She hadn't realized how thirsty she was.

Sophie watched as she drank, waiting for her to empty the glass. "Good. Now, you must tell me exactly what happened."

While Sophie tended to CJ's cuts and bruises, Ani related the whole story, from her run-in at school with Mad Millie's gang and Millie's near-fatal encounter with the Kalb, to the battle with the giant in CJ's apartment.

Sophie listened patiently, and when Ani's story concluded, she asked an unexpected question.

"You said you ran back to the Wakefield to help CJ. How did you know she was in trouble?"

Ani hesitated.

"Does this have something to do with your visions?"

Ani stared at her magical mentor, wide-eyed. She'd never told Sophie about the future memories. How did she always know?

"I too have premonitions sometimes," Sophie admitted, "when someone I love is in trouble. It's not as uncommon as you might think."

"But mine are not normal premonitions," said Ani. "Kahetay calls them future memories. I see things as if I were remembering them but they haven't happened yet."

"And these future memories of yours, they always come true?"

"Always. Usually within minutes or hours of having them."

"And the . . . Kalb," said Sophie, struggling to recall the unfamiliar word. "Is this the creature you spoke of when you told me about the scorpion incident in the desert?"

"Yes. Xephero says the Kalb can track me whenever I see the future. I saw CJ in my vision. That's how I knew she was in trouble. And that's how the Kalb found us at the school. My vision saved CJ but almost killed Millie. How is that fair?"

"All gifts have a shadow side, love. 'Tis the way of things."

"But what if Millie had died? It would have been my fault. How could I live with that? Knowing I'm the one who—"

"Millie is fine," interrupted Sophie. "That's what's important. For now, let us focus on the task at hand. After we have done all we can for CJ, we will explore ways to shield you from the Kalb's psychic reach."

Ani looked at her friend's cuts and bruises. "I thought Millie was cruel, but anyone who could do this to another person—"

"Joe is just a lost soul," said Sophie. "One of many."

"You didn't see the look in his eyes. He really meant to kill us."

"When so much hate clouds your vision, you see nothing but your own pain."

"He'll come looking for us when he gets free. I know he will. It's not over."

"You'll be safe here," said Sophie. "Joe's afraid to come near this apartment. Thinks I'll put some kind of hex on him."

"That would be good. Can you do that?"

Sophie gave Ani a disapproving look. "Stay here with CJ. I'll be a moment." She stood.

"You're not going to call the police, are you?"

"No. You have my word." She disappeared into the kitchen.

Ani felt something crunch in her back pocket as she sat beside CJ. Her mother's postcard. She'd carried it with her since her father handed it to her in the parking lot at Columbia University. Now she pulled it out and smoothed the crumpled edges. She had read it a hundred times, but her mother's words sounded different now, almost like a plea for help.

Dear Stan & Ani,

Arrived in one piece. We were met in Cuzco by a Guardian tribesman and led deep into the heart of the Amazon jungle to a place they call the "rim of the world." I'm beginning to think it is. Nothing here is what it seems. I'm afraid there are no earthly explanations for the impossibilities we now behold.

When we arrived at the Guardian's village, we were not greeted with the reception we expected as invited guests, but it is understandable that they would be wary of "the strangers from beyond," as they call us. Shortly after we set up camp, they posted sentinels at the perimeter. We have not yet been permitted to venture beyond the boundary. Interaction has been minimal. Our Peruvian guide is doing his best to translate, but it is slow going.

We're very alone here. Very isolated. They don't allow modern technology so we have no link to the outside world. I will send this postcard with our guide when he returns to Cuzco for supplies and hope it gets to you. But please don't worry. Everything's fine.

I send my love and will try to write more soon.

Miss you terribly.

I wish I could reach out and hug you both.

If only.

Love, Nan

Ani caught her breath as she reread the message. She hadn't noticed before, but now, as she studied the words more closely, there seemed to be a hidden meaning in them. What if mom had sent them a coded message? What did she mean by, 'Nothing is what it seems?' Was she trying to tell them something was wrong? Words now stood out as if they were written in bold type. Isolated. Alone. Impossibilities. Afraid. No link to the outside world.

Ani thought for a moment. *Not permitted to venture beyond the boundary? Interaction limited? Guards at the gate? Sounds like they're prisoners. And when somebody you love says 'everything's fine, don't worry,' the first thing you do is start worrying. Why would she tell us not to worry unless there's something to worry about?*

Another detail she hadn't noticed until now; a strange circular symbol, inked in red, had been drawn on the lower left-hand corner of the postcard. It had not been done with the same black pen her mother used to write the note, that was clear, and part of the mark overlaid the words as if it had been added after the fact, but why? What did it mean? And if mom didn't put it there, who did?

Sophie entered carrying a bowl of steaming hot water, swirling with herbs and spices. Ani looked up.

"Ani dear, what is it?" Then seeing the crumpled card in her hands, she said. "Your mother's postcard?"

Ani nodded. "Something's wrong. I know it. But no one will believe me."

"You sound certain."

"I am. At least I think I am."

"You've had a vision about your mother? You've seen her in some kind of danger?"

"That's just it. I can't separate them from my fears anymore. I keep seeing these horrible scenes, but it could just be—"

"Your imagination?"

Ani's shoulders drooped. "That's what my dad says it is."

Sophie soaked a washcloth in the herbal solution and laid it over the bruises on CJ's forehead. "Never underestimate the power of your imagination, my dear. It's a profound tool for accessing your magic."

"I know. That's how the Kalb got into my room the other night. I wasn't using magic, but I was imagining it. Do you think my mom—"

CJ stirred on the couch. Sophie took the postcard and set it on the coffee table. "I need you to put your concerns for your mother aside for now. My doctor friend will arrive soon. I want to do as much as we can for CJ before she gets here."

Sophie lit four candles and placed them in a circle around CJ. Then she stepped into the circle carrying a chalice of water.

"Are we going to do a spell?" asked Ani.

Sophie nodded. "I will need your help." With her free hand, Sophie sprinkled salt in the four directions uttering words in a language Ani had never heard. Then, with a graceful gesture she invited Ani into the circle. "Sit. Take hold of CJ's hand," she commanded. "And now mine."

"Sophie, I can't do the spell with you. The Kalb will—"

"It'll be alright, my dear."

Ani's eyes flashed around the room looking for any sign of blackness. "I can't."

"Still yourself, child. Release your fear. You are safe in this place. My home has a powerful protection spell around it. "

"As powerful as the Kalb?"

"Nothing can harm you here."

"Are . . . are you sure?"

"Yes. Now close your eyes," she began. "Clear your thoughts of all distractions."

When magic comes from a place of compassion, profound healing is possible. There is no greater source of power than the human heart.

-Xephero ✦ Tome of the Zielfah Ri

CHAPTER TWENTY-EIGHT

♈

LIFE AND DEATH

Obeying Sophie's command, Ani closed her eyes and tried to empty her mind, but it was impossible. She snuck one eye open to keep watch.

"Now, in your mind's eye," continued Sophie, "picture CJ completely healed. See her bruises fading, her cuts mending, internal damage repairing itself."

A sharp scent permeated the air, but to Ani's relief, it wasn't the smell of burnt flesh. Sophie had lit eucalyptus incense.

Ani began to hear flute music—a sweet, floating melody—and wondered if it was only in her head. It soothed her in ways she didn't understand and finally, she began to relax. Then, through this music, she heard Sophie's melodic voice again.

"I hereby request the activation of the elements,
Earth, Fire, Water, Air, for the purpose of healing
this young girl."

With one eye still open, Ani saw Sophie throw some kind of powder on a brick of glowing charcoal. It flared up and then began to smolder. She quickly closed her eyes as Sophie began to speak again, her voice taking on a low resonant tone:

"Spirit of the elements, keeper of the flame.
Heal this young girl of all injury and pain.
Let her wounds be mended by the power of will and choice.
This magic now created, with these words, by my voice.

And let this wish be granted for the greater good of all.

What's wrong will be put right again in answer to my call.

Heal her now and set her free.

And as I speak, so shall it be."

Sophie reached down and grasped CJ's hand, completing the circle once again. "Now Ani, say the last two lines aloud with me thrice."

"Heal her now and set her free.

And as I speak, so shall it be."

Ani chanted with Sophie.

"Heal her now and set her free and as I speak, so shall it be.

Heal her now and set her free and as I speak, so shall it be."

With the completion of the third and final round, the air in the room began to change, becoming denser somehow, harder to breathe. Ani felt buoyant for a moment, as if the gravity in the floor had weakened. Then, as though someone had suddenly opened a window, a fresh, clean breeze gusted through the living room. Ani opened her eyes.

The smoke from the incense curled about and then split to form two separate swirls. Ani glanced at her friend, amazed to find the ghostly image of two CJs floating just above her, one with cuts and bruises and the other entirely free of wounds. An instant later, the wounded CJ disintegrated, and the healthy one rushed back into the real CJ lying on the couch. She woke with a start.

"CJ!" Ani cried.

"Wh-where am I? What's going on?"

"You're downstairs, in apartment 13A," answered Ani.

"The witch's place? I can't believe you brought me here." CJ tried to get up but promptly fell back onto the couch.

"Slow down, dear," said Sophie. "Be still. Collect your strength."

"She healed you, CJ."

"It wasn't my magic that healed her," said Sophie, "it was yours. The bond between you is strong. It provided a powerful vehicle for healing. I've never felt anything quite like it."

"What's she talkin' about?" CJ's eyes narrowed on Ani with a dagger-stare. "I'm not gonna be a part of no magical mojo."

Ani grinned. "Too late."

"What'd you do to me?"

Sophie retrieved the white cloth that had fallen to the floor when CJ sat up. "How do you feel?"

"Strange."

"You should take it easy for a bit. You've been through quite an ordeal." Sophie checked the bruises on CJ's arms. The deep blues and purples were already starting to yellow, a clear sign of healing. "Astonishing."

CJ yanked her arm away and then rubbed her sore shoulder.

"It seems you'll be fine," said Sophie. "But we still need to have the doctor take a look at you."

"No hospitals."

"Yes, Ani told me as much, but—"

"Forget it. I won't go."

"You won't have to." Sophie snuffed the candles and placed them, along with the smoldering charcoal burner, on a serving tray. "I think I'll clean up in the kitchen and leave you two to talk," she said, gliding out of the room. "It would seem you have some things to discuss."

CJ looked at Ani. "What did she mean by that?"

"You can't go back there, CJ. To Joe I mean."

"Figured that one out for myself, Ponch." CJ picked the postcard off the coffee table. "Maybe I could stay with you guys, just until I can figure something out. Do you think your mom and da—"

"My mom never came back."

"What?"

"It's been almost three weeks since she missed her plane and no one's heard anything."

"Are they looking for her?"

"No. They say the lack of communication was expected."

"What does your dad say about it?"

"He doesn't care and neither does the university. They act like she's just on some kind of extended holiday."

While Ani and CJ talked, Sophie brought out tea and sandwich squares. The girls devoured the first batch and helped themselves to seconds when Sophie returned with another plateful.

Finally, after Sophie went back to the kitchen with a second empty plate, CJ turned to Ani, a determined look on her face.

"Well, are you going?"

"Where?"

"To Peru, stupid."

"My dad would never let me—"

"So."

Ani peered at CJ, finally comprehending what she was suggesting. Across the room, Solomon, who had been sleeping peacefully, now woke and stared at Ani from his spot on the rug.

"Look," CJ continued, holding up the postcard as evidence. "Your mom misses you. That much is obvious. She wants to be with you. And you want to be with her, right?"

"Yes, but—"

"Then who cares what your dad thinks?"

"But I don't have a plane ticket. I don't have money. I don't have . . . directions."

"You don't need anything but guts."

"Sorry, fresh out. Will stupidity do?"

"I'm serious."

"So am I." Ani stood and began to pace. "You expect me to get on a plane, fly to Peru, and somehow find my mother in the middle of the Amazon Jungle? With what? A compass?"

"Yeah, that's what I thought." CJ grabbed her jacket off the floor.

"What."

"You just don't have what it takes."

"If you mean I'm not stupid enough to think I could survive over there on my own, then yeah, you're right," said Ani, throwing up her hands. "I don't have what it takes."

CJ rolled her eyes. "You're pathetic."

"Thanks."

"You're still waiting for the punch instead of fighting back. For once in your life, Ponch, take a stand. Do something that doesn't make sense. Do it because it means something to you even if nobody else approves."

Ani's gaze fell to the floor. She wished she possessed even half of her friend's courage and determination. "I can't, CJ. I can't do it."

"Fine. Whatever. But if our situations were reversed, I sure as hell wouldn't be sittin' on my butt, waiting for the worst to happen."

Ani heard the tremor in CJ's voice and finally understood. If CJ had known even for an instant that her own mother really wanted her, she would have gone clear around the world to be with her. Ani sighed. She wished she could change what was happening . . . to both of them. With all her soul, Ani wished things could be different, but she was powerless to do anything about it. "I'm sorry," she whispered, and truly meant it.

As Sophie entered, Ani looked up, tears shining in her eyes.

"Ani dear, would you be a love and carry that to the kitchen for me. I'd like to talk to CJ for a moment." Sophie pointed to the large bowl of steeping herbs on the coffee table. "Careful, it's still quite warm. Use the towel."

Ani nodded, took the over-flowing bowl and, making sure not to spill its contents, carried it slowly to the kitchen.

"Thank you, dear" she heard Sophie call from the living room. "Just set it on the counter."

In the kitchen Ani paused a moment, staring into the dark liquid as the water swirled in a whirlpool of herbs. The steam rising from the surface clouded her vision. Root shavings and dried leaves began to form a picture like clouds drifting into shapes on a summer day. Ani saw a rock column jutting up in the center of an immense chasm. Surrounding the stone monolith was a wall of fire licking several hundred feet into the air. And trapped at the top was—

"Mom!" Ani screamed. The sound of the bowl shattering on the tile floor exploded inside her head.

"Ani," cried Sophie, running to her aid, "are you alright?"

Snapping back to reality, Ani saw the ceramic bowl in pieces, its contents slowly spreading across the floor. She gasped. "Oh no. I'm so sorry." She dropped to her knees and began sopping up the mess with the towel. "I didn't mean to—"

"Ani, it's fine."

"I'll clean it all up and I'll pay for the bowl. I promise!"

"Don't concern yourself, love. I have others." Sophie reached for her hand. "Come." She led Ani over to the kitchen table. "You're shaking. Sit. Take a deep breath and let it out slowly."

Ani did as she was told and then buried her head in her hands. "I'm so sorry."

"It's alright, dear. Truly. You saw something, didn't you? A vision? In the water?"

Ani nodded.

"What did you see?"

"I saw Mom . . . alone, trapped, surrounded by fire. Sophie, she was dying!"

"Are you sure?"

"This time it was real, not my imagination. I'm positive."

"Then you must talk to your father, make him understand."

"He won't hear anything I say. You know that."

"Ani. Listen to me." Sophie produced the folded Mapstone sketch from her handbag. "I figured it out—why these symbols look so familiar—and I think it has something to do with your mother."

"My mother?" Ani's jaw clenched.

"I know where I've seen this writing before. I have a friend named Nathanial Hayden. We met because of this building, in fact. He was the man who sold it to me."

"I don't understand. What does the previous owner of the Wakefield have to do with all this?"

Sophie unfolded the sketch and pointed. "These markings, or some just like them, are etched into the bottom of a drawing he made in Peru three years ago, but he didn't put them there."

The tiny hairs at the back of Ani's neck stood on end as Sophie spoke.

"He claimed they appeared after the fact, just like yours. His drawing is of a peculiar rock formation a mile or so north of Machu Picchu."

"Machu Picchu?"

Sophie nodded. "I've seen his drawing myself. It's framed and hanging in his office. But I never would have put the two together had it not been for this." She produced a crumpled copy of a newspaper called *The Record.*

Ani took the paper.

"It's the Columbia University newspaper," Sophie explained, opening it to an article on page four. She pointed to a photograph of a man sitting at his desk. "That's Nathanial. Look at the picture on the wall behind him."

Ani squinted at the large framed drawing behind the man.

"Here, use this," said Sophie, holding out an old-fashioned magnifying glass just like the one Ani always used in the rock shop back home.

With the magnification the convex lens provided, the photograph revealed its secrets in a complex arrangement of monochromatic dots. She could now make out the symbols at the bottom of the framed drawing on the wall. Ani caught her breath. They were the same! They were even in the same place on the drawing, but they spelled out something different.

"Did he translate it?" Ani asked, breathless and hopeful. "Does he know what it says?"

"No. He has been trying to decipher the language ever since his return. Until I showed him your sketch the other day, he had never seen another sample of it."

Ani read the caption under the photo. "Wait, it says Professor Hayden? But that's—"

"Yes," said Sophie. "Your mother's mentor and my friend are the same man. Dr. Nathanial Hayden."

"Are you sure?"

"I spoke with him, Ani. I showed him your sketch. He believes these symbols are be the language of the *Los Guardas.*"

"The Guardians? That's what my mom's doing in Peru. Studying the Guardians."

"I know. Nathaniel told me. He would have gone with them if not for the injuries he sustained on his last visit there. Something on that trip changed him. He was never quite the same after he returned."

"So he sent my mom instead? Even though he knew it was dangerous?"

Peering through the magnifying glass again, Ani shifted her focus from the wall behind the man, to the man himself. His face was strangely familiar, but it was the archaic suit he wore in the photo that gave it away. "Sophie, I recognize this guy. I've met him."

"You have?" Now it was Sophie's turn to be surprised.

"I met him on the train. He gave CJ a fifty-dollar bill to stop stealing. Two actually."

Sophie smiled. "That sounds like Nathaniel. He's on a personal crusade to reform the corrupted youth in this city."

"This is too weird," mumbled Ani.

"Ani, I don't think any of this is coincidence."

"What do you mean?"

"Remember the pinwheel I showed you on our first visit? Everything's connected. You. Your mother. The Mapstone. The Kalb. Xephero. Professor Hayden. The sketches. Peru. The Guardian tribe. It would seem this whole affair has been orchestrated somehow."

"Orchestrated?"

"I asked Nathaniel about your mother's expedition. He said the funding came from a private, anonymous source, and there was only one stipulation. One condition." Sophie reached out to touch Ani's arm. "The Guardian research grant was contingent upon your mother's participation."

"What? But that doesn't make any sense. She's not a famous anthropologist. She's just a student. Why would they—Oh God." A fire of sweltering panic burned through Ani. "It's a trap!" She shot out of her chair. "What I saw in my vision was real! My mom's going to die. I have to do something! I have to get to her!"

"Ani, wait. I think this actually has more to do with you than it does your mother."

"I have to find her, Sophie. I have to save her! This is all my fault! If I hadn't brought home the Mapstone, none of this would be happening. That's when it all started! I can't just sit around and wait for the worst to happen. My mom's going to die unless I do something about it!"

"Slow down, love. Take a deep breath."

"No! What CJ said was true. I'm always doing what everyone else thinks I should do. For once in my life I'm going to do what I need to do!" Ani marched into the living room and found CJ on her way out the door. "CJ. Wait!"

"I'm outta here, Ponch. The old lady called a doctor. No way I'm stickin' around for that." She slammed the door behind her.

Sophie hurried into the living room. "Ani, let's talk about this. There are things to consider—"

"No." Ani paused with her hand on the doorknob. "I'm sorry, Sophie. I can't. I have to do this." She opened the door and dashed out. "CJ! Wait up!" Ani ran to catch her in the hall.

"Look Ponch, I appreciate the backup and all, but I have to get out of Dodge, lay low a while, at least 'til Joe stops lookin' for me."

"You said I should go find my mom. Does that mean you're willing to help me?"

A mischievous smile spread across CJ's lips. "So then, you're up for a little adventure?"

Ani let out a groan. "The last time someone asked me that, my whole life changed, and not for the better."

"Well then, this is your chance to make it right."

"So you have a plan?"

"I always have a plan," said CJ.

Ani followed her through the lobby and out the front door.

"I know someone who can make it happen," said CJ. "He owes me a favor. A big one actually."

"What are you going to do?"

"Just leave the details to me. I'll get'cha to the airport, and I'll get'cha on the plane, but after that, you're on your own. Okay?"

The muscles in Ani's stomach contracted involuntarily as the reality of what she was about to do sunk in.

"Meet me out front in a half hour," said CJ. "If you need anything, now would be the time to get it."

"What about my dad?"

"Just tell him you're going to a party. Today was the last day of school. He won't question it."

They stopped at the bottom of the marble stairs. Ani peered up the steps. "I've never lied to him before."

"Well, it's about time then."

"But leaving him . . . without even—"

"You're not leaving your dad, you're just going to be with your mom for awhile, that's all. You can send him a postcard when you get there."

Fear clouds perception, yes, but the real danger is doubt. If one doubts the self in a crucial moment, failure is possible. The Light Master must banish doubt long before conquering fear, or the journey will be very short.

-Xephero ✣ Tome of the Zielfah Ri

CHAPTER TWENTY-NINE

ᵞ

SOLOMON'S FAVOR & THE GYPSY'S GIFT

Alternating tremors of insecurity, fear, and dread rumbled Ani's insides. The buzzing in her head wouldn't stop. Was she really going to do this? In her room, she found her backpack waiting for her. She had dropped it out in the hall when she ran in to save CJ and was relieved to see it back on the hook next to the door where she always kept it. But how did it get there?

She emptied the contents of its main compartment onto her desk. Books, spiral binders, pencils and pens spilled out. She didn't bother cleaning up the mess.

Ani quickly toppled the laundry basket of folded clean clothes onto the bed, separated out her socks, underwear, t-shirts and jeans and then stuffed them into her backpack. She tied her favorite red sweat jacket around her waist. She'd never been on a trek without it and she wasn't going to start now.

Spotting her wooden treasure box by the bed, she picked it up and opened the lid. She found the crisp one hundred dollar bill safe in its hiding place. For the first time since she found the Mapstone, she was grateful she had sold it.

She stuffed the money into her jeans and then set the open treasure box on her bed. Taking the photo from where it was propped on her dresser, she stared at her grandfather standing on the edge of the cliff. Ani let out a heavy sigh. That's where she was now. Standing on the edge of a cliff, getting ready to jump.

She suddenly realized she'd never asked Kahetay what happened directly after the picture was taken. Now she wished she had.

After flattening the photo between her palms, she placed it in one of the side pockets of her backpack and added the cell phone, fresh off its charger. It probably wouldn't work where she was going, but it might come in handy if they ran into trouble before they left the country. She retrieved the Roman coin her mother had given her before leaving for Peru and added it to her treasure box collection. On top, she placed the folded Mapstone sketch and the notebook paper with the first message.

Closing the lid, she set the tiny latch and nestled it amongst her clothes in the bottom of her backpack. Before zipping it up, she threw in her new polka-dot-less raincoat and a baseball cap her father had given her with the words 'Geological Society' silk-screened on the front. On top of these she put one of her barely used spiral-bound notebooks from school.

In the largest compartment, she found three candy bars and an unopened bag of beef jerky. She quickly checked the smaller pockets: gum, a ball of string, two pencils and a pen, a few paper clips, and a couple of rubber bands. Not much, but she couldn't risk going to the kitchen for supplies and raising her father's suspicions. It would have to do.

On her way out of the bedroom, her eyes fell upon a small glass bowl sitting atop her dresser. It held the three polished stones she took from the rock shop the day they left for the city. She scooped them out and stared at them in her palm, remembering happier times. A deep sadness welled up inside and nearly took her over. She shook it off, pocketed the tiny stones, and grabbed her backpack.

"What have you got there?" came a voice from the doorway.

Ani jumped. "Dad!"

He indicated her pocket.

"Oh. Um, just some stones from the rock shop."

"Ah. Glad you kept some. I did too. Just to remind me that it's not gone . . . although it feels that way sometimes."

"Yeah, I know," Ani mumbled.

He nodded to the backpack. "Found it in the hallway outside. Not a good idea Ani, leaving your things around for others to take."

"Oh. Yeah, sorry about that. I was in a hurry. Thanks for bringing it in." She looked down at the overstuffed pack.

Her father raised a brow. "Going somewhere?"

"A party. Last day of school thing. Sleepover." The lie sounded easy rolling off her tongue, but it tasted bitter.

"I think it's customary to ask your father first."

Ani felt like saying, *Oh, now all of a sudden you want to act like a parent?* But she didn't. She couldn't risk stirring things up. She just said, "So, is it okay?"

"Will there be adult supervision?"

Ani nodded. "A girl from school, Jenna—her parents. The party is at her house." That part wasn't a lie. Jenna was having a last-day-of-school party. Ani just wasn't invited.

"Where is it?"

"Not far. Just up the street. A bunch of us are walking over together." Ani hated being dishonest. It felt like the worst kind of betrayal.

"Jot down the address and phone number before you go."

"I will."

"Wow, my little gem's going to her first New York party." He sounded genuinely pleased. "Good for you, Ani. This move might have been wrong for me, but I think it was right for you. You're growing up and that's . . . a good thing, even if it scares me a little sometimes."

"Dad."

"I know this year has been tough on you, your first year in a public school, all the changes, and I know I haven't been there when you needed me—I've been too focused on my own problems—but you got through it and I'm proud of you." He fumbled around in his pocket. "I have something for you. Call it an end-of-the-school-year present."

He produced a tiny, palm-sized, cylindrical glass bottle. In it were four thumbnail-sized, untumbled rocks, ablaze with sweltering color. "Fire opals," he said, "raw." He held them up to the light. "These are especially vibrant."

He mumbled the last words. Ani could tell his thoughts were far away for a moment. He let the tiny bottle roll into his palm and then wrapped his fingers around it, making a fist.

"I've been carrying this with me since we left the rock shop. I guess I just didn't want to let go."

Ani thought of the three polished stones that had been in her pocket for the last few months. "Yeah," she said, "I know what you mean." She didn't want to let go either. And she didn't want to leave, but she had to.

"Well, I think it's time," he continued. "I . . . think you should have them now." He opened his hand.

214

"Dad, you don't have to give me a present."

"I want you to have them. I think maybe they were meant for you all along."

"Thanks," she said, accepting the gift with an aching heart.

"You'll always be my little gem, but I know I have to let that go too."

Ani's resolve wavered. Guilt rushed in to squelch her courage. Her backpack suddenly weighed half a ton. It sank slowly to the floor. How could she just leave without saying anything? She stared at him, open-mouthed, ready to tell him the whole truth.

"I know. I know. I shouldn't talk about such things," he said. "You're a teenager now. You have to be cool."

If he only knew how much she *wanted* to talk to him. But she couldn't. He would stop her from doing what had to be done. "Dad," she said, almost in a whisper, "I love you."

"I love you too, sweetheart."

I can't do this. I can't leave . . . leave him here all alone. Maybe if he knew the truth about Professor Hayden and the research grant, he would come with her. Maybe he really did care and was just hiding it like Sophie said.

Ani cleared her throat. "Dad?"

"Yes?"

"What if I had proof that Mom's really in trouble? Would you—"

"Ani, we've talked about this." He suddenly sounded very tired.

"But I found something out that—"

"We're following university protocol. Let them handle it. You know the plan. If we don't hear anything by the time their extension is up, we'll take the next step."

"But that might be too late!"

"We're sticking to the plan. End of discussion. Now wash up. I've made spaghetti."

Ani blinked. "Spaghetti?"

"Yeah, I want you to eat before you go to the party. No telling what kind of junk food they'll have there. Oh, and we need to talk about some . . . situations you might not be aware of."

"What situations?"

"This is the city, Ani. They may ask you to do things you don't want to do."

"Like what?"

"Like drugs."

"Daaad, you don't need to tell me to stay away from drugs. I'm not stupid."

"Yes, but well, sometimes it's hard to say no when the pressure's on. Just be strong, okay? Use common sense. Do what you think is right even if nobody else agrees. Don't let anyone tell you how to act or what to think and you'll be fine."

Ani knew he'd been talking about the party, but his words resounded in her mind and heart if he'd given his blessing for what she was about to do. "Thanks Dad, I will. I promise. And don't worry about me, okay? I can take care of myself."

"Yeah, you've always been good at that, haven't you?" He patted his daughter on the back. "I raised an independent girl."

Ani glanced at the clock. Ten minutes. She had to meet CJ in ten minutes.

"I left the noodles boiling on the stove. Dinner in five," he called as he hurried to the kitchen.

Ani sat on the bed, feeling like a rat trapped in a cage. *CJ won't wait. That much is certain,* thought Ani. *She'll just assume I chickened out. I have to get a message to her.*

Maybe I can help."

"Solomon!" Ani jumped up to open the window.

The fat cat bounded in, pouncing first on the desk and then on a chair before landing gracefully on the bed.

Hey girly-girl, said the cat. *Thought you might be in need of some assistance.*

"How did you know?"

A little bird told me . . . right before I ate it.

"Solomon!"

Kidding. Sort of. He licked his chops. *Okay, so give me the abbreviated version. What's up?*

"I have to meet CJ downstairs in ten minutes."

Uh huh.

"But my dad's out there making us dinner."

Uh huh.

"And we are leaving town without his permission."

Mmm, sneaky transgressions. Me likes.

"Can you get a message to CJ that I will be a bit late?"

Nope. But I could provide an effective diversion for your escape. It's one of my specialties, said the cat, puffing himself up.

Ani's nose crinkled. "What kind of diversion are we talking here?"

One that'll allow you to slip out the front door undetected, but you have to be in cat-stealth mode or it won't work.

"I can do that."

Good. Get ready.

"Solomon?"

The tabby stopped and glanced back at Ani.

"Do you, um, think I'm doing the right thing?"

'Mmmm, 'the Right thing' is sooo subjective. Sophie says for humans, it's more about 'the right choice.' Answer this. Are ya doing what you feel you really need to do?'

Ani nodded. "I think so. Yeah."

Wull then, how can it be wrong?

"But then why do I feel so bad?"

I think feeling bad is actually a good thing . . . for humans anyway.

"What?"

Deception, even when necessary, is not something humans should be comfortable with. For cats it's different. Deception is an art, an innate gift we are all born with. It is a cat's solemn duty to explore and express creative deception whenever possible, and we're good at it. But I'm the best there is. Solomon turned a circle and came to sit beside Ani on the bed. *Are we done? Can we commence with the fun?*

"Um, can I ask you one more question?

If it's all the same to you, I'd rather skip the Q&A and get to the mischief making part of the program.

"Just one more. I promise."

Alright, but make it quick. I have places to go, dogs to torment.

"Sophie says all cats have a secret name, different from the one we give them. Is that true?"

Yup, said Solomon.

"Well, I was wondering if . . . "

You want to know my soul name?

"Soul name. Yes, but I'll understand if you don't want to tell me. If it's something I'm not supposed to know."

Wull I trust ya' won't go blabbin' it all over the neighborhood.

Ani held up a hand. "Promise."

Okay then, my soul name is Nin-kiya."

"Nin kie yah," Ani repeated.

It means the supreme ruler of all things great and small, said Solomon, standing tall.

"Wow."

Just messin' with ya. Geez girl, d'you swallow a gullible pill at a pool party, or were you just born this way?

"This is all new to me," said Ani.

The cat scratched an ear and said, *We creaturekind don't attach meanings to names like you humans do. Nin-kiya is just a cluster of sounds strung together that resonate with the origin soul that connects my nine lives."*

"Wait. Cat's really do have nine lives?"

Of course. But not the way you think. Our nine lives are not consecutive, they're simultaneous.

Ani gave a blank stare.

You know, all at once.

"I know what simultaneous means, I just don't understand how—"

Right, okay, quick clarify and then we're outta here. Ready? There are nine Solomons running around in the world. All with different names. All me. Follow? You are two souls in one body, we are nine bodies with one soul, and Nin-kiya is the name of our origin soul. It's kinda like a secret password so we can all recognize each other. No cat-fights among soul-kind. Big no-no in the creature world. Get it?

"Got it," said Ani. "I like your soul name, Solomon."

Keep it safe, said the cat. *You may need it someday.*

Ani stood. "I'm honored that you shared it with me."

I'm honored that you asked. Solomon jumped off the bed and headed for the door. *Now that we've gotten the obligatory bonding out of the way, are you ready for some thrilling heroics?*

Ani leaned over her desk, took up a pen and wrote on a piece of notepaper: *Dad, really not hungry. Sorry. And please don't worry about me, ok? I'll be just fine. I promise to remember everything you've taught me. I love you, Ani.* Then she turned to Solomon. "All set."

Okay then, let's put my superior diversion skills to use.

"Thanks, Solomon, for everything. I'm glad you're my friend."

I trust our paths will cross again, said the cat, *when the* time is right, and with that, he dashed into the living room, placing himself directly in the line of enemy fire.

From the door, Ani could hear her father yelling, "Hey! How did you get in here? Damn cat. Shoo!"

She peaked through the crack in the door. Her father grabbed a broom from the hall closet and chased Solomon into the master bedroom. Her brave friend knew he'd be cornered there, but it gave Ani just the opportunity she needed. She took her backpack and slipped quietly out the front, leaving the door ajar so Solomon could make his escape.

"Hathanya wa nua, Nin-kiya," she whispered in Azimaran, and dashed to the stairwell.

When Ani arrived downstairs, CJ was already waiting out front with what might have passed for a car had it possessed a top, front and rear bumpers, and a lid for the trunk. Since this was not the case, however, Ani thought it looked more like a boat with wheels. She wondered what other parts of the car were missing.

On the hood of what she later learned was a 67 Mustang convertible sat Chet, an eighteen-year-old with a patch over one eye, an earring in the shape of a sword, and a knotted bandana holding down more hair than any one human should have on his head. Ani had never met a pirate before, but if pirates existed, surely this was one.

She paused for a moment in the lobby, not really sure she wanted to hitch a ride on a pirate ship just then but, she thought, if that's what it takes to find her mother, so be it. She summoned her courage and walked bravely toward the Wakefield's front doors.

"Ani?"

A gentle touch on her shoulder accompanied the soft voice.

Ani froze, poised to run.

"Wait. It's alright dear."

Sophie. Something made Ani turn and face her friend. It tugged at her heart to hear the love in Sophie's voice. She knew then, if she had left without saying good-bye, she would have regretted it.

"I wanted to say good-bye," said Ani, "really I did. I just didn't know if—"

"If I would try to stop you?"

Ani nodded.

"I'm not here to talk you out of it, dear one, although I want to." Tears filled Sophie's eyes. "I don't fully understand why, but I believe you need to do this, not just for your mother, but for yourself. This much I know; the road that lies ahead of you will be difficult, but it will set you on the path of your destiny."

"That's what I'm afraid of," mumbled Ani, so filled with fear and uncertainty that she thought she might be sick any second.

"Ani, I didn't get a chance to say this earlier, but something happened last night that convinced me you have made the right decision—so much so, that after you're gone, I give you my word, I will explain to your father what you have done and why. I will try to make him understand the importance of this journey."

"You will?"

"I promise."

"What changed your mind?"

"Last night your grandfather, Kahetay, visited my dreams."

"Yeah, he does that sometimes."

"I did not know he was a dream walker," said Sophie. "It is a very strong magic."

"What did he say? In your dream I mean."

"He said that you would be leaving soon and that I must let you go, and I must help your father to let you go. In the dream, I began to cry, and my tears became a river between us. I told him I was afraid for you. You're still so young. How can I protect you if I let you go? And you know what he said? He said that he loved you more than anything in this world, but he was not afraid for you. He said you have been preparing for this journey your whole life. He said you're ready."

Ani lowered her gaze to hide the tears misting her eyes. "I don't feel ready."

"He also said that there will be guides along the way and they will help keep you safe."

"I hope he's right."

"Stay your course, dear one. Trust your instincts. From that trust will come your greatest strength." Sophie unclasped the chain from around her neck. "But if you should lose your way, I want you to hold on to this." She pressed the tear-shaped ruby into Ani's palm. "It has always helped me find my way home."

"Sophie, I can't take this."

"It's only a loan. It has been given before, and always it has found its way back to me. Take it, love, and be well."

Ani blinked back tears. She threw her arms around the old woman and whispered, "I love you, Sophie." and then quickly turned to go.

"I will miss you, child," called Sophie as Ani pushed through the Wakefield's front doors.

"I'll miss you too," said Ani, hopping into the back seat of the pirate ship. "If I survive."

I have always thought; if I let go, I lose. If I open my heart, I risk heartache. If I accept what is, then nothing will change. I have discovered that the precise opposite is true. If I let go, I gain everything, if I keep my heart open, there is no pain . . . and the instant I accept what is, true change becomes possible.

-Naviga ✣ Tome of the Zielfah Ri

CHAPTER THIRTY

PIRATE TIES

All night they drove the New York streets, stopping a dozen times for what Chet called "necessary accoutrements"—once in the kind of seedy neighborhood where taking out the trash at night could be detrimental to your health, and several times in dark industrial looking areas where they were led into back rooms filled with electronic equipment, circuit boards, computer components and all manner of digital contraband. Each time, small packages were picked up and thrown into the trunk, and large amounts of cash changed hands.

On the last stop, Chet met with three men he referred to as "business associates," during which, two plain manila envelopes were exchanged. When they got back in the car, CJ gave Chet two fifty-dollar bills and he handed her the envelopes.

"We're even now," he said.

CJ nodded.

"Good luck getting out," said Chet. "If they come askin', I'll tell 'em you went to Pendejo, Mexico."

They both laughed at some shared private joke.

Ani didn't want to know.

Chet started the car and they were on their way again, this time headed, finally, for JFK International Airport.

"Where'd those fifties come from?" whispered Ani.

"None of your business," whispered CJ.

"They're from that man on the train, aren't they? The one who paid you to stop stealing."

"So what if they are?"

"I thought you said they were f—"

"You can shut up any time now."

"I'm glad you didn't spend them, CJ. Prof. Hayden was right. You're using the money to change your life. To change *our* lives."

"Prof. Hayden?"

"That was the name of the man on the train."

"How did you work that one out?"

"Sophie showed me a picture of him in an old newspaper. Prof. Hayden is the man who sent my mom to Peru."

"What?"

"Strange coincidence, huh?"

"I don't believe in coincidences," said CJ, dead serious.

"Neither do I," said Ani. "It's all linked in some way. I'm just not exactly sure how . . . or why."

By the time they reached the airport, it was nearly dawn. Ani and CJ stood on the curb and waved good-bye as Chet drove off.

"It was nice of him to take us all this way," said Ani.

"Nice?" CJ sniggered, turning toward the entrance. "Not a word I would use to describe Chet. He owed me. I collected. That's all."

"So, all those times you disappeared after school—?"

"I was working for Chet."

"Doing what?"

"You really need to mind your own business, you know that? One of these days it's going to get you in a crud-bucket of trouble." CJ looked down at the ruby necklace Ani now wore. "What's that?"

"It's from Sophie."

CJ's eyes grew wide. "Is it real?"

Ani clutched the ruby protectively. "Forget it, CJ."

"It's huge. Do you realize how much money we could get for that thing?"

"It's only a loan. She didn't actually give it to me." Ani tucked the ruby inside her shirt.

"Too bad. Could've made our trip a whole lot cushier."

When they entered the International Terminal, Ani gazed up in awe at the sheer magnitude of the structure. CJ grabbed Ani's arm just in time to yank her out of the path of a large man rushing toward an exit. "You need to watch where you're going, space-brain.

What's with the slack-jaw? You act like you've never seen this place before."

"I haven't."

"I thought you were here to see your mother off."

"I was. But all I remember is the pattern in the carpet."

"Well, you need to keep your eyes straight ahead now, got it?" CJ glanced behind her. "On second thought," she said pushing Ani down onto a nearby bench, "stay here." She held up a hand as Ani started to protest. "Stay," she repeated as if talking to a puppy, and then crossed to the ticket counter.

Waiting for CJ to return, Ani began to feel a new exhilaration. The atmosphere inside the international terminal buzzed with excitement. Passengers and packages, servicemen and suitcases going in every direction. Faces. Voices. So many separate lives in so many separate little worlds all meshing together.

CJ approached, pulling Ani from her reverie. "See that woman over there?"

Ani squinted.

CJ pointed to an elderly lady wearing several diamond bracelets and a mink stole. The woman stood at the ticket counter arguing with a reservations clerk.

"Right now she's demanding to have her two "children" sit with her on the plane." CJ used air quotes when she said the word *children*. "The crazy broad reserved the seats weeks ago, bla, bla, bla. Well, her so-called children are dogs. Literally. Two Afghan pups named Mandi and Mindi."

"You're kidding."

"No lie. The woman's a couple bats shy of a belfry. Of course the airline won't let the dogs on the plane with the passengers, so she was forced to give up the seats to stand-by. That's us." CJ held out a boarding pass. "Your ticket, ma'am."

"But how did you—?"

"The power of the Internet," whispered CJ, "and a few genius tech-heads who owed Chet."

"If this is my ticket, what's that?" Ani whispered, pointing to the paper in CJ's other hand.

"This? It's my ticket."

"Your ticket? Where are you going?"

"I thought Peru might be nice this time of year."

Ani's insides suddenly felt like bubbles popping. "Wait. You're coming with me?"

"Well, I figured someone's gotta watch your back over there. You sure as hell can't do it yourself."

"Hey, I can handle—"

"Don't even bother, Ponch. I've seen you fight." CJ checked a monitor screen above their heads. "Flight 311 bound for Lima. That's us. Come on. We need to make sure we're the last ones on as the gate closes. Give 'em less chance to ask questions. And remember, you're not Ani Jasper anymore."

"Who am I?"

CJ handed Ani her passport. "Got your picture out of the school yearbook. Pretty good, huh?"

Ani read the name and laughed. "Phoebe Guberwackle? That's my name? So who are you?"

CJ opened her passport and held it up. Ani smiled. "Ginger Guberwackle?"

"We're sisters. Chet's idea."

"So does that mean I can call you Ginger from now on? I think I'm going to like this."

"Well, get over it. You won't be doing any of the talking. Just stand there and look pathetic. Shouldn't be too hard for you."

"CJ?"

"What."

"Why are you doing this?"

"Sarcasm is a way of life for me."

"No, why are you helping me? You don't even like me."

"I do have my own reasons for wanting to get out of town, remember? You just provided the direction, that's all."

"Right," said Ani.

"Let's go. Plane leaves in thirty-five minutes and we still have to get through security. We're lucky it's so freaking early in the morning or we'd never make it through in time. You don't have anything lethal in that backpack of yours, do ya?"

"No. Unless you count the plastic explosives my dad gave me for my birthday."

"Ya'know, if you joke like that when we go through security, we'll never make it onto the plane. They take death threats very seriously here, even from idiots like you who are *just kidding*. Come on."

With CJ's coaching, they made it through security without incident, and exactly twenty-two minutes later, they were standing at the boarding gate to flight 311.

Ani found her feet had become leaden.

This is it. One more step and there will be no turning back.

"What's the matter?" asked CJ.

"I guess I didn't really think we would get this far. Are we really going to do this?"

"Listen, I've done my part. I got us here. The rest is up to you. But you better decide quick because we only have a few minutes before the gate closes."

"What if I don't want to go?"

"Then you go back to your single parent home, and I hit the road alone. I'm never going back to the Fragh."

"Is that your way of making me feel bad so that I'll go?"

"No, that's my way of telling the truth so that you have all the facts when you make your decision."

"You won't be mad at me if I change my mind?"

"I'll probably never speak to you again, but no great loss there."

A profound sadness came over Ani, warping her expression.

"Oh man, you should see your face. Told'ja looking pathetic wouldn't be a problem for you."

"CJ, I . . . I don't know if I can do this. It's wrong. And my dad, he'll think I ran away. He'll think it's because we haven't been getting along. But that's not what it's about at all."

"Why don't you just admit it," snapped CJ. "You're scared."

"Of course I'm scared. We're just kids. What are we doing?"

"Look, Ponch, I get it. This is epic. So do what you have to do. But before you decide, just ask yourself what it is about this that really bothers you? Is it really your dad? Is it really that we're just stupid kids about to go somewhere potentially dangerous without adult supervision?"

"All of the above," mumbled Ani.

"Or is it that for the first time in your life you might have to stand on your own two feet, make your own decision, and take responsibility for it?"

"You've been on your own for a long time now CJ, but things have been different for me."

"So you've led a sheltered life. Good for you. It's the perfect excuse. Don't take any chances. Oh and hey, maybe your mommy and daddy can pick out your clothes for the rest of your life too."

"You're saying I should grow up?"

CJ didn't answer, but the smirk on her face was enough.

"It's just not that simple," said Ani.

"Nothing ever is. I can tell you one thing, though; I know a fork in the road when I see one. Right or left, Ponch? What's it gonna be? Forward or back?"

Ani thought for a moment, glanced at the terminal gate, and then back at CJ. "Can I ask you a question?"

"You can ask. Doesn't mean I'll answer."

"What did Sophie tell you when she asked to speak with you alone at the Wakefield?"

"None of your business."

"But it was about me, wasn't it? That's why you're here?"

"I'm here because I choose to be. You never get anywhere without making a choice. I've made up my mind. Time for you to make up yours."

"Yeah, okay. Can you, um, give me a second?"

The loudspeaker announced flight 311, gate closing in five minutes.

"Consult your pocket guru, talk to God, I don't care. But whatever you do, make it quick."

Ani sat on a nearby bench and stared at the floor, her thoughts all ajumble. She'd never wished for a vision of the future before. They had always come unbidden. But now, in spite of the danger—in spite of the Kalb—she found herself wishing she could see the road ahead, even just a little —just enough to know if this was the right thing to do.

She stared down at her feet. The floor didn't swirl, didn't change. It remained the same interlocking pattern of red, blue and grey that it had always been. She remembered how she felt the last time she'd stared at this carpet. She would have given anything to get her mother to stay in New York.

Now her mother was in trouble. She was sure of it. But the truth was, Ani felt powerless to alter that fact. Getting on a plane and flying to Peru wouldn't change that. The only thing that was going to make a difference now was . . . courage. But she'd never felt less brave in her whole life.

She unzipped the side pocket of her backpack and once again pulled out the photograph of Kahetay standing on the edge of the cliff. She stared at it, trying to find the strength she so desperately needed. She remembered what he'd said about "taking a leap of faith."

Maybe she was wrong. Maybe she didn't need courage. Maybe all she needed was faith. Still, she should have asked Grandfather what happened after the photo was taken.

Ani's eyes fell upon the open compartment of her backpack where the photo had been stashed. In it was the cell phone her mother had given her. She fished the phone out and tapped it on, wishing she could just ring Mom and talk to her, but that wasn't going to happen. She sat staring at the glowing screen in a fog of indecision . . . and then she knew . . . knew what she had to do.

She punched in the number as fast as she could and then waited while the phone rang. "Please be there. Please. Please."

Two more rings and then—"Ani?"

"Kahetay. I know it's early. I'm sorry to wake you."

"I was not sleeping. I felt you reaching out to me."

Ani cleared her throat. "I want to ask you a question and I need you to tell me the truth if you can."

"There has always been truth between us, Granddaughter. Ask your question. I will answer if I am able."

"Do you remember that picture you gave me? The one where you're standing on the edge of a cliff?"

"The leap of faith. I remember."

"Did you?"

"Did I find my faith? Yes."

"Did you . . . jump?"

There was an impossibly long pause. Ani went still. Finally, she heard her grandfather take in a long breath.

"Yes," he said at last. "I did."

"And . . . you were okay?"

"Yes."

"Because . . . you can . . . fly?"

"Yes."

Ani's innards flip-flopped. "The hawk! That's you, isn't it? You're the grey hawk!"

"I am," said Kahetay.

"I knew it!" Ani finally had confirmation of what she'd always suspected. Her grandfather had the ability to alter his physical form like the skinwalkers in Navajo legends he'd told her stories about. Human to hawk and back again. What miraculous magic!

"I thought you might have guessed the truth," said Kahetay.

"Well," said Ani, "I didn't know for sure, but . . . it all makes sense now; why you don't have a car even though you own a garage. Why I never saw your footprints on the path when we met at the top of Boulder Dash Hill. How you got to New York so fast after that horrible dream we shared. And how you can call a hawk down from the sky without making a sound."

Ani smiled at the thought. It was thrilling to picture her grandfather soaring through Mojave skies. She wished she had more time to talk to him about it, ask him what it was like, but—

"Anani'nah," said Kahetay interrupting her thoughts, "you are standing on the edge of your own cliff now, are you not?"

"Yes."

"And you are wondering if you should take a leap of faith?"

After a grave silence she said, "*Eli* would. If he were here instead of me, I know he would get on that plane. He'd go save Mom. But I'm . . . I'm not . . . " She let out her breath. "It should be him here . . . not me."

"We all feel at times that we are not enough," said Kahetay, "but Ani, you will learn why it is you who must walk this earth and not your brother. Why you are meant to be here. Elijah is an important part of you and always will be, but it is *your* unique gifts the world needs now."

"I don't know if that's true," said Ani, "but . . . I guess I'm gonna find out."

"So . . . you have decided to take that leap of faith, little one?"

Ani looked up at CJ who was pretending to read the carry-on luggage warning sign. She didn't even have any luggage. She had nothing but her leather jacket and the plane ticket in her hand. That plane ticket gave her direction. Gave her purpose.

CJ needs to do this as much as I do, Ani thought.

The loudspeaker announced final call for flight 311 bound for Lima.

The gates were closing soon.

CJ whirled around and shot Ani a what's-it-gonna-be look.

"Yeah," Ani finally said into the phone. "I guess I am."

Kahetay sighed. "I believe in you, Granddaughter. Believe in yourself. You too can fly."

"Maybe," she said, glancing at the plane through the wall of glass, "but I think for now, I'll borrow somebody else's wings. Thank you, grandfather . . . for everything. I love you."

"And I, you, little one," his voice broke. "Journey well."

The line went dead.

Ani stared at the phone for a moment, then dropped it in her backpack and exhaled.

"Are you Ani Jasper?" asked a young man standing over her, fidgeting with something in his hands. His eyes shifted side to side as if he feared being caught. When Ani nodded, the boy offered her a tattered brown string-and-wax sealed envelope. "This is for you. I'm supposed to tell you to keep 'em safe."

Ani received the packet. "Keep what safe?"

The boy shrugged.

Ani touched a small mark inked on the front of the envelope in the lower right-hand corner. "I know this symbol. It was on my mother's postcard . . . from Peru," she said, more to herself than to the boy. She broke the wax seal, untangled the yellowed string that crisscrossed around two cardboard buttons, and retrieved the contents inside.

Tingles pricked the back of her neck. There, in her hands, were the missing pages of the library book the assistant had shown her—the one written by Wakefield Nick—*Places I've Seen That No One Believes*.

She flipped through the pages. "This . . . this is the translation key to the Mapstone symbols," she muttered in disbelief. "Who gave you these to give to me?" she asked, but when she looked up, the young man no longer stood over her.

Turning in her chair, eyes sweeping the terminal, she caught a glimpse of him weaving through the departing travelers.

"Wait!" she called out, but he vanished in the crowd.

She glanced at the entrance to flight 311. CJ, poised by the door, slung Ani a sneer and threw up her hands.

Ani quickly returned the pages to the envelope, folded it in thirds, and stashed it in the pocket of her red zippered sweat jacket.

Standing, backpack in hand, she called out to CJ. "Hey, you up for a little adventure?"

CJ gave one of her rare smiles.

The flight attendants began closing the doors to the ramp.

"Ponch! Hurry!"

They dashed through the gate just as it closed.

A Message From The Author

Dear Reader,

I hope you enjoyed Book One of *The LightBridge Legacy: The Secret Half*. I know. I left you at the airport. And I feel bad about that, so keep reading to find out how to get your hands on the first four chapters of *Book Two, The Hidden Gates*.

I must say, writing this series, I've become very passionate about its unfolding and evolution. It's really taken on a life of its own. I jot constant notes on the story, nearly every day of the week, even in my sleep (some of my favorite dreams are of Azimara). In fact, whole Azimaran scenes have come straight out of dreams (and I will take you there in **Books Three and Four** so you can dream-walk with me). All told, I've taken over 3000 notes on the series—a part of me is always working on it—and I have loved every second of it.

I've been inspired by Ani's courage and compassion, as well as CJ's spunk and spirit. Many readers have said the same, though more than a few fans have also written to ask me if **Kahetay and Sophie** will be around for subsequent books in the series.

Well, I'll let you in on **a little secret**. Kahetay and Sophie were inspired by two beloved mentors of mine and hold a very special place in my heart. I just couldn't bear to leave them behind. So even though Ani and CJ depart on their **grand adventure** without Kahetay and Sophie, I can promise you, they *will* find their way into **Book Two** (and subsequent books in the series as well), albeit in some rather unconventional ways.

The LightBridge Legacy has been a long, wonderful journey for me, a journey of a lifetime. It took 7 years to pen the initial 900 page story, 7 more to find the right publisher who promptly split it into 3 books (which I'm developing into 4, with a possible 5th book in the works). And another 5 to get here. When the 1st edition of Book One was finally published (you're reading the 2nd edition), I began to hear from readers who wanted to thank me for writing the book, and I thanked them right back, for what is a book without the hearts and minds that are moved by it? Soooo a big heartfelt thanks goes out to you, for if you're reading this letter, you stuck with it from page 1 to the last, and that is the best gift you could have ever given me.

Feel free to reach out to me too! I enjoy reading the ongoing comments, questions, and feedback from readers like you who enjoyed The Secret Half and are looking forward to subsequent books in the series. These comments have helped me engage with the story on a new and even **deeper level**, and in some cases, reader remarks and reviews have actually helped me **take the**

story in a new direction—one that was wholly unexpected but turned out to be a marvelous adventure. Sometimes, like Ani, you end up where you never thought you would go and realize it was where you were meant to be all along. I have to say that has been, and still is, **thrilling for me.**

In truth, you're the reason I'll explore the future of The LightBridge Series, taking it beyond the books that have already been penned into new, **unexplored territories**. So tell me what you liked, or didn't like, let me know what you want to see more of, send me a question, a comment or just say hi! [Pssst. I'm also looking for beta readers who can give feedback in exchange for free pre-publication copies.] You can write me at: ElayneJames.com/contact

And if you enjoyed the book, I'd love it if you would leave an honest review of *The Secret Half* on your favorite book site. Even one line can **make a huge difference**. You may not know it, but you, the reader, have great power. You have the ability to make or break a book. Word-of-mouth and reviews are vital. So if you'd like to help The LightBridge Series survive and thrive, here's where to start:

https://elaynejames.wordpress.com/reviews/

☞ That's my **Review Links Page** where you can choose your favorite book site to leave a review (the links on this page will take you directly to my book on each site—no searching required). Then you can scroll down to the book reviews section and click on "Write a Review."

Thank you so much for reading The Secret Half, and for spending time with me. I believe a book is a **window to the soul**, a bridge that connects us, reader and writer, in a way nothing else ever could. So you'll understand when I say I have enjoyed our time together, and I'm looking forward to seeing you again in Book Two.

In gratitude,

Elayne G. James

PS: **AS PROMISED,** if you would like a **SNEAK PEAK** of the first few chapters of **Book Two: THE HIDDEN GATES,** *and* would like to be kept in the loop on future LightBridge releases, PLUS get the **FREE SECRET HALF "EXTRAS" PACK** (it's like a book version of the behind-the-scenes "extras" on a movie DVD*)*, join my **EGJ Book News Email List** here: www.EGJ-BookNews.com (no spam or junk mail, just book related stuff. I'll guard your email address like a precious gem).

You've just read:

What's Next?

Book Two
"The Hidden Gates" is
Right Around the Corner!

The Adventure Continues...

Exclusively for LightBridge Fans:

Read a Sneak Peak of The Hidden Gates in the "Secret Half Extra's Pack" when you join my EGJ Book News email List!

Scan the QR Code Below/Right to get a heads-up when the next book in the series is comes out! Plus Free Goodies!

**Book Two
The Hidden
Gates**

**Book Three
The Lost Path**

**Book Four
The Dark Below**

*Visit My Website at
ElayneJames.com*

*Read my Blog at
ElayneJamesBlog.com*

*Join My Email List
EGJ-BookNews.com*

Heartfelt Gratitude

To the LightBridge Legacy's first editor, Greg Conway, who took time away from his own artistic endeavors to support me in mine. A true friend, with a gifted intellect and a courageous soul, Greg challenged me to become a better writer, and with his help, I did. I may never have found the courage and belief in myself necessary to complete the original 900-page novel. His mark and his heart are on every page of this journey.

To my beta readers: Jan, Cassidy, Archana, Kenny, Eoanna, Ishara, Rainbow, Mom, Dad, TJ, Raena, Noel, Liz, Bob, Paula, Jean, Slater & Grant, for their wonderful feedback and constant encouragement. I am so blessed to have in my family and circle of friends, people I love, trust and respect, whose opinions I value and take to heart. They helped me (and Ani) more than they will ever know.

To all those at the Millie Ames Writing Workshop for listening to me read Book One for months on end, and for offering honest and insightful criticism.

To my NY Historian friend John Schubert, for being my guide through new and unfamiliar terrains; for showing me the history, the beauty and the secret side of New York City.

A special thanks to Ishara, Raena, Michelle, Eoanna, Rainbow, Larri, and Cindy for their ongoing support and contributions to the evolution of both myself and my writing, which, all told, has spanned more than five decades.

To my fellow Muse & amazing editor, Cat Spydell, without whom this book might never have seen the printed page. Thank you for coming along with me on this incredible journey, and for believing in me *and* my dream to bring *light* to the world.

To my sister, Ishara, for being my *Sophia*—wise woman, confidant and best friend; for always being there with just the right words to heal my heart, calm my fears, and soothe my soul. For lighting my way, and always making sure I know I am loved.

To Gregg DeCastro for being my *Kahetay*; who became first my guitar teacher, then my friend, and then my soul's 'wise grandfather' during my teen and pre-teen years when, through the gift of music and words, he guided me on my journey of becoming and being.

To my sweetheart Henatay, for being my original inspiration for Kahetay's character. Of the Pueblo tribes in New Mexico, not the Navajo, Henatay (Cloud in the *Keres* language) is every bit as wise and noble as Kahetay in the LightBridge Legacy. He is an inspiration to me every day. I am blessed to have him in my life and by my side. Every moment a gift.

To my mother for being my *Nan J*; for passing on her gift of words, her love of stones, and her interest in anthropology and archeology to me when I was young. And for being the strong, intelligent, wise, beautiful, adventurous woman who raised me to be myself no matter what, and taught me, by example, to be courageous in the pursuit of one's dream.

To my father for being my *Xephero*; my wise counsel; for being the strength and core of a vast family; for challenging my mind to go beyond the accepted railways of thought and delve into the outer reaches where the tracks have not yet been laid.

And to both my parents for the rare and beautiful love and friendship they have given me; the incredible support of my writing and my dreams over the years, and for giving me the kind of childhood that sparked the imagination, and launched a life-long fascination with myth and dreams, quantum realities and inner worlds.

My deepest gratitude to all.

Hathanya wa nua,

Elayne

> *And a very special note of appreciation to my book foster partners, Chris Spurrell, and my brother Grant, who supported this work when Ani and I needed it the most, and who believed in me and my creative abilities so unquestioningly, that they fostered this book without ever having read even a rough draft.*

Author's Personal Note

I was raised within the sphere of influence of two great human beings, my parents. Both teachers, their greatness manifested in the form of heart, wisdom, intelligence, understanding, and acceptance. Freedom of speech and thought, though not commonly permitted in a child's confining existence, were their gifts to me and to the children they guided. To them, children had a voice, and they listened.

Between the ages of eleven and fourteen I had a series of thought provoking, life-altering conversations with my father, who had just completed his doctorate at the University of Southern California. I consider my father a rare individual, a singular original. He is a gifted conversationalist, an incomparable professor, a talented musician, a skilled craftsman, an affable gentleman, a playful genius, an intellectual humorist . . . uncommon in many ways, not the least of which, was his manner of conversing with his pre-teen daughter.

As a dyslexic child (a disability my father and I share) in a world which had no name for or knowledge of the now common learning disorder, I received such labels as "slow" and "inattentive" in school, getting low marks in every subject but art and creative writing. My self-respect and self-confidence would have suffered greatly had I identified with the labels I'd been given in school, but my parents saw to it that I never did. Far from treating me as a *learning disabled* child, my father instead challenged me to push beyond the thinking of everyday thoughts, to fathom the unfathomable. What's at the end of the universe? How do we know dreams aren't real? What exists beyond our five senses?

When I began to write down my ideas, and incorporate them into stories, it was my mother who encouraged me to take those stories and expand them into books. I finished my first book at the age of twelve—100 handwritten pages, misspellings and all. Even did a hand drawn cover. At this point, my father, who intercepted the little string-bound manuscript on its way to the round file, offered me a piece of sound advice; "Never throw away anything you write," he said, "no matter how silly you think it might be in the moment." When I asked him why, he said simply, "Someday you will be grateful." He was right. And I'm grateful to him, and to my mother, not only for encouraging me to take myself seriously as a writer, but for challenging me to be the kind of person that is not afraid to ask the big questions and imagine the answers.

When I was twelve I learned that imagination could open doors—real doors—to inner worlds. By the time I graduated from high school, I knew two things for certain; that I was a writer, and that I wanted to someday give the gift to others that my parents gave to me. This book is that gift. It is a favor returned. With love and deep gratitude, I dedicate The LightBridge Legacy Series to my father Jim, for starting me on this wondrous path and to my mother, without whose wisdom, love and support of my father and myself, this book would never have come to be.

A Note About the Quotes at the Start of Each Chapter

The quoted text from the Tome of the Zielfah Ri (book of wisdom) runs throughout all four books. Many have asked where the quotes came from. What is my source? My answer is simple; they stem from the same mysterious place that the story itself came from, the uncharted realms of imagination. I focused on each chapter and answered one question: What would the Light Masters say if they were here to help Ani through this chapter in her life? I wrote down the first thing that came to mind, and thus the legend of the Tome was born. In Book Four, The Dark Below, you will discover the role the Tome plays in preparing Ani for the challenge of mastering the magic of the Lightbridge.

A Note about Kahetay and the Natah

Although I am part Native American, and was raised to respect Native American wisdom and ways, the teachings of Kahetay in The LightBridge Series are not intended to be a reflection of Navajo beliefs and traditions. Out of respect for the Navajo Nation, I invented the Natah as a fictional device that could encompass all that Kahetay needed to teach Ani, drawing from the many sources of knowledge I have been exposed to on my journey through life.

ABOUT THE AUTHOR

Scribbler of words on paper napkins in corner cafes. Musician. Artist. Explorer of dreams, myth, and imagination. Passionate pursuer of creative expression. Curious surveyor of unexplained phenomena and the mysteries of the universe. Dyslexic time-traveler. Elsewhere Girl.

Like many of her main characters, Elayne G. James is an Elsewhere Girl. Born on the earth, but not of the earth, she's been searching for home ever since she first discovered she saw the world differently from those around her. And although she hasn't yet found where she belongs, through her writing, whole new worlds unfold, and she finds a little piece of home in each one of them.

She started her writing career at age 11 when she read The Hobbit by J.R.R. Tolkien and knew she wanted to spend the rest of her life pursuing the fine art of world building. That same year, she discovered her pop's old Yamaha guitar tucked away in the back of a closet, and fell immediately in love. Her love affair with writing and music has remained constant throughout her life. Being a novelist and a songwriter provides a place of refuge, a sense of home, a purpose-driven life, and a creative outlet to express her elsewhereness.

A Northern California native, Elayne visited NYC for the first time when she was 13, which planted the seed for Ani's move to New York City in The Secret Half. And though the trip made a lasting impression on her, it would be another 30 years before she would return. The journey from then-and-there to here-and-now has had many scenic detours, and some harsh turns, all of which were experiences she counts herself lucky to have had. She now lives by the Pacific blue in Southern California with her sweetheart and continues her study of myth, inner-magic, and the power of imagination.

Are you an Elsewhere Girl?

ElsewhereGirl.com